GUTTER

Also by K'wan

Gangsta
Road Dawgz
Street Dreams
Hoodlum
Eve
Hood Rat
Still Hood

Anthologies

The Game
Blow (with 50 Cent)

K'wan

GUTTER

St. Martin's Griffin 🔖 New York

This is a work of fiction. All of the characters, organizations, and events portrayed in this novel are either products of the author's imagination or are used fictitiously.

www.stmartins.com

ISBN-13: 978-0-312-36009-2
ISBN-10: 0-312-36009-6

First Edition: September 2008

30 29 28 27 26 25 24 23

This is dedicated to all
the gangsters I've met
in my life and travels.
There're two sides to every
coin, which one
will you choose?

GUTTER

prologue
My Father's Eyes

"**T**HIS IS so unfair!" I fumed, storming into my bedroom. I slammed the door so hard that the picture of me and Louis on prom night fell off the wall and cracked. I hadn't meant to slam it so hard, but I was tight.

"Watch that temper, Ken," I said to myself, scooping the picture off the floor. There was a hairline crack down the center, separating me from Louis. "How freaking ironic." I tossed the picture on my bed, reminding myself to get another frame from the ninety-nine-cent store.

I plopped down on the little stool in front of my vanity mirror and examined the face staring back at me. Ever since I was a kid people always told me how pretty I am, but I really didn't start to notice until junior year in high school. I'm five feet five, five feet six when I stand up straight, with thick black hair and lips that always make me look like I'm pouting, but what stands out about me most are my eyes... my father's eyes. My eyes are a pale green. Not like a contact lens green, but the color of new money. Mom says that's why she and my aunt nicknamed me Dollar.

Normally my eyes are clear and crisp, but not today. Today they were red and swollen because I had been crying for the last two hours. I had a golden opportunity waiting for me and my mother was throwing some serious blocks. The way she was acting you'd think I had just told my family's darkest secret, which in a sense I had.

I couldn't wait for the summer to end so I could start my first year of college. Mom wanted me to go away, but I opted to stay home and attend the University of Miami, on a partial scholarship. I could've gone to UNC or Howard for free, but Miami had a better journalism program, and I didn't have to wait until sophomore year to participate in the work study program. Besides that, it allowed me to be close to my mom and my best friend, Baby. Mom tries to front like it wouldn't bother her if I went away, but I know it would. For the first twelve years of my life, we were all each other had, then Arthor came along, but that's another story.

See, Mommy and me got the bomb relationship. Not only is she my mother, but she's like my best friend, next to Baby. I have the utmost respect for my mother and know that she's the law around here, but at the same time I know I could tell her anything and she's not gonna judge me. Lord, I thought she was going to trip when I told her about losing my virginity to Cedric last year. She went off about me not consulting with her before I did it to make sure I was safe, but she didn't condemn me as the whore of Babylon. When she finally calmed down, she took me to the clinic for a full physical and blood work and she buys me a box of condoms once a month. It's not like I need them. Cedric split my little ass open so bad that my first time was my last time. That might explain why we broke up a few weeks later.

I wanted to kill that fool for trying to play me out of pocket, but my mom helped me get through it. She knew all about heartache and how to get past it. Baby didn't take it so well though. They say that if Gunn hadn't been there he'd have shot that boy in front of all those people. Baby is a nut, but I know he'd do anything for me. That's my dawg for life!

With all the time we spend together, it's no wonder that people always thought that we were fooling around. Our mothers had even joked about us hooking up, but I think we all knew that wasn't nothing popping. Baby was a dime, and we had had some close calls, but we never crossed the finish line. Baby and I have a brother and sister relationship. Our mothers are best friends and we've lived next door to each other all our lives. We get along famously, but we're nothing alike. Me, I'm hood, but Baby is ghetto. We're both from a nice gated community in Florida and have both gone to private schools for most our lives, but for as much money as that boy's mother spent to give him a better opportunity, the heart of a gangster does and always will beat in his chest. I used to think he was a knucklehead, but after my little vacation during spring break I understand him a little better. Before he had even taken his first breaths his destiny was already written.

Mommy was from Harlem, and you could tell by her walk and her talk. She carried herself like a queen at all times and commanded the same respect she gave when dealing with people, anything less wasn't even an option. My mother was my ace, my superwoman. Whether it was me skinning my knee when I fell off my bike, or when those girls from the projects tried to jump me, mama love is always in my corner. My pillar of strength, giving of herself even when there's nothing left.

I used to look at my mother and wonder how she did it? How she mustered up the strength to smile at her enemies, and keep her faith in God when society was giving us a hard time. I wondered for a long time where that strength came from and about three months ago I found out.

"Break yo self, bitch!"

I spun around so quick that I knocked over my half empty bottle of Glo, spraying my freshly polished, hardwood floor with glass and perfume. I was about to scream for my mama when I looked up and recognized the peanut head that was poking in my bedroom window.

"You dick!" I yelled, throwing a box of sanitary napkins at him.

"Watch yo mouth, fool." Baby swung his long legs in the window. His Chuck Taylors left a dirty print on my windowsill, which I would surely make him clean before he left. As usual, Baby was decked out in a pair of tan Dickey pants and a white T-shirt. His long hair was braided in quarters, tied off by black rubber bands, meaning his mother had done it. When the hood rats did his hair they banded it in blue and white, but his mother wouldn't allow it. She didn't even allow him to dress in too much blue. Baby thought she was a nut about it, but I understood her phobia.

Damn, I hadn't even told him. Since we were old enough to talk we had told each other everything and here I was holding out on something that he had every right to know. Baby trusted me more than anybody and I repaid him by living the lie with our parents. I had to tell him, but how?

"Sup wit you, Dollar Bill?" Baby plopped on my bed, tossing the stuffed animals aside so he could get comfortable.

"You gonna stop climbing in my window like you pay rent here, Louis." I turned around on the stool so he could see the seriousness in my eyes.

"What'd I tell you about shouting my government like that,

woman? Call me Baby Loc or call me daddy." Baby smiled at me, flexing that dimple in his left cheek.

"Daddy? Nigga, please, you must think I'm one of them Carol City broads you be chasing." I gave him my no-nonsense stare. Baby knew my moods better than most, so he backed off a bit.

"Damn, everybody ass is snippy today. I spoke to ya mama when she came by the crib awhile ago and she looked at me like I kicked her dog," he told me.

"Yeah, she's going through a thing right now," I said, rolling my eyes.

"Sounded like more than a thing to me, Kenyatta. She looked really upset. I knew it was serious when Mom threw me the car keys and told me to get lost for an hour or two. What did your ass do now?" he asked me, as if he already knew the story.

"What makes you think I did something?" I folded my arms over my breasts so he wouldn't see that my nipples had started to stir beneath my T-shirt. It wasn't that I was cold, but I could feel Baby's eyes on my breasts and I wasn't sure how I felt about it just yet.

"Because I heard your name more than once and school. I thought you was doing ya thing in the white man's world?" Baby asked me. He always poked fun at me for going to college, saying college trained us properly in the etiquette of white folks. He didn't actually believe it, but it made his dumb-ass friends laugh when he said it. His mother had wanted him to go to college, but Baby's head wasn't really in it. He was always thinking about his next dollar, so it didn't really surprise me when he had caked off from a dot-com company he started. His mother let him take a year off to see how the business would pan out for him, but she made it clear that he would either be in somebody's classroom or on the streets for the new school year.

"Hell, I am. I'm in the top twenty percent at the university," I said, snaking my neck. I had a lot of bullshit with me, but I took school very serious. "I didn't mess up in school, I actually got an A plus on my thesis." I reached into my shoulder bag and took out the ring-bounded copy I had. Mom still had the original. I ran my thumb across the title line, as if blessing it, before tossing it over to Baby.

"It's the piece I wrote for my journalism class. Right before we broke for the spring, Professor Faulk gave us an assignment that we could take on for extra credit, so when I was on vacation in Cali, I started writing that." I pointed at the folder.

I watched him as he mouthed the title. "Gutter?" He looked up at me with questioning eyes. He knew what the word meant, as did I. Our mothers had never hid the fact that our fathers were gang bangers, but I don't think either of us understood the power they held, or the lives they'd altered.

"My thesis is about our fathers...my father really. They've even talked about publishing it," I confessed.

"Damn, congratulations, Dollar." He slid off the bed and leaned down to hug me. I could smell the chronic in his clothes, and for a minute I felt like getting high, until I remembered that I gave it up when school started. "So if the joint was this good, what they tripping off?"

"The truth," I said. "All my life I've thought of my father as just another thug from my mother's past, but I know better now, Baby," I leaned in to whisper. My heart was fluttering uncontrollably as I searched for the words. "For a long time I've wondered who my father really was and what he was about, so when me and Gunn flew out to L.A., I started asking questions. Most of the stuff I knew from the war stories in New York, but on the West Coast they filled in the blanks." I had to pause as the stories came rushing back to me. "Some of the stuff I learned I wouldn't dare tell my mother, but since she's read the story all cards are on the table now."

"Talk to me, Kenyatta." He touched my forearm. I could see the anticipation in his inviting brown eyes.

"Baby, if I tell you what I found out you've got to promise not to tell your mother, because it really ain't my place to be sharing this with you. They didn't want us to know the truth, so they kept it from us all these years. My mom found out about my little investigation and the paper, which is why she's pissed."

"Kenyatta, I know my father was killed, but I don't know the circumstances. I've asked Mom about it, but she gets all tight-lipped and shit. I want...no, I *need* to know, please?"

How could I say no to those eyes? "A'ight," I took a breath, "It all kicked off in Harlem...."

part I

BLOOD OATH

LENOX AVENUE was especially crowded that night. Summertime was in full swing, so the streets were alive with activity. A dozen or so young men crowded the park, either playing ball or waiting for next on the double courts. It was dark out, but children still ran in and out of the park playing tag or climbing the monkey bars. Even in light of the past few months, Harlem had gained back its luster.

Lloyd sat on the stoop, kicking it with several of the homeys and drinking a forty ounce. The Cincinnati Reds fitted that crowned his dome was tilted slightly to the right. The lesser soldiers sat around listening to him tell war stories. Some were factual, but most were fabrications of the truth.

"Word to mine, son, these niggaz is mad fake," Lloyd declared, swigging from the forty bottle. "Muthafuckas be acting like our click ain't the tightest out here, fuck Harlem!"

Lloyd fashioned himself as somewhat of a big man on the streets. Early on in his youth he made a name for himself by being a general knucklehead. He had been arrested several times, but had never done more than a few months in jail. He made his climb from a low-level nobody to a blip on the radar. Lloyd was eighteen and down with one of the largest gangs in the country, the Bloods.

"Yeah, fuck them niggaz," a young man wearing a Cleveland Cavaliers jersey added, trying to sound surer of himself than he really was. "But yo..." He hesitated for a minute. "Man, I heard they had this shit sewed up not so long ago."

"That's bullshit. They tried to get it popping, but we stomped them muthafuckas!" Lloyd declared. The young men stood around debating history of the B&C rivalry in New York and watching the world go by. Hearing their own voices, coupled with the sights and sounds of Harlem made them totally oblivious to what was about to go down.

Two mountain bikes were coasting along the shadows of the street in front of the building. The riders were dressed in oversized white T-shirts that laid flat across their laps, but if you looked closely you could see the slight awkward lumps. Hook and Noodles were the latest lost souls who had found something of worth in the "movement" as they liked to call it. They had murder on their minds and big things on their persons.

A kid by the name of Benny, who happened to have the misfortune of being with Lloyd, was the first to notice the duo. "Who them niggaz?"

When Lloyd turned around the beer in his mouth quickly dried into a paste as the cyclists drew matching .40 calibers. Noodles's face twisted into a mask of pure hatred as he skidded to a stop and jerked the trigger.

"Harlem muthafucka!"

The whole avenue seemed to stop moving as the sound of the

.40 cut through the night air. Benny clutched at his neck as a large chunk of it and his collarbone came loose. Blood sprayed over his comrades and a girl who was coming out of the building. The girl opened her mouth to scream, but another blast from the .40 sent her flying back through the door she had just exited.

The kid in the basketball jersey flipped backward as Hook gave him two to the chest. Lloyd thought about fleeing until he found himself staring down the barrel of two high-powered handguns.

"Chill!" Lloyd pleaded, crouching in the corner.

"Fuck that chill shit, nigga, you know what it is!" Hook hissed.

There was a coldness in his eyes that told Lloyd that he was going to die no matter what he did or said. He tried to bolt, but Noodles tripped him into a pile of garbage. Hook yanked Lloyd roughly to his feet and shoved the barrel of the .40 under Lloyd's chin.

"The big homey wanted you to have this," Hook said before pulling the trigger. Lloyd's body jerked once and his brains shot up through the top of his head. Hook cursed and wiped the blood and chunks from his face with the bandanna he had wrapped around his wrist.

"Damn, nigga, you almost got that shit on my whites!" Noodles scolded his partner for the mess he had made with Lloyd.

"Nigga, stop crying. The O.G. says the bodies keep dropping until he says otherwise," Hook shot back.

Noodles looked at the several dead bodies and shook his head. "All this over one dead nigga?"

"He wasn't just some nigga, he was a legend and you better not let the big homey hear you talking that crazy shit," Hook scolded. "Speaking of crazy shit though, why'd you pop the bitch?" He nodded toward the young girl sprawled on the steps.

Noodles just shrugged. "Casualty of war, my nigga. Let's get the fuck outta here."

KENYATTA KNELT on his balcony looking out at the sunrise. He touched his head to the ground, while he went into his third repetition of the prayer. His long braids swept gently across his naked back. Fallen Soldier was tattooed across his shoulders, while a portrait of his best friend stretched down his spine. After completing the prayer ritual, Gutter rose to his feet.

Gutter walked to the edge of the balcony and gripped the railing. Beads of dew—clung to his body, causing him to sparkle in the orange glow. Below people jogged and walked their dogs through the quiet Brooklyn Heights neighborhood. For the umpteenth time, he wished his comrade had lived to see what he had made of his life.

Kenyatta Soladine, aka Gutter, was the most troublesome son of Algerian immigrants. Born and raised in South Central Los Angeles, Gutter knew just what a hard knock life it was. After the death of his father and grandfather, it had been up to the streets to raise him. Gutter's mother did what she could to keep her son on the straight and narrow, but the hood had always been his first love.

Gutter ate, slept, breathed, and fantasized about the hustle. He was a man who had been through so much that the life of a square held no place in his world. Gutter believed in and respected Allah, but unlike most people, he wouldn't waste time on his knees waiting for the Most High to shape his destiny. He would do it himself.

He stepped from the balcony into his bedroom, feeling the warm rush of air on his neck and chest. There was a time when

Gutter would sleep through the sacred hour of prayer, but since the nightmares began he and sleep didn't always see eye-to-eye. The master bedroom of the duplex was dark, but the sun coming over the horizon was beginning to illuminate it. The first few rays had already crept up to the floor and gently touched the sleeping girl's face.

He leaned down and brushed a loose strand of hair from her forehead, and found that his fingers came away damp. Gutter couldn't help but wonder if Sharell's sleep was as fitful as his had been. He had literally taken her through hell and back and she was still with him. The murders, the drugs, him dying and rising again like the fabled Lazarus. She had been through it all. If he had it his way, she would never see another moment of hurt. Life would be good for his boo, but that didn't change the fact that he had business to handle. Blood would answer for blood.

Tucking his .38 snub into the waistline of his sweats, Gutter made his way down the stairs. The sun hadn't made it to the hall yet, so that remained dark. He didn't need any light though. Gutter performed this routine so often that he could do it with his eyes closed. He crossed through the spacious living room and retracted the metallic blinds. The orange rays of the sun seeped through the window and coated the living room in a soothing light.

The floors were made of mahogany and polished to an almost mirrored finish. The cream-colored sofa and love seat were made from butter-soft leather that had a sunken effect for the few privileged to sit in them. The apartment was decorated more for comfort than floss.

After securing the place, Gutter began his calisthenics. He started with push-ups, then went to sit-ups and back again. This went on for about a half hour or so. Often if he tried to work out too hard the old wounds began to ache. Cross had restored his body as best he could, but some of the wounds would still take time to completely heal. He hated the assassin for what he was, but was grateful that he had allowed him to breathe on his own again.

After the workout, he proceeded to the kitchen to make breakfast for himself and his lady. The meal consisted of eggs, waffles, and turkey bacon. No swine would be tolerated in the Soladine household. After completing the meal, Gutter proceeded to set the table.

SHARELL SAT bolt upright in the king-sized bed. Her gown was drenched with sweat, while her heart threatened to leap from her chest. She clutched the cross around her neck and tried to banish the fading images in her mind. It had been awhile since she had enjoyed a peaceful night's sleep. Every time she closed her eyes, she saw the faces of the dead. She always put God first in her life, but she knew she would have to atone for the part she played in the story that had unfolded.

Donning her robe and slippers, Sharell made her way into the hall. The first thing she noticed was the smell of breakfast being cooked. The scent greeted her nostrils and sent a signal to her stomach. Turkey bacon, she figured. She would know the smell anywhere. She enjoyed the tender strips of meat, but longed for her lost pork. There was really no comparison between the two.

When she got downstairs, Gutter had already set the table. The plates were decorated with fruits and dressing for appearance, and orange juice filled the crystal goblets. Smiling at her from the far side of the table was Gutter.

"Hey, baby," he said, getting up and pulling her chair out for her, "did you sleep well?"

"Like a rock," she lied. She didn't want to upset Gutter with tales of her nightmares. She had mentioned the dreams to him before, but had never told him the extent of them.

Gutter gave thanks to Allah, while she said a prayer to her god, before tearing into the food. They made small conversation at the table, but nothing significant. It had been this way for a while now. Gutter was still as attentive and caring as ever, but his mind always seemed to be elsewhere. It was no secret where that was.

"So, what you getting into today, baby?" Sharell asked, popping a piece of bacon into her mouth.

Gutter shrugged. "Probably bend a few corners. I got some things I gotta take care of on the set."

"The set," she repeated, shaking her head. "Kenyatta, you spend more time in the streets than a little bit. When you gonna give them corners up?"

"When the black man can get a fair shake in America." He winked.

She gave him a mock laugh. "I see you got jokes this morning."

"Ain't nothing funny about chasing a dollar, baby."

"Then why continue to do it?" she asked. Gutter gave her a look like he didn't understand the question so she elaborated. "Kenyatta, we've got money saved up and I'm no stranger to hard work. Why don't you get up out them streets?"

Gutter laughed, but Sharell's face remained serious. "Baby, you know I can't do that right now. I've got unfinished *business* to take care of."

She knew what he meant without him having to say it directly. She had been thrilled beyond words when he woke up from the coma. Through the grace of God her lover had been returned to her, but the man who got up out of that hospital bed wasn't the man she knew. On the surface he was still her Kenyatta, but there was a change in his soul. Though no one blamed him for what happened to Lou-Loc, Gutter felt otherwise. He believed that if he had been there his friend would still be alive. Instead of focusing on healing, his thoughts were consumed with revenge. No matter how much Sharell fought him on it he wouldn't let the vendetta go, blood would answer for blood. Sharell was forced to watch helplessly as her lover slipped further and further into the darkness. She could only pray that the Lord would deliver him from the insane quest before it consumed him.

"Kenyatta"—she placed her hand over his—"no matter how much work you put in, you can't bring him back."

"Come on, Sharell, don't start tripping this morning." He pulled his hand away.

"Kenyatta, I'm not the one tripping, you are. Baby, I know how you feel, believe me—"

"Sharell, ain't no way in hell you could know how I feel." His words were sharp, but the anger wasn't directed toward her. "My brother is dead...gone...fucking outta here. Them niggaz killed him like a dog in the street when all he wanted to do was get out of the game, and I'm supposed to let that ride? Fuck that, it's over when all them busters is dead." He slammed his fist against the table, nearly knocking over Sharell's orange juice.

"I'm sorry," he said softly. It took all of his concentration to stop the mounting rage from spilling over. "I see him every night, Sharell. Whenever I close my eyes I see my friend." Gutter placed his face in his hands and she almost thought she heard him sobbing. "He shouldn't have gone out like that, I should've been there."

Sharell got up from her chair and went to kneel beside Gutter. She moved his hands from his face and looked into his glassy eyes. "Kenyatta, the Lord decides who he calls home and when. Even if you had been there you can't say for sure that Lou-Loc would still be alive. It could've been two dead black boys instead of one.

Baby"—she ran her fingers through his nappy beard—"it's a sad thing that happened to Lou-Loc, but you can't change what has already come to pass. You weren't there with Lou-Loc so you could be here with me"—she placed his hand over her stomach—"with us."

This brought a faint smile to his lips. "Yeah, I gotta make sure my little man comes up right." He kissed her on the forehead.

"Or little girl," she corrected him. With Gutter's help, she got off the floor and moved back to her seat.

"Whatever, you know damn well my first child gotta be a son."

"All your first child has to be is healthy, Ken. Boy or girl it's still gonna be ours."

After breakfast Sharell cleared the table while Gutter went upstairs to prepare for the day. From their walk-in closet, he chose a pair of blue jeans and a white Air Force. After pulling on his white T-shirt, he retrieved his chain from the dresser. It was a thirty-inch platinum cable that twirled in on itself and around the diamonds. The piece was a script G that had sapphires embedded in the grooves. The last accessory was a black .40 caliber, which he slipped into his pocket. He was ready to hit the streets.

chapter 2

DANNY-BOY LEANED against the black Escalade watching the people watch him. Dressed in a blue hoodie and sagging blue jeans, he stuck out like a sore thumb in the upper-class neighborhood. It didn't offend him though. He got a kick out of their reactions. One woman nearly snatched her dog off its feet for wandering too close to the banger.

Daniel "Danny-Boy" Thomas got his name because of his youthful appearance. He was twenty, but looked fifteen. His skin was the color of caramel, and he always wore his hair in a wavy Caesar. He was one of the set's newest recruits. When Gutter found him, he was a young knucklehead looking for acceptance. Under the O.G.'s tutelage, Danny-Boy was becoming a true-blue soldier.

When Danny spotted Gutter coming down the steps of the brownstone, he immediately straightened his posture, so as not to look like he wasn't on point. He respected and admired Gutter, so he was always looking for approval. Danny put on his best mean face and nodded.

"Boy, you look like you just swallowed a lemon," Gutter joked.

"Why you always gotta clown me, cuz?" Danny asked.

"'Cause you're trying too hard," Gutter said, walking around to the passenger's side. "Lil homey, I know you're official so you ain't gotta come wit the mean mug."

"Nah, man, I know you know. I just want the rest of these muth-afuckas to recognize. When people see my face, they'll know not to try me."

"Danny, that's bullshit. If a nigga is gonna try you, he's gonna try you. It don't really make no never mind what's on your face. It's all about what's in your heart. Remember that shit."

Gutter had love for the young soldier, but sometimes Danny could be like a child. He was definitely one of the most dedicated little niggaz Gutter had encountered since being on the East Coast. Danny would put in work without question. His only hang-up was inexperience. He was always asking questions and speaking out of turn. Gutter tried not to be too hard on him, because he knew the boy was still young and didn't know any better. What Danny lacked in etiquette, he more than made up for in other areas. Before becoming a full-time banger, Danny was a boxer. He came up short during the Olympic trials, but he was lethal with his hands.

During the ride uptown Gutter and Danny smoked a blunt and made small talk. Danny did most of the talking, while Gutter half listened. He had a lot on his mind. During the time he spent in his coma, much had changed. L.C. Blood was still around, but their numbers had been decimated by Gutter's hit squads. Harlem Crip was still functioning, but not at peak efficiency. Pop Top had done what he could to hold the set together, but he was more of a soldier than a general. They had lost lives and money under his reign. Now it was up to Gutter to put things in order.

They exited the West Side Highway at 125th and coasted

through Harlem. Gutter sat in the passenger side of the truck taking in the scenery. The weather was warm, so people were out in numbers. Shoppers shoved their way up and down the strip, visiting the stores or making their purchases from the vendors.

They made the left on Lenox Avenue, and headed farther into the hood. It seemed like every block was popping that day. People were either outside barbecuing or just shooting the shit. Every hood they went through, someone acknowledged Gutter. They either waved or just stared. His exploits in Harlem had made him both known and feared uptown.

Cutting across 132nd, they made their way east. Danny suggested they not take that route, but as usual, Gutter insisted. They had been shot at on several occasions passing through some of these hoods, but Gutter wasn't easily spooked. How could you scare a man that had already died once? Even though it wasn't the safest way, he wanted his face to be seen. It was to be made clear to each and every hood that he went wherever he pleased.

When they approached the Abraham Lincoln housing projects, Gutter placed his gun on his lap. He had quite a few projects on smash, but Lincoln wasn't one of them. The project was once totally dominated by Bloods, but the increased work the Crips were putting in had caused their control to slip. The project became a free-fire zone coveted by both sides.

When they crossed Madison Avenue, some local hardheads in front of the bodega tried to ice Gutter. He turned his soulless eyes on them and threw up his hood, causing the boys to turn their heads.

"Punk-ass niggaz." Danny snickered. "We should go back and set it on them faggots."

"For what?" Gutter slouched a bit in the seat. "We already got they hearts. Ain't no thrill in busting on a nigga that's scared."

Gutter noticed the questioning glance Danny gave him, but continued looking out the window. He would learn in his own time.

They finally arrived at their destination. It was a storage facility on Park Avenue at 125th, right next to the Metro-North. The young woman behind the reception desk didn't even look up from her magazine when the two bangers came through the front door. Gutter and Danny boarded an elevator and took it to the third floor. When they stepped off they were greeted by home boys smoking blunts and shooting the breeze. Gutter nodded at a few of them and proceeded to the rear storage unit.

The man Gutter had come to see sat on a crate in the last unit. Also inside the unit were Young Rob, Hollywood, and a female named C-style. The room was filled with wooden crates, marked from different ports in the Middle East, and loose sheets of bubble wrap. Some of the crates were sealed, while others sat on the floor open. In the center of all this, Pop Top was hunched over examining a Russian machine gun.

"Sup, O.G. Gutter?" Top asked, looking up from his inspection. A crown of dusty black hair sat atop his head. It had begun to thin in the middle from the stress of hard living, but Top refused to cut it. He was never big on appearances.

"Maintaining," Gutter said, making a mental note of how many boxes were stacked in the room. "Sup wit all that traffic out there?"

"That ain't 'bout nothing," Top said, putting the gun down. "A few of the homeys came by to spend something wit Harlem. Them niggaz is hyped off the new hardware we got."

"If they copped already, why they still here?" Gutter questioned.

"It's blue, cuz. They just kick'n it," Top responded.

"It ain't blue, cuz. You sitting in here on a shitload of illegal burners and you got muthafuckas smoking, congregating in the hall. This ain't no hangout, Top."

"I'll tell the homeys to bounce," Hollywood said from behind his shades. He had been down with the set since the days when Lou-Loc was around. He was a lanky yellow dude, who always dressed in flamboyant gear. Even his jewels were different. From the iced-out globe he wore around his neck, to his bracelet that spelled out his set, Hollywood was a fly nigga. The former hoops star strode from the room to pass along Gutter's decree.

Top and Gutter made eye contact, but no challenge was issued. When Gutter had gotten hit up, Lou-Loc had turned Harlem Crip over to Pop Top. At the time it seemed like a wise decision, but it soon turned sour. Pop Top was a warrior to the heart, but he lacked the diplomacy skills to efficiently lead the set.

Havoc reigned in the coming weeks. Top allowed the homeys to run wild and do as they liked. It didn't take long before the police started riding down on the team, snatching up quite a few of their number on charges. Top solidified Harlem Crip on the streets, but he also sent a blue flag up for the police.

"What we looking at?" Gutter asked, looking over the shipment.

"Shit, ya peoples done set it out," Top replied, pulling out an invoice. "We got all kind of shit up in this piece. Rifles, handguns, the whole shit, cuz. The regular shit is already sold on the streets, but we got some choice clientele for the pretty shit. We doing the damn thang, cuz."

"That's what's up. Sell off whatever you can and hit the homeys off with the rest. I don't want nobody on the set to be without a strap. You hear me?" Gutter slapped his hands together.

"I got you, homey." Pop Top nodded.

"The boy, Diamonds, get wit you on that yet?"

"Yeah, he said he needs like seven and a half this rip."

Gutter thought on it for a minute. "When he comes to cop, give him eight. I like that country muthafucka's style."

"Y'all need to let a bitch hold one of these down," C-style added, picking up a nickel-plated .22. "I got some lingerie to go with this here."

"Bitch, please." Top snatched the gun from her. "You hoes ain't trying to pop nothing."

"Fuck you, nigga! Do you call your mama a bitch, bitch?" C-style had a supermodel figure and the features of an Egyptian princess. High cheekbones sat behind her cinnamon face. Though she was a fun-loving chick, she had a low tolerance for disrespect, which Top had to be reminded of all too often.

"Yo, cuz," Young Rob spoke up. "I heard the young boys Hook and Noodles put the heat to them niggaz from over on Lenox last night." His youthful brown eyes looked at Gutter eagerly for a response.

"Word?" Gutter replied in a very uninterested tone. When Gutter had gotten the wire the night before he knew it was a good move to bring Hook and Noodles in. They were like he and Lou-Loc had been when they were young and didn't give a fuck, which made them the perfect protégés. He currently had them tucked away up in Yonkers until the heat in the city died down.

"Straight gangsta," Rob continued. "Harlem ain't to be fucked with."

Gutter ignored Rob's praises and continued to inspect the arsenal. He was pleased that two more "dead rags" had been taken out of the game, but he didn't show it. To him, the movement wasn't about praise; it was about power and old scores. Before it was all said and done, the other side would pay for his friend's murder a thousand times over.

"I'm taking these," Gutter said, holding up two German assault rifles.

"Drama, cuz?" Top asked.

"Nah, a birthday present for a friend. Let's go, Danny." Gutter said his goodbyes and led Danny from the unit.

NOT LONG after Gutter left, Sharell got ready to start her day. It was her day off and as much as she wanted to sleep in, she knew she couldn't. After taking a long hot shower, Sharell sat on the edge of the bed and began to apply lotion to her body. When she got to her protruding stomach, she smiled.

She and Kenyatta were expecting their first child. The pregnancy wasn't planned, but abortion was never an option. God had blessed them with the most precious of all gifts and she had no intentions on going against his will. With all the stress she had been under, it was a wonder she hadn't miscarried. With Gutter being hell-bent on his insane quest for vengeance, she feared that the child would grow up without a father. She just hoped that fatherhood would get him to calm down.

Since Lou-Loc's murder he had ate, slept, and breathed revenge. Diablo and Cisco were dead, but that wasn't enough for him. In his heart, Gutter felt like he was responsible. Sharell tried to convince him that he wasn't at fault, but he still carried the burden. He was determined to make anyone affiliated with the rival gang feel his pain.

"Pain," Sharell said aloud. She was no stranger to it, physically or emotionally. Since she was a little girl it had always been with her and it probably always would.

Sharell was a devout Christian, putting God and family above all else, but it hadn't always been like that for her. She came up hard on the Harlem streets, right off of 143rd and Lenox Avenue. Her father was a hustler and her mother was an on-again, off-again junkie. Daddy spoiled Sharell when she was little, making sure she was always fly and wanted for nothing. Though her mother spent most of her time nodded out, Sharell had a relatively pleasant childhood. But all that came to an abrupt end shortly before her thirteenth birthday.

Her father had been murdered by a rival drug crew over some money he owed them, or so the police had deduced. The streets told a different story: one where his right-hand man and lieutenant had set him up so he could take his spot. Her father's soldiers promised to make sure Sharell and her mother were good, but of course it didn't play out like that. For a while they would come by to check on things or drop a few dollars off, but as time went on and the memory of her father began to fade from the streets, the visits slowed and eventually stopped altogether.

Though Sharell took the death hard, her mother became completely unglued. She stopped going to work and let herself go physically. She wouldn't eat or wash her ass for days on end. All she did was sit in her room shooting up. As her mother's grip on reality began to slip, so did her hold on her children. Her younger brother, Malik, took to the streets, determined to pick up where his father left off, while Sharell was left to explore the very same ghettos her father had always tried to keep her sheltered from. It wasn't long before she was staying out all night, trying different drugs, and living life at a million miles a minute.

It was the freest Sharell had ever felt in her life. For the next few years she was on a high horse that no one could knock her off. This newfound feeling of liberation lasted up until the point when they got the call that Malik had been killed. You would've thought that losing her baby boy would've sobered her mother up, but it didn't.

She would go to rehab just to come back out and relapse. What most people don't realize about addiction is that it's something that never leaves you. No matter how long you stay clean, you always hear the call in the back of your mind. There was only one real escape from addiction, and Sharell's mother found it when her heart finally gave out on her.

Sharell now found herself a nineteen-year-old high school drop-out, alone in the world. She would spend her days hiding under the covers and her nights clubbing and smoking weed. Her life seemed to be heading in the same direction as her parents and sibling until a chance meeting with a homeless woman one night.

It was about three in the morning when she and her friends were staggering out of a club, drunk and high as kites. As was their ritual, they stopped by White Castle on 125th for a late night–early morning snack. Outside there was a homeless woman begging for change. Her friends passed the woman by, but Sharell stopped and gave her a dollar, which from the woman's reaction might as well have been a winning lottery ticket.

"Bless you, child." The woman smiled, revealing a mouth full of crooked and yellowing teeth. "Bless your heart."

"It's all good," Sharell told her, about to rejoin her friends.

"The Lord is truly gonna shine on you for your kindness," the woman called after her, stopping Sharell short.

"The Lord?" Sharell snorted. "Ma, your god ain't got a whole lot of love for little ghetto kids."

The woman's face took on a look of shock. "No, child, you're wrong. The Lord loves everyone, we are all his children. All we gotta have is a little faith."

"Well, I guess that rules me out because I'm all outta faith."

The woman looked at Sharell sadly. "Don't fret, child, we all waver in the faith from time to time, but whether we know it or not it's always there. But don't you worry none, I'm gonna pray for you and the Lord will show you that he has not abandoned you, no matter how bleak it seems."

"I hear that hot shit," Sharell said, walking away.

"I'm gonna pray for you, child!" the woman called after her. "The Lord loves you, all you gotta do is let him in."

Sharell was dead tired when she got home, but found that she couldn't seem to get to sleep. The old woman's words kept ringing in her head. "The Lord loves you," yeah right. God had taken everything she ever cared about and left her alone in the world. If that was the kinda love he showed than she didn't need it or want it.

Before she knew it, the sun had risen high in the smog-filled sky. Sharell decided to take a walk and try to tire herself out so she could crash. Though she didn't have a particular destination when she left the house, she found herself on the corner of 132nd and Fifth Avenue, staring up at a huge stone church. For reasons that she still couldn't put into words, she stepped inside the house of worship. Sharell hadn't been inside that church in almost ten years and even that was on Easter. Her family had never been very religious, but her mother made sure she and Malik were in church every holiday. The inside was the same as she had remembered it. Wooden benches polished to a high shine, and stained-glass windows that reflected rainbows on the floor.

She walked down the aisle, gently touching the backrest of each bench as she passed it. She could almost see her mother sitting there decked out in her good blue dress and white handbag. Being forced to go to church had always been a pain in the ass for her and Malik, but they dealt with it because it was one of the few days that their mother was guaranteed to be as sober as a judge. A lone tear rolled down her cheek, snapping her out of her daydream. She wiped it away with the back of her hand, but there was another one behind it. The next thing she knew the tears were flowing freely down her face. She tried to walk away, but found that she didn't have the strength to do more than plop down on a bench at the foot of the aisle.

"Why, God," she whispered, looking up at the large cross that was mounted on the wall, just behind the diesis. "I haven't been the best person, but I could be worse. I was going to school and trying to live my life the right way, even if people around me weren't. If you love me so much then why shit on me? Why leave me all by myself?"

"Something that is a part of you can never leave you," a voice called behind her. Though he was a little heavier and his hair had gone completely gray, Sharell still recognized Reverend Greene. He was dressed in a black long-sleeved shirt and gray slacks, his ever present Bible tucked under his arm.

"I'm sorry, Reverend Greene, I didn't mean to intrude," Sharell said, trying to compose herself.

"This is just as much your house as it is his." He pointed his Bible heavenward. "I haven't seen you in a while, Sister Baker."

"I've been kinda busy," she said, avoiding his gaze.

"So I've heard." He sat down on the bench behind her, so she had to turn around to speak to him.

"And what's that supposed to mean?" she asked defensively.

He shrugged. "It means that just because you don't come by to check up on me doesn't mean I haven't been keeping abreast of you." She was about to say something, but he raised his hand and silenced her. "Sharell, I've known your family since before you were born. I've watched you go from a promising young lady to a lost little girl who doesn't know trouble when it's staring her in the face."

"I'm a big girl, I can take care of myself," she told him.

"Just because your ID says you're grown doesn't mean you are. I'm fifty-something years old and there's still much that I have to learn before my time is done here. What's weighing so heavy on you, child?"

"You wouldn't understand," Sharell said. She wasn't even sure that she did.

"You'd be surprised what I understand. I've been around a long time, Sharell, and have seen a great many things."

"No offense, Reverend Greene, but I don't think me and you have seen the same things, the hood is a little different than the church. I don't think you could even begin to grasp my grief."

Reverend Greene laughed and placed his Bible on the bench next to him. "Grief," he said, rolling the sleeve of his shirt up and holding it out so Sharell could see the old track marks and scars. "I live with grief every day. The grief of what I've done and what I'll never do. See, this church wasn't always my life; I was a child of the streets. I've sold dope, coke, and my body for all in the name of the devil and his vices. I ain't proud of it, but neither am I ashamed. We make mistakes so that we can learn from them and pass the lesson on to others."

"And what lessons would you pass on to me, Reverend," Sharell asked, in a half sarcastic tone.

"That there is light at the end of even the blackest tunnels," he said seriously. "Listen, Sharell, I know your grief, and God knows that my heart goes out to you, but you can't let the devil and your own sadness take you out of the fight. You've got to go out into the world and make something of yourself. You've got to show your family that you learned from the lessons they passed on to you."

Sharell shook her head frantically. She tried to maintain a cool façade, but couldn't hold it together. "I can't," she sobbed. "I can't tackle this world by myself."

"You don't have to." He hugged her. "Sharell, you aren't too far gone to pull it together. If you need a crutch, I'll be there for you to see you through it."

"I don't want charity, Reverend."

"It ain't charity, Sharell, I owe this to you."

She pulled away and looked up at him. "Owe it to me?"

Reverend Greene nodded. He took a few minutes to examine a scuff on the hardwood floor before speaking. "Thirty years ago this up-and-coming little punk came to me to front him a package. The boy didn't look old enough to be off his mama's bosom, but he was hungry, and I liked that about him. So, after a little bit of convincing I fronted it to him, which turned out to be one of my biggest regrets in life. Three decades later I find myself looking into the face of his ailing daughter, trying to figure out how to help her pick up the pieces."

"But, Reverend, you didn't take my family," she told him.

"Oh, but I did. I might not have tied your mother off for that last hit, or put them bullets in Malik, but I set off the chain of events. Sharell"—he took her by the shoulders and stood her up—"I couldn't save your father, but I will save you. Let me help you, child. Let us help you." He nodded toward the cross.

A million and one thoughts flashed through Sharell's mind as the weight of his words washed over her. Looking up into the eyes of the man she had known since birth, but actually didn't know anything about, she felt a tingling in the center of her chest. The tingling became a swelling so intense that she felt as if she was having trouble breathing. "I can't do it."

"You can and you will." He tightened his grip on her arms. "All things are possible through God, but you have to be willing to let him in. Are you willing to accept the lord Jesus Christ as your savior?"

With tears stinging her eyes, Sharell looked up and whispered, "Yes." Just like that the bubble in her chest burst and she sucked in the cool air. For the next two hours she sat in the pew with Reverend Greene and talked about her life. It felt like the things that had been weighing her down for years began to fall away piece by piece the more she talked. Sharell went on and on and the reverend sat quietly and listened. He wasn't preaching or judging her, just listening, which is what she needed more than anything else.

True to his word, Reverend Greene helped Sharell get her life back on track. He gave her a part-time job at the church to help her keep up the rent on her parents' apartment and got her into a nursing program that allowed women to take their GED test while studying to be a registered nurse. From that point on, Sharell devoted her life to the church and helping others find their way. Ironically, the soul she was having the most trouble saving was that of the man who was to be her soul mate, Gutter.

Most of her friends thought that she was out of her mind falling for a gangster, but Sharell saw more than just what was on the surface. In Gutter she saw a brave and loving man who would go above and beyond to provide safety and shelter for his family…a man much like her father. Gutter was way rougher around the edges than her father had been, but still she found comfort and love in his arms. At the end of the day it didn't really matter to her what the church or anyone else thought about Gutter, what was important was that she would ride for him whether he was right or wrong. The heart was funny like that.

After dressing in a peach sweat suit, Sharell went downstairs and got into her vehicle. It was a candy-red X5 that Gutter had bought her when they moved to Brooklyn. He wanted to keep her sheltered from the violence that was erupting in Harlem, but she still wanted to be in arm's reach of her friends, so Brooklyn was the compromise.

The ride to Connecticut took her about two hours. Sharell hated driving long distances, but it was for a noble cause. She pulled up to a security booth that sat in the center of a block-long iron fence. After giving the security guard her identification and the name of the patient, Sharell was buzzed through the gate. The grounds of the facility were well kept and smelled of fresh-cut grass. Sharell parked her car in a visitor's space and began the short walk to the main building.

Orderlies patrolled the grounds and escorted patients on walks. A woman of about thirty gave Sharell a childlike grin. Sharell replied with a wave and a smile. She felt bad for the people who made their home at the facility. As much pity as she felt for them, she knew it was a necessary evil.

Sharell walked through the front doors and made her way down a long corridor. At the end of the corridor was a spacious waiting room. A few people sat around in hard plastic chairs, but the room was relatively empty. When Sharell approached the desk she was greeted by a portly nurse.

"Hello, Ms. Baker." The nurse smiled. "How are you?"

"I'm fine," Sharell replied.

"I see you made it this week."

"Yeah, I'd like to come more often, but it's hard for me to get off from work on visiting days. How is she?"

"Up and down." The nurse sighed. "Some days it seems like we're making progress, while others she's totally nonresponsive. She's eating on her own now, but not doing much else. Come on, I'll take you to her."

The nurse led Sharell to a door that required a card to be opened. Beyond the door was another hall with rooms on either side. Each room contained one patient. Some were busy with different activities while others just occupied space. Sharell tried not to stare too long and followed the nurse to the last door.

"You can go on in," the nurse said, opening the door. "If you need anything, just ask one of the orderlies. Enjoy your visit."

"Thanks." Sharell smiled. After the nurse had gone, she took a deep breath and entered the room.

Satin sat in a recliner, staring out the window. Whether she heard Sharell come in or not, she didn't acknowledge her. It had been about a month or so since she had last seen Satin. She would've liked to spend more time with her, but in addition to it being a long drive to the facility, the visits were painful. She couldn't bear to see what Lou-Loc's soul mate had become.

Before the murder Sharell hadn't really had a chance to get to know Satin. They had spoken on the phone once or twice, but that was about as far as it went. They all planned to vacation in Miami Beach when Gutter came out of his coma, but they never got the chance. Gutter had come to visit her when she first came to the facility, but he too found the scene heartbreaking. His visits became less and less frequent, but Sharell still came when she could.

"Hey, baby," Sharell said, pulling a folding chair beside Satin's. "How you been?" Satin turned and smiled at her, but she didn't respond. Sharell was used to this. Sometimes she and Satin would pass a few words between each other, but most of the time, Sharell did most of the talking.

Satin didn't look anything like the pictures Sharell had seen of her and Lou-Loc. Her hair was uncombed and she had deep circles under her eyes from sleepless nights. She was still beautiful, but she looked worn. The glow appeared to be returning to her color, but she was still pale. Her lips were chapped and she looked like she had put on a few pounds since Sharell's last visit. At least she was eating.

"Do you feel like talking today?" asked Sharell. Satin just continued to stare. "Satin"—Sharell took her hand—"I know you can hear me. Baby, I'm not even gonna front like I know what you're going through, 'cause I've never walked a mile in your shoes. You're probably still in a lot of pain, but trust that the Lord will make things right."

More silence.

"Okay," Sharell said, pulling a small Bible from her purse, "you don't have to talk, just listen." Sharell proceeded to read a passage from the Bible.

▬ ▬ ▬ ▬ ▬ ▬ ▬ ▬ ▬ ▬ ▬ ▬ ▬ ▬ ▬ ▬ ▬ ▬

chapter 3

DANNY PULLED the truck up in front of the bodega and killed the engine. He wanted to accompany the O.G. inside, but Gutter instructed him to wait. He never brought people into the stronghold of his partner. After retrieving the duffel bag containing one of the German machine guns, Gutter walked into the store.

Inside, the store was buzzing with activity. People were browsing through the aisles, while others were paying for their purchases. As usual, Roc was at his post behind the counter. Noticing Gutter, he motioned for Hassan to relieve him. The skinny boy still looked the same as he did during their first meeting.

"*Al-salaam alaykum,*" Roc greeted Gutter, coming from behind the counter.

"*Alaykum salaam,*" Gutter replied.

"Anwar awaits you in the war room. I trust you remember the way?"

"All day, cuz," Gutter said, cutting through the aisle. He pushed open the door to the storeroom and proceeded to the freezer. Stepping inside the freezer, Gutter punched the numeric code into the keyboard. It took Anwar awhile before he trusted him enough to reveal the combination. The Al Mukalla valued their privacy, which is why Gutter never brought anyone within their hall with him.

The elevator went dark, but the metal detectors didn't sweep him this time. He had given Roc prior notice of the parcel he was carrying. He stepped off on the ground floor and made his way down the infamous hall of eyes. The hidden cameras observed his approach, but he didn't spare them a second look. Approaching the door to the war room Gutter looked at the Arabic writing and chuckled. "Freedom for the sons and daughters of Allah," he read it out loud. Bush had yet to withdraw the troops so it looked like the freedom wouldn't be coming anytime soon. Gutter removed his shoes and knocked on the iron door.

After a brief wait, the door clicked partially open. Gutter pushed it the rest of the way and stepped inside. As usual the room was dimly lit. The conference table and sofa were gone, but the desk and vast wall of monitors remained. Sitting cross-legged on a prayer rug was Anwar.

The leader of the Al Mukalla swept his long hair from his face and looked up at his visitor. "Enter and be welcomed, child of the Soladine family," Anwar said, in a formal tone.

"Greetings, young prince, I come to you in friendship and thank you for your hospitality." Gutter matched his tone.

"Please, come and be seated," Anwar said, motioning to an empty space on the rug.

Gutter adjusted the duffel bag and took a seat on the rug with Anwar. "A gift for the birthday boy." Gutter smiled, handing him the bag.

Anwar smiled and accepted the gift. He examined the machine gun and nodded in approval. "Very nice."

"I thought you might like it."

"Indeed," Anwar said, setting the weapon off to the side. "How goes things?"

"Another day, another hustle." Gutter sighed. "Things are still a little crazy, but it's coming together."

"Glad to hear it." Anwar nodded. "For a time, we were concerned about the state of our agreement. No disrespect to your comrade Pop Top, but I did not relish the idea of having to do business with him."

"Top means well, but not everyone is skilled at diplomacy. He's served his purpose, but I'm back running the show now. I'm gonna do what I gotta to make sure the set flourishes."

"Indeed," Anwar agreed. "How's Sharell?"

"She's good. She still hasn't gotten used to the idea of living in Brooklyn, but it's for the best. I love that girl with everything that I am, so I need to keep her out of harm's way."

"As you should. Tell me this though, when are you going to make it official?"

"Come on with that." Gutter waved him off.

"I'm serious. Even if she wasn't carrying your child, I think she has more than proven her loyalty and love for you."

"I plan to marry her one day; it's just that the time isn't right yet."

"Kenyatta, that's a weak excuse and you know it. Though you lost your way for a time, you are still one of Allah's children. Living with a woman and giving her a child outside of marriage is an American custom. Being as we are, a wife completes the foundation of life. She is the earth which you have planted your seed in and should be cherished as such."

"I know, but there's just so much going on with me right now," Gutter explained.

"Speaking of which, how are you?" Anwar questioned.

"I'm fine," Gutter shrugged. "Still got a few aches, but I'll be okay."

"Not your physical, my brother, your soul. I see much unrest in your eyes. The devil tries to worm its way into your spirit and you welcome him with open arms."

"It ain't like that, Anwar. It's just that a lot of shit has to be made right before I can move on."

"And what constitutes making it right? Since you've come back on the scene, much blood has been spilled in the streets. The murderers of your brother are dead and gone, yet you carry on the siege. Will it take your own death to end it?"

"If need be," Gutter said very seriously. "Lou-Loc was the only friend I ever had. They cut him down like a dog in the streets. I can't let that shit ride. They gotta pay!"

"Kenyatta"—Anwar placed his hand on Gutter's forearm—"I understand your need for vengeance, but what about your need for peace? How can one pay a debt that has no denomination? You have swimmed through rivers of blood to reach this point. You have money and an army behind you. I implore you to abandon this quest before it consumes you."

"I wish I could," Gutter said, trying not to get choked up, "but I can't. These busters gotta feel what I feel. I wanna hurt them, Anwar."

"Gutter," Anwar said, using his street name. "Your father and his father before him were both very wise men, but I fear the trait wasn't passed along to you. Only a fool has everything, but still feels it isn't enough. You must ask yourself, are you killing for vengeance or is it something deeper than that?"

Gutter felt his anger clawing its way to the top. He was sure Anwar saw the rage flickering in his eyes, but he still sat motionless, staring at the ganglord. Had this been anyone else, Gutter would've pummeled him for speaking so freely. But the man sitting before him wasn't anyone else. He was the prince of a city within a city. More important, he was right. The killing would have to end at some point, but it wouldn't be today.

"I gotta go," Gutter said, rising to his feet. He made for the door, while Anwar remained seated.

"I'm sorry, Kenyatta," Anwar called behind him. "Not sorry for expressing myself, but for the conflict that continues to poison your soul. May Allah walk with you on whatever road you choose."

GUTTER WAS tight when he left the bodega. *Leave it to Anwar's little philosophical ass to rain on a nigga's day,* Gutter thought to himself. He understood what Anwar was saying about losing focus, but why didn't Anwar understand what *he* was saying? Anwar was beginning to sound like Sharell.

Just thinking of his boo drained some of the anger from his face. If nobody was in his corner, she was, even when he was on his bullshit, which was most of the time lately. Still, she rode with him and had been just as solid as when he'd met her.

He and Lou-Loc had only been in New York for a few months and still trying to get the lay of the land. It didn't take them long to open up shop and get a short crack flow popping out of this base head's house on Lexington. It was the first of the month and they had sold out of product just after sundown. Being that they wouldn't be able to re-up until the next day they decided to hit the party scene and blow some of their newfound wealth.

They tried to hit up some popular spots in Midtown, but because they were dressed in boots and jeans instead of button-ups and loafers it didn't go too well. They ended up rolling through this spot on Eighth called the Sugar Shack. It was a small spot, but the atmosphere was mellow. There were some birds in the joint, but for the most part it was a light crowd. Gutter was about to suggest that they bail when the night suddenly started looking up.

Lou-Loc was leaning against the bar, jabbing with a thick Spanish chick while Gutter played the cut, brooding over his Heineken when Sharell walked in with two of her peoples. Gutter could tell they were squares by their conservative dress, when most of the other chicks were in man-catching gear. Still, all three chicks were fine and Gutter was lonely. As they passed he tried to capture them with his alluring green eyes, but the first two passed without giving him so much as a glance. It was the last one who looked over at him. The look couldn't have been for more than a heartbeat, but in that heartbeat something passed between them.

"Say, cuz." Gutter tapped his partner. "Check them joints right there." He nodded toward the trio that had taken one of the tables in the back.

Lou-Loc kept his hand on the girl's thigh and leaned over to his friend. "Who, them square bitches?"

"Yeah, man. Yo, I think I'm about to move on baby girl in the green sweater." He rubbed his perspiring hands against his jeans.

"Man, that broad ain't fucking wit yo old thug-ass. Kick back, cuz, I'm 'bout to see if baby here got a friend." He jerked his head toward the girl he was talking to.

"Man, fuck that bitch; I need you to help me break the ice with baby girl," Gutter said, not really caring if the current object of Lou-Loc's affection heard him.

"Man, you tripping. I ain't 'bout to go over there looking in no projects when I got prime real estate right here." He traced his finger down the girl's arm, causing her to giggle. Lou-Loc was about to lean over and whisper something in her ear when Gutter grabbed him roughly by the arm. He was surprised to see the seriousness in Gutter's eyes.

"Cuz, you know I wouldn't even put you out there unless it was serious," Gutter told him.

"Damn, you really snagged, huh?" Lou-Loc shook his head.

"Nigga, I ain't asking for your firstborn kid or no shit like that. All I want you to do is go over there and ask honey if I can speak to her for a minute."

Lou-Loc twisted his lips. "Dawg, not only do you want me to smile and nod for these lame hoes, but you got me on some high school shit at that?" Gutter's eyes were almost pleading now. Lou-Loc whispered something to the girl he had been talking to. From the way she stormed off you could tell that she didn't take rejection well.

"A'ight, loc, I got you on this here, but I ain't tricking no bread on getting these chicks faded. You got the crush, you buying the damn drinks." Lou-Loc swaggered over to the table.

Gutter fumbled around on the bar stool, trying to find a cool-ass position while Lou-Loc approached the table. The girls looked up at him with everything from lust to disgust as he spoke, moving his hands to punctuate his words. One girl, who Gutter would later come to know as Lauren, rolled her eyes while the other two broke out into a fit of laughter. Gutter felt like he had played hisself and wished he'd listened to Lou-Loc. The girl in the green sweater tugged him down by the arm and whispered something in his ear. Lou-Loc shrugged and made his way back to the bar with a smirk on his face.

"What she say, cuz?" Gutter asked, trying not to make eye contact with the girl in the green sweater because she and her friends were staring over at them.

Lou-Loc took his time before answering. "She say that I need to take you home."

"What?" Gutter looked confused.

"Home girl said that anybody who is still sending his friend to step to girls for him ain't old enough to be in no bar." Lou-Loc slipped and let out the laughter he had been holding.

"Fuck you, Lou-Loc." Gutter shoved him.

"My fault, man, but you should've seen your face when I told you you'd been shot down!"

"I ain't stunting that broad." Gutter tapped the bar to get the bartender's attention.

"G, why you just go over there and holla at her?"

"Why, so them bitches can get another good laugh off me? Nah, I'm good."

Lou-Loc stopped laughing. "Cuz, I know you ain't scared of no broad? Oh, hell nah, not big muthafucking Gutter from Harlem! Nigga, fuck licking your wounds about this shit, you want shorty then you go get her. You know how we do it on the left, cuz." Lou-Loc knew just the right things to say to get his friend motivated, because right after Gutter downed the shot of Crown Royal the bartender had set down, he was on his feet and on his way across to the spot where the three girls were sitting.

Gutter's heart was slamming against his chest so rapidly that it's a wonder it wasn't visible through his shirt. Lou-Loc and Crown Royal had put the battery in him, but he was already committed to the move so he couldn't back out. All eyes were on him as he crossed the room, but when he arrived at the table only the girl in the green sweater kept his gaze.

Gathering his courage Gutter said, "Sup, baby, they call me Gutter. Why don't you let me buy you a drink of something?"

"No the hell he didn't," Lauren said.

"Tired, tired, tired," the other girl mumbled.

Green sweater turned around in her chair and looked Gutter up and down. "Can I ask you a personal question?"

"Fo sho," he said, figuring he had her.

"Are you a virgin?"

Gutter looked at her quizzically. "Hell, nah, why?"

"Because it's a wonder that you can get a woman to sleep with you approaching her like that. No, I don't know if you prefer hood rats or ghetto girls, but I don't fall into either category. So if you're really trying to get my attention you need to rethink your approach." Without another word, she turned her back to him and went back to her martini.

"What? Man, fuck this shit." He stormed away. He was halfway back to the bar when he glanced over his shoulder. Lauren and the other girl were laughing at him, but the young lady in the green sweater was giving him a look somewhere between pity and curiosity. He looked over at Lou-Loc who just threw his hands up. "I ain't no chump," Gutter said to himself before busting a U-turn and heading back to the table.

"Excuse me," he said when he got back to the table. "I didn't mean to interrupt you ladies, but I just had to come over here and tell you what a vision you were. My name is Kenyatta"—he extended his hand to the young lady in the green sweater—"and you are?"

The girl in the green sweater looked up and smiled at him for getting it right that time. "Sharell." She took his hand and held it for a minute.

"Well, Ms. Sharell, if I'm not overstepping my bounds, I'd like to invite you to the bar to join me for a drink."

"I can't run out on my girls like that," she answered. His eyes flashed disappointment but it was only for a second before she continued. "But you're more than welcome to join us."

Lauren took this time to press her hate campaign. "Sharell, you don't know this thug from a hole in the wall. Ain't no way—"

"Lauren, knock it off," Sharell cut her off. "Gutter," she called him by his street name to ease some of the tension mounting in his face. "Please pay my friend no mind, she's off her meds today. You can sit with us."

"Yeah, especially if you bring your friend with you," the third girl added.

Lou-Loc was reluctant at first, but Gutter promised him a half ounce of haze for his services so he came over. There was an instant connection between Gutter and Sharell. They were from two totally different walks of life, but their personalities seemed to go together like peanut butter and jelly. The five of them had a good time that night, even with Lauren hating on the sidelines. When the lounge closed Gutter and Sharell went for breakfast, while Lou-Loc agreed to drop her girls off. Gutter had heard whispers that Lou-Loc had convinced Lauren and her friend to get into some freak shit that night, but none of them would ever admit it.

Gutter and Sharell stayed together that night and well into the next day, just enjoying each other's company. For as much as he wanted to taste Sharell's fine ass, she made it clear from the gate that she didn't rock like that. Gutter was so into her that didn't even matter to him. He was willing to wait a lifetime for her, but luckily they only put off sex for a month, and by then they were an exclusive couple. Gutter had engaged in the random fling, but ever since the night he'd met her, Sharell would always have his heart. The street, however, had a receipt for his soul.

SINCE GUTTER had gotten back in the truck, he had hardly said a word to Danny. It wasn't usual for him to get quiet after a visit to the suspicious bodega, but this time it was different. He seemed almost hostile. Even when he gave Danny their next destination, there was an edge to his voice.

When they arrived in Fort Greene, Gutter punched in a number on his cell phone. When the caller answered, all Gutter said was, "I'm here," and hung up. After a few minutes, two young men came walking out of the projects. Danny didn't know the dark-skinned boy, but he recognized the Puerto Rican.

Louie was a professional thief. He and a few of his associates were former members of the Low Lifes, turned Crips. They made paper hustling other people out of theirs. They robbed everything from stores to supermarkets. It really didn't make a difference to them. If Gutter was coming to see him, he either wanted something stolen or wanted to purchase a hot item.

"Sup, cuz," Louie said, leaning into the truck.

"You got that for me?" Gutter asked, lighting a cigarette.

"All day, my nigga. Come on."

Gutter told Danny to keep the engine running while he followed Louie around the corner. They cut through the projects and found themselves in a parking lot. Louie led Gutter to a gray Honda Accord. The car had seen better days, but it would do.

"Yeah, this should work," Gutter said, handing Louie a roll of bills. Gutter got behind the wheel and started the engine.

"My sister works at the DMV, so I was able to get you a temp plate," Louie said, pointing at the orange sticker in the back window. "Just make sure you snatch it out when you dump the car."

"I got you, cuz." Gutter gave Louie dap and pulled out of the parking lot. When he pulled up next to the truck, Danny was already reaching for his hammer. "Easy," Gutter said, rolling down the window. "Follow me. We're gonna park the truck, and then I want you to drive this muthafucka."

"A'ight, G," Danny said, putting the car in gear. "Where we going?"

"To bust on some slobs." Gutter mashed the gas pedal and pulled out.

Danny grinned as he tailed the Honda to the B.Q.E. The crew was dropping bodies throughout the five boroughs, but Gutter mostly pulled the strings. If he was about to ride out, it must be a big fish. Danny didn't care either way. As long as he was getting a chance to earn his stripes, he was wit it.

"YOU KNOW I don't be doing this kinda shit," C-style said, undoing her bra.

"I know, baby, but moms ain't go to work today," Rob said, planting kisses on her now exposed breasts. C-style was a slim girl, but had just enough of everything in all the right places.

"A'ight, but hurry the fuck up. I don't want nobody to catch us and start spreading rumors about me being a ho, you know it ain't that type of party." She turned to the staircase wall and braced her hands against it. Had it been anybody else there was no way in hell C-style would've agreed to have sex in a stairwell, but she had a soft spot for Young Rob's handsome ass. She wasn't sure if she'd ever been in love before, but what she felt for Rob was the closest thing to it.

"Baby, I'd put lead to any nigga who ever called you out your name," he said, slipping her sweatpants down passed her waist.

"Hold up." She looked over her shoulder at him. "You got a condom on?"

"C, you know I ain't got nothing. We got tested at the same time, remember?" he reminded her.

"It ain't about catching nothing, Rob, but I ain't trying to end up no damn teenage mother like the rest of these bitches."

"Don't worry." He kissed her passionately. "I'll pull out when I cum." Before C-style could protest further, Rob was inside her. Rob was so thirsty to get it going he didn't take into consideration that she was still mostly dry, so it hurt when he first entered her, but once her juices started flowing, it was all good.

Rob humped away like a man on a mission while she tried her best to keep from skinning her face against the concrete wall. Though Rob was well hung and C-style enjoyed their little fuck sessions, he had a lot to learn about tact. He wasn't trying to make it pleasurable for her, just working to get his nut off. She made a mental note to herself to talk to him about it as soon as she got a chance. Before C-style could even tell him to slow down, she felt Rob's body go stiff and him dump out inside her.

"Oh, hell no!" She pushed him off her. C-style looked between her legs and saw semen running down her thigh and into her sweatpants.

"My fault, ma. That shit got so good I couldn't hold it." Rob was leaning against the wall with his pants around his ankles. His dick was swinging freely with leftover cum dripping from the tip.

"Rob, you are so fucking irresponsible. I told you I don't want to get pregnant!" she barked, taking a sanitary wipe from her bag and trying to clean up the mess he'd made.

"Damn, why you tripping. It's not like I wouldn't be there for you if you got pregnant. I'd handle mine," he assured her.

C-style gave him an angry look. "Rob, how the hell you gonna handle anything when all you do is run the streets with the set? You ain't even got a job."

"I sling stones for mine, baby, you know what it is," he said proudly.

"Rob, your ass is too smart to be so stupid. You think you can play the block forever?"

"Nah, not forever. Just until I get my cake up. Fucking with Gutter we all gonna be rich."

"Fucking with Gutter you're more likely to end up dead than rich," she said seriously. "Rob, you know I love the big homey too, but he's gang-banging on a whole 'nother level."

"So, what you trying to say? You don't think I can hang?"

"Rob"—she touched his face—"I'm not saying that at all. What I'm saying is to get where Gutter is, you've gotta be willing to go to hell and spit in the devil's face. When I look into your eyes I see life and promise, when I look into his eyes I don't see *anything*."

Rob sucked his teeth. "Whatever, man. One day you're gonna see that your man is just as down as anybody else, you watch." He pulled his pants up and started walking down the stairs.

"Where are you going?" she asked with an attitude.

"I gotta meet the homeys," he called over his shoulder. "I'll get up with you later, ma."

C-style stood in the staircase not knowing whether she should be mad at Rob or herself. He had pulled a typical nigga move, getting his then leaving her without so much as a hug or a kiss, just to go be with the set. Being down used to be fun, but that was before the killing. Gutter promised to bring prominence back to the C-nation, but all he'd brought was death. She and Rob were both down with the movement, but it was Rob's determination to prove himself that scared her. She knew how Gutter and Pop Top broke in their shooters and knew that Rob couldn't handle that kind of pressure.

HOLLYWOOD STEPPED out of his smoke-gray Chrysler 300 Limited. The vehicle resembled a Bentley, but the design was more squared.

He fitted it with whitewalls, but left the factory rims on it. He would always tell people that the factories on that particular car gave it nobility. Hollywood had what people would call refined taste. He liked his cars plush, his women seasoned, and his money new. This is what pulled him from between a young girl's thighs to the block.

Hollywood gave himself the once-over in the vehicle's tinted reflection. He ran a manicured hand down the waves that rippled through his dark hair. The laces of his Nike Airs looked as if they had been bleached, while the cuffs of his jeans were perfect. After adjusting the collar on his smoke-gray blazer, he stepped off the curb.

He saw B. T. and a few of the other homeys congregating in front of the store. The timing couldn't have been better. B. T. owed him some money through one of his girls. She had swung an episode with the Crip, but he couldn't pay all of the money. After dropping Hollywood's name, and agreeing to repay the rest, she let him rock. Now, it was a week later and B. T. didn't have Hollywood's bread. The set was the set, but this was business.

Hollywood adjusted the pistol tucked in his pants, near his kidneys, and headed in their direction. As he passed the bus stop, he was confronted with a vision. The young girl was brown-skinned with hair that tickled her shoulders. She had nice round breasts and a shapely ass. She was reading a copy of *Section 8* over her glasses.

"Hey, baby girl," Hollywood said, easing around the advertisement to stand next to the girl.

She glanced at him with a look of disgust on her face. After looking up and down at him, she snorted and went back to her book. Now someone in the know might've taken this as rejection, but Hollywood always dug deeper than the surface. The fact that she had even bothered to look him over meant that she was considering it. That was incentive enough for him.

"I didn't mean to come between you and your reading, but I'm a lil lost at the moment," Hollywood lied. "I just wanted to know if you could point me to building Two Fifty-nine?"

"I ain't from around here." The girl had a soft voice.

"A blind man could see that. You came from heaven right?" Hollywood flattered her.

"Yeah, right." She blushed.

"True story"—he eased closer—"I'd be thankful for the directions, but I'd be thrilled with a moment of your time."

The girl looked Hollywood over once more. She found him very attractive, and from the looks of his gear, he was getting some type of money. The bus came and went, but the girl remained. After about ten minutes, Hollywood was letting her into his car with instructions to wait for him. Then he stepped back across the street to handle his money.

"Damn, you don't play," China said, slapping Hollywood's palm. He was a brown-skinned cat with slanted eyes. Originally from San Francisco, China was the product of a black whore who had the misfortune of having the condom break while turning an Asian trick.

"You know how it is, man. I gotta stay one step ahead of the competition," Hollywood replied. "Sup, B. T.?"

"Ain't nothing," B. T. said. His beady little eyes kept going from Hollywood to the car. If you looked closely, you could still see the scar on his head from when Lou-Loc had pistol-whipped him. Though he never said it out loud, he wasn't sad to see him go.

"Say, I need to holla at you, T," Hollywood said.

"So, talk." He shrugged.

"Dig, you and one of my ladies came to an understanding over some paper, and she says she ain't seen it yet."

"Oh, I told shorty I'd square up with her." B. T. brushed him off.

"Yeah, I dig that. Thing is, you ain't made no moves to settle the debt."

"Yo, you stunting me over a few dollars?" asked B. T., sounding a bit hostile.

"Listen, man," Hollywood said, hooking his thumbs in his belt. He kept his hand close to his gun. "You know I don't do nothing but count money. Them few dollars you skipped with don't mean shit. This is about principle. Pay to play, cuz."

"Damn, kid. All that shit you slinging in the hood and you shorting bitches," China clowned.

"Fuck you," B. T. snapped, "and for damn sure fuck that bitch!" He tried to give Hollywood his coldest stare, hoping it would rattle the pretty boy. It didn't.

"Yo, I think you need to watch your tone, cuz," Hollywood replied, removing his shades. No matter how flashy Hollywood was, there was nothing sweet about him.

"Fuck y'all bitch-ass niggaz arguing about?" Pop Top came out of the store, breaking the tension.

"Ain't nothing," Hollywood said, never taking his eyes off B. T., "just a little dispute between the homeys."

"B. T. owes Wood some paper and he stunting on the debt," China confessed.

"Why don't you mind ya muthafucking business?" B. T. turned on China.

"Them stitches in the side of your head ain't taught you nothing." Top nodded toward the scar Lou-Loc had given him shortly before his murder. "Either pay, cuz, or go head up for it, but ain't gonna be no extra shit. That goes for both you muthafuckas."

B. T. sized Hollywood up and weighed his options. True, he owed the girl some money, but he wasn't really feeling how Wood was coming at him. He had been down with the set longer, so he figured his seniority should've been respected in that right, but Hollywood was about his paper. He reasoned that he could take Hollywood in a fight, but if he lost he would've been embarrassed as well as wrong. Reluctantly B. T. reached into his pocket and gave Hollywood what he owed him.

"Now, was that so hard?" Pop Top patted B. T. on his back. "Y'all niggaz always going at each other instead of dropping these dead rag chumps. You got the young boys showing you up."

"I heard Hook and them dropped some brims the other night?" China asked.

"Square biz," Top confirmed.

"That nigga Gutter got this shit like the Wild West. Soon we ain't gonna have nobody to bang on," Hollywood joked.

"Some niggaz know how to hold a grudge." Top shrugged.

"Shit, he fucking up our paper." B. T. snorted. "Police running all up and through the block and shit, how we supposed to sling?"

"Same way you been doing it. With caution," Top said. "Gutter gonna keep riding for his nigga until he gets it out of his system. I know it's hard on y'all, but that's how the homey wants it."

"Man, fuck that," B. T. spat. "That nigga been dead how long? I'm trying to get money, fuck that ol' mourning shit."

"Watch ya mouth, cuz." Top glared at him. "That nigga you wolfing 'bout is a ghetto legend. I know you still salty over that ass-whipping, but you had it coming. Learn when to shut the fuck up!"

B. T. was uptight, but he didn't say anything. Awhile back he and

Lou-Loc had a dispute over his relationship with Satin. The end result was him getting pistol-whipped and stripped of his rank on the set. He had tried to have the assassin murdered, but his people were sent back in bags. Before B. T. could make a second attempt, someone blew Lou-Loc's brains out.

"Well"—Hollywood popped his collar—"I'd love to stay and chat with you fellas, but I got some new pussy to sample. Nice doing business with you, B. T." Hollywood winked at him and went to join the young lady waiting in his car.

chapter 4

OOK AT this shit," Ruby said, slapping a copy of the *New York Post* down on the table. Highlighted in the corner was an article about a gang-related shooting in Harlem. "Three more soldiers gone. These crabs is getting out of hand."

"Relax," Supreme said, tearing into a piece of chicken. "Their little run is gonna come to an end soon enough." Supreme was a chunky cat who wore his hair in braids. The sleeves of his red shirt were rolled up slightly, advertising the iced-out watch on his right arm. He commanded a small army of soldiers from Hillside, Queens, that had been called in to lend aid against the rival set. Supreme and his soldiers had proven to be efficient killers, and were respected even by the Crips.

"I don't see it," she continued. "We've been dancing in place for damn near three years and we're still getting our asses kicked. Then that stupid little fuck Cisco stirs up all this shit. 'Once Lou-Loc is gone, Harlem will be wide-open.' Bullshit. What we went through with him was like a light slap on the ass compared to what Gutter is putting down. He took that shit *way* personal."

"Yeah, I gotta give it to him. Gutter turned out to be a real headache," Supreme confessed. "What I wanna know is, how the hell he got back up when Scales and them laid him out?"

"That's what a lot of people wanna know," Ruby said, pushing a strand of red hair from her face. "No one expect him to live, let alone be running around shooting muthafuckas. Shit, even the big boys are scratching their heads about this one. I heard a rumor that their thinking about calling in some help. Some of us are gonna find ourselves without a set to run."

"Fuck it." Supreme wiped his hands on a napkin. "We put him down once, we can do it again. Ain't nobody gonna come in here trying to tell me how to conduct my shit. When I put a bullet in that muthafucka, they're gonna give me a promotion."

Supreme had already begun putting a plan together to get at Gutter. He had successfully murdered several key players in the Crip army and he reasoned it would only be a matter of time before he snagged the prize. After dropping some money on the table, he and Ruby exited the restaurant.

Supreme smiled proudly as he held the door for Ruby. She was hard as hell, but she still had it. Ruby was the color of a Hershey's Kiss, with a body straight off sticky pages. The tight shorts she wore exposed just enough ass cheek to make a man do a double take. In addition to being set leaders, she and Supreme were also fuck buddies.

The sun was beginning to set, but Jamaica Avenue was still buzzing with activity. People were either going in and out of stores, or just on the strip stunting. Supreme smiled proudly as he followed Ruby to her car. No sooner than he walked around to the passenger side, a gray Honda skidded to a stop beside them.

"Say, Blood, you looking for me?" Gutter asked, aiming his

.40 caliber over the roof of the car. When Supreme turned around, Gutter shot him once in the face and twice in the chest.

Blood splattered on the car as well as a shocked Ruby. Seeing Supreme get splattered stunned her, but it didn't last long. She pulled her .380 from her handbag and returned fire. The back window shattered, but she didn't hit Gutter or the driver. Ruby walked around the car and looked over what was left of Supreme. As she watched his life drain into the gutter she vowed that there would be a reckoning.

NIGHT HAD fallen and the fiends had come out to get their blast. In the depths of the jungle you cop whatever you needed to escape whatever troubles you had. They readily sold their souls for a temporary release. Even with the increased police patrols, business was still able to be handled. B. T. and China sat on the bench, passing a blunt back and forth watching it all.

"These niggaz is a trip," China said, taking a toke of the blunt. "How can you know crack is gonna fuck your life up, and still smoke it? These people ain't got no scruples."

"Man, fuck these niggaz," B. T. said, spitting on the ground. "They can get as high as they want as long as I got a fat pocket."

"You're a sick dude." China laughed him off. "Say, what was that shit wit you and Top earlier?" Being fairly new to the set, China didn't know B. T.'s story.

"Fuck that nigga," B. T. replied. "He riding a dead man's dick."

"Everywhere I go I hear about this Lou-Loc cat," China said, passing the blunt.

"Man, he wasn't nobody. If he was so muthafucking hard, them brims wouldn't have aired his ass out."

A fiend walking up on them broke up their conversation. She

was a Hispanic girl with a pretty, round face. The effects of drug abuse had begun to make her lose weight, but she still had a very nice shape. Her eyes held a look of hunger that both men understood.

"What's up, fellas. Got some coke?" she asked, wiping her nose with her sleeve.

"Bitch, you better go see them lil' niggaz like everybody else," B. T. snapped.

"Come on, B. T. Don't do me like that, you know we go way back."

"Marisol, you better get the fuck away from me."

"We can work something out," she said, touching his knee.

"You must be out ya fucking mind." He slapped her hand away. "You just as grimy as ya sister was. I slide with you, and I'll probably wake up with a pistol to my head. Get out my face!"

Marisol sucked her teeth and walked away. She knew she was playing herself by being out there like that, but what choice did she really have? Her boyfriend had lost his position at the firm for drug abuse, then he up and left her to move back with his family. She found herself out on her ass and broke. The fall from diva to dopehead was a short but hard one. She started out snorting with her boo in the high-class circles then ended up stalking a fix on the block like the rest of the fiends. The sick part of her addicted brain told her that the actions of her sister Martina had cast a black shadow over her family.

The downhill spiral began when Lou-Loc was murdered. Though she knew her sister was hurt over the loss of her meal ticket she never thought she would take it to the extremes she did. Martina couldn't accept the fact that Lou-Loc didn't want her so she concocted a plan to punish him. Though Marisol and Lou-Loc had never seen eye to eye she still didn't believe he should've been murdered, especially like that. After his death Martina was found dead. The police still had no clues as to exactly what had happened, but Marisol knew. The devil she had served for so long had come back to swallow her. It was just too bad that she had set him on everyone else's heels in the process.

Marisol wiped the long tear from her cheek that the stroll down memory lane had left her and moved deeper into the trenches to see who else she might be able to offer her services to for a blast.

"YO, YOU twisted that faggot, son!" Danny squealed. "That boy head exploded like *boom*! Yo, I think a piece of his brain was stuck on the window."

"Danny, anybody ever tell you that you talk too much?" Gutter asked, lighting the blunt that was hanging from his mouth.

"It's blue, cuz. I was just trying to give you your props. You pushed son's wig back. That shit was dope!"

"Let me tell you something." Gutter turned on him. "Ain't nothing glorious about murder. Blood don't wash off, lil nigga. You ever shot somebody?"

"Nah, but I would," Danny quickly shot back.

"But the point is, you *haven't*. You ain't never seen death up close and personal. Baby boy, you don't know what kind of demons haunt me everyday of my life. You're a good soldier, Danny, but don't be so quick to sell your soul for stripes." Gutter leaned back in his seat and busied himself looking out the window.

Danny felt kind of foolish being chastised by his mentor. All he was trying to do was give it up to Gutter on his flawless execution of Supreme, but he ended up getting flipped on. Everyone doubted him because he was young, but Danny was eager to prove just how 'bout it he was. When his time came, he would surely step to the plate. Danny dropped Gutter off in front of his building and drove off into the night.

When Gutter got into the duplex, he noticed that the light was still on in the study. He had hoped to come in and wash the gun smoke from his body, then ease into the bed with his lady. Unfortunately, Sharell was still up. He walked into the makeshift office and greeted his lady.

"Sup, boo," he said, kissing her on the cheek.

"Hey, Ken"—she patted him on the leg—"I left dinner in the oven for you."

"I'm not hungry," he said, turning to leave the room.

"Everything okay?"

"Yeah, everything is blue. How's Satin?"

"Still the same." She shrugged. "The nurse said she's up and down, but no major changes. She's putting on some weight though. Probably all that medication they're giving her. My heart really goes out to her. Lord knows I'd probably lose it if something were to ever happen to you."

"You ain't gotta worry about that. I ain't going nowhere," he assured her.

"That's easy to say, Ken, but no one can foresee God's plan."

"I don't know about God's plan, but I know about *my* plan. I'm gonna be here to be a father to my child and a husband to my lady."

"Not if you keep running like you do, Ken."

"Don't start this shit again, Sharell." He massaged his temples.

"The truth is the light," she said, turning her chair around to face him. "You can say what you want, but ain't no good gonna come from the way you're living. The devil is always busy, Kenyatta. More often than not he uses troubled souls like you to do his will. The Lord says—"

"Man, miss me with that 'the Lord says' shit," Gutter snapped.

"The Lord ain't said a muthafucking thing when my partner got blasted. His ass was silent as the grave."

"Kenyatta Soladine, don't you be in here blaspheming," she warned. "It was a terrible thing that happened to Lou-Loc. I loved him like family and didn't nobody cry harder than I did at the funeral. That still doesn't change the fact that it was the Lord that brought you back to me. I prayed by your bedside everyday and he let you come out of your coma. You should be thankful for that."

"Oh, I'm thankful, but not to the Lord. He ain't have shit to do with me getting up out that bed," Gutter said, in a matter-of-fact tone.

"And what's that supposed to mean?"

"Nothing." He sighed. "Look, it's been a long day. I'm going to bed," Gutter turned and walked out of the room.

Sharell felt like crying, but she promised herself she wouldn't. She and Gutter had the same argument more times than she cared to recount. With each passing day, he seemed to become more and more obsessed with his mission. Sharell knew Gutter was a good man at heart, but she was hardly a fool. Every time she read about a gang-related shooting, she knew just who was behind it.

Gutter had the homeys putting in overtime on the streets of New York. No matter how much blood was spilled, his thirst never seemed to be sated. It had gotten to the point where her friends from church refused to be seen publicly with her. They feared that her man's reputation would land them in a cross fire. Regardless of his wrongs, she loved him and would stick by him no matter the outcome.

HAWK LEANED against his car, watching while Ruby punished a bottle of Jack Daniel's. Even before he had gotten her phone call, he knew about Supreme's murder. In the streets, news traveled fast.

No one really understood why Ruby was taking his death so hard, but Hawk understood. He was one of the few people that knew about their secret love affair.

"I want him dead!" Ruby said in between sobs. "Gutter has finally crossed the line!"

"Ruby, calm down," Hawk said in an even tone. "We're all upset about what happened to Supreme, but drinking yourself into a stupor isn't going to bring him back. I need your head to be clear so you can command your troops. Get it together."

"Fuck that," she slurred. "This shit is war. Y'all can keep playing with these crab niggaz, but I'm taking it to 'em. He's going down."

"What're you gonna do, march into Harlem and single-handedly take the whole set?" he questioned.

"If I have to. That nigga should've been put down a long time ago. Y'all kept playing with it and look what happened. We lost three set leaders and God knows how many soldiers. We gotta do something, Hawk."

"Something has already been done, Ruby. This problem with Gutter is officially out of our hands. We'll be getting some outside help from the West."

"Just what we need, some Cali clowns coming out here trying to tell us what to do." She guzzled her bottle.

"This clown comes highly recommended," Hawk said, taking the bottle away from her.

"I don't even give a fuck no more." She slumped against the car. "I just want him dead."

"Soon, I don't think that'll be much of a problem."

IT SEEMED like Gutter had just gone to sleep when he heard his cell ringing on the nightstand. He grumbled something in Arabic under his breath as he reached for the phone. It was four o'clock in the morning and he wondered who the hell could be calling him from a 310 area code.

"Hello?" he rasped.

"Kenyatta?" the caller asked.

"Who the fuck is this?"

"Ken, it's Rahshida," the woman replied. Rahshida was his aunt who lived in Watts.

"Auntie, it's one in the morning out there. Everything okay?" he asked, sitting up.

"Ken, oh God, I've been trying to get in touch with you all day."

"Rahshida, what's wrong?"

"It's Gunn. He's been shot!"

Gutter almost dropped the phone. As if things couldn't get any worse. Big Gunn was like the surrogate father for all of the lil homeys on the set back home. It was because of him and his tutelage Gutter and Lou-Loc were able to come up through the ranks. He taught them what banging was really all about. In their eyes Gunn was invincible, now his aunt was on the phone telling him he'd been wounded.

"Kenyatta, are you still there?" Rahshida cried.

"Yeah, I'm here. How is he?"

"Not good. They're saying he might not make it. Oh, Ken, he was just going to the store and some Swans rolled up on him. They just started—"

"Don't even say no more over the phone," he cut her off. "I'm catching the next flight out." With that, he ended the call.

"EVERYTHING OKAY?" Sharell asked in a sleep-laden voice.

"Yeah, go back to sleep," he replied, sliding out of bed.

Sharell was about to call out to him, but didn't. Whatever had stirred her man at this hour had to be of the utmost importance, but he would tell her when he was ready. Sharell tried to go back to sleep but couldn't. The early-morning phone call rattled her, but it was her visit with Satin that was nagging at her.

She was used to the wordless visits, but there was something different about Satin physically that she couldn't quite put her finger on. She had some sick days she needed to use anyhow so she decided to make another trip to see Satin the following day.

AFTER MAKING himself a drink, Gutter stepped out onto his balcony and lit a blunt. The news of his uncle's shooting was unexpected and ill-timed. There was a full-scale war raging in New York so he couldn't really afford to dip out, but his family came first. Taking a deep drag off the blunt, he looked out at the water.

It had been more than two years since Gutter had last walked in the California sunshine. He always knew he'd return, but not under these circumstances. Nearly his entire family was Crip'd out, but Big Gunn banged the hardest. Now that he was out of commission, the weight of restoring order would fall on Gutter.

He thought about Sharell and how the situation would affect her. She didn't really know his family, but she had love for them off the strength of him. When he broke the news of Gunn's shooting and his trip back home, she was sure to insist on going. It would be a tooth-and-nail fight when he told her no, but it was for the best. Gang life in New York was harsh, but nothing compared to the escalating feud in California. Los Angeles was truly the land of the heartless.

Gunn was an O.G. Touching him was a blatant sign of disrespect and justice would have to be dispatched swiftly to save face.

There was no doubt that the homeys were going to loc up and he would be smack-dab in the middle. He had already put Sharell through enough and wouldn't subject her to that. As the weed numbed his physical, his mind began to make preparations for the events to come.

THE PRIVATE room at the facility was completely dark and quiet. The only sound that could be heard on the floor was the small television that played in the nurse's station. The duty nurse and one of the orderlies watched a sitcom and drank beer, waiting for the end of their boring shift.

Satin tossed and turned fitfully, but she did not awaken. The unannounced visitor crept silently into her room as he always did. A chain hung from his belt, but made no sound as he moved across the tiled floor. The visitor looked down at the girl's sleeping form and wondered what she saw when she slept. The visitor reached out to touch her, but withdrew when she stirred. On more than one occasion he thought about intervening, but Satin's injury wasn't a physical one. For all of his gifts, there was nothing he could do about a broken heart.

"If only he'd taken the bargain," the visitor whispered.

The floor nurse thought she heard voices coming from Satin's room so she went to investigate. Cautiously, she entered Satin's room sweeping her flashlight back and forth. The room was empty save for the young girl who occupied it.

▬ ▯ ▬ ▯ ▬ ▯ ▬ ▯ ▬ ▯ ▬ ▯ ▬ ▯ ▬ ▯ ▬ ▯ ▬ ▯ ▬ ▯ ▬

chapter 5

WE'VE BEEN waiting here for forty-five minutes," Eddie complained.

"Shut up, man." Tito waved him off.

"Eddie's right," Miguel added from the backseat. "The flight landed twenty minutes ago, and the guy still hasn't shown. We don't even know who we're looking for."

"Please believe we'll know Major when we see him," Tito assured him. "Y'all just chill." Tito leaned back and lit a cigarette. He too shared their impatience, but that didn't change the fact that he had been ordered to pick up their guest. A council had been called to deal with the recent Crip insurgents and the murder of El Diablo, who had been a respected East Coast general. This suited Tito just fine. He wanted everyone who could connect him with the double cross to disappear anyhow.

Cisco had recruited Tito to double-cross El Diablo. He was to make it so the old L.C. leader was found with dirty guns in his car and get sent off to jail. During the set up, things went wrong. El Diablo ended up getting smoked by his crazy-ass sister before the police could get to him. The bonus was that one of their greatest adversaries ended up getting clipped in the process. It seemed like a fair exchange. The only problem was, Cisco got whacked right after and the L.C. was thrown into disarray before he could make good on any of his promises. Instead of the promotion Cisco had assured him of, Tito found himself starving with the rest of the set.

A knock on the rear window startled the trio. They turned as one and saw a man standing beside the car. He was a stocky yellow cat who wore his hair parted into quarters, with four thick braids crowning his face. Dressed in a red leather varsity jacket and construction-colored Timberlands he didn't look like much, but a smart man knew that you never judge a book by its cover.

"Holy shit!" Miguel gasped.

"Who the fuck is that?" Eddie asked, being new to the click.

"Major Blood," Tito said with a slight edge to his voice.

"Right on the money." The stranger smirked. "The *real* Major Blood, homey. Tito"—he glared at the young Latino—"I hear you been out here embarrassing my name?"

Drayton, or Major Blood as he was called, was one of the meanest cats you could ever have the misfortune of going against. He was born and raised in California, in a one-story stucco home off Piru Street. His father was a wayward Mexican, whom he had only met once, and his mother was a home girl, claiming the 900 block Bloods.

Just about everyone in the hood was either a Blood, or a supporter. It was usually what block you lived on that determined which side you chose, if any. Maria had always been attracted to the hard-ass street thugs, so when she and her parents moved to a Blood hood, it seemed only natural that she threw her lot in with them.

Her parents were always warning her against the gangs and the violence that came with their lifestyle, but it was hard to monitor the comings and goings of a wild young girl, and work three jobs between them. Maria's older sister Essie was reserved and obedient, but Maria was wild. Even when they forbade her to hang with the local gangsters, she would just sneak off every chance she could. This eventually led to her period standing her up, six months after her fifteenth birthday.

Her parents were irate. Her father would've beaten her to death had it not been for her mother's interference. They were disappointed with her, but they didn't cast her to the streets. Six and a half months later, she gave birth to Drayton.

A girl so young could never fully understand the burdens of parenthood, which is what happened with Maria. She eventually grew tired and frustrated with having her wings clipped at sixteen. She began going off and staying out later and later, putting the baby off on her parents. Her mother eventually had to quit her jobs to stay home with the child.

Drayton grew up watching his mother's antics as well as the violence and absorbed it. A child's mind is so very like a sponge in those early years, taking in whatever it comes into contact with. Drayton had the full "red" print on how to bang accordingly, but it wasn't until he was about five that his life would be defined.

On a rare night, Drayton had accompanied his mother and a group of her friends to a local fair. The only reason she had him along was because her parents had flat-out refused to babysit. Reluctantly, she took her son to the fair, and as it turned out had a pretty nice time. The home boys adored him and were very generous in showering him with popcorn and candy till his stomach hurt. He got on the makeshift rides, while they smoked pot and drank Old English.

As the day wound down the group made to leave the park. On the way out, one of Maria's people got into it with a group of Hoover Crips over an incident that was at least six months old. The beef was broken up when the sheriffs and their dogs started to bully their way toward the altercation. The two groups parted with violent glares and threats. One young man in particular radiated an especially menacing vibe.

His hazy green eyes looked down on young Drayton and studied him for what felt like an eternity then broke off. A cold chill ran down the child's back, even as the big man stormed away.

The new excitement, mixed with the weed and drinks, sent everyone into a fit of laughter. The Bloods poked their chests out and traded stories about what they would've done if the sheriff hadn't come. They weren't worried, because they had "straps" in the car, which was parked right outside the fairgrounds. The group of Crips walked in the other direction, deeper into the fair. Maria held the seat up, and Drayton hopped into the back of the Chevy.

The next few seconds would be embedded in his mind until the end of his days. He could remember his mother, with a cigarette hanging out of her mouth, laughing at a joke someone told. Suddenly everything seemed to move in slow motion. Those same eyes he had seen at the fair were approaching from the rear. His bulky form was hunched over and moving swiftly. It was just like the army movies he had watched with his grandfather, he recalled. Everyone in the group was smiling, but the man wore a mask of pure hatred.

The tipsy group noticed him just as he was pulling a long revolver from beneath his blue sweatshirt. Bottles fell from hands and joints were abandoned as everyone tried to find cover. Drayton saw the man's lips moving, but he couldn't make out all the words.

The two he did catch would be his newfound purpose in life. "Hoover, nigga!" the man shouted. Then came the blood.

The revolver barked over and over, trying to touch everyone assembled. Some made it under cover, while others weren't so lucky. Maria fell in the latter. Her face had gone from a smile to a mask of terror. She was halfway in the car when the bullet exited her heart, and struck the seat right next to Drayton. Blood stained his face and clothes, but he didn't seem to notice. All he saw was his mother's cold, dead eyes.

The police rushed to the scene, but as usual, the shooter had already vanished. There were several injuries throughout the group, but only one fatality. At the funeral, his father showed up to pay his respects, but if he had knowledge that he had sired Drayton, he didn't show it. The lean mirror double of him looked the boy over once and disappeared. That was the last time they ever saw each other. Drayton would spend more than enough time in and out of foster care, while his grandparents fought the system for him. When they finally did get him home permanently, the seeds had already been planted.

Drayton began his career early and quickly excelled at it. He had been around gang-banging since infancy, so it was a part of who he was. He tried his hands at drugs and a few other hustles, but found that his real strength was in murder. Drayton didn't have the patience to stand around and sling stones. He wanted his money long and fast, and that didn't seem quick enough for him. Drayton capitalized on the one thing he had carried with him since early. Hate.

Murder came easy to him. It was a gift of sorts. Drayton would find new and innovative ways to kill his victims. Whatever his methods, they were always very bloody. As his calling card, he would leave the bloody clothes of his victims on the doorsteps of their families or crews. This is what got him the nickname Major Blood.

The thirty-something-year-old had been putting in work since he was old enough to get "quoted," a real live career banger. He was an iron-willed killer with a pack of wild young dawgz that wanted to be just like him, the most promising student being Young Reckless, his aunt Essie's only child. Just as Major had been poisoned, he passed it off to his little cousin. After a while he got his kicks from just kicking back and watching Reckless smash shit. It was around that time that Tito had adopted the nickname Lil Major Blood. It was a name that until recently he had held down with valor.

"One of you niggaz get my shit," Major said, walking around to the passenger's side. He stood on the curb waiting for Eddie to get out, but Eddie just stared defiantly. "You gonna move or what?"

"What for? There's room in the back," Eddie pointed out.

"See, I can already tell you New York niggaz got the game twisted." Major Blood smirked. "Where's the respect for seniority?"

"Blood, I don't even know you. These niggaz say you supposed to be official, but what kinda credentials you come with?"

"Okay, tell you what"—Major's arm shot out in midsentence. He snapped his elbow and caught Eddie in the nose with the back of his hand. Eddie's head bounced off the headrest and his hands covered his face.

Major snatched the door open, and pulled Eddie out. "Get yo ass out." He shoved him and Eddie slunk out of the car and climbed into the backseat. Without being asked, Miguel got Major Blood's bag. Major pushed the passenger seat back to where it would be on Eddie's knees and relaxed. He stuck his hand down into his underwear and pulled out an ounce of sticky green. Without looking, he tossed it into the backseat.

"Roll that," he ordered. "Tito, drive this muthafucka before I catch a case."

IHOP ON Seventh Avenue was as crowded as usual. It was only eleven thirty, but people filled the booths as well as stood in line trying to fill their bellies and seeing who was out. The wait time was twenty minutes, but Gutter and his crew were seated as soon as they entered. Hollywood was fucking the hostess. The men climbed into the booth and placed their orders. When the waitress had gone, they got down to business.

"That's some heavy shit, cuz," Hollywood said from the corner. "How bad is he hit up?"

"I don't know yet." Gutter tugged at his beard. He had run a comb through it before hitting the streets, but it still made him look like a wild-ass mountaineer. "My aunt just told me that some Brims dumped on him. Shit!"

"Man, Gunn is a stand-up dude. That was some bold shit them busters pulled, but they gonna catch it. I'm rolling wit you, cuz," Pop Top declared.

"Nah." Gutter shut him down. "I ain't going to war; I'm going to see my fam. When I get the story, this shit is gonna get handled. In the meantime we keep up the effort over here. They call themselves Bloods, so make 'em bleed!"

"You know I got you faded all day, my nigga," Pop Top assured him.

"True indeed." Gutter nodded. "Now, y'all know them niggaz is gonna be out for blood behind what happened with Supreme so move smart about it and be on constant alert. No cowboy shit, just tactical hits. If these muthafuckas even look like they wanna frog up, put the love on 'em." Gutter crumbled his napkin for emphasis.

"You know we gonna keep it funky out here while you're gone," Danny assured him.

"You're coming with me," Gutter announced to everyone's surprise, including Danny. "We about to step off into some heavy shit and I don't know who I can still trust out there other than my family and Snake Eyes."

"Aw shit, I might even get a chance to put it on one of them West Coast niggaz," Danny joked.

Gutter looked at him seriously. "Danny, this ain't no game. We about to step into a war-torn city, where these little niggaz ain't got a problem caving your fucking melon in just for the stripes."

Danny sucked his teeth.

"You better listen to what the homey is telling you. Think about it like a trip to the Holy Land, nigga," Pop Top added.

"If my uncle dies you're likely to see more gunplay than you're ready for," Gutter said seriously.

chapter 6

‎■■■■■■■■■■■■■■■■■■■■■■■■■■■■■■■■

HAWK STEPPED into the lobby of the W Hotel and gave a casual glance around. He had been to a few of their hotels and compared to the rest, the Lexington Avenue location didn't measure up. Still, he wasn't a guest, he was only there to handle business so he wouldn't have to endure it long. With him were Tito from L.C., and Hawk's guard dogs, Red and Shotta. The two men looked like day and night, with one being tall and slightly chubby, while the other was almost pitch-black and sported long dreads. For as odd a pair as they appeared to be, they were both very handy with the steel.

Hawk was a man of high standing in most underworld circles so it was rare that he ever had to unleash the two, but when they killed they did it well. That was before Gutter. With the way he had things popping in New York, Shotta and Red found themselves with their hands full. Gutter didn't discriminate against rank when it came to taking out his enemies, which Hawk had a feeling was part of the reason he was down at the W that afternoon. A very important, and very dangerous, associate of his gang was visiting New York City and that meant trouble for anything blue.

As soon as he got the word that Major Blood would be visiting the city he knew something major was about to go down. His instructions were to act as a liaison while Major Blood was in the city, but he hadn't been told what the mission was. Adjusting the bulge under his butter-soft, red leather jacket, Hawk led the way into the elevator.

They got off on the sixth floor and filed down the carpeted hallway. Even if they didn't know what room Major was in, the unmistakable sounds of N.W.A. would've led the way. Hawk motioned for Shotta and Red to hang in the hall while he knocked on the door. The music dropped to a respectable level, and he could hear people shuffling around in the room. When the door opened a thick cloud of marijuana smoke floated into the hall.

The girl who opened the door was a shapely Puerto Rican. Her thick thighs pressed against her light blue Lady Encyes. She took her colorful fingers and brushed a strand of feathered blond hair from her face as she looked them over. Without waiting to be invited in, Hawk stepped into the hotel living room. Sitting across the room was Major Blood.

Major was sitting on the floor with his back against the love seat and his head resting on the inner thigh of a big-breasted girl, with heresy skin. She was pulling a comb through his long silky hair, finishing up the last two braids. Major Blood looked up at Hawk with lazy eyes, smoke billowing from his mouth to his nose in two tiny jets. Resting against the crease of his tan Dickies was a chrome 9.

"My nigga, Hawk," Major greeted him, his face smiling but his tone flat. "I know you ain't bring ya goons with you to see lil old me? We Blood, homey, I ain't no threat to you."

"Nah, it ain't like that. We got some other business to handle when we leave here, but I ain't want them in here while we talked," Hawk lied, hoping Major Blood didn't see through it. "Welcome to New York, Blood." Hawk pounded his fist. "Sorry I wasn't there to meet you at the airport, but I'm sure you've been making out okay."

"I've been keeping myself occupied." Major patted the chocolate girl's thigh. "Ladies, go in the back for a sec. I gotta talk to my dawg." The girls went into the sleeping area, closing the door behind them and turning up the television. "Now, down to business; I hear you niggaz got a crab infestation you can't handle?"

"That's not totally accurate," Hawk said, pulling up a wooden chair. "We've just been having some difficulties with a pocket of Crips in Harlem."

"I don't call getting most of your team greased, *difficulties.* Word is, Harlem dusted damn near all of L.C. and is making short work of the rest of you muthafuckas too. That sounds like a problem to me, hommes."

"With all due respect, Major, you ain't from out here, so you really don't know what's up."

"Well"—Major sat upright—"*with all due respect,* Hawk, my O.G.s say y'all losing face out here and they ain't feeling that." Major Blood got to his feet and walked over to where Hawk was sitting. "Don't trip, man." He draped his arms around Hawk, causing him to tense up. "The old heads know you get down, Hawk, so you're good money, baby. Now, it's these little bastards y'all got flagging that's becoming a problem. No disrespect, but you guys are looking like a bunch of pussies to the niggaz back home, repping this." He tugged at the red belt that was looped through his Dickies.

Hawk got up out of the chair and positioned himself so that his back was to the wall. "What do you want me to say? Niggaz die every day, all over the world. Sometimes we get one up on them, some times they get one up on us. That's how this shit has always gone. Gang-banging ain't gonna change, fam," Hawk defended.

Major Blood stared at Hawk long enough to make him uncomfortable before responding. "See, that's the kind of half-ass thinking that's got your monkey-asses in a sling now. Hawk"—Major took the seat Hawk had just vacated—"you of all people know this shit y'all putting down ain't what we come from. I mean, we all criminal muthafuckas at the end of the day, but there was a time where the people who lived in our neighborhoods were off-limits. We didn't prey on our own, we protected them and smashed on the rest. We made long paper and made sure that niggaz knew they couldn't come through our hoods tripping. Fuck is New York promoting? Purse snatching and cutting civilians for stripes? Them fruits don't come off no tree that I know of. Show me one muthafucka other than you and maybe Tito that's banging accordingly."

Hawk was usually the one giving the homeys lectures on Blood etiquette, so Major flipping the script had him tight, but he held his composure as best he could. "Man, we're working with what we got in New York City, Blood. This ain't California so the same rules don't apply. It ain't a problem with Crips; it's a problem with Harlem. Gutter is on some bullshit."

"And that's just why I'm here," Major Blood rocked the wooden chair back on two legs. "My orders are real simple, homey: Harlem Crip is getting shut down. I need any information you got on them fools. Sets...numbers...the works. I'll take care of the rest, you think you can handle that?"

"I'll have somebody get it to you," Hawk assured him.

"I need anything you got on Diablo's murderer too."

"His sister killed him, Blood," Tito spoke up for the first time.

"I don't give a fuck who killed him. He was one of ours. Fuck is it when our generals can get they shit pushed and nobody do nothing? On everything, I always fill my contracts. As far as I'm concerned she's a Judas and wasn't fit to share the same womb as a down-ass damu like Diablo. That bitch is going to sleep, Blood."

Tito cringed at the ice in Major Blood's voice. He could understand bringing it to Gutter and his lot, but why bother with Satin? She had lost her sanity as a result of the shooting and surely couldn't be a threat to anyone but herself. Tito would stand with his people when it came time to ride on Gutter, but he would have no part in Satin's execution.

SHARELL THUMBED through her outfits trying to pick something comfortable to wear for her trip to see Satin. She could still fit into some of her stuff, but the babyweight limited her choices.

She was still a bit upset at Gutter for planning to fly out without her, but she understood where he was coming from. A respected member of the Hoover Crips had been shot and the shit was definitely going to hit the fan. Gutter had no way to tell exactly what the situation was and he didn't want Sharell to get caught up if things went sour. Still, she didn't know how she felt about Gutter running off into God only knew what.

Gutter had always lived his life like two people. This was one of the only similarities that he shared with Lou-Loc, other than both being down for the set. One side was the light, where he was Kenyatta, the loving husband and father. The other side was the darkness, where he murdered and ordered men murdered. He chose to keep her in the light.

Sharell might've been a churchgirl, but she wasn't a twit. She knew that Gutter had bathed in a river of sin, yet she stood by him. She was his woman, and it was only right. For the most part, she knew there was good in him, but he showed it less and less as the need for revenge grew. Still, she prayed for his salvation.

Sharell quietly reflected on how things would be with Gutter being all the way in California, while she was stuck in New York. She knew he had a life before her and wondered if he would pick up where he left off? Maybe there was some old flame awaiting his return with open arms. Would she be the one to console him?

She was thinking nonsense. Even suggesting that Gutter was going off to some secret rendezvous as his uncle lay mortally wounded was selfish on her part. If she spent his time away conjuring scenarios she would surely drive herself crazy. What she needed to do was get herself on the road to go see about Satin.

Her soul was wounded in ways beyond what no woman should endure. To be sentenced to a lifetime of sorrow seemed a fate worse than death. Sharell wondered what Satin now saw in her mind's eye. Was she aware? Or in some far-off place that existed only in her mind?

When she finally finished dressing and stepped outside her building, the sun blared mercilessly down on her. Throwing on her Chanel shades, she continued on to her car. Mohammad was at his usual post, sitting in his Maxima thumbing through one of the several newspapers that he devoured each morning. He was a youthful-looking man with copper skin and a beard that hung slightly longer than Gutter's but was far more kept. He smiled politely at her then went back to reading.

Since the conflict, Gutter insisted that she be under constant guard. One of the homeys had occupied the job in the beginning, but that turned out to be a disaster. Mohammad was one of Anwar's. He was always with her when Gutter wasn't around and sometimes when he was. Other than the fact that he greeted her in the mornings, she never knew he was there. He didn't talk to her and he never revealed his exact location. He only made direct contact with her when necessary. Mohammad was the equivalent of having your own personal ghost.

Sharell walked to her car, which was parked a few spaces up, and got behind the wheel. She checked herself over in the mirror and pulled into traffic. Mohammad followed shortly behind her.

SATIN SAT at the foot of a waterfall, looking at her reflection on the surface of the water. Her hair hung down to her shoulders, but had begun to frizz from the light drizzle that was sprinkling her. Her face was as beautiful as it has always been. There were no dark circles around her eyes and her cheeks still held a youthful glow. Running her hand through the water, she waited as she always had.

A figure approached from the direction in which the sun was setting, she couldn't see his face due to the glare, not that she needed to. She'd know him anywhere. He approached, with his hair neatly braided and his khakis heavily creased. His brown face smiled at her lovingly as he occupied the patch of grass next to her.

"Lou-Loc," she whispered, to which he gave her his infamous smile. His face was still as smooth as it had been before the shooting.

"Hey, baby," he said, his voice being little more than the hum of a mosquito's wings, but she was able to hear him perfectly. His breath smelled of the sweetest flowers, with a hint of tilled earth. When she laid her hand against his cheek it felt warm, not the cold flesh of a dead man. Every rational part of Satin's mind told her that he was dead and that the man sitting beside her couldn't be her forever lover, but when she pressed her body against his it seemed very real.

"God, I miss you," she sobbed.

"I miss you too, ma," he replied. "More than you can imagine, Satin." His form wavered then became solid again. "Satin, you gotta go back, ma."

With tear-filled eyes she looked up at him. "I know, baby, but I can come back tomorrow, or the day after."

He looked down at his All Stars before turning back to Satin. "No, baby, I mean you gotta wake up. This ain't no life for you, and the more you come here the more of yourself you lose. I can't let you end up like me." He motioned toward his body, which was starting to take on the clarity of a bootleg movie.

"I won't leave you, Lou-Loc." She tried to grab hold of his Dickies shirt, but her fingers passed right through. "Why can't I stay here with you?"

"Because you gotta water the seed, ma." He tried to touch her stomach, but his body was rapidly losing substance.

"Water the seed, what are you talking about?" she asked his fading form.

"You can't sleep anymore, Satin, sleep is for the dead. This place"—he motioned at the fading scenery around him—"it ain't for you, baby. Life is for you."

"Baby, a life without you ain't a life," she pleaded. "I wanna stay here with you, Lou-Loc. Just about everybody I ever loved is dead, ain't nothing out there for me. I don't wanna lose you too."

"Baby, as long as you water the seed you can never lose me, don't forget that," he said before his form faded completely.

SATIN AWOKE with a start. Her eyes darted around the room, searching for the mountains and the waterfall, but there were only the dull hospital walls, and the morning sun coming through the picture window. Lou-Loc's words again rang through her mind and the meaning suddenly became clear. With a trembling hand Satin touched her stomach and felt the faintest hint of a flutter.

chapter 7

A S SOON as Sharell stepped off the elevator she heard the shouts and sounds of furniture being overturned. A burly orderly rushed past her so swiftly that he almost knocked her over. Down the hall she saw a small cluster of people gathered around Satin's room. An orderly stepped inside, but immediately backpedaled out, followed by a lamp, which shattered against the hallway wall.

"What's going on here?" Sharell asked as she approached the duty nurse. Her youthful face wore a worried expression.

"Step back please, miss, we're dealing with a situation," the nurse told her as she pulled a syringe from her pocket along with a small glass bottle. Her hands were shaking so bad that she almost dropped the bottle when she tried to slip the needle through the corked top.

"I'm Sharell Baker, and that's my sister in there." Sharell tried to step around the nurse so that she could see into the room, but one of the orderlies blocked her path. He was a thick-necked cat whose arm and neck were covered in tattoos.

"I can't let you in there, ma'am," he said in a bass voice. "It's too dangerous. Ms. Angelino attacked one of my people a few minutes ago." He motioned to the splatters of blood on the floor that she hadn't noticed before.

"Attacked an orderly? The last time I was here she could barely feed herself, let alone be a danger to anyone." Sharell looked from the orderly to the nurse for an explanation.

"Tell that to the young man who's downstairs getting his hand examined." The nurse folded her arms over her small breasts. "Ms. Angelino came out of her stupor some time this morning and when the orderly went in to administer her medication she attacked him with a pencil."

"Jesus." Sharell covered her mouth in shock.

"Ms. Baker, I'm just as shocked as you are, but it still doesn't change the fact that she's become a danger to herself and my staff. She has to be sedated." She held up the syringe that was now filled with a greenish fluid.

"Wait, can I try and talk to her first?" Sharell asked.

"Can't do it, Ms.," the tattooed orderly spoke up. "If you were to go in there and something happened we'd be held responsible, and I ain't trying to lose my job." He folded his arms, letting her know that it was nonnegotiable. It was just then that she spotted the six-pointed star tattooed on his elbow, with two numbers crowning it.

"Can I speak with you for a minute . . . in private?" Sharell asked politely. The orderly gave her a distrustful look, but agreed to hear her out.

"Make it quick lady," he said, leading her off to the side. The nurse gave him a look, but he motioned that he had it under control. "What's up?" he asked when they were out of earshot.

"Where're you from?" Sharell asked, slipping into the venacular she'd often heard Gutter use.

He gave her a quizzical look. "The Bronx, why?"

"Young man, I'm not here to give you grief or jeopardize your job, but I really don't have time to play. Now, where're you from?" She nodded toward the tattoo.

The orderly absently placed his hand over the tattoo. "Seven-Duce gangster, but I'm not in the life anymore," he said just above a whisper. She could clearly see he was lying, but it wasn't her place to judge.

"Listen, have you ever heard of Gutter?" she asked.

The orderly lowered his eyes. "Yeah."

"That's my husband, and the woman in there is his sister."

The man snapped his head up and looked at her with fear-filled eyes. "Listen, lady, I don't want any problems, I'm just trying to do my job." He raised his hands in surrender.

"I don't doubt that, but like I said, that's Gutter's family, and I'd hate to think how he'd feel if something happened that could've potentially been stopped." She looked him directly in the eye. "Just give me a minute to see if I can calm her down before y'all run up in there. I'd look at it as a personal favor."

The orderly stood there and pondered it for a minute. Everyone, Crip or Blood, knew just who Gutter was and what he was about. If the patient truly was Gutter's family and something happened to her there was no doubt in his mind that he was a dead man walking. Though he valued his job, he valued his life more.

"A'ight," he told her. The orderly looked over at the nurse and motioned that it was okay to let Sharell in. "You got five minutes, and we do what we gotta do if she tweaks again," he warned.

"Thank you so much." She took one of his massive hands in hers. Sharell hurried to the doorway only to be stopped by the nurse.

"Terrence, are you crazy?" she shouted at the orderly. "If somebody finds out we let her in there all our asses are gonna be fired! I got kids to feed and I need my job."

"Trish"—he took her firmly by the arm and moved her out of Sharell's way—"I got this. Give her a minute." Trish started to protest, but the warning look Terrence gave her kept her silent. Reluctantly she allowed Sharell to enter the room.

Sharell stepped around them and entered the room. She was totally taken aback when she saw Satin, pacing near the window, with a crazed look in her eyes and a bloody pencil in her hand. "Satin?" Sharell called to her.

"I want to go home!" she shouted. "What am I doing here? Why won't they let me go home?"

"Satin, calm down baby. I'm here," Sharell said, stepping closer, but not close enough to taste the end of the pencil.

Satin turned her animal-like glare on Sharell. For a minute it looked like she was going to attack, but her eyes softened when she recognized Gutter's girlfriend. "Sharell, why are they keeping me here? Why won't they let me go home?"

"Baby, you're sick. They've been treating you here since the shooting. Don't you remember?"

Satin rocked on her heels for a minute then continued her pacing. "I want to go home, Sharell, I can't stay here. Lou-Loc says I have to water the seed."

If Sharell wasn't convinced that Satin was insane before, she was then. Lou-Loc had been dead for months so it was impossible for him to have told her anything. "Satin, Lou-Loc is dead. There's no way he could've told you—"

"No, no, no!" Satin threw her breakfast tray against the wall, painting it with processed eggs. "He's not dead, he's alive, alive inside me. I gotta water the seed!" she insisted, covering her stomach with her free hand.

"Satin, what seed? What are you talking about?"

Satin's motion was so swift that Sharell took a step back when she moved in her direction. "The seed, Sharell, *our* seed." She pointed to her stomach. "Lou-Loc says I have to water the seed! I have to take care of our child."

Child?

Sharell thought back on her dreams and the overwhelming urge that she go back and visit with Satin. Could Lou-Loc have been speaking to her from beyond the grave? For as outlandish as it might've seemed, Sharell knew that dreams always held a hint of the truth, be it yours or someone else's. Back when she was a child, her dead aunt used to visit her dreams in an attempt to warn her of some danger to the family. A short time later her little brother, Malik, was murdered.

"Nurse!" Sharell called. The duty nurse came into the room, still holding the syringe and glaring at the violent young woman. "Has Ms. Angelino been given a pregnancy test?"

The nurse's face held a look somewhere between nervousness and confusion. "Pregnancy test?" she asked as if it was something she didn't quite understand. "No, we don't do that here. When we check patients in they get EKGs, blood work, respiratory, all tests that fall under our standard policies, a pregnancy test not being one of them. Furthermore, she's shown violent tendencies and will be sedated so that she doesn't harm any more of my staff or herself."

"No, no more drugs until she's tested."

"Look," Trish said, glancing at Satin's chart. "Apparently they didn't feel it necessary to give her a test when she came in, and I wasn't here for that. Any complaints you have you need to take them up with my supervisor. Now, what I plan to do is—"

"What you *will* do is hold off on any more medication until Satin is given a pregnancy test, unless you want to explain to my lawyer why you've been giving a pregnant woman medication that could be harmful to her fetus. I need her tested, immediately."

"The lab is closed but first thing in the morning—" Trish began.

"What part of immediately don't you understand?" Sharell snaked her neck, matching her attitude. Trish made to say something, but Sharell raised her hand for silence. "You know what, never mind." She stormed past the nurse over to where Terrence was standing. "I hate to ask, but I need one last favor." Sharell leaned in and whispered something in his ear.

"Oh, hell nah, Gutter's old lady or not, you're asking for a little much." He shook his head.

Sharell palmed a bill into his hand and said, "I really need this done."

Terrence looked in his palm and nodded at the hundred dollar bill. "A'ight, I'll be right back."

"Terrence, where are you going?" Trish called after him.

"Trish, hold it down. I'll be right back."

She sucked her teeth and turned her attention to Sharell. "I don't know what y'all are up to, but I'm going to call my supervisor." She stormed down the hall.

"Yeah, you do that," Sharell said, going back into the room to sit with Satin. Sharell held Satin in her arms and stroked her face. Under the watchful eyes of the remaining orderlies, Sharell waited for Terrence to come back from the pharmacy, listening to Satin tell her of waterfalls and tilled earth.

TWO HOURS later Sharell found herself zipping through traffic heading back into the city. She had cried, shouted, and cursed but it didn't change what she had discovered or do anything to resolve the situation.

As soon as the two strips appeared on the stick Sharell demanded that Satin be released to her custody so that she could receive the proper care, but the nurse wouldn't budge. She fed Sharell a line about procedures and the girl's release clearing the proper channels. No matter how you sliced it, Satin was still a murderer. Snake Eyes would fight the good fight in court, but there was no getting around the fact that Satin would have to stand trial and eventually go to jail.

The news of Satin's pregnancy was both a blessing and a curse. It was a blessing because she was about to bring a child into the world, but a curse because of the circumstances. A million things ran through Sharell's mind, but the most relevant thought was how to get Satin out of that hospital. Sharell was a churchgoing girl and a law-abiding citizen, but this was a situation that needed to be handled outside the law. Flipping her phone open, she called Gutter. After the third ring he picked up.

"Baby?" she said, trying to calm herself. "I need to talk to you. It's about Satin."

NIGHT HAD fallen over the streets, taking with it some of the humidity the day had brought on, but the cool air did nothing to ease the heat building in the pit of Gutter's stomach. The only time he ever visited that end of Manhattan was to get new tattoos, but even those hadn't been often since Wiz's cousin Spider came over from out west. The boy was nasty with the ink.

The news Sharell had dropped on him hit like a ton of bricks. It was bad enough that he had to deal with his uncle's situation on the West Coast, now he had to deal with Satin. Though he was glad to hear that she was coming back to her old self, the timing was lousy. For as much as he would've loved to stick around and deal with the situation personally, the attempted murder of his uncle was top priority.

Lou-Loc would've been happy as a sissy in Dick Town to hear that he was about to be a father. He always talked about wanting kids, but he was too deep in the game to really entertain it. The thought of the streets claiming him and leaving his child fatherless was one of the few things that terrified him, and ironically that turned out to be exactly the case. One thing was for sure, Gutter would be damned if he'd allow Lou-Loc's child to become a ward of the state. He vowed that Lou-Loc's child would have the same privileges in life as his own seed. The obstacle was that to get Satin out of the hospital he'd have to use unconventional means. This is what brought him dredging through Lower Manhattan in the middle of the night.

Anwar had tracked down the address for him, but even without it Gutter would've probably been able to find the run-down West Village bar. Though it appeared to be barely a step above being a shack, the hairs standing up along his arms told Gutter there was more to it. Gutter climbed from behind the wheel of his car and made his way across the street to the hole-in-the-wall. The entire block was empty except for two young men loitering in front of the bar. The first was tall and thin, sporting a thrift store vest over a red T-shirt, while the other was dark and dressed in baggy jeans. Gutter nodded, but they only stared as he entered the bar.

The interior was pitch-black with the exception of the glare from the jukebox and several wall-mounted televisions broadcasting rock videos. There was a light sprinkling of people along the bar or at various tables and all eyes turned to Gutter when he entered.

It took a minute for his eyes to adjust to the darkness of the place, especially behind the black sunglasses. A faint light emitted from an old-school jukebox that was belting out something

Gutter couldn't even identify, let alone groove to. He could see bodies moving around in different sections of the bar, but there wasn't enough light to make out numbers, or sex. Ignoring the lingering stares he could feel on him, Gutter made his way over to the bar.

A withered old man stood behind it, wiping a glass with a dingy towel. He took his time letting his milk-colored eyes wash over Gutter. Had it not been for the intensity of his stare one might've mistaken him for blind. After completing his inspection, he shuffled over to where Gutter was sitting and rested his knuckles on the bar top.

"Say, man, let me get a shot of yak," Gutter ordered.

"We don't serve no yak here," the old man said in a raspy voice.

"Then how about a beer?"

The old man looked past Gutter as if he could see something going on in the dark corner that no one else could, then turned back to Gutter. "Listen," he said just above a whisper. "You're either not from around here or one dumb son of a bitch. Take an old man's advice and go get yourself a drink at that spot down the block."

Gutter leaned in and matched the man's tone. "I fear nothing but Allah. Now, why don't you go get me that beer, homey, I'm waiting for somebody."

The bartender made to say something, but the young lady who was now standing beside Gutter silenced him. She was dressed in ripped jeans and a red satin corset. Her platinum hair was slightly cropped on one side, while the top and back were long. Pale blue eyes moved seductively from Gutter to the bartender.

"Moses, it's no wonder this bar doesn't get much business, the customer service sucks." Even though it was an insult, her voice seemed to ooze sex.

"Nadia, don't you go starting nothing in my bar. You know what Kane said about not needing the heat." Moses waggled a gnarled finger at her.

"If you don't watch that finger you might lose it." She clamped her pearl-white teeth together. When she was done teasing Moses, she turned back to Gutter. "So, what's a nice young boy like you doing in a dive like this?" She tried to run her finger along the side of his face, but he grabbed her by the wrist.

"First of all"—he removed his sunglasses and looked Nadia in the eyes—"I don't allow women to touch me uninvited. And second, I ain't been a boy in a long time, so why don't you keep it moving, shorty."

"Mmm, feisty," she purred before grabbing his crotch. The pressure was so intense that he couldn't even cry out. "I think I'm turned on." She leaned in to lick his earlobe, but paused as if she had just smelled something rank. Using her free hand she turned Gutter to face her and looked into his rage-filled eyes. "Somebody is keeping secrets." She made to taunt him further, but the feeling of cold steel pressed under her chin gave her pause.

"Bitch, either you let go of my sack or I'm gonna paint the fucking ceiling wit yo brains," Gutter grunted.

Nadia's eyes narrowed to slits. "A tough little bastard, huh? That's okay, I like to play rough." She smiled, flashing jagged white teeth. The situation was about to turn ugly when a voice boomed through the darkness.

"Some people gotta keep sticking their hands in the fire, even after they know it's hot." The speaker came to stand beside Gutter, facing Nadia. He was tall and had shaved his black curls, but still wore the leather duster.

"Cross, how ya doing, baby?" Nadia released Gutter, allowing him to catch his breath. With the fluidity of a cat, she slipped off the stool and looped her arm around Cross's waist. "I didn't know you were here tonight."

"I'm here every night," he said, totally unmoved by her phony display of affection. "This one is spoken for, you know the rules."

"I just wanted to play with him, that's all." She chuckled, trying to mask the fear beneath the joke.

"I'll bet," he said in a humorless tone. "Take a powder."

"Can't knock a girl for trying," she said before vanishing into the darkness of the bar.

When the girl was out of earshot the stranger turned back to Gutter and spoke harshly. "What do you want here, ganglord?"

"I need to speak to you, Cross," Gutter said.

"We have nothing to talk about," Cross shot back.

"I need a favor."

Cross laughed. "You muthafuckas kill me. It's not enough that I save you from the worms, yet you still come around seeking the devil's bargain. Gutter, you're pushing your luck coming in here. Nadia is harmless, but there are others here who might not think my mark is enough to keep you in one piece, and I ain't about to get my ass tore up trying to rescue you. Take Moses's advice and get your crack-slinging ass back to Harlem."

"Check this fly shit, Cross," Gutter began. "If I had it my way you and me would never see each other again, but I need this solid. . . . It's about Lou-Loc."

Cross's sparkling green eyes flashed anger as he leaned in to Gutter. "Dawg, off the strength of my man, I'm gonna allow you to walk out of this place without tearing your fucking head off, but for as long as your asshole points to the ground you'd better never drop his name trying to sway me. He's gone and our debt is settled." Cross turned and headed back the way he came.

Gutter shook his head in frustration. As bad as he wanted to put a slug in the back of Cross's head, he was Satin's last hope. "Cross, if you ain't gonna do it off the strength of his memory, do it for his seed," Gutter blurted out. This got him Cross's undivided attention.

part II

PILGRIMAGE

chapter 8

▪▪▪▪▪▪▪▪▪▪▪▪▪▪▪▪▪▪▪▪▪▪▪▪▪▪▪▪▪▪

THE FLIGHT from JFK to Long Beach had been anything but comfortable. Gutter hated to fly, but did so reluctantly when he had to. If they'd driven or took the train, Gunn might've been gone. Flying was definitely their only option.

The trouble started from the moment Gutter got to the metal detectors at the terminal. A beefy, red security officer played with a jaw full of tobacco and glared at Gutter. He produced his identification, boarding pass, and emptied his pockets like everyone else. The guard looked down at his driver's license and read Gutter's full name: Kenyatta Usif Soladine. Glaring at the young man he asked flatly, "You a Muslim?"

"Yes," Gutter replied politely.

The guard tossed the wallet on the gray table and motioned for Gutter to walk through. Immediately the machine went off. Gutter stepped back through and took off his wide-buckled belt and jewelry. When he made to step back through, the guard stopped him.

"Step over here, you've gotta be specially searched," he said, motioning toward a small roped-off square.

"Is there a problem?" Gutter asked, still keeping his tone polite.

"I said, you've gotta be specially searched."

"I emptied my pockets, why can't I just go through like everyone else?"

"'Cause you got your ticket off the Internet. Regulations and all." The beefy guard smiled wickedly.

Danny was about to open his mouth, but Gutter waved him silent. He didn't want to risk missing the flight due to an argument with the guard. Casting a glare at the guard, he stepped over to the square.

The guard stood in front of him with a wand, shooting Gutter a hateful look. He slowly ran the wand from his feet to his torso. When he got to Gutter's chest, the wand beeped faintly.

"It's lead. I got shot a while back," Gutter told him.

"Is that right?" the guard said with a raised eyebrow. "Take your shirt off."

"You can't be serious," Gutter said in disbelief. "I told you I got shot!"

"Regulations, *sir.* For all I know, you could be concealing a bomb. You can either take your shirt off to prove you're clean, or I can have you detained."

Gutter could feel all of his blood shooting into his arms. He balled his fist so tight that his knuckles began to crack. A haze of red swept over his vision, as he contemplated putting his fist through the man. He knew if he got into it with the guard, he would surely be jailed. God knew when he would be released, but Gunn might be gone. It took all of his self-control to silence the voice that screamed for death. Ignoring the crowd that had formed, Gutter stripped down to his tank top.

"Lift it," the guard demanded, giving Gutter a look that made his flesh crawl. Gutter did as he was told, exposing the multiple scars from the shooting. They were all healed, but they had left ugly keloids. "Jesus, you must be one scandalous son of a bitch to make somebody put this many holes in you!"

"Man, are you finished?" Gutter asked, finally having enough.

"Yeah, I'm done, Tin Man," the guard said with an obnoxious snicker.

Gutter snatched his goods, and moved to find his boarding gate.

The flight didn't go much better than the boarding. The people in the first-class section looked at the two men as if they didn't belong. They ignored the rude stares and made their way to the seats. Once everyone was seated, they went through the usual routine. Emergency exits, how to properly buckle your seat belts, the whole nine. After the mechanical speech, the plane was lifting off.

Takeoffs always made Gutter uneasy. He hated the dropping feeling in his stomach when the plane left the ground. Once they were in the air and coasting, he tried to relax a bit. The flight attendant came through and set two glasses of Hennessey in front of the two men and continued with her rounds. Danny's questions seemed to come without end. Gutter wanted time to think, but the youngster kept at his insistent gibbering. He tried to escape the boy's questions by dozing off, but that proved to be another dead end.

As soon as he went to sleep, he was assaulted by nightmares of his own attempted murder, as well as Lou-Loc's horrible fate. He was able to see with clarity the men who gunned his friend down. He felt everything that Lou-Loc must've felt when it happened, including Satin stroking his head. Gutter didn't fear much, but he feared these dreams. At times he wondered if it was because of the bond he now shared with Lou-Loc and Cross.

For the hundredth time he wondered how his friend and the demon called the Cross had become so tight. Cross was rude, arrogant, and downright creepy, but Lou-Loc had a knack for finding friends in the most unlikely places. For as much as a scumbag as Cross might have come across as, Gutter knew if anyone could complete the task he could.

After a few restless hours the plane began its descent into the land of the heartless. Against his better judgment Gutter lifted the blind and peered outside. The clouds looked like the softest cotton as the aircraft cut through them on its way back to earth. The 110 freeway looked like a child's racetrack from that height. Seeing the California skyline brought a feeling of nostalgia to him. He was home.

AFTER THE long flight, everyone wanted to get off the plane. People were pushing and trying to yank bags from the overhead compartment. Gutter and Danny waited patiently until it was their turn to exit the bird, and hurriedly got off.

It was nearly three o'clock when they landed in Cali, but Long Beach Airport was packed. Danny shoved and cursed people on the way to the baggage carousel, while Gutter quietly brought up the rear. Danny began the task of identifying and retrieving their luggage, while Gutter called home to check on Sharell.

The phone rang four times, then the machine picked up. He dialed it again, with the same results. At first he was nervous, but remembering that Mohammad was with her, his mind was at ease. For as soft-spoken as the bodyguard was, he was also a trained killer. Mohammad had been trained from his earliest days in the art of death, and his skills only increased when he was brought over into the death cult Gehenna. If it came down to it Gutter knew Mohammad would kill or die protecting Sharell, which gave him some solace. Knowing Sharell, she was probably asleep. He left her a brief message, then hung up and waited for Danny. After snatching their bags from the belt, they picked their way to the exit, where someone would be waiting to pick them up.

As soon as Gutter stepped out into the night air he could feel the difference. The weather was humid, with a warm breeze carrying the salty smell of the Pacific Ocean. The strip was filled with taxis and private cars. Drivers stood around, chatting and holding signs with the names of their passengers. None advertised Soladine.

"It's hot as hell out here," Danny said, adjusting the collar of his button up. "Where the fuck is our ride?"

"Someone will be here," Gutter said in nearly a whisper.

As if on cue, an electric-blue Lincoln Navigator rumbled up the strip. The windows were tinted, so the occupants were hidden from view. The sounds of the popular group The East Sidaz blasted from the stereo. Tray Dee and Goldie Loc spit pro-Crip lyrics over heavy riffs and Doctor Dre–like horns. When the truck stopped a few feet away from where Gutter and Danny were standing, the chrome rims kept spinning. Danny reflexively took a step back, but Gutter held his position. One of the customized doors lifted up and out, and the driver stepped around to greet them.

Tears was a year or two Gutter's junior and hailed from Eighty-eighth Street, stomping grounds of the Eight Treys. His skin was the color of night, and his teeth bone-white. Even though he had been banging since before he was technically old enough, his face was still pleasant and youthful. Though from two different sets, he and Gutter had stood side by side in many firefights.

"Sup, fool?" Gutter smirked.

"So, the dead do walk." Tears smiled. He hugged Gutter then

held him at arm's length and examined him. "Damn, cuz. The homeys wrote me and said you got hit up something terrible, but you look okay to me."

"You know I'm made of blue steel. Wounds heal, man," Gutter replied.

"Shit, in under a year? When I got hit in the gut, it took me six months to get right. I heard you got aired out and left for dead, but I can't see it."

"You know how niggaz exaggerate," Gutter deflected.

"Right, right," Tears said suspiciously. "I hear you kicking up major dust on the East, kid?"

"You know I'm true to this." Gutter formed a *C* with the fingers of his left hand and placed them over his heart. "We're trying to come up like everybody else."

"Yeah, getting money and trying to make the funeral director a rich man," Tears joked. "Dude, what's with you riding on these slobs so hard?"

"It ain't about nothing." Gutter placed a cigarette in his mouth and fished for a light. "Niggaz touched mine, and I ain't standing for it. We ride on my side."

"I hear that. Say, I'm sorry about missing Lou-Loc's funeral. County wouldn't give a nigga a pass, ya know?"

"Don't trip. I know you would've been there if you could. Say"—Gutter motioned to Danny—"this here is Tears from Eight Trey. Tears, this is Danny from Harlem." The two men nodded. "Now, if you don't mind, I'd like to see my uncle."

DANNY STARED out the window like a starstruck kid. This was his first trip to the West Coast. He had heard stories about what California was like, but it was nothing compared to actually seeing it.

They rode down Melrose where there were quiet streets and palm trees. They had rented two suites at the Double Tree Inn, out in Westwood. It was an upscale-looking strip, lined from end to end with different hotel chains. Danny was designated to check them in. Luggage was left in the truck while he got the keys. Danny looked around and thought how overrated Cali was.

After the keys were secured, the trio hit the 405 south, heading to Los Angeles. Danny sat in the passenger seat as Tears gave him a brief overview of L.A. Danny paid close attention to the various monuments, such as the Capital Records building. When they exited the freeway the scenery began to change.

The pleasant suburbs turned into middle-class vinyl houses. From that the landscape turned into liquor stores and shabby stucco houses. Spray paint scarred the walls of supermarkets and other buildings. Even at that late hour, groups posted up on corners and porches, eyeing the truck wearily. Most were young men, drinking or talking among themselves. Danny searched some of their faces and only found the eyes of hardened men on the faces of boys. Some even threw up their hoods trying to gauge a response from the mystery convoy. Danny quickly realized that he had been rash in his assessment of California.

They passed through L.A., and on through Carson, but to Gutter's surprise they hadn't stopped. Tears dipped back around and headed toward Torrance, which was notorious for Blood activity at one time. Most of the houses were dark, save for a few porch lights. Deep within the horseshoe of a nondescript street, they pulled up into the driveway of a small lavender house.

"This is it," Tears said, turning to face Gutter, who was meditating in the backseat.

Gutter looked around at the scenery in disgust. "Man, y'all got my uncle laid up in a slob city? What the fuck was y'all thinking?"

"It's all good, cuz. Slob activity ain't like it used to be around here. And the few muthafuckas out there that's still connected got a truce with us 'cause we hitting 'em with birds. As long as we ain't trying to move in we got an understanding. Besides, had we kept him at the hospital niggaz might've tried to come back and finish the job. We got medical equipment and round-the-clock nurses on call. He's in good hands."

Gutter nodded and stepped out of the truck. He looked up and down the block and felt as if he was out of place. He took a few moments and examined the house. It was a two-story house, situated in a still-under-construction housing development. From the average cars in the few driveways, he deduced it was a working-class neighborhood. There were men dressed in blue Dickies and jeans, holding automatic weapons outside the front door. He should've known that the homeys would make sure Gunn was well protected. They started forward when they saw him, but resumed their positions when Tears waved them back.

As he stared at the door his heart began to pound. He had no idea what to expect. He decided to let Tears go before him. Tears knocked on the door, while Gutter waited with anticipation. There was a brief wait and finally the sound of footsteps. The peephole jingled then bolts were slid free. When the door finally opened Gutter lost his breath.

chapter 9

CROSS THE ocean, another scene was unfolding. Though it was well past midnight the warm weather had the park on 145th and Lenox packed. Two local groups were running a full court for unnamed stakes. Hollywood sat behind the wheel of his Chrysler, while the girl from the bus stop occupied the passenger seat. Young Rob occupied the back, blowing haze smoke into the air.

"This is some good shit." Rob smiled.

"You know Hollywood only smokes the best grass." He smiled, referring to himself in third person. "Matter of fact, I gotta have the best of everything. Gear"—he popped his collar—"shine"—he touched his chain—"and ladies." He rested his hand on the girl's exposed thigh.

"I know that's right." Rob looked on hungrily.

"Hollywood, stop being nasty." Sonia giggled.

"See, Rob. When you get to be a nigga of my stature, you'll realize what I'm rapping about. These niggaz is always complaining about spending money to have the finer things in life, but that's only because they're uneducated. Me, I live by the philosophy of: Take care of life and it'll take care of you. Dig it?"

"Yeah, man," Rob said, passing the blunt, "I dig it."

"Talk that shit, nigga," Sonia said, leaning over and licking Hollywood's neck. Without missing a beat, she took her hand and began to massage his crotch.

"Say, Rob," Hollywood called over his shoulder, "I'll get up with you later."

"Sure, Hollywood," Rob said, catching on. "I'll see you later, fam." Rob slid out of the car and headed up the street.

Hollywood gazed at Sonia lazily. She returned his stare with a hungry one of her own. He could tell the potent weed was beginning to loosen her up. Slowly she kissed his cheek and neck, she tried to kiss him on the lips, but he turned his head. Sonia moved her kissing further south to his chest. His jeweled hand guided her steadily down, while she undid his pants. Within a few seconds, he felt her warm mouth on him. She had come across as a schoolgirl when he met her at the bus stop, but Hollywood had a nose for freaks. Sonia was rank to say the least.

ROB STROLLED across the avenue, trying to figure out what he was going to do with the rest of the night. Hollywood had his hands full and China was probably somewhere with B. T. Though he was a down soldier, there weren't that many members of the set he hung out with on his personal time. Rob decided that he would go cop some weed and maybe get up with C-style. It had been a few days since he'd had a taste of that sweet pussy.

After purchasing a twenty of haze, he headed to the store for a forty and some Dutch Masters. On his way out of the store, a passing group of young ladies caught his attention. They had on tight shorts that exposed a good portion of their asses. Rob was so caught up in trying to be cool, that he never saw the two young men run up on him.

When Rob turned around, the first of the young men smashed a fist into his face. Rob tried to fall, but was held up by a second young man, who punched him in the stomach. They gave him a few more good blows, before dragging him to the curb where a green Ford was waiting. The men tossed him roughly into the backseat then climbed in behind him. Before anyone knew what was going on, the car was gone.

In the backseat of the car, the two thugs took turns slapping Rob across the face. The world began to spin but Rob still managed to stay conscious. The beating had stopped and his vision was finally beginning to clear. He looked up and saw a pie-faced man staring down at him.

"Don't pass out on me now, nigga." Major Blood poked him with the barrel of his gun. "We got some things to discuss."

"YOU KNOW who I am?" Major asked, pacing the parking lot.

"A fucking dead rag!" Rob spat.

"Wrong." Major Blood punched him in the face. "I'm a fucking headache. Look, lil nigga, I know youz a nobody in the organization, so you get to keep your life...at least for today. I've got a special job for you my friend. You get to play the go-between for me and your set."

"I ain't doing shit for you, nigga!"

"Wrong again." Major punched Rob in the stomach, but held him by the jaw so he couldn't fall. "You're gonna do just what I tell you for two very simple reasons." He pulled his gun and placed it to Rob's head. "For one, you're a smart kid. For two, you don't wanna die."

At the sight of the gun and the cold glare in his captor's eyes, Rob's knees began to involuntarily shake. For as hard as he might've tried to come across, he was still a child. He felt the water begin to form in the corners of his eyes and prayed the tears would spare him the humiliation.

"You scared?" Major whispered. "Tell me you scared." He rubbed the gun against Rob's sweat-covered temple. "Yeah, you scared muthafucka. Fake-ass gangsta. You think wearing that flag makes you a true banger?" He pressed the barrel of his gun deeper into Rob's temple. "Boy, youz a pussy in wolf's clothing," he slapped Rob with his free hand.

Rob's head snapped back, causing him to lose his balance. He was so hurt and embarrassed that he could no longer keep the tears at bay. If he'd had a gun, he'd have emptied it into his tormentor, but he was unarmed. Moisture ran down his cheeks, but he continued to glare at Major.

"I know that look." Major leaned in close enough for Rob to feel his breath on his face. "You're probably thinking how much you'd like to blow my brains out, but you can't. You got caught without your strap, if you even own one. First rule of thumb in the gang-banging handbook; never get caught without a weapon." He tapped the barrel against Rob's skull for emphasis.

"This nigga is a mess," Tito said, stepping from the shadows. "He's probably shitted his pants. Faggot-ass crab!" Tito hit him in the ribs.

Rob doubled over in pain. Every time he tried to breathe his ribs throbbed. He knew that he had no wins against the odds, so he didn't bother to try and scrap back. He did study all the faces and commit them to memory. If he survived the ordeal, they would all answer for what they'd done.

"We should just kill this fool and get it over with." Miguel cocked the Beretta he was carrying.

"Nah, it's like I said. He's gonna be my messenger. Hey"—Major slapped Rob and held him upright—"you listening?" Rob nodded. "Tell your boys that it's a wrap for Harlem." Without warning, Major hit him in the face.

Rob collapsed where he stood. The force of his face hitting the ground shook his brain. Spots flashed before his eyes as sweet blackness engulfed him. The last thing he saw was the booted feet of his attackers disappear into the night.

chapter 10

MONIFA WAS a five feet nine brown goddess who oozed sex appeal without even trying. She had long dark hair, with flakes of gold scattered throughout it. The lime sundress she wore hugged her hips and plentiful breasts. Her full lips looked as if they couldn't decide whether to smile or cry at the arrival of the guests. Caramel eyes swept over the trio, but lingered on Gutter.

"Sup," he said, breaking the silence.

"Same ol." She stared down at her airbrushed toes, peeking through her sandals. "Heard you took a few?"

"Shit happens."

Another uncomfortable silence.

"So, you just gonna stand there, or show me some love?" She spread her arms.

Gutter hesitated at first then moved in to accept her embrace. Monifa's skin was warm against his. When her hair brushed against his face, he could smell the faint traces of jasmine. During the embrace, age-old feelings rushed to the surface.

Monifa and Gutter had been lovers when California was still his state of residence. More accurately, they had been a couple. She lived on 101st and Hoover, not far from Gunn. Though she never officially joined the set, she was a firm supporter of the Crip movement.

During the early days you could always find her at Gutter's side, rallying the troops and helping him plot on his enemies. Monifa's little brother, Half, was also a Crip who ran with Harlem. Not long after joining, he was killed in a drive-by shooting. After her brother's death Monifa began to change. Her love for Gutter was unwavering, but her attitude toward the movement had soured. She was beginning to wonder if the banging was as senseless as her mother always warned her.

The more detached Monifa got from banging, the more entrenched Gutter became. He and Lou-Loc were so intent on coming up through the ranks that gang-banging consumed their every waking thought. If he wasn't committing murders, he was planning the take over of enemy territory.

The change in personalities put a serious strain on their relationship. Monifa had gotten tired of playing second fiddle to the set, and demanded that he change. Being from California, she understood that he couldn't just walk away from the gang, but she also knew that he had already proven himself to be a G. It was no longer necessary for him to ride every night. Gutter promised to change, but never really did. The relationship became more and more frayed, but they stayed together. Each knew the other was doing their thing on the side, but publicly they still professed their unity. Then came the murder.

She never really got the full story, but from what she gathered he was being sought for questioning in the murders of two Los Angeles detectives. The whole set was tight lipped about the incident, only telling her that all would be taken care of. One day Gutter and Lou-Loc up and disappeared.

For a while he would send her letters letting her know he was all right. She could never pinpoint his location because the postmarks came from various points on the Midwest and East Coast. Eventually the letters stopped coming and she lost contact with him. About a year ago, she learned from a friend that he had relocated to New York City. She thought about contacting him, but never did. In time she learned not to hate him, but the resentment still lingered. He had left her with a broken heart.

"You look good." He smiled.

"I'm a'ight," she said flatly.

"Monifa . . . I wanted to call you, but—"

"Save it"—she cut him off—"we can discuss our past another time. Right now, your family needs you. Everyone is in the living room."

He was a little stung by her sharp tone, but he couldn't blame her. He just nodded and stepped through the doorway.

The living room was packed. Friends and relatives were crammed into the tiny space, talking in hushed tones or praying. Some people lingered near the kitchen area, while others hung out in the back, smoking weed and cigarettes. Though they tried to carry on normal conversations, they couldn't hide the grim faces they all wore.

"Kenyatta," his aunt Rahshida called from the corner. She was a short woman with dark skin and their family's trademark green eyes. She wore street clothes, but kept her head covered by a silk wrap.

"Auntie." He hugged her. "How's he doing?"

"Up and down." She wiped her eyes. "Thanks for getting here so quickly."

"That's my fam. You know I'm gonna be here in his time of need."

"Young Gutter!" a voice called over his shoulder. A short man, who was shaped like a building, came through the crowd. He was clean-shaven, wearing a white mock neck and blue slacks. His blue Stacy Adamses glided across the carpet to where Gutter was talking to his aunt. He gave them his too-big grin and slapped Gutter on the back.

"Blue Bird, what it is, cuz?" Gutter returned the gesture.

Blue Bird was an older homey, claiming 9-4 Hoover; a close ally of Gunn's set 107. He was about the same age as Gunn, but carried himself like a teenager. Blue Bird enjoyed putting in work almost as much as he enjoyed convincing other people to do it for him. He was loud, ignorant, and disrespectful, but more important he was a straight-up G. Blue Bird was an old head of the old codes, where human life meant nothing.

"Man, we all fucked up about what happened to Gunn," he said, sipping his can of Budweiser. "Them slobs don't respect nothing, man. That's okay though. We gonna ride on them fools for Gunn. That's on the nine!"

"Why don't you sit your drunk ass down!" Rahshida snapped. "My brother is back there fighting for his life and you're still talking that *who-ride* foolishness. More violence is not what's needed right now."

"Rah, ain't mean no disrespect. I'm just trying to let nephew know the hood is with him."

"I appreciate that, cousin. Gimme some time with my fam and we'll rap," Gutter suggested, trying to defuse the situation.

Blue Bird nodded, and made his way back through the crowd. As he passed the homeys he notified them all of Gutter's return. Soon Gutter was swamped with old friends and new faces welcoming him back to the set. It seemed as if all at once everyone in the room was either trying to pass Gutter a blunt or inquire about life in New York. The homeys were just trying to show love, but Rahshida was clearly getting frustrated. After shaking a few hands and assuring them that they'd all be addressed promptly, he managed to disperse the crowd.

"Damn fools. Every one of them." Rahshida folded her arms.

"Don't trip, Auntie." He patted her back. "You know they don't mean no harm."

"Sup, Rah." Tears approached, followed by Danny.

"Trying to get these rowdy fools to show some respect. They need to take they asses home."

"Yeah, it is a gang of muthafuckas up in here," he said as he observed the crowd. "Any word?"

"Same thing," she said in a defeated tone. "Blocks from all over been tripping on Bloods, but nobody saying who the shooter was. Bloods blame it on the Mexicans, and vice versa. Hoover been tripping on both sides. I heard they even blasted on some Sixties who were rumored to have something to do with it."

"Sixties didn't do this," Gutter disagreed. "Gunn had homeys from that side. When that shit popped off with them and the Treys, he didn't get in it."

"That's possible," Tears agreed. "Gunn wasn't never for that Crip-on-Crip shit."

"Crips bang on Crips out here?" Danny asked, shocked.

"Please believe it." Tears faced him. "It started because of this kid getting killed for his jacket years ago. The next thing you know muthafuckas started choosing sides and a civil war jumped off between the sets. Shit got real ugly," Tears recalled. "Personally, I never got involved with it because I feel like the homey Gunn did. At the end of the day we're all Crips, so it seemed backward for us to be taking each other out. It ain't as bad as it used to be, but some of these stupid muthafuckas just can't let it go."

"That's some crazy shit."

"More like genocide," Rahshida added. "I don't know when y'all are gonna learn about playing in them streets."

"Come on, Auntie, don't start wit that," Gutter said.

"Kenyatta, please, don't tell me what to say out my mouth, I'm your aunt, not one of your little hood rat friends. Besides, I'm only telling you the truth. You see what happened to your uncle and he wasn't even in the streets anymore. You gotta pay it all forward one day, Kenyatta."

"Can I see him, Rah?" Gutter asked, trying to change the subject.

"Yeah, come on." She headed toward the back rooms. Gutter followed, while the rest remained behind.

The hallway was narrow, but had high ceilings. There were pictures on the wall of Gunn and other home boys who had come and gone over the years. This was no doubt one of many safe houses Gunn had access to. The fresh paint and hardly worn carpet suggested that this one was new. At least Gunn hadn't owned it when Gutter was still living in L.A.

Sitting outside the door at the end of the hall was a man lounging on a wooden chair. He had his long legs stretched and crossed, rotating one of his white Chuck Taylors. A wool skully was pulled over his head and ears, stopping at the beginning of his thick beard. His dark face twisted into a mask of disgust at the intrusion, but softened when he recognized his nephew.

"Oh, shit." He leapt to his feet. "Little Kenyatta!"

"What up, Uncle Rah." Gutter hugged him.

Rahkim was Rahshida's twin. The whole Soladine clan was gangsta, but Rahkim was a triple O.G. Much like Gutter and Gunn,

Rahkim rebelled against the responsibility of being a Soladine as well as the teachings of Islam. He fell in with the street gangs, right after Gunn did. Though he was younger, his name had more horror stories attached to it than any of them. Rah had been catching bodies since he was eleven years old, only taking an occasional break to do time in someone's prison. The majority of his cases had been as a minor, so there was only so much time he could do, but his most recent had proved to be his undoing.

Rah and some of his click had gotten high off PCP, and decided they were going to go ride on some Bloods. After appropriating a car, or stealing depending on who you asked, they drove deep into enemy territory. While sitting outside a bowling alley that was rumored to now be under the sway of the rival gang, Rah and his troop spotted a group of people coming out of the alley. They were all wearing red shirts, and walking in the direction of two more men, who had already been confirmed as the enemy.

Getting out of the car, Rah and four other men crept across the parking lot. The two enemies were sitting on the car with their backs to them, so they never saw the approach. Rah got low, dangling his .45-long at his side. The other three men played leapfrog between shadows and parked cars. When the group dressed in red got close to the two men, Rah raised his pistol and dumped.

The shots sounded like thunder splitting the quiet of the night. The first of the enemies never even saw it coming when the bullet entered through his back and exited his chest. The other enemy tried to raise his own gun, only to have one of Rah's men cut him down with an Uzi. The group tried to scatter, or plead, but Rahkim had given orders that no prisoners would be taken.

When it was all said and done, there were seven wounded, and five dead. As it turned out there were only two real enemies. The red-clad group was a part of a bowling league that held a tournament that night. The cashier at the bowling alley had identified the car carrying the shooters when the police arrived. Rah and his people were so high off the sherm that they were still sitting in their car, parked across the street and laughing hysterically when the cops found them. For his roll in the caper, the judge handed Rahkim a lengthy sentence.

"Damn, nigga, you trying to get swoll on me." Rah gave him the once-over.

"You know how it is." Gutter flexed. "Say, when you come home, man?"

"About three weeks ago."

"You gonna stay out this time?"

"Nephew, I just did a dime flat. My days of going to the pen are long over," Rahkim said seriously.

"I know that's right." Gutter gave him dap. "Look, I'm 'bout to go in here and see what's up with your brother."

"Prepare yourself, cuz. He's in a bad way. I almost broke down when I seen him."

"Uncle Rah, I done been to hell and back this year. Can't nothing I see in there make me feel in no way." With that being said, Gutter followed his aunt through the door.

When Gutter entered the room, his heart sank. It was a large space with various machines plugged into every outlet. Gunn's hulking frame was laid out on the bed, with tubes running into just about every hole imaginable. His entire body, including part of his face was covered by blood-caked bandages. Gutter almost faltered as memories of his own assault rushed back to him. There were three nurses in the room. One who monitored his vitals and two more to attend to his daily needs.

Gutter moved timidly across the room and slid a wooden chair to Gunn's bedside. He hesitated for a long moment, staring. Gunn's body was as huge as it had ever been, but he didn't seem the same. The Gunn Gutter remembered was animated and alive. The man before him seemed anything but that. Finally Gutter took the chair.

"Gunn," he whispered. "It's Kenyatta, can you hear me?" Gutter placed his hand over Gunn's.

Gunn opened the eye that wasn't covered, and blinked. He tried to speak, but winced against the pain of the breathing tube. Gunn nodded at Gutter and drifted off again.

"I see them slobs tried to put you down. They should know they can't stop the unstoppable." Gutter paused again, trying to find the right words. He wanted to tell Gunn that it would be okay, but in all honesty he didn't look good. Gutter counted at least five holes, and only God knew how much lead he still had floating around inside him. He knew firsthand what kind of damage a bullet could do, bouncing around in your organs. "Don't trip, family. Ya nephew gone ride for you, that's on the turf." He patted Gunn's hand.

At some point, Monifa had entered the room. He didn't have to turn around to know it was her. The scent was embedded in his brain. She placed a hand on his shoulder and before he could stop it, he placed a hand over hers. There was so much still unsaid between them. That would have to wait for another time. Seeing his uncle laid out like that only made him conscious of one thing: revenge.

"I STILL don't see why we didn't kill him. I mean, that's what you do, right? Murder?" Miguel asked sarcastically.

"Don't get cute, muthafucka. I know what I'm doing," Major Blood said coldly. "It like I told him: he's a messenger. That whole snatch and grab wasn't about dropping no bodies. They'll be enough of that soon enough. I wanted to see what kind of niggaz I'm up against, so I'll know how to move."

"Yeah, but by not killing shorty, he's gonna tip Gutter off that someone is after him," Tito added.

"You think Gutter doesn't know he has enemies?" Major Blood lit a cigarette. "He's gonna chalk this shit up to Bloods tripping."

"I've seen that kid hanging around Gutter. He not gonna like the fact that we touched one of his young boys. He's gonna ride hard on the hood," Miguel said.

"Well, that's something we won't have to worry about any time soon." Major blew smoke in his face. "Gutter has his hands full at the moment. Now on to the next order of business; what do we know about this Satin bitch?"

"After she whacked her brother, they shipped her off to the nut-house." Tito shrugged.

"Where?"

"I don't know."

"Get on that. Next"—Major counted off on his fingers—"divide and conquer. We got anybody posted up on that side of the fence?"

"Yeah, a lil nigga that's got a hard-on for Gutter," Miguel recalled.

"Set up a meeting with him. He's gonna play an important part in all this."

"And what about Pop Top?" Tito asked. "He's Gutter's new general."

"Yeah, I've heard stories about that kid," Major recalled. "Supposed to be a real animal." He faked fear. "Fuck that nigga too. When the time comes, we'll do him up real special."

GUTTER STOOD on the front porch taking in the California night air. Though there was a slight chill to it that night he could still smell the faint traces of salt carried from the Pacific Ocean. Seeing his uncle twisted the way he was had hit him harder than he expected. In Gutter's eyes, as well as all who came in contact with Gunn, his uncle was invincible. He was a nigga that couldn't be faded, but someone had faded him. Not long ago he had been in the same predicament, but Cross had resurrected him. Unfortunately for Gunn there was no cursed blood to heal his wounds.

"Sup, duke?" Danny-Boy stepped out onto the porch.

"Chilling, man. I'm just trying to get my head together," Gutter told him.

"How's ya uncle?"

"He all fucked-up, cuz. Them slobs did him in," Gutter said, trying not to get too emotional.

Danny placed a hand on Gutter's shoulder in an attempt to comfort him. "We gonna make this shit right, man. These West Coast cats is gonna see what this East Coast swagger is all about."

"Spoken like a true protégé of the Soladine family." Tears came out, sipping a forty ounce. "How you be, my nigga?" Tears asked Gutter.

Gutter shrugged. "I'm a'ight. It just fucked me up seeing him like that."

"You ain't the only nigga feeling some type of way about this, G. The hood is demanding blood."

"I hear niggaz is nut'n up over this?"

"Yeah, these lil muthafuckas is bust'n ass left and right, screaming it's for the homey. The funny thing is that most of them are too young to even know who the fuck Gunn is. All they know is that an O.G. got touched and that's a good-enough reason to pop off. C.R.A.S.H been kicking red and blue asses because of all this damn heat these lil ones are bringing down. Then when you got niggaz like Blue Bird instigating it really doesn't help."

"I was surprised to see him inside. I thought sure someone would've killed his ass by now," Gutter half joked.

"Nah, bald-headed son of a bitch has got more lives than a fucking alley cat."

"Fuck the both of you niggaz, out here talking 'bout me like I ain't got ears." Blue Bird staggered onto the porch, which was now beginning to get crowded.

"Go 'head wit that shit, Blue. You know you stay starting some shit," Tears told him.

"Man, I don't never start the drama, but I can sure as hell finish it," Blue Bird said, making the shape of a gun with his fingers. "Fuck is y'all standing around looking all sad and shit for?"

"In case you hadn't noticed we're in the midst of a tragedy," Gutter said seriously.

"Aw, I'm just fucking wit you, cuz." Blue Bird draped his arm around Gutter, causing him to frown at the potent stench of alcohol coming off him. "Look, we all fucked-up about what happened to Gunn, but this shit is gonna get handled. These young boys is out here putting in much work."

"These fools is dumping on everything moving, but we still ain't no closer to finding the shooter," Tears reminded him.

"In due time, my nigga. Say, in the meantime the home boys is having a set over in Twenty-first in the beach. Let's mash over there and get cracking wit 'em."

"I ain't really up for no party," Gutter said.

"Come on, G, stop acting like that. Sitting around here sulking ain't gonna change Gunn's situation. We might as well go on and have a few drinks and shoot the shit." Seeing Gutter's reluctance Blue Bird pressed the issue. "Dude, it's been over two years since you've been home and it would really pick the homeys' spirits up to see the living legend. We'll stay for an hour then you can go back to your pouting."

Gutter thought on it for a minute. He really wanted to be with his family, but Blue Bird had a point. Sitting around the house wouldn't do much to change Gunn's condition. Besides it had been awhile since he had seen the old crew and Danny would need some downtime to prepare him for the heap of shit that was about to be thrown into his lap.

"Fuck it." He finally gave in. "One hour and I'm up."

"That's what I'm talking about." Blue Bird clapped him on the back. "We're gonna get faded and fuck wit some bitches, just like old times."

Blue Bird stepped off the porch, followed by Tears and then Danny. Gutter hesitated for a minute before stepping off. He glanced over his shoulder and saw Monifa watching from the living-room window. He gave a half smile to which she responded by closing the curtains.

"Just like old times," he mumbled to himself before joining the group.

chapter 11

WHEN THEY reached Twenty-first Street there were cars lining both sides of the block. People staggered up and down the sidewalk drinking and carrying on as if it wasn't a residential block. Tears navigated the big truck through the traffic and parked on someone's front lawn. No sooner than they got out of the car, their ears registered a series of whistles, the Crip call. Within seconds they could see shapes moving in and out of the shadows. Even in the darkness their weapons could be seen in hand. Danny tensed up, but Gutter got out as if he hadn't even noticed the armed men.

"Where you from, homey?" one of the men asked Gutter, having never seen him before. Gutter just looked at him as if he was stupid. "Nigga, you hear me talking to you?"

"Put that muthafucking strap away before you get your little ass killed, Dion!" Blue Bird snapped, climbing from the backseat next to Danny.

"Aw, I ain't know he was with you, Blue," Dion said, tucking the small revolver back into his pocket. "I ain't never seen homey so I ain't know if he was friend or foe, you know how muthafuckas be out here tripping."

"Cuz, ain't you up on what's happening? This is Gutter, Gunn's nephew," Blue Bird informed him.

"Gutter?" Another one of the armed men stepped up.

"The same Gutter who put the work in on that pig from narcotics?" Dion asked.

"Don't go believing everything you hear, cuz. I don't know nothing about no cop getting killed," Gutter said, brushing through the crowd.

"Hold on, man. I didn't mean no disrespect," Dion said, catching up to Gutter. "It's just that you're a legend around these parts."

"I ain't nothing but a soldier, just like everybody else," Gutter said modestly.

"You hear this muthafucka?" Blue Bird joined them on the front lawn. "You sound like you're accepting a Grammy or some shit."

"Dude, they said you rallied over two thousand troops in New York," a nameless cat wearing a blue lumber jacket said.

"More like two hundred," Gutter informed him.

"Man, you can tell your war stories later. Let's go on in here; I got someone I want you to meet." Blue Bird pulled Gutter into the house.

The inside of the house was just as packed as the outside. There must've been at least a hundred or so of the homeys from different sets getting their party on. The smell of weed and PCP made the air almost impossible to breathe without catching a contact. The sounds of the old Partna Duce cut, "That's My Partna," blasted through the tower speakers that were placed in each corner, causing the china cabinet to rattle.

"Yeah, yeah, that's my partna though! Yeah, yeah, that's my

partna!" Blue Bird sang along with the chorus, throwing up Hoover, and bumping through the crowd. Gutter followed closely behind, occasionally nodding to the few heads he knew and ignoring the rest. For a few minutes he was able to survey the crowd anonymously until some fool holding a bullhorn shouted, *"Big welcome home shout to Gutter from Harlem!"* The whole crowd went crazy, throwing up their respective sets and shouting their blocks. It seemed like everyone was trying to bulldoze their way over to him and shake his hand. In a strange way he felt like a celebrity. The only things stopping him from being mauled were the combined efforts of Blue Bird and Tears.

"Damn, these muthafuckas act like you a rapper or something!" Danny shouted over the noise.

Gutter brushed him off, but he couldn't front like he wasn't flattered by the reception. His crew in New York always showed him love, but it wasn't like this. California was his birthplace, the epicenter of all that he was. People feared the men and women gathered that night, but among the wolves, he was home.

"Who's the dumb muthafucka coming 'round here causing shit at my party?" a raspy voice came from their left. The speaker was a man of about twenty-six or seven, with skin the color of olive leaves. He was wearing a tank top and denim shorts. There was a blue bandanna tied around his neck, just above the short gold necklace he had taken to wearing. His hair was cornrowed on a slant and tied at the ends with blue and white beads.

"Jynx, what it is!" Blue Bird spread his arms.

Though Jynx appeared to be nothing more than a lanky juvenile, he was one of the most feared men in Southern California. Jynx, like Lou-Loc, was a contract killer, and also like Lou-Loc, it was tragedy that brought him into the fold.

Jynx's brother had been a high roller, seeing major paper off the weed trade in Southern Cali. One night a group of Bounty Hunter Bloods broke into their home searching for drugs and money. When they didn't find anything in the house they shot his brother and slit young Jynx's throat, leaving him to die. Jynx lived through the ordeal, but the cut left a nasty scar and caused some damage to his vocal cords. When he was able to get up and around he went on one of the most talked about killing sprees on the West Coast. It was said that more than a half dozen Bounty Hunters died by his hands, and as a result Jynx was placed on their most wanted list, to be killed on sight.

"I should've known." Jynx embraced him. "Blue, why you always gotta break up some shit?"

"Man, I ain't come here tripping. I brought somebody here to see you, man. I know you know Gutter from Harlem?" He nodded to the man standing behind him.

Jynx squinted at the bearded man standing beside Blue Bird. "Gutter? Blue, you been smoking that shit you selling? That nigga bought the farm in New York."

"So I keep hearing," Gutter said.

"On the turf, this *is* Gutter," Blue Bird said.

"So you're Kenyatta Soladine?" Jynx said, continuing his examination. The unwavering green eyes were more than proof enough of his lineage. "Homey, we never met but I owe you." Jynx shook his hand. Seeing the confused look on Gutter's face Jynx went on to explain. "A few years ago that cop O'Leary murdered a little boy and left him strung up in the hood. The little boy was my cousin and the last blood relative I had left in the world. You settled that score up for me, cuz. Thanks."

Gutter just nodded, but he didn't accept credit for the murder. "It was fucked up the way they did the little homey. O'Leary got what he had coming."

"Listen, I heard what happened to your uncle and I can't tell you how sorry I am. Crip, Blood, Chicano, whoever did this is going down. You've got my word on that. Anything you need, just ask."

"Thanks," Gutter said.

"Enough of this sap shit, where the fuck is the drinks?" Blue Bird asked.

"Spoken like the lush that you are." Jynx laughed, motioning for the men to follow him to the makeshift bar area. To get to where the drinks were being poured they had to pass a small bathroom, just off from the kitchen. When they got within spitting distance of it a pungent odor assaulted all of their nostrils. Each man in the group made a disgusted face, but it was Jynx who vocalized his displeasure.

"Who the fuck is in here trying to kill my plants?!" he barked, banging on the bathroom door.

"Stall me out, cuz. That Carl's Jr. I had earlier is running through a nigga!" someone shouted from the other side.

"Damn, cuz, put some water on that shit or something." Blue Bird put his two cents in it.

"Stinking-ass nigga." Jynx gave the door another kick and proceeded to the kitchen.

Inside the kitchen the air was a little less smoky, due to the back door being propped open. The counters were lined with various brands of liquor and a few half empty bottles of soda and juice. Tears bypassed the liquor and headed to the far corner where there was a tall garbage can filled to the brim with forty ounces. He opened an ice-cold Old English and took a long sip.

"Damn, thirsty, were you?" Blue Bird teased.

"Fuck you, nigga." Tears wiped his mouth with the back of his hand. "Them squares be having a nigga dehydrated."

"That and the fact that they'll kill you is why you need to quit smoking," Jynx said, firing up a blunt.

"Look who's talking," Tears shot back.

"This here is for my glaucoma, fool," Jynx joked, exhaling the smoke. "Y'all niggaz go on and get right. The yak over there and we got that Crip-notic on ice."

"Say, man, where you hiding all the bitches?" Blue Bird asked, pouring himself a healthy shot of Hennessy.

"Shit, take your pick." Jynx nodded toward a group of young women who were talking to some guys in the doorway. "Wit all these hood rat bitches running 'round here, somebody'll give your ugly ass some pussy."

"Fuck you, Jynx. If you wasn't my boy I'd blast yo ass," Blue Bird joked.

"Friendship ain't got nothing to do with it, Blue." He pulled up his tank top and exposed the butt of a very large .45. "You fools help yaselves to whatever you want." He grabbed a light-skinned girl that had been walking past and pulled her close. "I'm 'bout to get into some grown shit." Jynx swaggered toward the bedrooms.

Gutter laughed at Jynx's antics and went back to observing the party. Blue Bird had slipped off to the backyard with a freak, and Danny was ogling the scantily clad women like he was ready to catch a charge. The music was jumping and everyone was having a good time.

"Fuck it," he said, grabbing a forty out of the bucket and leading his troops out into the throng of people. Gutter and his team drank the best liquor and smoked the best weed well into the A.M. before deciding to mash back to the pad. The crowd embraced Gutter like he was family, though most of them had never even met him. Everybody wanted to be close to the legend. Two big booty Mexican chicks were trying to get Gutter and Danny to join in on a freak show, but Gutter declined for them. Danny was tight, but he'd get over it. For as much as Gutter wanted to stay and freak off he knew he couldn't—there was killing to be done.

chapter 12

WHEN GUTTER woke up the next morning it felt like he had just gone to sleep. Tears was supposed to drop them off at the hotel, but Blue Bird's greedy ass insisted on stopping at Jack in the Box, where they bumped into some more of the homeys and ended up smoking two more blunts. The sun was damn near up when they finally got back to Westwood.

After showering, Gutter dressed in jeans and a long-sleeved T-shirt. The bulletproof vest he had gotten from Tears would bulge a bit, but it was better than getting caught slipping. When he removed the contents of the black box resting on his bed he couldn't help but laugh. Inside the box was a Glock and two clips, but not just any Glock, the very same Glock he used to keep at Monifa's. He wondered if it was his ex's idea of a joke, or some ironic reminder of the past he had left behind.

The hotel phone caused Gutter to jump. The front desk informed him that there was someone waiting for him in the lobby. He had no idea who it might be because he didn't tolerate unannounced guests. After ringing Danny, Gutter tucked his strap in his pants and headed for the hotel lobby.

"AIN'T THIS a bitch?" Gutter beamed as he stepped off the elevator and greeted the mystery visitor. He had been ready to come through the lobby shooting until he saw the smiling face of his old friend.

There stood Snake Eyes in all his glory. He was decked out in a blue, striped, Nautica polo. His jeans were starched and creased, cuffed over his white Nikes. His hair was faded almost perfectly into his smooth brown skin. Standing there in a pair of wire-framed glasses Snake Eyes looked every bit of the egghead lawyer that he was. He had become such a square peg over the years that you almost forgot that he was once a killer and dope peddler. The little boy from 102nd and Hoover had done okay for himself.

"My brother," Gutter said, embracing him.

It had been years since he had last embraced his crime partner. The last time they had been in each other's company Gutter had been lying in a pool of his own blood, fighting for his life. Snake Eyes had come to his rescue, laying down the would-be executioners. Back when Snake Eyes was still putting in work he, Gutter, and Lou-Loc had been as thick as thieves, but their lives had gone in different directions. Snake Eyes now did his fighting through the judicial system and Gutter was still putting in work for the turf.

"What that be like, my nigga?" Snake Eyes struck a mock-thug pose.

"You know it's Harlem-Hoover all day and then some." Gutter threw up one set then the other.

"You mean Hoover-Harlem." Snake Eyes threw them up in reverse. An elderly couple that was checking into the hotel gave them a disgusted look, but kept about their business. "Man, I ain't seen your monkey-ass ever since, baby boy!"

"Shit, if it wasn't for you I wouldn't be here now. Dawg, I never got to really thank you about—"

"Man, knock that shit off." Snake Eyes waved off his thanks. "Family does for family; you know how we do it. What it is, home boy?" Snake Eyes addressed Danny, who was staring at him curiously.

"Harlem," Danny said proudly.

"Danny"—Gutter draped his arm around the young man—"this is my homey, Snake Eyes."

"Yeah, I heard of you." Danny smiled. "You 'bout ya shit, huh?"

"That was a long time ago," Snake said evenly. "I have a law practice in Miami now, dealing with a select few clients. I do a lot of wills and trusts for the homeys out here too."

"Bet that's profitable," Danny joked.

"Unfortunately."

"So, what the hell you doing here?" Gutter interjected.

"I heard you flew into town last night, so I came to check you." Snake Eyes informed him.

"You should've come by the spot. It was enough niggaz in there."

"Nah." Snake shifted his weight on the cane. "You know I don't rock with just anybody. Besides, I ain't really wanna let niggaz know I was in the town just yet."

"You see something that I don't?" asked Gutter.

"We'll talk about it on the way," Snake said, heading for the door.

"Where we going?" Gutter questioned.

"Carson. I got some things I want to bounce off you. Besides, I got somebody who I think you'll wanna talk to."

"And who the fuck might that be?"

"Just come on," Snake Eyes urged.

"SO, WHAT'S your take on this, Snake?" Gutter asked from the backseat.

"Honestly, I ain't come up with much more than y'all did," Snake Eyes admitted. "I made some phone calls and probed into a few people, but don't have much to go on. There's a bunch of rumors, but nothing solid."

"I heard that some Mad Swans rode down on him, but I ain't confirmed nothing yet." Gutter stroked his thick beard.

"Interesting." Snake rubbed his chin. "I did some legal work for B-Boy. You know Blood, he was claiming the Gardens before them niggaz chased him up out and he started sucking Swan dick. He ain't denying that slobs did the shooting, but he put it on the hood that his people were clean of the killing."

"Somebody's ass is lying and I'm tired of chasing my fucking tail about it. What are the big homeys talking about in the way of payback?" Gutter asked.

"Nothing yet," Snake Eyes replied. "Nobody wants an all-out war over some knuckleheads tripping, you know how it is."

"The fuck I do. I know that somebody gonna taste steel over popping my uncle. I don't give a fuck if I gotta mash on every nigga in every hood to flush that wormy muthafucka out. It's on a cracking!" Gutter declared.

"I see getting dropped off on heaven's door hasn't quenched that thirst of yours." Snake Eyes commented.

"Don't start that shit, man. I get enough of it from Anwar."

"Wise young dude."

"Fuck you, nigga. This ain't about me and my business in New York. This is about some slobs touching my uncle, and these old muthafuckas who govern us playing United Nations out this bitch."

"This shit with Gunn has ruffled quite a few feathers, but all the right moves need to be made to fix it. The old heads is having a hard enough time containing the fighting that's kicked off since the shit happened. Man, these lil niggaz is out here breaking fool, making the hood all hot and shit. The G's are just trying to keep the peace." Snake Eyes said.

"I hear you, Snake, but I'm a warlord. I don't know nothing 'bout that peace shit. My uncle is a shell of the man I knew, and even if he does live through the injuries, he'll never be the same. Someone has got to answer for this. A debt is a debt."

Snake Eyes could've argued the point with Gutter until the following summer, but the result would be the same. Trying to change the subject he asked, "How's Sharell?"

"Man, she's getting big as hell. I don't know if she's having a baby or a damn elephant." Gutter smiled, thinking about his boo, but the smile quickly faded when his mind went back to Satin.

"Everything all right with the baby?" Snake Eyes asked with concern in his voice.

"Oh, everything is cool with Sharell, but it's Satin I'm worried about." Gutter gave him the short version of what he'd learned from Sharell.

"Muthafucka." Snake Eyes shook his head. "Pregnant? Gutter, why didn't one of you call me? Dawg, I gotta get the ball rolling to get her out." Snake Eyes said, pulling out his two-way and scrolling through the numbers.

"Man, you know the laws don't work in favor of the blacks.

They'd have you tied up in red tape for God only knows how long, not to mention the fact that the girl has got that murder beef still hanging over her head. Nah, we need to get her out ASAP, but ain't no need to trip because I got somebody on the job already."

"Who?" Snake Eyes asked.

Gutter's cell going off drew his attention. He glanced at the caller ID screen and smiled when he saw the 347 area code. Before flipping his phone open, he looked to his friend and said, "You don't even wanna know."

CARSON WAS a small city situated on the border between L.A. and Compton. It was composed mostly of Samoans and Filipinos, but also hosted a Latino and black population. Though a seemingly quiet town its location and the large mall in its center made it a rest haven for gangs. Since its construction it had been contested territory between the Crips and Bloods. Over the last few years the East Coast Crips had been the controlling faction.

Snake Eyes piloted the Regal down Carson Avenue and banked a left onto Dominguez. About a half mile down they turned into the mall parking lot. The large IKEA sign loomed overhead like an open invitation. The morning sun was still beaming in full effect, so the lot was filled almost to capacity. Snake Eyes parked the car near the edge of the lot and killed the engine.

"Nigga, we got planning to do and you wanna shop?" Danny asked.

"Danny, shut up, please." Gutter eased out, and joined Snake Eyes. "What's this all about, Snake?"

"I'll explain it to you as we walk," Snake said, cutting across the grass leading to a small walkway. They followed a long wall, which served as the divider between the mall parking lot and a grungy-

looking suburb. Below the level on which they stood was a basketball court, which had a crowd of young men gathered in the center.
Apparently, two of them were squaring off over a dispute.

"Snake, where are we going, man?" Gutter asked, following
him down the stairs.

"Like I told you before we left, there's someone here who I
think you might like to see," Snake Eyes continued. "It's a cousin of
yours flew in to be with the big homey in his time of need."

"Snake, I got a lot of cousins in town. What's so special about
this one?"

"Just watch," Snake Eyes said, leading them toward the crowd.

When they had almost reached the crowd of spectators, one of
them branched off and moved to join the trio. He looked to be
about seventeen or eighteen years old, sporting a blue Dickies suit
and short cornrows.

"Sup, cuz," Marv greeted them.

Snake Eyes shook the young man's hand. "What's going on over
here?"

"Shit, De Shawn is going head up with the lil homey from Suicide. He tried to punk the lil nigga, but shorty is getting 'em up
like a true G."

Gutter and Snake Eyes followed Marv to the circle, where on-
lookers watched the fight and took bets. In the center were two com-
batants. Both were breathing hard, but neither was ready to give.
The dark-skinned combatant had a busted lip and a bruise was
beginning to form under his eye. The light-skinned combatant
also sported a bruised face, and his nose didn't seem to wanna quit
bleeding.

The light-skinned one shot out a right, which the dark-skinned
one feinted and then launched a powerful left. The blow connected,
but didn't drop him. The two men circled each other like angry

dogs, every so often throwing a punch. The light-skinned boy out-weighed the dark-skinned one, but couldn't intimidate him.

Growing impatient, the light-skinned one shot out of his corner throwing combinations. The dark-skinned one deflected most of the blows, but still took shots to his chest and head. He staggered back, seemingly ready to drop. The light-skinned one decided to take advantage of the opportunity and move in for the kill.

"Who's the lil nigga there, Snake?" Gutter asked curiously.

"You mean, you really don't know?" Snake asked, surprised.

"Nah, cuz. Should I?"

"I would think so. Y'all share the same genes."

De Shawn came at the dark-skinned boy with an overhand right, trying to knock his head off. The dark-skinned boy waited until the last moment and moved out of the way. The momentum of the swing took De Shawn off balance. When he tried to right himself, the dark-skinned one came in raining blows to the back of his head. De Shawn swayed but didn't fall. He feebly tried to mount a defense, but a well-placed haymaker ended the fight. He was out cold.

"Suicide, bitch!" The dark-skinned boy bellowed, planting his foot on his opponent's chest.

The crowd erupted into cheers and patted him on the back as he was steered through the mob. Outside the ring, he was greeted by the man whom he knew to be Snake Eyes and two others he didn't know. He stared at the bearded man and tried to place his face. Seeing this familiar face staring at him made him uncomfortable. It wasn't the way the man was looking at him, but the way he *looked*. The young boy had smooth dark skin and their eyes were almost the same shade of green, but he couldn't think where he knew him from.

"Sup, Snake," the dark-skinned boy addressed Snake Eyes, but never took his eyes off Gutter.

"Sup, lil nigga. I see y'all fools out here banging on each other." Snake Eyes gave him dap.

"Fuck this nigga." The dark-skinned boy spat blood on the floor. "Bitch nigga trying to put shit on Suicide, so I had to school 'em out." The young man paused for a minute and then turned to Gutter. "Sup, cuz, we know each other or something? Where you from?"

"Say what?" Gutter asked, surprised.

"Watch yo mouth, Lil Gunn," Snake cut in. "That ain't no way to talk to your family."

"Gunn?" Gutter said with recognition finally setting in. The reason the young man looked so familiar was because Gutter had been there the day his mother had given birth to him.

Tariq "Lil Gunn" Soladine was the child of Big Gunn and a woman named Stacia, who originally hailed from Watts. Back when Big Gunn was on a come-up, Stacia had been his ride-or-die bitch. She loaded the guns and he dropped Brims with them. She knew Gunn was on his way to being a ghetto superstar, and wanted her piece of the pie. Everything was gravy until she got pregnant with Tariq. Stacia felt that since she was now Gunn's baby mama that she had papers on him. She began trying to press Gunn to marry her and square up in a big house. Gunn, being married to the streets, wasn't trying to hear it. Eventually, she absconded with the child and moved to San Francisco. She claimed it was to keep them safe from the violence Gunn was bringing to their doorstep, but most people felt it was done to spite Gunn for not marrying her. He saw the child from time to time, but other than the checks he sent once a month, they really had no contact.

"I'll be damned. Lil ass Tariq!" Gutter said in disbelief.

"Snake, who is this nigga?" Lil Gunn asked, not really making the connection.

Snake Eyes smiled. "This is your cousin, Gutter."

Lil Gunn looked Gutter up and down, and his face began to soften. "No shit?"

"Come here, lil muthafucka." Gutter embraced him. "Man, I ain't seen you since you was about eight or nine years old."

"Cuz, I heard you got smoked out in New York!" Lil Gunn said excitedly.

"Don't believe rumors, fam. I took a shitload of lead from some stunting ass Brims, but can't no bullet kill a Soladine," Gutter joked.

"I'm glad to see a real Crip among us." Lil Gunn shot a glance over his shoulder. "My old man is taking his last breaths and these niggaz ain't trying to do shit but get faded and *talk* about shooting muthafuckas. If you ask me, the only thing these busters is shooting is their mouths."

"Not everybody is built like us, little cousin." Gutter stroked his beard.

"I know that's right, man. But I ain't tripping. My big cousin Gutter is home and these faggot-ass oh-las better run for cover. Man, your name is ringing all over the Coast. Yo shit is the stuff of legends. With you and me together, we gonna ride on every Brim hood in retaliation for my dad." Lil Gunn tried to hide the pain in his voice, but Gutter caught it.

"All in due time, cousin." Gutter placed a reassuring hand on his shoulder. "For now, let's get you cleaned up and us reacquainted."

chapter 13

"**Y**OU GOT that info I asked you for, poppy?" Major Blood asked Tito as he entered the hotel suite.

Tito reached into the pocket of his jeans and handed Major Blood a folded piece of paper. Tito narrated as his superior read the printout. "My home girl tracked that down for me. The top is a job address for Gutter's girl, Sharell."

Major nodded as he looked over the sheet. "Bet I got a lil nigga I can put on Sharell's case and see what pops off. I'm just gonna have him watch her for now, but when I lower the curtain, I'm gonna do it real ugly on Gutter's bitch. What about that turncoat ho, Satin?"

"The address on the bottom is the hospital where she's locked up," Tito told him. "I still don't see what you want with her though. The girl can't even wipe her own ass."

Major nodded. "Ain't your job to wonder, T. You just handle your end of this; I got the Satin situation from here. In the meantime rally the troops and let's get ready to mash out, Blood. It's time we made our presences felt."

POP TOP sat in the emergency room of Harlem Hospital flanked by China, B. T., and Hollywood. The staff shot funny glances at the ragtag bunch, to which they responded by throwing up their sets or middle fingers. Though several people had complained to security about the noise they were making, no one dared ask them to leave. As much business as they brought the hospital, they were given ambassadors' status.

C-style came from the back where Rob was being treated for his injuries wearing a grim look. She was dressed in sweatpants and a white V neck. Her hair was wrapped and pinned under the powder-blue scarf she wore. When they had called her she was already in bed, so she just jumped in her sweats without bothering to primp. Her eyes were red from crying and lack of sleep, but she didn't seem too broken up.

"What they say?" Pop Top asked.

"He took a hell of a beating." She sighed. "They blackened his eye, and he'll look like Jimmie Walker for a while, but he'll live."

"Did he get into a fight or something after I left him?" Hollywood asked.

"That's the thing, he said he got snatched up," she explained. "Supposedly, some of them niggaz from the other side rolled up and tossed him into a car."

"If he was kidnapped, why didn't they ask for a ransom?" China questioned.

"I was getting to that," C-style said. "He said they wanted him to take a message back to Gutter. 'It's a wrap for Harlem.'"

"These niggaz got nerve," Hollywood said, picking his tooth

with a manicured pinky nail. "Trying to tell my dude how to do what he do. You'd think that after we laid down damn near an entire set that they'd finally realize that we ain't to be fucked with."

"Them niggaz knew he was with us, and they fucked him up anyway. They outta pocket." B. T. shook his head.

"Yo, they fucked him up real bad, fellas. What're we gonna do?" C-style asked.

"Okay, okay." Pop Top stood up. "The last time I checked, I was running Harlem. We gonna handle these niggaz who touched our brother. They're gonna learn the hard way how we play."

"Maybe we should call Gutter?" China asked.

"Nah, we ain't gonna do that," Top said quickly. "I can handle this shit. Was Rob able to ID anybody?"

"Yeah, Tito from L.C. and some other dudes. He said he'd never seen them around before so maybe it was a joint effort," C-style told him.

"Fuck 'em all then," Pop Top declared. "Snake-ass muthafucka, we should've killed his ass years ago. But you know what; I got a trick for that bean-eating muthafucka. They wanna touch our fam, we gonna touch their pockets." Everyone looked at him curiously, but he didn't elaborate. Pop Top was always secretive when it came to murder, as everyone should be.

Rob was the hardheaded son of a square mother, but he was like a little brother to most of the members assembled. The group filed out of the emergency room, each lost in his or her own thoughts about what would come of Rob's beating and the seemingly endless war with their sworn enemies. B. T.'s cell going off caused him to slow up. When he looked at the caller ID he hung back a bit from the group. Only when he was sure the crew was out of earshot did he pick up the phone.

"Yo?" he answered.

"Sup, son?" the voice on the other end taunted.

"Man, I can't talk right now I got something on the ball." B. T. tried to rush the caller.

"Well, yo shit is gonna have to wait cause I need to get up with you, *now*," the caller insisted.

"Loc, I told you I'm in the middle of something. I can't just dip off to come meet you."

"Nigga, you can either come meet me or I can come to you. Imagine how it's gonna look to your homeys to see me and you chopping it up like old friends. You know the deal, son," the caller shot back.

B. T. was so angered by the threat that he could've roared. He had been doing side business with the caller for the last few months without anyone finding out, and now that was threatened because his partner wanted to flex his power. He made a mental note to address the issue once he was in a better position. Before he could utter a response, he heard footsteps behind him.

"Nigga, what you doing?" China approached.

"Ah, nothing," B. T. stuttered. "Just taking care of something. Look," he said into the phone, "I'll be there." He ended the call.

"Man, why you look all irritated?" China questioned.

"These hoes getting on my last nerve." B. T. gave a fake chuckle.

"You need to be more like Hollywood. He's got his hoes in check," China pointed out. "Now, let's hit the block so we can get to the bottom of this Rob shit."

"I can't," B. T. blurted out. "I mean, I got some shit I gotta handle."

"What's more important than handling business for the crew?" China raised his eyebrow.

"Stop being so nosey, slant-eyed muthafucka. Man, I'll hook up with you later."

B. T. strode from the emergency room exit, while China looked on. There was something about B. T.'s behavior that didn't sit right with him. B. T. was always a shifty-acting cat, but something was different this time. China decided he would keep an eye on his comrade and see what he could discover before taking his suspicions to the crew.

B. T. STOOD in the parking lot of Western Beef, chain-smoking. Every time he heard a car, or saw a group of people, his body tensed up. The last thing he needed was for someone to spot him and report it back to the homeys. He had been a Crip for a long time, since even before Lou-Loc and Gutter came to New York. In those days, he was a respected member, and even had his own territory. The Cali native had changed that.

Lou-Loc had not only whipped his ass in front of his friends, but he had also stripped him of all rank and title. B. T. was reduced to nothing more than a soldier, trying to keep his head above water. When the opposing team had come to him, he was skeptical about the whole idea. He was a Crip, but what had it gotten him so far? He gave them loyalty, and was rewarded with disrespect. His plan was to work with the Bloods until he got what he wanted, then set out a piece of the pie for his comrades. He never planned for anyone to get hurt in the process, but he reasoned that you had to break a few eggs to make an omelet. What he was doing was beyond fucked-up, but the fact that no one from his gang respected him was his motive.

B. T. spotted the car he was waiting for, and tried to pull himself together. The red Taurus pulled into the lot and parked a few cars from where he was standing. There weren't many cars in the lot at that hour, but they found two to hide between. Tito came walking in his direction, followed by Miguel, Eddie, and a man he didn't know. His antennas screamed danger, but he brushed it off and stepped out to meet his partners.

"Sup, Big Time." Tito extended his hand.

"Cut that small talk, Tito. What you want, man?" B. T. looked around.

"Damn, you niggaz is antisocial 'round this bitch," Major commented.

"Fuck is this nigga?" B. T. looked him up and down.

"This is the cat I called you out here to meet," Tito explained. "Major"—Tito turned to him—"this is our inside man. B. T."

Major Blood studied B. T. momentarily before speaking again. "So, you the turncoat muthafucka that's willing to sell his crew down the river?"

"Fuck you. Dead rag-ass nigga," B. T. spat. "You don't know me."

"You're right. I don't know you, and don't wanna know you. These niggaz said you could help further our cause, and that's the only reason I'm here. Don't flatter yourself, young'n."

"Yo, Tito," B. T. addressed his contact, "I ain't come all the way out this bitch to be insulted by this chump. If you got some business, let's talk about it. If not, I'm out."

"Everybody be cool," Tito said, trying to defuse the situation. "We're all on the same side. Major Blood is from the West Coast, so his style is a little different. He ain't mean nothing by it."

"Whatever. So, what y'all need?"

"What we need is information," Major cut in. "They say you know the ins and outs of Gutter's operation, so spill. I need names and addresses, starting with that Bible-toting bitch of his."

"Sharell? I really can't say. I know he moved her out of Harlem. Brooklyn, I think," B. T. replied.

"Where in Brooklyn?"

"Didn't I just say I don't know?"

"Okay. What about a mistress?"

"Gutter fucks with bitches here and there, but nobody he really gives a fuck about."

"What about his routines." Major tried a different angle. "Where does he hang out? What restaurants does he take his broads to?"

"He ain't got no set patterns. Mostly he just bounces in and out of the hood. Beyond that, I don't know." B. T. shrugged.

"Tito, I thought you said this nigga was useful?" Major Blood asked over his shoulder.

"Yo, you got a lot of sideways shit with you, fam," B. T. said angrily.

"B. T.," Tito cut in, "Major Blood is here to help us knock Gutter off his high horse. Now, if I remember correctly, that's what you wanted, wasn't it?"

"Yeah, but that don't mean I gotta listen to this faggot pop shit. Besides, I don't think Gutter is gonna take too kindly to you niggaz doing his young boy like that. You might wanna watch ya back," B. T. said smugly.

Major Blood laughed at that. "You let me worry about Gutter, homey. I'll deal with King Crip when the time comes, but right now he ain't an issue. Dismantling your fag-ass set is the order of business, so play your fucking position, crab."

B. T.'s eyes flashed rage, and he thought about taking a swing at the stranger, but the coward in him stayed his hand. "Check this shit out, cuz, I've been helping y'all niggaz take out key players, and I think that counts for something, so you might wanna stop talking all crazy to me. When I get some more info, I'll float it to you."

"Fair enough." Tito nodded. "If Blood ain't got no more questions for you, we out."

"Actually, I do have a question," Major spoke up. "Why?"

"Why what?" B. T. asked, confused.

"Why cross yo peoples like this? I know they've done some greasy shit, but you're still a Crip. How can you set your own up to be slaughtered?"

"Gutter ain't mine. Him and his faggot-ass man came out here acting like they running shit. It's about time somebody checked his ass. Besides, this shit ain't personal. It's strictly business."

"Strictly business." Major laughed. "I'll be sure they put that on your tombstone." Out of nowhere, Major Blood hit B. T. with a left. He staggered from the blow, but it was the right hook that put him on his ass. He lay on the ground, dazed and leaking from his nose.

"I never could stand a rat." Major Blood shook his head while kneeling over B. T. The turncoat suddenly found it very difficult to focus his eyes, but he caught flashes of Major Blood taking something out of his pocket. B. T. tried to say something, but all that came out was a wet, gurgling sound as Major Blood cut his throat.

chapter 14

GOTDAMN, MAJOR, we could've used that nigga!" Tito fumed.

"For what? Man, I wouldn't use that snake-bitch to wipe the shit off my shoes," Major Blood spat. "I came here to put in work, not play muthafucking I Spy, nigga! Fuck B. T. and fuck Harlem. What you need to do is spin Harlem so I can get a line on this monkey muthafucka, Pop Top. As far as everything else, I got this nigga."

"I hope so, Blood," Miguel mumbled.

"Y'all niggaz stop acting like faggots and show some nuts," Major barked. "Now pay attention while I put that little info you gave me to some good use, Tito." Major Blood pulled out his cell and punched in a few numbers. After a brief pause someone picked up on the other line, but didn't say anything, not that Major needed him to. "Sup, Blood?" Major greeted his watchdog.

THE MAN known as B-High was a piece of shit even by a piece of shit's standards. Born in Compton and raised on different Blood sets throughout the surrounding area, all he knew was gang-banging and his love for his hood ran deeper than the love he had for his own mother. To him there was nothing outside of the set.

Major Blood had originally come across the wild young man barely into his fifteenth year and had no problem turning him out. The seeds had already been planted in B-High so all Major Blood had to do was add a little water. Of all the young Bs he had under him, B-High was the most down to ride, which is why he was now on the East Coast living like a fugitive.

When Major had finally reached O.G. status he decided it was time to deal with his mother's murderer. It was public knowledge that Big Gunn from Hoover had killed his mother, so he found himself stumped that when he'd approached the governing body about laying Gunn they had denied him justice. Some of the old heads felt him on wanting to ride for his old bird, but there were two in particular who fought him tooth and nail on the matter, Swoop from the Jungle, and Bad Ass who represented the 900s. They spit a bunch of political shit about letting old beefs die and Gunn's status, but Major didn't even listen. In his mind, if you weren't for him then you were against him and you had to go, Blood or not. It was that night after the meeting that he plotted Swoop's and Bad Ass's deaths.

Major knew he would be under the magnifying glass, because of the ruling and his reputation of having a hot temper, so he had to seek help elsewhere and this is where B-High came in. He loved Major Blood as if he had been the one to push him from the womb. All it took was the spiel of crabs killing Major's parents and Bad Ass and Swoop trying to protect them. B-High was a powder keg and Major Blood lit the fuse.

Three nights after Major Blood and B-High's meeting Swoop was found shot to death in the parking lot of his apartment complex. Bad Ass got roasted the next evening. He was found at an hourly motel in Hollywood sporting a bullet hole in his left cheek. The whore he had been with took one in the back, but unfortunately she lived. Five minutes after scrolling through the LAPD's gang file, she had fingered B-High and made him not only a fugitive from justice, but with his name crossed out on every wall in the hood. The set had marked him for death.

Major Blood knew that he would have to get rid of anything that could've tied him to the murders, but he had a soft spot for B-High. Instead of murking him he put B-High on the first thing smoking to Florida. B-High was supposed to lay low until things had cooled off, but of course he couldn't. He went from selling coke on South Beach to sniffing and taking contract hits for short paper in Miami, and finally a fugitive from both ports. Now he made his home in New York, living off the occasional bone Major Blood threw him and his wits.

He was thoroughly surprised when he'd heard from his old mentor, Major Blood. Every so often Major would throw him a piece of business, but that was always done by phone or coded letters. They hadn't actually seen each other in almost a year, so he wondered what his intentions really were for coming to New York? His first thought was that Major had finally confessed and bartered B-High's life for his, but when he mentioned Gutter his fears were put to rest.

Gutter had been notorious in California, but he was becoming a street legend in New York. He had brought to the Big Apple what hadn't been seen in L.A. for almost ten years, banging...full frontal murder over turf. His gangsta wasn't to be tested, but it was his ability to unify the sets that made him dangerous. Could you imagine a man like Gutter with ten thousand troops? No, it made perfect sense for Major Blood to be put on his ass. Use a sociopath to kill a sociopath, how ironic was that?

The nation must've been pissed with Gutter, considering Major's rep and the fact that he hated every Soladine. But the logic behind it, nor Gutter, were B-High's concerns at the moment. What his mind was focused on was the fact that Major had promised him thirty grand for this assignment. Fifteen up front and fifteen when the job was done. B-High took the money, went and bought a quarter-piece of white, and had been getting blasted and sitting on Sharell ever since.

His cell phone vibrated, tearing his eyes off the entrance of Sharell's building. He started to let it ring until he saw that it was Major. His mentor told him that it was time to go to phase two, which brought a smile to B-High's face. He needed the cash, but he was lazy as hell, preferring to sit in his tiny apartment, playing Madden or sniffing with one of the hood rats off his block. Laziness aside, B-High enjoyed putting in work and the heavy paper Major was gonna drop only got him more excited.

WHEN SHARELL felt the faint throbbing in her temples, she knew a headache would be coming soon after. It was bad enough that the baby was sucking all the calcium out of her, causing god-awful toothaches, but the strongest thing she could take was Tylenol... *regular* strength at that.

Between the kung fu master in her stomach, who felt the need to kick her every time she tried to doze off, Satin being pregnant, and her man on a suicide mission, Sharell found that her nerves were quite frayed. "French onion dip," she said aloud. The draining sound that emitted from her stomach said that the baby agreed. Rolling off the couch, which she had been lounging on all morning, Sharell decided to take a walk to the store.

She didn't bother with any sort of primping, opting to just jump in her sweatpants and slip on an overcoat. She could only imagine how she looked with her frayed ponytail and no makeup, but she didn't really give a damn. She was fat, her feet hurt, and she felt like she would need chiropractic therapy for months by the time she gave birth. How someone felt about the way she looked going to the store was the furthest thing from her mind.

The weather was decent, but the wind was in full effect, whipping at her overcoat. She was able to button the coat at the neck and chest, but after that it was a wrap. When she had bought the form-fitting coat she was a size nine or ten, but the baby had her pushing a fourteen. She knew she truly loved that man when she allowed him to move her up four dress sizes.

Across the street she saw the dome light go on in Mohammad's car. With a practiced hand gesture she motioned for him to stay put. She was only going to the store and doubted that some wayward assassin would be waiting for her among the throng of upper-class whites that lived in her neighborhood, especially in broad daylight.

Sharell trekked the short distance to the grocery store on Remsen, which was the only one for blocks. Something else she hated about living in Brooklyn. Granted, it was a beautiful neighborhood, but it lacked the convenience of her beloved Harlem. Uptown you had a store on damn near every corner, and most of them were open twenty-four hours. Still, it was a relatively safe neighborhood and that's what mattered most in light of everything that was going on in her life.

She was going through the freezer of the store, trying to find a pint of Ben & Jerry's banana nut ice cream to go with her chips and dip, when the bell over the store's entrance jingled. The young man who strode into the store looked totally out of place in the neighborhood. He was wearing oversized jeans and a red sweat-shirt that looked a little stretched at the collar under a bulky leather jacket. The Korean couple behind the counter glared at him suspiciously, while the few white shoppers in the market did their best to move out of his way. Sharell sucked her teeth at the way the people reacted to the young man when he came in the store. She wondered if they looked at her the same way when her back was turned. Trying not to tell them about themselves, Sharell decided to grab her stuff and get out of the store. She told herself that she would have to track down another market somewhere in the neighborhood because she didn't know how she felt about giv-ing them her money anymore.

She happened to be coming out of an aisle when the young man was coming in. He gave her a smile as she passed, showing off his badly stained teeth. Sharell gave him a weak smile of her own and kept on to the counter.

Sharell stood in line behind a woman who had decided to pay for her purchase with change, rubbing a coin across a Scratch-Off, when she felt a presence behind her. The young man was looking at her strangely, holding a forty ounce in his wiry mitt. It wasn't a threatening look, but something about it still made Sharell un-easy. Slowly, he unscrewed the top of his beer and took a long swig, never taking his eyes off Sharell. When she got to the counter she was in such a rush to get out of the store that she almost forgot her change. Only when she was outside did her heartbeat start to slow down.

"Excuse me!" a voice called from behind her.

Sharell turned around and saw it was the young man from the store. He was slowly bopping toward her, with his free hand tucked deep into the pocket of his jacket. Sharell's had dipped into her bag and landed on the small .22 Gutter insisted she carry at all times.

She'd been against it at first, but it seemed like it would come in handy. By the time he was within spitting distance of her, Sharell's hand was on its way out of the purse with the pistol.

"Could you tell me where I could find the circuit court?" he asked, pulling a folded piece of paper from his pocket.

Sharell stopped the ascent of her hand. "Oh, it's two blocks over," Sharell said, nodding in the direction of Court Street. She hoped she didn't sound as embarrassed as she was.

"Thanks, ma'am." The young man nodded, heading up the block. He gave a brief glance around and took another swig of his beer.

Sharell stood there for a minute trying to compose herself. She had almost shot a man for nothing because of her paranoia, which seemed to be getting more out of control throughout the course of her relationship with Gutter.

God and the church aside, Sharell was a straight hood chick and never forgot where she came from, but she wasn't used to this. Gutter was a marked man, not only by rival gangs, but the police as well. From narcotics to homicide, they all knew Gutter from Harlem, but had yet to come up with a way to pin him down. Outside of his street name and his gang affiliation, the NYPD had no idea who he was. Even when he was in the hospital it was under a fake name. He was one of their greatest unsolved mysteries, and an embarrassment to the department, which is why he had to be removed from the equation. They had already made it clear that be it by prison or death, Gutter was going down.

Every day of Sharell's life was spent with the fear that she would be gunned down or snatched over one of Gutter's beefs. Her friends all thought that she should leave him alone, but love was a mutha-fucka. She knew he was a bad seed, but she also knew that there was good in him just waiting to be brought out, and that's where she came in. Though it was going to take some doing, she would peel away the hard layers and expose the jewel beneath.

B-HIGH CHUCKLED to himself as he took another swig of the beer before tossing it into the trash can. For as protected as Gutter thought his wife was he had just proven that anyone could be gotten to if you were patient. He could've blasted Sharell right there if he so chose, but Major hadn't given him the green light. No matter, he would bide his time and appreciate the reward when it came. Thinking back to the sexy pregnant woman, B-High envisioned himself violating her before she died.

AS SOON as Top confirmed the whereabouts of his marks, he contacted his partner in crime, High Side. All of the homeys loved High Side because he was just as vicious as he was loyal. He and Pop Top had come up together and joined the set together. Their bond went beyond just being a part of the same gang.

Next they recruited China. Though China was still fairly new to their gang, he was eager to prove himself. Everyone from the crew dug the little mutt, but steered clear of him because of his ties to B. T. Until then, he had participated in a few petty capers, but nothing heavy. Now it was time to see if he was ready for the next level.

The two men he and his cronies were currently stalking were from the Grant projects, and rumored to be two up-and-coming ghetto stars. They made tons of money for Tito slinging crack up and down Amsterdam Avenue. Top had heard of their exploits, and respected their gangsta. They were young, but would never live to see old age because of the side of the color line they had chosen.

"Yeah, we gonna twist these muthafucking slobs shit," High Side said anxiously, placing the last bullet into his Uzi clip and sliding it into the machine gun.

"True story," Pop Top agreed. "These fools act like they don't know what that C like, but we gonna show they asses who run shit uptown. Say, lil nigga"—he turned to China, who was seated in the back—"you ready to get yo stripes?"

"All day." China tried to sound confident. The truth of the matter was, he was terrified. As a minority among minorities China had been fighting his whole life, but he wasn't sure if he had the heart to murder in cold blood.

All three of the men tensed as their marks came out of the barbershop, laughing together. The first was a tall kid with a chipped tooth, who called himself Vlad. The other was of medium build, with a wide flat head. His mother named him Jonathan, but his gang called him Pook. Both men were known for their triggers and their tempers, but when you went against a nut like Pop Top, neither counted for shit.

Pop Top was the first one to step from the vehicle and head across the street. He didn't crouch, or try to mask his approach, he just walked. High Side walked a little farther north, before crossing Eighth Avenue. His stride was as calm as Pop Top's, but his eyes made continuous sweeps of the two-way traffic. China brought up the rear, cuffing a shotgun under his Pelle leather.

"Son, I heard they having a locked door up on Webster tonight." Pook tapped Vlad.

"Yeah, I heard about that shit. That light-skinned porno bitch is supposed to be taking on twenty niggaz in one shot." Vlad rubbed his hands greedily.

The two men continued to walk and talk, never noticing the trio closing in from all sides. High Side approached from the north,

Pop Top from the east, and China closed in from the south. Pop Top drew his weapon and held it at his side, still advancing on the unsuspecting victims. Those who noticed him, moved for cover. It was clear by the look of hatred in his eyes that he meant to do something wicked and no one wanted to be a part of it. Raising his black Glock 19, Pop Top fired on his rivals.

As soon as the first shot was let off, people began to scream and break in all directions, trying to avoid catching a stray. Vlad ducked for cover, while Pook was frozen. High Side didn't mind this a bit, as it made his job easier. Firing his Uzi from the hip, he tore into Pook's chest and face.

"Fuck you, nigga!" Vlad wailed, producing a .45 automatic from his belt. He began backing toward the shop, alternating return fire between Pop Top and High Side. High Side managed to duck behind a Volvo, narrowly escaping a bullet. Pop Top wasn't that quick. He took a slug to the shoulder and went down. Vlad turned and boated in China's direction.

China watched the whole thing unfold as if in slow motion. Pop Top had collapsed into the street, but he was still moving and there was no sign of High Side. He was alone to face off against Vlad who was charging right at him with a smoking gun. China fumbled with the shotgun and was finally able to establish some type of aim. He leveled the shotgun and pulled the trigger with all his might.

The shotgun seemed to silence every other sound in the world. The screams, traffic, it was all muted under the roar of the gauge. The force of the thing sent vibrations through China's hands and wrist. The shot came up awkward, but dealt a crippling blow. China looked on in horror as Vlad's thigh exploded. Chunks of meat flew in the air and smeared whatever they encountered. Vlad was down to one knee, but was still able to get China in his sights.

China saw his whole life flash before his eyes, as he stared down the barrel of the gun, which was pointed right at his chest. When he joined the gang, he never imagined it coming down to this. All he ever wanted was to belong, but he never considered the price. Now he was faced with a mortal decision. It was his life or the life of his enemy. China closed his eyes and pulled the trigger.

The gun rocked his small hands once again as he staggered back. For a moment, he kept his eyes closed, expecting to feel the hot lead piercing his body. Several seconds passed, and still there was nothing. China opened his eyes and dropped to his knees. Tears streamed down his face as he took in the measure of what he had done. It wasn't the sight of Vlad missing his entire right arm, and part of his chest. It was the sight of the little girl who had been coming out of the bodega lying in a pool of her own blood. The buckshot had passed through Vlad's arm and hit her square in the chest. She still clutched the bag of nachos she had been eating as her lifeless eyes stared up at China.

"Bitch-ass nigga!" Pop Top shouted, as he limped to the curb. There was blood leaking from his wound, but it didn't hinder his shooting arm. He leveled his pistol and fired two shots into Vlad's face.

"We out!" High Side shouted, jogging back to the car.

"Let's go, lil nigga." Pop Top limped past China. Seeing that China was rooted to the spot, Pop Top tried a different method. He grabbed China by the collar and slapped him across the face. "Nigga, unless you plan on spending the rest of your life in the fucking joint, you better get on your fucking feet and move!"

China looked at Pop Top as if he were seeing him for the first time. He looked from the smoking rifle to the two dead bodies, before he was able to stagger to his feet. He still felt like he was trapped in a dream, but he understood the prison time that came with what he had done.

SHARELL WAS just about to find out who the baby's father was on *Maury,* when the news came on unexpectedly. A tanned gentleman with mouse-brown hair and almost perfect teeth was covering a gruesome homicide in Harlem. She could tell from the barbershop in the background that he was on 132nd and Eighth.

The newscaster went on to tell the story of a shoot-out that had taken place there not long ago, leaving three people dead, one of which was a little girl. Tears ran down Sharell's face as a family member tried to console the grieving mother of the little girl. Touching her stomach, she knew she would surely die if something were to happen to her little one. The police suspected that it was over drugs, as usual, but something in the pit of Sharell's gut told her that it wasn't. She recognized one of the boys' names and knew that the shooting was gang-related.

Even on the other side of the country Gutter was still managing to keep the chaos going in New York. She flipped her cell phone open to call him to deliver the news of what he had caused.

▮ ▮

chapter 15

W HEN THE two-car entourage arrived back at the house there were people scattered in front of it. Some were standing around laughing, while others were getting in their cars and preparing to leave. Snake Eyes, Danny, and Gutter looked on to see what was going down. Tears stood out front, puffing a cigarette and looking highly irritated. Gutter stepped from the Regal and addressed his home boy.

"What it is, cousin?" Gutter rolled up to the front of the house.

"Man, I'm glad you're here, G. Yo peoples is in there loc'n." Tears sighed.

As Gutter listened, he could hear shouting from the partially cracked front door. More and more people began to file out of the house, all wearing looks of frustration or disgust. When Gutter spotted Monifa among them, he grabbed her arm.

"Man, who in there making all that noise?" he asked.

"Who you think?" She sucked her teeth.

In answer to the question, a woman came stumbling out of the house. She was tall and thin, with bleached blond hair. Her eyes were lined in black mascara and partially covered by a pair of dime-store glasses. She had yellow skin that had begun to splotch in certain areas from lack of care. Gutter looked on in shock, while Lil Gunn just turned his head.

"Ol thug-ass niggaz," Stacia slurred, as she staggered out onto the front line. "Posted up in this muthafucka like it's some kinda damn clubhouse."

People laughed or stared at her like she didn't have any sense, but Gutter just shook his head. It had been quite some time since he had seen Big Gunn's baby mama, but from the looks of things she was still as wild as hell. Stacia had always been a pretty girl, and still was to that day, but those who knew her back in the day could tell she was slipping. Her clothes and hair were crisp as always, but she looked worn.

"Well, I'll be damned," she said, noticing Gutter for the first time. "Nigga, I heard you was dead and gone. 'Course I'm not surprised to see you here, being that none of you evil green-eyed muthafuckas know how to lay down and die."

"Nice to see you again too, Stacia," he said sarcastically.

"I'll bet. So, what you doing back out here? Them New York niggaz showed you what a real thug was about?"

Gutter started to bark on her, but remembering Lil Gunn was with him he kept it cordial. "Nah, baby girl, business is business like always. I'm the man on whatever coast I stomp through. You ain't that drunk to where you don't recognize this Crip'n." He flashed Harlem, then Hoover.

"Whatever, nigga. Tariq"—she turned to Lil Gunn—"what the hell happened to your face?"

"Nothing, Ma, I fell riding a bike," he lied.

"Young nigga, who you think you fooling? I ain't flew here, I grew here. You probably got your lil ass whipped trying to play gangsta. You better quit while you're ahead, unless you wanna end up like yo daddy. You see that nigga in there knocking on heaven's door." She took a sip of her drink.

Gutter immediately checked her. "Hold that shit down, Stacia. Don't disrespect my uncle like that, especially in front of his seed."

"Y'all niggaz just can't handle it. See, I'm a real bitch. I call it like I see it. Big Gunn is always gonna be my boo, but the truth is the light. This gangster shit got him living between two worlds right now. That's the reason why I moved Tariq away from this shit. I call myself saving him from the streets." She looked Lil Gunn up and down. "As you can see, that didn't pan out too well."

"You need to go somewhere and sober up," Gutter said, getting frustrated.

"Sober up? Muthafucka, I ain't even *nice* yet. Don't get me started, lil Kenny," she taunted him. Stacia sat her drink on the floor and scowled at everyone assembled.

Gutter could feel the fire in his gut expand to his face. Reflexively his hands curled into fists, and he shot daggers at Stacia. Monifa must've felt it, because she moved to his side and placed a calming hand on his shoulder. Just like that the anger drained away. She could still work that magic on him.

"I ain't even trying to hear this shit." Lil Gunn stormed past her and into the house.

"I'm going for a walk." Gutter turned and headed down the block.

"Hold on, I'll go with you," Monifa called after him.

Snake Eyes already knew what time it was, so he took Danny into the house, leaving Tears alone with Stacia. Tears knew her from back in the days, when she used to kick it around Hoover with Gunn and his lot. She was always a little outspoken, but now she was just plain rude. He didn't really fuck with her back then, but he absolutely couldn't stand her now.

"Fuck you looking at, Scarface?" she spat.

Tears sucked his teeth and walked toward the house. As he passed Stacia, he swept his foot out and "accidentally" kicked her drink over. "Bitch," he mumbled, before disappearing behind the screen door.

AFTER CHANGING into a pair of jeans and a black sweatshirt, Lil Gunn came lumbering down the stairs. There were still a few people lounging around the living room and in the backyard. Stacia sat near the kitchen entrance, sipping yet another drink. He scowled at her and went in the opposite direction toward the backyard.

Blue Bird stood off to the side with several other young men and women. The ladies were working the grill and playing cards, while the homeys were gathered around Blue Bird. Though he was a loudmouth, and more often than not a troublemaker, he had his stripes in the hood. Lil Gunn slipped into the crowd, and grabbed a forty ounce from the cooler.

"Look at this lil nigga." Blue Bird nodded toward the youngster. "Out here trying to drink with the grown folks. Put that forty down, young'n."

"I got this, cuz," Lil Gunn said, turning the bottle up and taking a deep swig of the beer.

"You see that boy do that there?" Charlie beamed proudly. He was from Grape Street.

"That boy got it honest." Blue Bird patted him on the back. "Man, we all rooting for yo daddy. Them Swans disrespected the G, and we got to C them behind that shit."

"That's what the fuck I'm talking about." Lil Gunn took another swig. "I'm ready to ride on these fools!"

"Shut yo lil ass up. You ain't 'bout no one-eight-seven," Charlie teased.

"Fuck you. I'll dump on any Blood or *Crip* on any set!" Lil Gunn said heatedly. Gaining the respect of the older heads was crucial to him, so he put an extra production on it.

"Quit talking crazy, killing ain't for children." Blue Bird nudged him.

"I ain't been a kid since I joined up. I'm ready," Lil Gunn declared.

"You serious?"

"As a heart attack."

Blue Bird studied the young man for a moment. He looked into his eyes and saw no fear. The man-child was ready to make his bones.

"A'ight." Blue Bird nodded. "We 'gon C."

GUTTER WALKED down the block with his hands tucked firmly in the pockets of his jeans. He was mad, but all of his anger wasn't directed at Stacia. He knew what kind of woman she was, so he expected her to come out of her face. What really had him uptight was the situation.

His uncle danced on the brink of death, and everything was in total chaos. There were dozens of people visiting him at the house off and on, but they weren't really helping the situation. Some of them were sincere, while others just talked for the sake of hearing themselves. No one was actually doing anything to make the situation right.

Gunn had love from many sets in California as well as the

Midwest, but so far no one had stepped up with a solid plan for retaliation. Even if they had, who would they retaliate against? The word was out that it was the Mad Swans who did the shooting, but no one knew if it was true or exactly who did the shooting. They could ride on the whole set, but that would make things worse. Though Mad Swans and Hoover were from opposite sides there was a mutual respect between their O.G.s and the old-school Hoovers from the seven and the nine. They didn't have an official truce but had been known to exchange passes. If they went at the whole set without having their facts together it was sure to get real ugly real soon.

"Penny for your thoughts?" Monifa crept up on him. With so many things flooding his mind at one time, he had almost forgotten that she was with him.

"Just thinking how much I miss this place." He stared up at a palm tree.

"Yeah." She stood next to him. "There's something about the West Coast that makes you fall in love with it."

"True, if you can overlook all the dumb shit that goes on out here. This is the land of the heartless."

"It ain't the land, it's the people that make it this way," she said, watching a group of young men ride by in a Chevy. "Kenyatta, I've been blessed to have seen many different places in my short life, and they all fall short to Cali. This place is both the most beautiful of states, yet the ugliest."

"Girl, you tripping." He waved her off.

"I ain't the one tripping. These niggaz that's out here terrorizing decent folks and killing off all our young men are the ones that are tripping. Makes you wonder when all this will end."

"Man, gang-banging ain't gonna never end." He stroked his beard. "This shit has been going on since before we were born, and it's only gonna get bigger. Muthafuckas kill me talking that stop the violence shit. This ain't gonna end until we wipe them out, or they wipe us out, period."

"You don't know how fucking stupid you sound." She laughed. "Kenyatta, you don't even believe what you're trying to feed me. That's just you trying to be difficult, as usual."

"Go ahead with that. I'm just stating my case."

"Well, if that's your case, then that ass is guilty. Don't try and front for me, cause I know you, *Gutter.* When you know someone is telling you right, you throw up this ignorant ass gang-banger persona. Nigga, please."

"What you talking 'bout, woman? I'm a Crip to the heart. Don't never forget that."

"Oh, I would never doubt your love for your hood, but I also know that you've never been a dummy. If you were, I would've never given you any play."

"Gave me no play?" He raised his eyebrow. "Monifa, don't try that. If I recall correctly, *you* pursued *me.*"

"That chronic got you all twisted. I wasn't the one at Universal Studios talking about, 'Aye, sis. Let me rap to you for a minute,'" she imitated him. "You followed me and my girls around that whole lot, trying to get at me. You were so cute, with your starter kit braids."

"Fuck you, Mo," he joked.

"Fuck you right back."

They both slapped at each other and burst into laughter. He instinctively reached out and touched her hand. It was warm, and smooth as silk. For a second, it was as if they were still teenagers, dating at Jack in the Box. Each one's eyes shone with lost passion, creating an uncomfortable silence. Monifa's eyes flashed indifference, and she quickly snatched her hand back.

"Mo…"

"Don't." She turned her back to him. "Kenyatta, leave it alone."

"Monifa…we need to talk about it. There was so much left unsaid."

"I think you said it all when you left me wondering what happened," she said, a bit more scornfully than she meant to.

"Mo…I don't know what to say," he admitted. "Shit got a lil crazy. Things happened that I won't go into, but I had to jet. You know how it get in the hood."

"Fuck the hood!" she said heatedly. "You're always putting the hood before me."

"It wasn't like that."

"Then what was it like?" She spun around. "Gutter, please don't try and feed me some shit that you had two years to mull over. I was supposed to be your girl, Ken. Your heart! 'Be my forever lady,' remember that?"

He turned his eyes away.

"Well, I do. You took me to up to Sacramento to celebrate my twenty-first birthday," she recalled. "We had a beautiful dinner, and you fed me ice cream. Everyone at the restaurant kept saying how cute we were. We went for a walk on the strip and talked about a life together and how you wanted to do right by me. 'Be my forever lady,' that's what you whispered to me…right before you pushed me to the ground and shot that boy, because he was an *enemy* as you called him. On a night when we should've been making love until the sun came up, we ended up fugitives." She gave a weak chuckle.

Gutter was so overcome with shame that his head felt like a lead weight when he raised it. Tears danced in the corner of her eyes, and he could tell that she was doing all she could not to cry. All she had ever tried to do was love him and he'd shitted on her. He couldn't help but feel like a real asshole. With some effort, he managed to swallow the grapefruit-sized lump that had worked its way into his throat.

"Monifa," he began, "I never misled you, or told you anything I didn't mean. You deserved way better than what I gave you. Believe me, I've thought about you and what happened to us ever since I left."

"Did you think about me when you made that New York bitch your wife?" she spat.

He should've seen that one coming.

"Don't get all quiet on me now," she continued. "What, you think I didn't know about her? People talk, Kenyatta. I might be naïve, but I have ears."

"Monifa, let's just go somewhere and talk," he pleaded, while reaching for her hand.

"I think we've both said enough." She stepped back. "I ain't mad no more, baby. But I'm a lot wiser for the experience. See you at the house, *Gutter.*" Monifa strutted away.

Gutter was about to go after her and tell her how much he'd loved her and how the old feelings still lingered when his cell went off and the name on the screen brought him back to his senses.

"SHE WAS only seven," Sharell sobbed into the phone.

"Baby, calm down," Gutter said, not really being in the mood for hormones. "I know you're upset about what you saw, but that's why I don't watch the news, it's too damn depressing. Look, it's a damn sad thing when a child is killed, but there ain't a whole lot we can do about it. All we can do is say a prayer for the little girl and watch over our own family."

"We can do something to stop it, Ken, but we don't want to," she shot back.

"You talking real reckless on the horn, Sharell," he warned.

"Kenyatta, I'm upset not stupid. These kids are getting cut down left and right over this street shit, and everybody turns a blind eye as long as it's not somebody they knew. It's bullshit and you know it. I don't want this for my family, Gutter, no white sheets."

He sighed. "It's not gonna be like that for us."

"I can't keep doing this." She sounded exhausted.

"So what you trying to say?" he asked defensively.

"Calm down, Kenyatta, I'm not trying to say anything.... Baby, we got a good life together. Kenyatta, you move my spirit in a way that a man hasn't been able to do since my daddy was alive, but something has got to give."

"Sharell, it's going to get better," he said as if the line had been rehearsed.

"Oh, I don't doubt that, but in order for it to get better we've got to change the formula. In a hot minute, we're going to be somebody's mommy and daddy, and this child is gonna need us...both of us. I really ain't trying to have the 'your daddy was a good man' talk with my baby, Ken."

Gutter tugged at his beard in frustration. "Sharell, you know what it is, so don't come at me with this. I know what you want, and I know what I gotta do to get it, but I gotta be who I am."

"Ken, I know who you are and I'd never try and change that, but I'm asking you to look at the bigger picture. I'm tired of not being able to shop at the mall or go out to dinner without having a bodyguard. I want a life, Ken, a life and a family. I deserve as much."

"I know," he said, more to himself than anyone else.

"Then act like it."

"A'ight, Sharell, we'll talk about it when I get back. I gotta get back to the house, fam is waiting for me."

"Umm-hmm." There was doubt in her tone. "I know you're in the middle of something right now, Kenyatta, but best believe when you get back from California we've got some talking to do."

"You got that, baby. I love you."

"I love you too, Ken, and keep that in mind while you're out there with them big braid-wearing West Coast broads," she remarked. Gutter laughed, but she didn't. "I'm serious, Ken. I'd hate to have to come out there and clown, you don't wanna see my ghetto side."

"Nah, I don't wanna see that. Don't even trip, ma, you know this bone belongs to you." He grabbed his crotch as if she could see him through the phone.

"You better know it. Now go ahead and handle your business, I'll talk to you later." She ended the call.

Sharell's ass is a trip, he thought to himself. She was the only person he knew who would use something she saw on the news to prompt a lecture on life issues. She had to know that the set flowed through his veins, and was a part of him. Still, hearing about that child getting caught up in his turf war struck him like a physical blow. Though he wasn't the shooter, he still felt in some way responsible for her death. He had passed the death sentence on the other side, so whether he had been there or not, the blood was on his hands.

"Dawg, you tripping," he said to himself. He was at war, and sometimes in war there were casualties, but that still didn't justify that mother having to bury her child. "Fuck it, just one more I owe them hoes," he reasoned as he headed back to the house.

chapter 16

B ACK ON the streets, straight blue and gray, cuz I rep-re-sent like every day," Charlie sang along with the track. He loved to bump the *Murder Was the Case* soundtrack just before they went on a mission, and "Who Got Some Gangsta Shit," had become his and Blue Bird's theme song.

Lil Gunn sat as low as he could get in the backseat of a bor-rowed Grand Cherokee. His wool skully was pulled down on his head, nearly covering his eyes. He took long drags of his Newport, which had been dipped, and felt the fluttering of little wings in his gut. He normally didn't smoke PCP, but the circumstances were anything but normal. He had shot at enemies in his lifetime, but that was always from a distance. He knew Blue Bird was an old-school killer and would want to make this up close and personal.

"Yo a'ight back there?" Blue Bird called from the driver's seat.

"I'm good," Lil Gunn said flatly.

"Little nigga, take you another hit of this stick." Charlie tried to pass him another dipped cigarette, but Gunn waved it off. "Man, let me find out yo ass is claiming blue when you really yellow?"

"Fuck you," Lil Gunn spat at Charlie.

"Don't go bitching up on me, lil cuz," Blue Bird added, taking the sherm stick from Charlie.

"He gonna bitch up." Charlie snickered.

Lil Gunn continued to stare out the window.

After cruising for a while longer, Charlie suggested that they make a beer run. Blue Bird pulled into the parking lot of a local package store. There were several cars parked with people posted up and killing time. The Grand Cherokee bent the corner to park at the rear of the store. As they passed the last row of cars, Blue Bird recognized one of the loiterers. His name was Shorty and he was a respected member of Mad Swans.

"Say, there go some of them ho-ass niggaz right there," Blue Bird nodded toward where Shorty was standing with two other men.

"Aye, pull 'round back and let's creep on these niggaz," Charlie said excitedly.

Blue Bird nodded and backed the car into a parking spot. He retrieved a Colt revolver from under the seat and got out, leaving the engine running. Charlie handed Lil Gunn the 9 from the glove box while he went with the bulldog. The three men skirted along the edge of the store, back toward the front. Shorty and his crew were sipping beers and trying to holla at some of the females in the lot. A five feet five light-skinned dude with caramel eyes, Shorty considered himself a pretty boy. One of the young ladies was in the process of writing down her phone number when she spotted the killers creeping. When Shorty turned to see what she was looking at, a bullet hit him in the left bicep.

"What's up now, niggaz!" Blue Bird screamed, firing his Colt.

People began running for cover, trying not to end up on anyone's wall. Shorty ducked behind a car, leaving his comrades stunned and on their own. One of the red-clad men tried to get Blue Bird in his sights, but Charlie laid cover fire and forced him back.

The sound of gunfire and the smell of smoke made Lil Gunn dizzy. The youngster fired his gun one-handed, feeling the rush of the hunt. Seeing the fear in his enemy's faces was like a high for him, and in the name of his father, he planned to overdose that night.

A soldier, whom no one had noticed in the backseat, leaned out the window, spitting from his pistol. Lil Gunn dashed forward, military-style, and leapt behind a metal garbage can. Crawling on his belly he slipped up under the car the shooter was held up in and slithered out from under the other side. When the shooter looked down, Lil Gunn blew the top of his head off, raining brain matter all over his face. The goop was sticky and uncomfortable but Lil Gunn was so high that he didn't even seem to notice. The only thing that mattered to him at that moment was the kill.

A man wearing an Atlanta Hawks jersey let off with his .32. The low-caliber bullets sparked off brick and metal as he tried to take Blue Bird out of the game. The seasoned warrior returned fire, hitting the shooter in the jaw. The man clutched uselessly at his jaw and spilled to the ground.

A second man managed to get to the driver's side of the car and came up holding a Mac-11. He swept the lot, hitting glass and bystanders. Blue Bird got low just as he was making a second sweep, but Charlie got caught out there. Bullets danced up his chest, spinning him. Charlie was dead before he hit the ground.

The two men were exchanging fire with Blue Bird, so they never saw Lil Gunn creeping from the rear bumper of their car. He leveled his hammer and blew the back of the machine gunner's head off. His partner spun on Lil Gunn and popped off. Lil Gunn would've probably been dead had Blue Bird not grabbed the shooter in a headlock just as he pulled the trigger. The heavier man grunted once and broke the man's neck. To add insult he blasted him twice in the face with the Colt.

Lil Gunn took a moment to observe the scene, and found himself pleased. The lot was in total chaos. Bodies of the dead or dying were strewn all over, and the survivors were terrified. He noticed Charlie stretched out, and rushed to his side.

"Charlie, man!" Lil Gunn shouted.

"That nigga dead." Blue Bird lifted Lil Gunn to his feet. "Come on, Shorty trying to lose us!" Blue Bird jogged back toward the car.

Shorty half ran, half hobbled down a dark backstreet. He would've stuck to the main road, but he didn't want to chance being chased down. His lungs burned, and his whole left side was numb, but he wanted to live more than anything. It seemed like the harder he tried to run, the more his arm bled. He knew it would only be a matter of time before he collapsed from the loss of blood. He had almost made it to the end of the block when he heard tires screeching behind him.

"There that nigga go!" Lil Gunn pointed his gun excitedly, while bouncing up and down on the passenger seat like an unruly child. The sherm was now working in overdrive, making the whole ordeal seem like a video game. "Lay that pussy for my pa, Blue. Run that muthafucka over, cuz!"

The closer Shorty got to the corner, the weaker he became. By the time he reached the streetlight, he was seeing spots. Coughing up globs of blood, Shorty turned around just in time to see the headlights of the Jeep coming right for him.

AFTER SPENDING almost five hours in the emergency room, Pop Top was finally patched up and ready to be discharged. As per procedure, the police were brought in to question him about how he had gotten shot. The story he fed them was that he was walking out of a grocery store on 155th and got caught in a cross fire between two crews. Being that the bullet that struck him went in and out, the police had nothing to match against the shoot-out at the bodega.

He knew the police would want to question him about the shooting, so he had the homeys stay away so as not to arouse suspicion. When he came out of the examining room, Maxine was waiting for him. She was a high yellow chick who hailed from Flatbush. She was thick in the right places and didn't talk much, which suited him fine.

"All done?" she asked, looking up from the copy of *Hood Rat* she was reading.

"Yeah, we can boogie now," he replied.

The couple stepped out into the night air, and headed up the street in an attempt at catching a cab. Maxine stepped off the curb and tried to flag one, while Pop Top stood off to the side. A car slowed to a stop in front of them, but when Pop Top peered inside, he knew it wasn't a cab. With limited mobility, he was slow on the draw. The occupant that aimed his shotgun out the back window wasn't.

"I wouldn't do that," Major Blood said, getting out the passenger's side. "You reach for that piece, and I'm gonna let my man air this pretty bitch out." He nodded toward Maxine, who stood there shocked. "I came here to talk, but if you wanna make it a gangsta party, then reach for it."

Maxine stood frozen in place. She got with Pop Top, hoping to get some action, but this was more than she bargained for. Her life flashed before her eyes as she stared down the barrel of a shotgun.

Pop Top looked from the car to the man standing in front of him, and weighed his options. He could take his chances and try to gun the man down, but even if he did, the shotgun would surely be fired. He really didn't give a fuck if Maxine took it, but he was worried that he might not make it out of the line of fire. Reluctantly, he relaxed, but he still kept both the man and the car in front of him.

"You're Pop Top, right?" Major asked, in an all-too-easy tone.

"Who the fuck are you?" Top shot back.

"Me? The name's Blood. *Major* Blood. And I'm asking the fucking questions."

Pop Top scanned through his mental rolodex and tried to remember where he had heard the name. There were several rivals who used Blood in their name, but there was something unique about this man. He remembered that Tito from L.C. went by that moniker, but he knew Tito when he saw him, and this was definitely not Tito. As he looked deeper into the man's cold eyes, it dawned on him. He had heard tales about the notorious killer from Cali when he was still trying to come up. If this was the same Major Blood, he knew he was in a world of shit.

"I can tell by that stupid-ass look on your face that you've heard of me," Major said, "but we ain't here to discuss my résumé, crab."

"You a long way from home to be talking all crazy, my dude. What the fuck do you want in my city?" Pop Top glared at him.

Major chuckled. "*Your* city? Knock it off, home boy. Everybody knows Gutter is holding sway 'round here. You just a crazy muthafucka who's looking for a purpose. Now, let's get back to business. There're some people that're hella pissed by this little war you lowlife muthafuckas got going on out here. Y'all killed one of ours and we took one of yours, but you couldn't leave it at that, could you? Nah, y'all wanna press your luck, and act like this don't mean nothing." He raised his right arm, exposing the red five-pointed star tattooed on his forearm.

"Nigga, get to the point," Pop Top insisted.

In a motion that was almost too fast for Pop Top to catch, Major Blood produced a pistol and put it to his enemy's head. "You're doing a lot of talking for a nigga that could be a memory in a matter of seconds."

"I ain't scared to die. If it's my time, be done with it," Pop Top said defiantly. Had this been anyone else Major Blood would've taken it as just a tough guy act, but he knew what time it was with Pop Top. He was a straight rider and really didn't give a fuck if he lived or died as long as it was in service to the set.

Major lowered his gun and eyed Pop Top curiously. "You really are crazy, ain't you? Look here, man. I'm gonna make this shit short and sweet. It's over. You understand? You know who I am, so you can guess what the fuck I was sent here to do. But see, I ain't a complete asshole, so I'm gonna give you a sporting chance. Shut it down, or I shut y'all down."

"So, you think you're just gonna walk in and make us close up shop?" Pop Top asked with a grin.

"You must not be hearing me?" Major Blood leaned in to whisper. "I ain't Cisco, nigga. I'll kill you and everything you love. I don't give a fuck about you, me, or anything else, that's why I'm the best at what I do. This is your first and only warning. And just in case you think I'm fucking around." He motioned toward the men in the car.

Miguel got out, followed by Tito and Eddie. Tito trained the shotgun on Pop Top, while his two cohorts went to the trunk.

They popped it open and struggled to remove a large rolled-up carpet. They carried it to the sidewalk and dropped it between the two men. Eddie leaned in and cut the rope that held it in a roll.

"I think this belonged to y'all." Major kicked the carpet open, exposing B. T.'s corpse. His face was bruised, and his neck was splayed open like a gutted fish. "Don't feel bad though. He was a fucking snake. Your comrade has been feeding us information for the last couple of months. Seems that my associates made him a deal, but I can't stand a fucking rat, so I changed the agreement. Food for thought, *Blood*." Major strode casually back to the car, followed by his henchmen.

When the car was well away from the block, Pop Top began breathing again. He had come within a hair of losing his life, and escaped through the grace of God. He looked from B. T.'s body to the receding taillights of the car and wondered what he was going to tell Gutter.

"WHAT'S THE matter, honey?" Rahshida asked as Monifa stormed across the kitchen.

"Nothing, Rah, I'm good." She grabbed a Corona from the fridge and plopped down on the wooden chair, across the table from where Rahshida was sitting.

"Monifa, you hardly drink and I've never seen you do it before sundown so I know something is bothering you, what's up?" Monifa didn't answer, but the look in her eyes told the story. "It's Kenyatta, isn't it?"

Monifa sucked her teeth. "Fuck Gutter."

Rahshida shook her head. "Monifa, why do you keep doing it to yourself? I watched you go through the motions when he left, and just when the wounds finally start to heal you wanna pick at the scab."

"I don't know why I keep doing it to myself, Rah. I tried to tell myself that I could handle him being here and that the old feelings are gone, but no sooner than he gets me alone I go to pieces." She took a light sip of the beer and made a face. "Am I stupid or what?"

"You're not stupid, Mo, just a young girl in love," Rahshida told her. "Baby, I know how you feel about my nephew, but you gotta let it go. He's a different man than you knew, with a different life."

"Yeah, a life with his New York bitch."

Rahshida narrowed her eyes. "Monifa, that isn't called for. You know you're bigger than that."

"Rah, I feel like I fell and bumped my head for the way I'm allowing myself to feel about Gutter, especially after the way he dissed me. There's something about him that I just can't seem to let go."

Rahshida propped her elbows on the table. "For as much of a good man that I know my nephew is, or wants to be, he isn't ready to let go of his mistress . . . the set. I pray that he's grown up enough to do right by that girl, but at the end of the day he's gonna do what he wants. Monifa, that's my nephew and I love him no matter what, but he's still a Soladine man, and the only woman he'll ever give his heart to totally is the street." Rahshida nodded outside, to where Gutter was congregating with the homeys. "Let that train go, baby."

There was so much truth in Rahshida's words that Monifa only felt stupider for the way she was carrying on. She knew Gutter had a new life and a new woman, but what about old promises? It was clear that that chapter of their life was at an end, but it wasn't yet closed.

chapter 17

GUTTER'S NIGHT was spent very fitfully trying to sleep. After the heated word exchange, he had retired to one of the upstairs bedrooms. After firing up blunt after blunt of chronic, he fell asleep. During his rest he was plagued with terrible nightmares. It was the same death scene that had played out for his comrade, except he was the one being fired on. It seemed so real, that he thought he even felt the bullets tearing through his skin.

It seemed as if he had only been asleep for a little while when he was awakened by a commotion downstairs. He was irritated about the noise breaking his rest, but grateful for it awakening him from the nightmare. He made his way down the stairs and found a group of spectators crowded around the back door. After elbowing his way through the crowd, he was surprised by what he saw.

Tears, Danny, and Snake Eyes stood among some of the other homeys in a semicircle. In the center of the circle Rahkim and Blue Bird were going head up. Blue Bird was a skilled boxer, but Rahkim was a straight animal. For every blow Blue Bird landed,

Rahkim hit him with two. Seeing that exchanging punches was getting him nowhere, Blue Bird changed his strategy.

He rushed Rahkim, trying to scoop him up from the waist, which proved to be his undoing. He was heavier and stronger than Rahkim, so he had no problem getting him off the ground. The only problem was, every time he tried to lift him, Rahkim rained punches on his exposed face. Several vicious blows brought him to one knee. Rahkim hauled his leg back and kicked Blue Bird in the jaw. It was a clean knockout.

"Tears, gimme ya strap!" Rahkim demanded.

"Hold on, cuz," Tears protested.

"Fuck that shit, I'm 'bout to smoke this dumb muthafucka!"

"Rahkim, what the hell are you doing?" Rahshida cut through the crowd, and stood between her brother and Blue Bird.

"Rah, mind your business. This ain't got nothing to do with you," he warned.

"The hell it doesn't. Our brother is up in there fighting for his life, and you're out here about to murder a man in his yard. Hasn't there been enough violence?"

"Rah, this greaseball muthafucka took our nephew, Gunn's baby boy, on a fucking hit. The shit is all over the hood and the goddamn news!" he explained.

"Oh, my . . . Tariq, bring your ass here. Now!" she shouted.

"Sup." He stepped from the crowd with his head down.

"Are you crazy!" She slapped him across his face, shocking everyone especially him. "Why would you let someone talk you into such foolishness? Haven't you learned anything from what has brought us here?" She shook his arm.

"Yeah." He jerked away. "I learned a lot of niggaz talk about gangsta shit and codes, but most of 'em is bitches. Some Brims fired on my daddy, and I fired on some Brims. Fuck them niggaz!"

"Watch your mouth, Gunn," Gutter interjected. "Rah is telling you right. Blue Bird had no right to take you roll'n. Who y'all dump on?"

"Some busters." Lil Gunn shrugged. "Blue said they was Swans, so we blasted them niggaz. I think one of them was named Shorty."

"Shorty?" Snake Eyes rubbed his chin. "Yeah, I know that cat. A real loudmouth that's always itching for a beef. If they didn't ride on them, somebody would've."

"That don't change the fact that this nigga was wrong." Rahkim nodded toward Blue Bird, who was finally beginning to stir.

"Fucking dummies, both of you," Gutter said. "Who else was down with this lil G ride?"

"It was just me, Blue, and Charlie. We lost him in the battle," Lil Gunn said sadly.

"Police are supposed to have found the body and linked him to the Crips." Rahkim added.

"There's gonna be a shit storm behind this," Snake Eyes shook his head.

"Who the fuck you telling? This is the reason why this had to be handled with finesse," Gutter reminded them. "The last thing we need is the LAPD laying their pressure game down on us. It'll make setting this shit right that much harder."

Danny added, "Man, y'all got so many sets and gangs out this muthafucka, you really think the police is gonna be looking at y'all in particular?"

"I'm sure of it," Snake Eyes said. "Like I told you before, this shit is politics. Even though they wear badges, the LAPD is a gang, same as ours. They know what's going down in the streets, and who it's going down with. The Bloods are rumored to have shot Big Gunn, and they found Charlie's body at the scene. Even though he's with Grape Street, he's connected to us. It's only a matter of time before they start snatching Grapes and Hoovers, 'cause we allies for the moment. They'll be poking around here soon enough and that could be bad business for some of us." He glanced at Gutter, remembering the murder they had both played a part in.

Before they could ponder it further, one of the nurses attending Big Gunn appeared in the doorway. She was a motherly looking Mexican woman with salt-and-pepper hair. Her face was sullen and blood spatter stained the front of her uniform. Tears twinkled in her eyes, as she motioned for the Soladines to come with her. Once she had led them into the living room, she began speaking.

"It's Mr. Gunn," she sobbed with a heavy accent.

"What's wrong?" Rah asked frantically.

"We thought we had stabilized him, but he started hemorrhaging internally."

"Move!" Gutter barked, rushing past her.

"Wait!" she called after him, but Gutter kept going.

When he got to the bedroom where Gunn was being kept, he heard orders being barked and metal scraping. Ignoring the nurse and his aunt who were both following closely behind him, Gutter barged into the room. When he stepped through the threshold, a lump formed in his throat.

Doc Holliday was a homey, who had pulled his way through the sludge of the ghetto and had graduated from medical school. He worked at St. Vincent's Hospital in Pasadena, as a resident. Big Gunn had schooled him to the game back in the day, so he was more than willing to take some time off to tend his former mentor in his time of need.

Doc Holliday stood over Gunn's bed in a bloody lab coat, working expertly trying to stop the bleeding. Sweat ran from his forehead into his eye, which one of the attending nurses wiped. He tried a variation of clamps and stitches, but the bleeding just seemed to continue. It wasn't looking good for Gunn.

"Doc, what the fuck is going on?" Gutter approached.

"Gutter, not now," he said, applying pressure to one of the wounds. "I'm trying to save your uncle. Get these people out of here and let me work!"

Reluctantly, Gutter led the entourage from the room and back into the hallway. Everyone looked nervous, but none more so than Lil Gunn. You could see tears in the corner of his eyes, but he wouldn't allow them to fall. Gutter placed an arm around him and led the youngster into the living room. He tried to convince him that his father would be okay, but he didn't know if it was more to set the youngster's mind at ease or his own.

Blue Bird had been helped outside, and held ice wrapped in a cloth against his face. Stacia had appeared from where ever she was and taken up a seat in the living room. In her hand, she held a glass of wine, which she kept swirling between sips. Monifa stood in the corner, dressed in jeans and a tank top. She looked sorrowfully at Gutter, but didn't approach. The rest of the homeys stood around, trying not to look terrified.

After what seemed like an eternity, Doc appeared in the living room. His scrubs looked as if they had been painted red. Removing his glasses, he looked out over the inquiring faces. He opened his mouth to speak, but couldn't find the words. When he couldn't hold it any longer, the tears came.

"*Nooooo!*" Stacia screamed before collapsing to the ground.

DOC FOUGHT as hard as he could for his mentor, but in the end his injuries proved to be too severe. He might not have been able to prevent his death, but he pumped him so full of drugs that it was painless. It was the least he could do for the man who had literally kept him alive during his stint with the Hoover Crips. When his contact from the mortuary arrived to take the body away, he slipped him a wad of hundred dollar bills, and thanked him for the role he played.

Everyone took the loss of Big Gunn hard, but his son appeared to be hurt the worst. He overturned furniture, and cursed the rival set, while his family looked on. Rahkim made to stop him, but Gutter held his uncle back. The boy needed to let it out, and if this was his way, then so be it. Stacia cried and carried on, between freshening her drinks. For all the bullshit she talked, she still loved Gunn. Everyone except the immediate family and closest friends were asked to leave the house.

Gutter tried to hold it together, but it was too much. With tear-filled eyes, he threw his cell phone against the wall, shattering it. All of the Soladines were close, but he and Gunn shared a special bond. When his father died, his middle brother stepped up and made sure that his nephew was prepared to deal with the ugly world that awaited him.

Rah and the women sobbed as they lit candles around a make-shift altar supporting a picture of Big Gunn in the yard at San Quentin. The sun was just beginning to rise in the eastern sky, blanketing the yard in an orange glow. Rahkim stepped into the backyard, followed by the men who were left in attendance. Danny, Tears, Snake Eyes, and Doc hung back while Rahkim led his family to the front. Three prayer rugs were placed on the grass, which Gutter, Lil Gunn, and he knelt upon. With tears streaking all their cheeks, they made Saullat and asked that Allah accept Big Gunn into his bosom.

chapter 18

BY THE time Gutter rose from prayer, his knees ached and he had trouble walking from the lack of blood flow for so many hours. He bypassed everyone who was gathered in the living room and made his way upstairs to the bedroom. The women cried and sobbed over Gunn's loss, while the men cursed and vowed revenge against their sworn enemies. None of this moved Gutter. Though he knew he was supposed to be sad he couldn't find it inside himself, only the cold darkness that came before the storm.

Somewhere along the way he had managed to grab a bottle of vodka. It wasn't normally his drink of choice, but it would do. He took a long swig, letting the sting cleanse his insides. It felt like a small fire had started in his chest, but it still didn't help the coldness in his heart. All he wanted was to be alone and reflect on the man who had meant so much to him over the years. With Gunn's passing Gutter had lost more than an uncle. He'd lost a father, friend, mentor, and icon.

A soft knocking snapped Gutter out of his daze. Ignoring it, he took another deep swig of the bottle and stared blankly out the window. Instead of the intruder taking the hint and going away, he heard the door creak open. Gutter was about to flip over the invasion of his privacy, but the words stuck in his throat when he saw Monifa standing there.

"Sorry, I didn't know anyone was in here," she said sheepishly.

"It's all good," he told her, taking another drink. From the way her eyes were puffy and red he could tell she had been crying. Monifa and Gunn were very close when he was alive.

"I was just trying to get some space to clear my head. I can go somewhere else." She started back the way she'd come.

"Nah, you ain't gotta bounce, Mo," he told her. "Come on in," he beckoned, patting the space on the bed next to him. She gave him a weak smile and sat down. For a minute there was an awkward silence, neither really knowing what to say to the other, but it was Monifa who broke it.

"So, how ya doing?" she asked, looking at the worn carpet.

"Shit, I'm fucked-up. We just lost the most stand-up nigga ever to claim a set," he said emotionally.

"Yeah, I'm gonna miss the shit outta Big Gunn, that was my folk. Remember when he let us hold his Bonneville to drive out to Disneyland?" she recalled.

"Do I? Man, that muthafucka broke smooth down halfway there. I thought I was gonna catch a heatstroke waiting for Rahshida to come pick us up off the side of the highway."

"I remember. You was mad as hell because you got motor oil on your Magic Johnson jersey trying to be Mr. Mechanic." She giggled.

"Damn right. I paid a grip for that joint." He smiled and shoved her playfully. A small static current passed between them, causing Monifa to flinch.

"Guess that old spark ain't totally dead, huh?" She rubbed her arm.

"Guess not," he replied. "Mo, about the other day—"

"Gutter, there ain't no more to be said about it. You've got your life in New York and I've got mine out here," she told him, getting off the bed to go stand by the window. Monifa only called him Gutter when she was angry or trying to put distance between them.

Gutter sucked his teeth. "I love how you try to make shit all black-and-white."

She glared at him. "Gutter, you left me without a word and started a life with your new bitch in New York. It don't get no more black-and-white than that."

"Ain't no need for name-calling," he said. He sat the bottle on the ground and became a bit more serious. "Watch ya mouth, hear?"

Monifa laughed. "What, you getting sensitive because I'm talking about ya bitch?"

"I ain't gonna tell your ass no more." He slid off the bed and stood nose to nose with her, his green eyes flashing anger. A few years ago, Monifa would've shrunk under his gaze, but this was a whole new day and a whole new Monifa.

"Gutter, you can miss me with that mean-mug shit, because I'm hardly impressed. Save that for them buster-ass niggaz y'all be tripping on. I ain't scared of you, Kenyatta."

"Monifa, don't push me," he warned.

"Push you? Push you? Kenyatta Soladine, you've got hella nerve after the way you *pushed me* right out of your life. You're lucky I didn't try to kill your ass when you showed back up on the West." She went to mush him, but he grabbed her wrist, causing her to wince.

The moment Monifa felt the pain shoot up her arm she knew she'd gone too far. There was a look in Gutter's eyes that she'd only seen before he was going out to "put in work." Though they had once been lovers, she didn't know the man who stood before her. She expected him to strike her, or at the least toss her across the room, but to her surprise he kissed her.

Gutter's lips pressed against hers so hard that she thought her teeth would pierce her upper lip. The kiss was not a soft passionate kiss of a lover, more like that of a rapist conquering his victim. Never one to be outdone Monifa nicked his bottom lip, almost drawing blood.

Monifa's body suddenly felt weightless. The room became a swirl of colors, devoid of sound save for the beating of two lovers' hearts. She raked her nails along Gutter's neck, to match the iron-like fingers that were digging into her back. A cool wind caressed her cheek and she thought sure that she was falling down a bottomless pit, until the softness of the bed's mattress touched her back.

Looking up into his eyes, those same eyes that often made her feel loved or terrified, Monifa found that it was hard for her to concentrate. She promised herself that she wouldn't let him back in, that she would carry the hate with her forever, but she couldn't. Though Gutter had done her wrong, she still wanted him... no, she needed him.

With a tug, Gutter had torn off her tank top fumbling with her bra strap. Tiring of his clumsy fingers she popped the latch, exposing ripe cinnamon breasts and brown, silver-dollar nipples. Gutter suckled her breasts like a starved child, while she moaned in ecstasy. Grabbing a fistful of his braids, she yanked his head back and bit into his neck, drawing a yelp from him. The bite wasn't hard enough to draw blood, but it was hardly friendly. Strangely enough this seemed to turn him on more.

Grabbing her by the waist he flipped her over onto her stomach. Monifa's back arched as he ran his tongue down her spine.

Gutter proceeded to pull her jeans off and plant kisses on her ass cheeks. She thought she saw spots when he pulled her thong to the side and started lapping at her kitten from behind. His tongue moved in and out of her pussy like a hot spear, hitting spots that he was clueless to when they were an item. He had obviously been practicing. She shook him off and flipped over, wrapping her legs around his neck and pulling his head further into her love cave, and he happily gorged on her. At that moment he was one of Jesus' apostles and she was the last supper. As waves of pleasure rode her like a jockey she wondered how the hell she could've ever let him get away from her in the first place.

Slowly, he slid up her body, tickling her with his beard. His cat-like eyes twinkled as he whispered, "I missed this so much."

"Not as much as I did," she panted. Monifa raised her head as much as she could under his weight and kissed him. Her juices tasted like sweet nectar on his lips. "I need you inside me, baby," she pleaded. "Please, let me feel you."

Aiming with his thumb, Gutter slipped inside the warmth that was Monifa. Her walls felt like warm silk, gently tightening on his muscle as he dipped a bit deeper into her. Monifa hissed like she was in pain, but that didn't stop her from pulling him in deeper. She raked her nails across the picture of Lou-Loc that he had on his back, begging him to go deeper still. Even when Gutter reached the furthest and deepest parts of her she begged for more.

Monifa's eyes rolled back in her head as Gutter slipped in and out of her in a steady rhythm. She let her tongue roam his neck then his chest, but stopped when she saw the tattoo above his heart. Sharell is what it said in Gothic letters. It was just another reminder of what Monifa had lost, which pissed her off. It was at that moment that the intense pleasure mixed with the mounting rage took over. Digging her nails into the back of his neck she began slamming herself against him like she was trying to break his penis off inside her.

Gutter saw the change come over Monifa, but he was too lost in the warmth to care. He didn't know what had gotten into her but if she wanted to be *fucked* then he would gladly oblige. Gutter slapped her hands away and moved his upper body out of the girl's reach. Using his arms he locked her legs around his waist and started plowing into her. Monifa tried to scream, but he leaned in and silenced her with his mouth. They half kissed, have devoured each other while still slamming their bodies together.

Not bothering to remove himself from her, he flipped Monifa on her side, with one leg resting on his shoulder and the other pinned between his legs. Gutter cursed, snarled, and damn near foamed at the mouth as he could feel all the energy in his body concentrating itself in his privates. Monifa felt so good that he wasn't ready to come, but when she bounced her heart-shaped ass against him it stole the choice from him. Gutter exploded inside Monifa like a small geyser before falling on the bed next to her, still inside her cave.

Monifa snuggled against Gutter's body and wrapped his arm around her. She could feel his heart beating erratically against her back. Monifa felt like all the tension she had carried around for the past two years was finally released. Though she didn't fool herself about what had just happened it was still nice to be touched by someone she loved. She knew that as soon as Gunn's business was concluded he would be back on a plane to New York where his girl was waiting, but didn't ruin the moment by dwelling on it. Sharell had obviously won his heart, but at that moment his body belonged to her.

chapter 19

H E'S STILL not picking up his phone," C-style said, flipping her
cell closed. "First B. T. and now China has gone missing, what
the fuck is happening to our troops?"

"We need to get a line on China," Pop Top said, thinking of how
funny he started acting after the murder. China was one of their
click, but if Pop Top even thought he might snitch he was going to
kill him. "C, I want you to swing by his mama house and see what's
up with the boy. If he ain't there we gotta assume he's flipped."

"Nah, not China, he's one of us," C-style defended him.

"So was B. T.," Hollywood reminded her. "I always knew that
nigga was shady, but wasn't nobody trying to hear me."

"I can't believe that nigga was working for the other side,"
C-style said in disbelief.

"Fucking rat." Pop Top slammed the glass of Hennessey he'd
been sipping. "He's probably been sucking that L.C. dick since Lou-
Loc whooped his fucking ass, so ain't no telling how much they
know about us."

"Damn, you think he gave up addresses or anything like that?" C-style asked nervously.

"Shit, it wouldn't surprise me," High Side spoke up for the first time. "You can't put nothing past a cocksucker, ma, no offense." He smiled.

"Fuck you, Side." She punched him in the arm.

"I'm glad you muthafuckas see this as some kinda playtime when we got the fucking devil on our heels. If Major Blood is here that means we managed to piss off somebody real important."

"What's the skinny on this cat?" Hollywood asked.

"Before today I had never met him personally, but he's supposed to be official wit his murder game, since a shorty. Him and Lou-Loc had an ongoing beef; that's how he got the scar behind his ear."

Hollywood whistled. "If he was able to get at Lou, he must be one bad muthafucka."

"So, what are we supposed to do?" Rob asked, sporting two fresh black eyes.

"We war," a voice to their rear answered. Bruticus was a hulk of a man, who wore a clean-shaven head and a thick gold chain bearing a transformer emblem. Bruticus was one of the founding members of the Decepticons back in the late eighties. He was notorious for his violence, so it was a brilliant strategic move when Lou-Loc suggested they recruit him for the cause. Bruticus and his team from Brownsville had been instrumental in the fall of L.C. Blood, with him having murdered at least four of their members personally.

"I can agree with you on that one." High Side nodded. "But how do we find this nigga, Major Blood?"

"That shouldn't be too hard. We ride on enough of his punk-ass boys; he'll poke his head out again. Then we bust it open." Bruticus chuckled. "Matter of fact, I got the perfect mark in mind. He's a pussy, but he brings in a lot of money for them cats uptown. The best way to hurt a nigga is to cave his pocket in."

"Bet. Arm up and make it happen, my dude," Pop Top told him. "C"—he turned to her—"hop in a cab and go see what up wit young China. You know where he lives, right?"

"Yeah, I'm on it." C-style grabbed her purse and prepared to bust her move.

"I'm ready to rock when y'all niggaz are." Hollywood cocked the hammer of his pearl-handled .357. "How you wanna do this, cuz?"

"We gonna mash on these niggaz, on some guerrilla warfare shit." Pop Top ground his fist into his palm. "I gotta a little nigga I've been hearing about that should make things real uncomfortable on them slobs."

"You know how Gutter don't like bringing in no outsiders on family business," High Side reminded him.

"I hear that, playboy, but Gutter is in Cali and I'm holding the reins. Check, right now ain't but so many niggaz on the turf that's 'bout that body count. Niggaz is shooters, but they ain't killers. Make no mistake about what I'm telling you, cuz. Major Blood is a stone killer and to combat a killer we need killers, smell me?"

"Yeah, I got you, Top," High Side told him. "So who you gonna call?"

Pop Top grinned wickedly and said, "The Outlaw."

C-STYLE HOPPED out of the cab in front of China's building and slammed the door with an attitude. While all the men were making plans for the war, she was reduced to playing the roll of errand girl. When she had joined the set, it was in search of adventure and stripes, but so far all she was used for was braiding hair and slinging weed. It wasn't the most exciting roll, but it was better than getting passed around like some of the other home girls.

There was a group of young men posted up on the stoop, passing a blunt and trying to look hard. To an outsider they'd have been intimidating, but C-style was unmoved by the tough guy antics. They were as much a part of the scenery as the wilted tree planted on the curb.

"Sup, C-style?" one of the young men asked as she approached.

"Shit, everything is blue," she replied.

"Damn, girl, you getting thick than a muthafucka," another young man reached out to pinch her thigh, but she slapped his hand away viciously.

"Nigga, you must be trying to lose that," she snapped.

"Aw, its like that, ma?"

"I ain't ya mama, nigga, and respect my space."

"Stall her out, cuz, you know Young Rob got that pussy on smash," the first young man taunted.

"And *smash* it he does," C-style said smugly before going into the building and up to China's apartment. She rapped heavily on the door and waited.

Lucy Maynard snatched the door open with a scowl on her face and a Newport dangling from her mouth. She was a slightly plump woman with dark skin and full black hair, which she wore in a stylish cut. Her mouth was pursed to spew something hateful, but she relaxed when she recognized C-style.

"Oh, hey, Cory, I thought you was somebody else." She stepped aside to let C-style into the apartment.

"You got drama, Ms. Lucy?" C-style asked. She and Ms. Lucy had always gotten along famously. She often hinted that she and China should hook up, but C-style never entertained it. China was cute, but she wasn't trying to get passed around Harlem Crip like some of the other home girls.

"Yeah, but as usual it ain't my bullshit, it's China's. The police came around here looking for China again earlier and I thought you might've been them making a return trip. I swear, if it ain't one thing it's a fucking nothing. You know why they looking for his ass this time, Cory?"

"No, ma'am," C-style lied.

Lucy gave her a disbelieving look. "I'll just bet. You know, y'all seem to forget that I ain't much older than you so I ain't completely ignorant to what's happening in the streets, it's the same as when I was coming up. In the eighties we thought we knew more than the people coming out of the seventies, same as y'all do today, but what we ended up learning is that it's the same bullshit. You understand where I'm coming from, *C-style?*"

"Yes, Ms. Lucy." C-style nodded, a bit embarrassed at Ms. Lucy's use of her gang name.

"Good. Come on." She turned toward the hallway. "I just got back so I don't know if China is here, but if he is he better not be up to no good in my damn house!" She said the last part loud enough for China to hear through his bedroom door. Ms. Lucy knocked twice before pushing China's bedroom door open. The first thing she noticed was the rank smell and promised herself that she would make China clean his nasty room. But when she looked over at the bed her mind snapped. The bellow that came from Ms. Lucy was like nothing C-style had ever heard. Chanting, "Not my baby," over and over again she rushed to her departed son.

China was lying on his bed with his arms tucked peacefully behind his head and his ankles crossed. His face was calm and his eyes glassy, staring up at the ceiling. Had it not been for the fly perched undisturbed on his foam-crusted lips you could've mistaken him for sleeping. C-style had seen dead bodies in her lifetime but never someone close to her, never a friend.

There was an empty pill bottle lying near his leg, and a folded piece of paper on his chest, labeled MOMMY. While Ms. Lucy grieved for her son, C-style picked up the slip of paper and read it. In the note China had gone on to explain to his mother how he had done some terrible things in life and was sorry for not being a good son. Apparently the weight of what he and Pop Top had done became too much to bear and he took the coward's way out. C-style slipped the note into her pocket and went to console Ms. Lucy. There wasn't much she could say to ease her pain, but the least she could do was hold her for a time. She kept her eyes on the top of Ms. Lucy's head to keep from looking at China. She would make her report to Pop Top later, but the only thing that mattered at that moment was being there for Ms. Lucy.

chapter 20

BEDSTUY, BROOKLYN

NORMALLY, IT was against Gutter's policies to seek outside help with problems involving the set, but Gutter wasn't in charge at the moment, Pop Top was. A young man, riding a motorcycle composed of parts from different bikes, cruised up Marcus Garvey Boulevard. He was smiling behind the face mask, but you couldn't see it because of the skeleton's face airbrushed onto the visor. Hanging from the handlebars of the bike were two blue bandannas, the calling card of the Crip army, but he wasn't a banger, he was an outlaw, the last outlaw, let the streets and the obituaries tell it.

Johnny Outlaw was a man barely out of his teens, but had already earned a reputation as being brutal and cold. He was among the elite in his field, which was killing. Pop Top had paid him a handsome fee, but he knew if anyone could get his point across, the Outlaw could.

The young killer coasted to a stop at the corner of Jefferson and Marcus Garvey. There was a cluster of young men in the block between Jefferson and Throop shooting dice. There were about five of them in all, and none had the slightest clue as to what was about to go down. The Outlaw checked his Ingram M-10 9mm to make sure that the silencer was secure and one was in the chamber. It was a different weapon than he was accustomed to using, but Pop Top had promised him a few extra stacks per slob he dropped, and he intended on breaking the bank with the M-10. Satisfied that he was battle-ready, he revved the bike, emitting an eerie wailing sound from the custom exhaust pipes fitted onto it. Startled by the high-pitched sound the young men looked up from their game and the block burst into bright flashes.

"MAN, I got fifty he four or better!" A kid wearing a beat-up Yankee hat called from the sidelines.

"Ain't nothing, I don't mind taking ya money and ya man's," the man shaking the dice said. He was a portly young cat, just out of his teens and dying to make a rep for himself.

Surrounding them were other thieves and hustlers from the block. Some had money tied up in the game and some were just watching. Almost three thousand dollars lay on the ground, tucked under feet or piled near the center. No one worried about anyone being stupid enough to try and rob the dice game. At that end of Jefferson Avenue, they didn't play that old bullshit. There were dozens of Blood sets in New York City, but the boys from Jefferson boasted one of the most notorious. Between their little group they had accumulated more than a dozen bodies, and too many robberies to count. Their click was strong and they had the block on smash.

"What the fuck was that?" the kid with the Yankee hat said,

scanning the block for the source of the strange noise. It sounded like a cat being dragged over a barbed-wire fence. When the kid shaking the dice popped his head up, the side of his face was caved in by a bullet.

JOHNNY OUTLAW dipped into the block, going against the flow of traffic, spitting with the M-10. It looked like someone was pelting the men with rotten tomatoes as they lost body parts and vital organs. One cat tried to run and had his leg torn clean off by one of the high-powered slugs. Satisfied that he had done enough damage, Johnny prepared to make his escape when something slammed into him, knocking him off the bike and sending the M-10 skidding.

Now, for as vicious as Johnny Outlaw was rumored to be, he couldn't have weighed more than 160 pounds on a good day, and the man who had dismounted him was almost double that. Johnny rained rights and lefts on the man who was trying to pin him down until his comrades got there, but the brute was too strong. Seeing that his fists were getting him nowhere, Johnny tried a different tactic. Dipping his hand into his boot he came up holding a stiletto, which he shoved up into the man's gut with all his might. The man coughed blood onto the airbrushed visor and fell to the side.

"See what the fuck you made me do?" Johnny said, getting to his feet. Though his voice was distorted by the small microphone built into the helmet, his intentions were clear as he retrieved the M-10. "Couldn't lay down like the rest of them, could you? Trying to fuck up a perfectly good killing, huh?"

"P-please, man. Don't kill me," the brute pleaded.

Johnny looked at him almost compassionately. "You got heart, man, and that's a good thing. But you chose the wrong side of the color line to throw in your lot with, which means you're fucked. My niggaz from Harlem say y'all forgot your places on the food chain, and I gotta remind you. Nothing personal, baby," Johnny assured him before cutting loose with the M-10 and finishing the young banger.

Even with the sirens in the distance Johnny took a moment to admire his handiwork before heading back to the fallen motorcycle. The smart thing would've been to leave the patchwork bike, but it held sentimental value to him. It was the first thing he could ever call his own, since leaving his old life in Mississippi as a young boy. He built it with his own hands and refused to leave it.

People were starting to stir, coming to their windows trying to be nosey, but when Johnny sprayed the front windows with the M-10 they thought better of it. True, it was overkill but Johnny Outlaw had made his bones by overdoing it. Satisfied that he had temporarily deterred any Good Samaritans from aiding the police, Johnny hopped back on the bike and floored it, leaving a trail of bodies and a ghostly howl in his wake.

HARLEM

J. B. BOPPED down Morningside Drive with his right-hand man, Steve. They had just come from the spot copping two twenties of haze and had two prime freaks waiting to help them smoke it up. When they got a dose of the date rape that J. B. had scored to drop in their drinks, the party would really be in full swing.

"You think they'll go for it?" Steve asked J. B.

J. B. smiled reassuringly. "I don't see why not. This shit is supposed to be off the chain. My man, Harv, gave a bitch a half of pill and she took cock damn near till the next morning."

"I can't wait!" Steve said excitedly. "I'm gonna fuck the shit out of one of them hoes."

"Fuck that, Blood." J. B. held up the baggie containing several white pills. "Once they get a dose of these, you're gonna fuck both of them."

As the two young men continued to walk and talk, a white Chevy Lumina was coming up behind them. There were three men in total occupying the vehicle, all motivated by one thought—murder. When the car was coasting along next to them, the driver's side window rolled down.

"CRIIIP!" THE driver sang in a high squeal. When J. B. and Steve turned to identify the source, Bruticus stuck his arm out the window, letting the sun wink off the barrel of his .45. At first there was only silence and then came the thunder.

Two slugs entered Steve's chest, cracking his breast plate, decorating the bench behind him with bits of heart and lungs. When Bruticus turned his hammer to J. B., J. B. was already sprinting in the other direction. The Lumina screeched and reversed after him, while another shooter leaned over the top of the car and tried to lay J. B. Trees splintered and glass shattered, but the shooter never hit his target.

J. B. DUCKED and zigzagged like a hunted animal. He recognized one of the shooters in the car as a member of a rival gang. Even though he had gone on a few outings with his new family, he had never done anything directly to any of the men in the car. He found himself running for his natural life, because he represented a different color. When he joined the gang, he thought it would be fun, but he would soon realize that banging was not a game; it was a way of life.

"FUCK IS wrong with your aim?" Bruticus barked at the shooter. "Lay that nigga down!" He steered the Lumina with one hand, watching the fleeing man over his shoulder. A taxi came around the bend on 116th, causing him to swerve and slamming the car into a parked Explorer. "Shit," Bruticus spat, sliding from the car. "Take the wheel."

THE EFFECTS of all the cigarettes had begun to catch up with J. B. as his chest started to burn. He knew that the only way for him to escape would be to cut through the park. That was easier said than done, because the next entrance was more than four blocks away. The loud crash to his rear caused him to spare a glance over his shoulder. The nose of the Lumina was jutting out into the street, while its rear was hooked on the bumper of an Explorer. He thought that luck might finally be swinging in his favor, but knew it to be a lie when he saw the driver climb out of the car and begin pursuing him on foot.

The fear of being gunned down in the middle of the street made J. B.'s mind race. He knew he only had one chance of escaping, but he didn't like it. He looked over the wall of the park, at the grass that was easily twenty feet below street level. Swallowing the lump in his throat, he leapt over the stone wall.

BRUTICUS WAS a large man, but he was by no means slow. J. B. had a head start on him, but he was closing the distance in good enough time. He watched the young boy veer from the street, and head for the wall. He knew that there was a long drop and figured he had him cornered. He slowed to a jog and made to dispatch his victim, until his mark suddenly jerked and leapt over the wall.

Bruticus ran to the wall and looked over in time to see J. B. picking himself up from the ground, and preparing to continue his sprint. Bruticus knew that if the boy got away, it would upset Pop Top's plan. Leveling the .45, he got J. B. in his sights and squeezed the trigger once. J. B.'s calf exploded, knocking him to the ground. Bruticus pulled himself over the wall and dropped down to finish him.

The force of the impact sent shock waves from Bruticus's ankles to his lower back. It hurt like hell, but he didn't feel like anything was broken. After gathering himself, he walked casually over to J. B. who was trying to crawl away. The bullet had totally destroyed his calf muscle, but the fear of death wouldn't let him give in to the pain.

Bruticus kicked him square in the ass. "Turn the fuck over, nigga!"

"Chill, man," J. B. cried.

"Fuck that chill, shit. You knew the rules when you joined up, kid. You wanted to be a soldier, so now yo bitch-ass is a casualty of war."

"I don't want no beef with y'all. You got it!"

Bruticus chuckled wickedly. "Nah, I don't want it, you take it." Bruticus squeezed the trigger. Bullets tore through J. B.'s body and struck the ground below. A dust storm rose up around J. B., coating his face and body. The boy lay in the dirt with plum-sized holes in his chest and legs. Bruticus took a moment to spit on his corpse, before limping across the park to his waiting getaway car.

IT TOOK more than an hour, but Sharell had finally managed to fight through the traffic and make it to Harlem. Though she was officially off, she still found herself at her place of employment, St. Luke's Hospital. She could've waited until she came back to pick up her check, but it allowed her time out of the house, which is what she needed since Gutter had her feeling like a sardine trapped in the house.

Instead of going directly to her station she decided to cut through the emergency room so she could holler at her girl, Rhonda, who worked as a triage nurse. When she passed through the automatic doors her senses were overwhelmed with the bullshit that was the emergency room.

As usual it was overcrowded with people in need of medical attention. In the far corner, an addict rocked back and forth, sweating like a runaway slave, waiting to see if there was an available bed in their detox wing. Another man was hunched over near the pay phone, nursing his hand, which was wrapped in bandages that were splotched with blood. A girl who didn't appear to be more than seventeen or so cradled a newborn in her arms, while two more kids who couldn't have been more than a year apart tore through the emergency room as if it was their own personal backyard.

"Welcome to the jungle," Sharell mumbled, as she stepped over a bum who was either passed out or sleeping, and made her way to the triage window. A woman, whose profile was familiar to her, sat at the window exchanging words with Rhonda. Though it had been a while, she'd know Tameeka anywhere.

"Look, I've been sitting here for two hours and my son still hasn't been seen, this is unacceptable," Tameeka was saying.

"And like I've been telling you for the last ten minutes, we're overcrowded and understaffed today. We're seeing the priority patients first," Rhonda replied.

"And my child ain't a priority? My boy has been throwing up all morning, and he's running a fever!"

"Look, we've got people in here suffering from everything from gunshots to the shakes, your son's flu symptoms aren't a priority right now." Rhonda was still being polite, but Sharell could tell she was losing her patience with Tameeka so she decided to step in.

"What's up, Tameeka?" Sharell said, moving to stand over her.

Tameeka's eyes flashed surprise then embarrassment before she uttered a weak, "Hey."

Until about a year or so ago, she, Lauren, and Sharell had been like the three amigos, but when she got serious with Gutter all that changed. Lauren, though she never really cared for Gutter and still didn't, held her down when people tried to crucify her for her choice of a life mate, but Tameeka fell in line with the Joneses. The few times they had spoken on the phone Tameeka always had an excuse about how busy she was, but Sharell knew it was just so she didn't have to state the obvious—she was afraid. Everybody knew who her man was and what he represented, but they also knew that her love for him was unwavering.

"Sup, mommy." Sharell tapped on the window Rhonda was sitting behind, and gave her a warm smile.

"Chilling, preg-o," Rhonda teased. "I'm just trying to get through the day without having to get fired." She cut her eyes at Tameeka when she said this.

"Take it light, Rhonda, you only got a few hours left until your shift is over. Breathe, girl," Sharell told Rhonda, but placed a hand on Tameeka's chair.

"No doubt." Rhonda nodded in understanding. Reluctantly she turned back to Tameeka and said, "Give me a minute and I'll see if I can get somebody to see your son."

"Well, I just came to pick up my check and skate, call me later though," Sharell said to Rhonda before heading deeper into the hospital. She was about to go through the double doors in the back when Tameeka stopped her.

"Hold on, Sharell," she said, catching up. "Thanks for looking out."

"It was nothing, you know how I do it," Sharell reminded her. "So what's up, how's everything with you?"

Tameeka shrugged. "I'm just trying to make it like everybody else. But listen, can I talk to you for a minute, in private?"

"Sure." Sharell took her by the hand and led her outside the emergency room. "What's up, Meeka?"

Tameeka took a minute to examine her shoes. "Listen, I know I haven't been the best friend over the last few months, but you know that hasn't changed how I feel about you, right?"

"That's what I like to think," Sharell said. There was another short silence.

"You know, for a long time I didn't see what it was about Gutter that made you stay with him. I mean, he's thugged out and you're sweet. If anything I always figured you'd end up with a doctor or some square dude."

"We ain't got a whole lot of control over our hearts, Tameeka," Sharell told her.

"Don't I know it." Her eyes said something. "I didn't understand it until life threw me a curveball and I ended up in a similar situation." Tameeka paused as if she wasn't sure of how much she wanted to share with Sharell.

"You wanna talk about it?" Sharell asked, sensing her uneasiness.

"Not much to tell, really. My heart belongs to a nigga who refuses to do right. If it ain't the beef, it's the bitches and I'm starting to feel like I can't get a word in edgewise."

"That's a hard pill to swallow, baby girl."

"Yet I do," she said in a shameful tone. "Don't get me wrong, my man takes care of me and my son. We ain't rich, but we don't want for nothing. But this lifestyle"—she paused—"it's just hard to deal with. I call myself doing him a favor and went and picked up some work from uptown and end up getting stopped in the cab. I had to call my mother to pick my son up from school, because my ass was down at the precinct."

"Jesus, girl, is everything all right?" Sharell asked, genuinely concerned.

"Yeah, I'm still going back and forth to court over this shit though. Sharell, in my whole life I've never been one to be twisted up with the police, but it seems like lately they're always over my shoulder." She looked around as if they were being watched. "How do you cope with this shit?"

Sharell thought for a minute before answering. "Honestly, if Jesus wasn't my backbone I'd have probably snapped a long time ago. I can't speak on your situation because it's not my situation, but Gutter draws a very clear line between his street antics and the life we're trying to build. It ain't no secret that Gutter is a criminal, anybody who watches the news knows that, but the streets have no place in our home. I'm not gonna go as far as to say that it's impossible for me to get caught up, but Gutter goes the extra mile to try and ensure that I never find myself in that position."

"I feel you, but do you ever feel like it'd be easier for you to just cut your losses?" Tameeka asked.

"All the time," Sharell confessed. "But you know what, I knew what he was into before I committed to him, and I still fell in love with his ol thug ass." She rubbed her hand over her belly. "My guy goes the extra mile for me, so it's only right that I hold him down through thick and thin. The question you need to ask yourself is, how far is your man willing to go for you? Once you know the answer to that then you'll know where you stand."

"That's deep." Tameeka nodded.

"That's real. Meeka, I can't tell you what you should or shouldn't do, but always make sure you put you and your son first."

Before the conversation could go any further there was a loud popping in the distance. It sounded like a firecracker at first, but when several more pops followed everybody knew them to be gunshots. Sharell hurried back inside the emergency room with Tameeka on her heels, and almost got knocked over as security came rushing out.

chapter 21

"WHAT UP, y'all?" Jesus said as he approached the bench where Tito and Miguel were ping-ponging a blunt. He had put on a little weight, but was still on the slim side.

"Sup, Blood," Miguel replied. He noticed that Jesus had winced a bit at the term. Though he was still officially a part of the set, he didn't hang around so much. After Lou-Loc had waxed him with a lead pipe the prior summer, gang-banging no longer seemed to appeal to him. The young man still sported a thin scar along his jaw from where the doctors had to wire it.

"I can't call it." Jesus invited himself to a seat. "Let me hit that, yo." He reached for the blunt only to have Miguel snatch it away.

"Surgeon general says that smoking can be detrimental to your health," Miguel teased as he took another drag.

"Let the lil nigga hit it, hype." Tito nudged him. Miguel grudgingly complied, handing the blunt to Jesus. "Ain't seen you around in a while, J. Everything good?" Tito continued.

"Yeah, man. I just been busy taking care of my aunt. She ain't been so good since Satin went away," Jesus informed him. At the mention of Satin, Tito turned away.

"So what's up, when you gonna stop acting like a girl and get back down for yours?" Miguel capped.

"I'm always gonna be down for mine, dawg, don't get it fucked-up," Jesus told him. Though he tried to make his voice firm there was no conviction in his statement. "It's just that...I don't know, a nigga been trying to finish school and all that, Blood. You know I love my hood, but I gotta think about what I'm gonna do when all this shit is over."

"Over?" Miguel sat up with a questioning glare in his eyes. "T, you hear this nigga?" Miguel nudged his partner. "Check this shit, shorty," he addressed Jesus. "This shit ain't never gonna be over. For as long as its crab-ass muthafuckas trying to stop our shine, we're gonna be out here banging the fuck out. You better stop fooling ya self and get out here and get this paper."

Tito glared at his best friend, realizing at that moment just how ignorant Miguel really was. "Jesus, don't listen to this warped muthafucka. Son, you gonna always be a Blood and ain't nothing that none of us other than God or a bullet can do about it, but always think outside the box. You ain't gotta be no killer or play the corners to support your hood. Be down for yours by blowing the fuckup one day. You can make more paper owning your own business than you can out here pitching stones."

"You sound like Satin." Jesus laughed. "She was always telling me the same shit, but I never listened to her."

"You should've. Satin has always had a good head on her shoulders." Tito nodded.

"Yeah, she did." Jesus got silent for a minute. "Blood, that shit fucks me up every time I go see her. I look at the chick up in that place and think that this can't be my fucking sister," he said emotionally.

"Don't trip, man. She'll come around sooner or later," Tito lied. "You just keep doing what you gotta do and take care of that aunt," Tito said, reaching into his pocket and pulling out a knot of money. "Go buy her some flowers or some shit." He handed him some folded-up bills.

"Thanks, man." Jesus accepted the money. "Tito, you should come up with us and see her one of these days. You know we're all we got left."

Tito fidgeted. "I know, my nigga, I just be crazy busy. I'll tell you what, how 'bout we drive up there next week?"

"That's a bet." Jesus smiled. "Yo, I gotta burn it, but I'll hit you later on." He gave Miguel dap then Tito.

"A'ight, Blood," Tito said. As he sat there watching a young man who had been like a little brother to him make his way out of the projects he couldn't help but feel like shit. He knew damn well that he wouldn't be going to see Satin next week, nor would anyone else. By that time the next day Satin Angelino would be dead.

THERE'S A place in our minds somewhere between sleep and awake where reality and dreams overlap and your senses are slow to recognize which is which. This is where Satin found herself at that moment. She had come out of her stupor, but things were still jumbled in her mind. It was as if a whole year had been wiped away and she struggled to make sense of what had happened.

"Life," she heard the word whispered somewhere in the back of her mind. It was the last word her lover had spoken to her in the dream, but it was not his voice.

"Life," she mouthed in her dream, but there was no sound. She recognized the word, but it no longer held any meaning for her. A life without him was a cheap imitation.

For the millionth time she tried to shut out the world around her and escape to the sleeping place, but it had rejected her. Within the recesses of her mind she had been able to escape the world around her, but thanks to Lou-Loc's last visitation she had been barred and forced to face the world around her. She had a life growing inside her, a life she and Lou-Loc had created. If she hadn't believed in miracles before, she did then. For as thrilled as she was about becoming a mother, and getting back a part of what she lost, the fact remained that she was the property of the state of New York. If she didn't escape the hospital, chances were that she would never get to know her child.

"Life," the voice said again. This time there was something more to the word, as if a hand had slapped her across the face, without actually touching her. "Remember his warning child. You must be here to water the seed, sleep isn't for you. Life, Satin."

Lou-Loc, Michael, her parents. The faces of everyone she had lost flashed through her head like a cheap movie reel. They were all dead, but the sleeping place allowed her to be with them. Did this mean she wanted to die too? *No!* There would be no more sleeping, her seed needed her. Feeling a presence in the room Satin's eyes snapped open. She was about to roll over to see who was there when she was suddenly lifted violently off the bed.

THERE WAS hardly anyone on the floor save for the nurse, who sat at her usual post in front of the portable television. She was so engrossed in her show that she barely gave the young doctor's badge a second look as he strode past whistling a tune. Had she been on her job she'd have noticed that the picture on the ID card looked nothing like the man who had it clipped to his white lab coat.

Major Blood had taken out his braids and brushed his mane back into a neat ponytail, bringing out his handsome features. Once inside the hospital he had swiped a pair of scrubs and the lab coat from a laundry cart that had been abandoned in the hallway. No one gave him so much as a second look when he helped himself to one of the computers to find out which room Satin Angelino was being kept in.

Glancing up and down the hall to make sure no one was watching Major Blood slipped into Satin's room. He waited for his eyes to adjust to the darkness before pulling out his silenced .22. Satin had her back to him, sleeping peacefully. Moving stealthily, he made his way to the bed and leveled the gun.

In all truth he knew that killing the girl was totally unnecessary, but the money had already been dropped. "Nothing personal, shorty, but I always fill my contracts," he whispered before squeezing the trigger.

SHARELL HAD been in her duplex crying and praying all evening. The word had come down about Big Gunn passing and she took it pretty bad. Though she'd never met him personally, they enjoyed a few phone conversations and she knew that he and Gutter were close. She expected Gutter to be just as broken up over his uncle's death, but he was surprisingly calm. So much so that it made her nervous. She knew that he had been a warrior all his life and death was the norm for the children of Los Angeles, but there was an edge to him that chilled her. Without having to be told she knew a shit storm was about to rain over L.A. and she just hoped her man would make it back to her in one piece.

After receiving her condolences, Gutter dropped the bomb on her. She couldn't say that she was too surprised though. When Gutter got motivated enough about something he wasted no time in putting a plan in motion. He wouldn't go into detail about how he had managed to pull it off, but she knew that there would be consequences because of it. Still, he had called on her to do her part and she would answer without question.

There was a nasty chill to the wind, but it was to be expected for the hour of the night it was. A shadow in her peripheral vision made her jump. She breathed a sigh of relief when she saw that it was just a cat slithering between the trash cans. She gave a cautious glance to her left and saw nothing, but she knew he was there. Mohammad had been against the idea and he expressed this to Gutter, but Sharell insisted. For something as important as this, she was the only one who could be trusted with the task.

Sharell could see headlights in the distance making their way toward her building. Mohammad stepped out of the shadows and moved to stand in front of her with his gun dangling at his side. His muscles tensed beneath his long-sleeved shirt ready to attack or defend. A pea-green cargo van pulled to an easy stop at the cub and killed its lights. The driver, who was a balding man with a double chin, stared straight ahead, not even casting a curious glance at Sharell or her armed bodyguard.

A slender man dressed in a tight black T-shirt came around from the passenger side and regarded Sharell and Mohammad. He looked at her curiously, but there was something about the way his emerald-green eyes lingered on Mohammad. Mohammad didn't move, but Sharell noticed that he'd tightened his grip on the pistol. Whatever passed between them she was completely oblivious to it. Fearing there was about to be violence Sharell opened her mouth to say something, but her breath caught in her throat when the man in black slid open the side door to reveal his cargo.

SATIN WAS huddled on the moldy seat in the back of the van, wrapped in a leather duster. It provided her with more protection from the night chill, but her bones still felt cold. She squinted against the glare of the streetlights as if they were a dozen tiny suns. When she stepped from the van she found that her legs weren't quite ready to support her weight. With an exaggerated sigh, Cross scooped the frail young woman into his arms and started toward Sharell.

"Stay where you are, assassin." Mohammad leveled his gun at Cross. There was a tension to his movements that Sharell wasn't familiar with, which could've almost been mistaken for nervousness, but Mohammad wasn't the nervous type. Something about the taller man had him on edge.

Cross looked at Mohammad comically. "For as much as Gutter claims to detest the children of Gehenna I'm surprised that he has entrusted one of its initiates with the well-being of his wife. Tell me, what is your name, little one?" Cross took a step forward, causing Mohammad to take two steps back.

"I am Mohammad Al Haj, firstborn of Sharif Al Haj, and right arm of the Al Mukallah Prince and guardian of the Soladines. On my oath, I will die or kill in service of my prince!" Mohammad said defiantly.

Cross just shook his head. "And to what end? Have they promised you the devil's bargain, or assured you safe passage into Mecca upon your death?" Cross taunted him. "Had murder been my purpose here, you'd have never heard me coming. Don't test me, Mohammad, or I'll surely see that you receive your reward earlier than you'd like."

As Cross spoke the sound of his voice echoed in Mohammad's ears like someone was beating a drum right next to him. The small voice in his head that we call reason begged for him to step aside, but he held his ground. Mohammad was a killer, but Cross was something else all together. He had been warned of the assassin since his earliest days studying the path of death and knew full well what Cross could do to him, but he had taken an oath and not even impending death could make him dishonor his prince, or risk what Sharif had promised him.

"It's okay, Mohammad," Sharell said, stepping between them. For this man to put fear into Mohammad's heart she knew that he was dangerous, but she also knew that Gutter would not have trusted him with the mission had he posed a threat to her or Satin.

"Tell Kenyatta that our business is done," Cross said, handing Satin over to Mohammad, who was still holding his gun, but speaking to Sharell.

"Thank you so much," Sharell said with tears of joy in her eyes. "God bless you."

Cross gave a faint chuckle. "I think we're too late for that, but I'll take it." Cross climbed back into the passenger side of the van and motioned for the driver to pull off.

For a long moment the trio just stood there in silence. Satin was a little dusty, but appeared to be fine. There was still a glaze to her eyes, but there was also an awareness that Sharell hadn't seen in a long time.

"Satin, are you okay, baby?" Sharell touched her cheek.

Satin looked at her and gave a faint smile. "I'm ready to wake up now."

chapter 22

GUTTER SAT on the front porch, looking up at the California sun. The weather was a warm eighty-three, and there wasn't a cloud in sight. The sky looked like the clearest blue ocean, with a red-orange jewel resting in the middle. The trees were thick and green with the smell of fresh grass floating on the air. This place would never know the icy touch of snow, or the frigid winds that swept through New York every year. California would be forever green and warm, if not scorching. It was hard to believe that a place so beautiful could breed such ugliness.

The Soladines had prayed through the dawn, well into the day. Lil Gunn had finally stopped crying and gone off to bed. Gutter felt for his cousin, because he was no stranger to the pain of loss. Like his brother Rahmil, Gunn had died prematurely. The difference was Gutter's father was an active participant in that war, and had been ready to lay down his life for that cause. Gunn was done fighting, but it didn't stop the conflict from claiming him.

It had been a horrible year for him. He had been shot up, lost his best friend and his uncle, all in succession. And let's not forget the murders, dozens of murders. When Gutter had awakened from his coma and discovered the events that had transpired, something inside him clicked. The darkest side of him had been unleashed, and it demanded compensation. Be it by his order, or by his hand, blood flowed in rivers. How many would die before it was all said and done? The snubbing of human life had become the norm. Not just in the hood, but all over the world. Ironically, death and the practice of it dictated how the world was run. From Pakistan to Inglewood, the touch of the reaper had no bounds.

He touched his hand to his neck and felt the scratches Monifa had left the night before. He hoped that they would heal by the time he went home to Sharell. Just thinking of her and how he had violated their relationship made him feel low. He was wrong for sleeping with Monifa, but it felt so right. Sharell had always tried her best to know his heart, but Monifa knew it a little more intimately. They had come up through the good times and the bad, before New York had even been a thought on his mind. In that moment of weakness he craved her familiarity and like men tend to do he let his little head do the thinking for his big one. He wondered to himself how that would change the already complex dynamics of what was going on in his life.

He ran his hands through his wild mane. It would be even more of a mess if he didn't get it done before the sun began its merciless noon onslaught. His clothes and sneakers were soiled from the grass in the backyard and there would be nothing he could do about it before Danny and Tears came back from the hotel with the rest of their stuff. It had already been decided that they would stay at the house for the remainder of their trip. His family needed him and he needed them.

Gutter picked up the forty of Old English that was sitting by his foot, and swigged thirstily. "So much death," he whispered.

The creaking of floorboards caused him to turn around. Monifa was standing behind him, with her arms folded across her breasts. Her hair hung loosely, fanning out over her shoulder. Her lips were lightly coated in a peach shade, like remnants of something she drank. Monifa's eyes stared down at him, but there was no malice, only hurt and need. She motioned toward the step one level above him and he nodded. Giving a slight tug to her denim shorts, she took the seat.

She was silent for a minute, just staring at him. He looked like a warrior prince with his wild hair and sharp ebony features. Monifa had always found Gutter beautiful, even when he tried to come off as hard and insensitive. She knew both sides of the man and had long ago come to terms with who he was and what he was about. This was one of the reasons she found herself so hopelessly in love.

"Hey," she said weakly.

"Sup," he replied. "I thought you got up outta here?"

"I did. I went home to change clothes, but came right back to see if Rahshida needed anything."

"You're a sweet kid." He chuckled.

"Oh, so now I'm a *kid*, huh? I don't know, Gutter, I seemed old enough this morning."

He was quiet for a moment. "Mo, about that—"

"Save it." She held her hand up. "It was a onetime thing, Gutter. It wasn't that serious," she lied. On the outside Monifa tried to carry it like the night was just nothing but a nut, but they both knew it was more than that. Her soul craved him, but she knew that Gutter would never again be hers.

"Your hair looks a hot mess," she joked, changing the subject.

Gutter managed to muster up a smile. "I didn't do this on my own," he said sarcastically. "Besides, I ain't really had a whole lot of time for grooming."

Monifa pulled a comb from her back pocket and patted her inner thigh with it. "Sit back and let me tighten you up, smart-ass." She took the step just above the one he was sitting on. Gutter slid back and rested his head against her leg. Slowly, Monifa began the task of untangling his hair and rebraiding it. "So, where's Danny this morning?"

"I sent him and Tears back to the hotel, then they gotta stop over at the mall to get me a new cell phone. With everything going on . . . I kinda smashed my old one."

"You and that temper." She popped him on the head playfully with the comb.

"You know, this reminds me of back in the days, us sitting out and you braiding my hair," he recalled.

"Yeah, seems like so long ago." Monifa paused. "Ken, what happened to us? What happened to you?"

"The hood," he said honestly. "I got so caught up in this shit that I couldn't think of anything else. Not my family, my loved ones. Nothing was more important to me than the set."

"Even me?"

Gutter paused momentarily, gathering his thoughts. He thought about feeding her another line of bullshit, but he owed her more. He owed her the truth. "Mo, you gotta understand the circumstances surrounding my leaving Cali. A cop and his partner died and their blood was on my hands." He proceeded to tell her the whole story about what had happened that night in the O'Leary house. Monifa was shocked, and had a thousand questions, but she let him finish his story. When it was done, she was crying and his eyes were moist.

"My God, I never knew," she sobbed.

"Not many people did." He took another drink. "The LAPD rode down on the hood, pressing niggaz for a killer. It was only a matter of time before one of these fools started running their fucking traps. The big homeys decided that it was best for me and Lou to get low for a while. Lou-Loc had had enough of Cali anyhow, so it was cool for him to relocate to New York. Me, shit I couldn't wait to get back to the hood. The thing is, we started getting money on the East Coast. We blew up real fast, baby. The next thing I knew, years had passed and neither of us was in a rush to get home."

"You could've called or written me, Kenyatta," she insisted.

"And said what? 'Hey Monifa, I moved away from Cali to become an even worse criminal on the East Coast.' Nah, baby, I had already done enough damage to your life and didn't want to cause more. I figured in time, you'd forget about me and move on. Maybe find yourself a good working dude. I ain't the kind of nigga you need in your life."

"Kenyatta, that is the most selfish thing I've ever heard," she said seriously. "How do you know what kind of man I need in my life? Jesus, I can't tell you how many nights I laid awake thinking about you. I've been with other guys since you, but none measured up. You were my first and *only* love."

Gutter craned his neck to face her. "Monifa, I—" his words were swallowed when she placed her mouth over his. Monifa kissed him deep and passionately, and he returned it. They stroked each other's faces, and for just a few seconds everything was as it had been. The moment was shortlived as they heard a series of whistles coming from the house, followed by Tears appearing in the doorway.

"What the fuck is going on, cuz?" Gutter asked, ready to answer the war call.

"The sentries bagged a slob creeping through," Tears said, lumbering down the stairs, tossing Gutter a pistol as he passed. The homeys were hot on his heels.

"Is he still alive?" Gutter asked no one in particular.

Rahkim pulled the slide on the sawed-off pump, "For the moment."

Gutter looked from the jogging forms of Rahkim and Criminal to Monifa. Her eyes pleaded with him not to follow, but she knew better. Gutter was a soldier, and thus had to be in the trenches. When she nodded in understanding he took off after his comrades.

BY THE time the trio had made it to the end of the block, Mad Man and Lil Blue Bird were coming their way. Both the youngsters were dressed in dark sweatshirts and jeans. The young men were wearing the confident smiles of game hunters that had just bagged a prize. Walking between them was a soldier that Gutter recognized from the other side.

Pudgy was a portly young man, with a round face and thick neck. He was a highly respected member of the Mad Swans, who had spilled his fair share of blood over the years. Usually when a set was planning a raid they used cannon fodder as scouts. They would never send a soldier of Pudgy's value for fear of losing him. Gutter wondered why they had chosen him, but his curiosity would soon be satisfied.

"We caught this nigga creeping, cuz," Mad Man lisped. A few years prior he had had his two front teeth knocked out by some cops, so he whistled a little when he spoke.

"Yeah, old boy was riding in a mean Benz," Lil Blue added.

"Punk-ass slob." Rahkim raised the sawed-off. "My brother

ain't even cold yet and you got the nerve to show your stinking face round here. Y'all little niggaz move so I can peel this bitch!"

"Easy, Unc." Gutter stepped between Rahkim and Pudgy. "Pudge, I know you ain't got a death wish, so I assume you got a good reason for being here? Start talking before these hammers do." Gutter motioned toward his heavily armed entourage.

Pudgy was clearly as nervous as a rabbit in a pit of vipers, but he tried to steady his voice when he spoke. "Listen, man, I didn't wanna come here to die, but they said it would be a show of good faith."

"Who the fuck is they?" Criminal asked.

"The homeys from Swan, Trik wants to meet with you guys."

"Fuck Swan!" Rahkim raged, stepping around Gutter and placing the sawed-off to Pudgy's large stomach. "You niggaz killed my brother, ain't shit to talk about."

Pudgy fought to control his bowels. When the homeys gave him his mission, he told them that he'd wanted no part of it. The Soladines were a wild lot and there was no reasoning with them. Still, Trik had insisted he do it. It was either that or be tried as a traitor. Now, Pudgy found himself about to be executed for trying to do his duty. His only hope would be to reason with the more sensible member of the clan.

"Gutter, man, tell dude to stall me out," he pleaded.

"And why the fuck should I?" Gutter glared at Pudgy. "Swans shot my uncle and y'all knew he wasn't riding no more. Fuck you and your whole set. Mad Man, Lil Blue, take this faggot somewhere and waste him. When you're done, dump his body in Swan hood."

"Wait, man!" Pudgy pleaded, as the youngsters grabbed hold of him. "We didn't hit Gunn."

"Yeah, so who the fuck put the work in on my uncle, Santa

Claus? Don't change the fact that a fuck nigga in a red suit did it."

"Gutter." Pudgy tried to compose himself. "Please, just meet with Trik. He can clear this whole mess up."

"Don't listen to him," Rahkim said. "Trik is probably just trying to lure us out. Let's smoke this muthafucka for the big homey, nephew."

"It ain't like that, man," Pudgy insisted. "Trik just wants to bring an end to all this shit. On my kids, we ain't lay hands on yo people."

Gutter mulled it over for a few. Though Trik was quite a few years older than him, Gutter knew what he was about. Back in the day Trik had the reputation of being one of the most savage niggaz in the hood. If he wanted to get at the Soladines he wouldn't have sent a messenger, he would've come in with an army. But for as savage as Trik was, he was one of the few niggaz left who respected the old codes.

"Okay, we'll meet with Trik," Gutter agreed. Rahkim started to protest, but Gutter waved him silent. "When and where?"

Pudgy visibly relaxed. "Trik said y'all could meet at the Beverly Center."

"Fuck that nigga, who say he get to pick where the fuck we meet? Them ol ho-ass niggaz probably got something cooked up over that way."

"Dawg, I wouldn't play wit y'all or my life like that, Trik ain't plotting," Pudgy tried to convince Gutter.

"Nah, cuz, I'm wit my uncle on this one. We pick the spot or it don't happen." Gutter thought on it for a minute. "That Beverly Center shit is out; we'll meet in the Beach...the old church on Fourth."

"Okay, man, you got that. I'll go tell him." Pudgy made to leave, but Gutter stopped him.

"Hold on, cuz. I'm reasonable, not stupid. *Call* Trik and tell him. Your ass is staying here. Mad Man, Lil Blue"—Gutter turned to the youths—"take this fool somewhere and sit on him until you hear from us." He turned back to Pudgy. "If this does turn out to be some funny shit, I'm gonna let my niggaz take turns fucking you up. Then I'm gonna cut your throat from ear to ear."

Pudgy didn't know Gutter that well, but he knew from the young man's reputation that he was serious. Trik seemed sincere about his intentions, but Pudgy hadn't been willing to bet his life on it. Now it seemed that he didn't have a choice in the matter.

AFTER PUDGY placed the phone call to Trik, he was escorted to an abandoned house on the outskirts of town. Gutter, followed by Criminal and Rahkim, made his way back to the house. Rahkim complained the whole time, saying how they should've just blasted Pudgy, and Gutter did his best to ignore him. He knew that they could keep killing Bloods from now until the end of the year, but there was no guarantee that they'd be any closer to catching Gunn's killer. He would meet with Trik to see if his words held any truth, but if they didn't, he'd be another dead slob.

When they reached the house Monifa was still standing on the porch where he had left her. At first she appeared rattled, but once she noticed they had all come back in one piece she relaxed. She knew better than to ask Gutter what had happened in front of Rahkim and Criminal, so she stored it away for later. She informed him that she had to make a run, and she'd be back in a little while. After kissing him on the cheek, she got in her car and pulled off.

Gutter had been in the house for about fifteen minutes when Snake Eyes came in. The young attorney's cane clicked against the hardwood floor as he crossed the foyer into the living room.

Though his limp had improved over the years, he still sometimes depended on the walking stick for balance. After speaking to everyone, he made his way to the backyard where Gutter was sitting on a lawn chair talking to Criminal.

"What up, Harlem?" Snake Eyes dapped him.

"Ain't shit, we got a lead on Gunn's killer so we gonna mash in a few." Gutter filled him in.

"Well, you're gonna have to fill me in because I got something a little more pressing to holla at you about." Snake Eyes took Gutter gently by the arm and steered him out of earshot of everyone else. "I got a call from Sharell today, she says she's been trying to call you, but keeps getting the voice mail."

"I kinda smashed my phone. I'll call her when I get in the house. Is everything okay?" Gutter asked.

"Yeah, she was ecstatic actually. Satin is at your house," Snake Eyes told him. Gutter just smiled. "G, you wanna explain to me how you were able to get her released from the hospital?"

"Trust me, cuz, you don't even wanna know, loc. But check, they say Trik from Swan wanna jaw about who bust on Unc."

Snake Eyes raised his eyebrows. "Straight up?" he asked, momentarily forgetting about the fugitive.

"Square biz, homey. He say he got some information on who popped him up and he wanna meet with me."

"You think he trying to plot?" Snake asked.

"Man, if he don't play fair Ima let Criminal and them niggaz break that power saw in on Pudgy's fat ass."

"Shit, I'm rolling with y'all," Snake Eyes declared. He had a fire in his eyes that Gutter hadn't seen in quite a few years.

"Nah, Snake. It might get ugly, and you're too valuable to get caught up in some bullshit," Gutter explained.

"You can't cut me outta this one," Snake Eyes insisted. "Big

Gunn was always looking out for me, and I want to see his killer brought to justice, *hood* justice."

Gutter couldn't even argue the fact that Snake Eyes had a very valid point. Of all his comrades, Snake Eyes had been the closest to Gunn. Not only did he school him to the streets, but he was the main reason why Snake Eyes didn't fall under the sword after the O'Leary murder.

There were several gang factions, Crip and Blood, that didn't appreciate the heat the cop killers had brought down on them. Lou-Loc and Gutter were safely tucked away on the East Coast, but Snake Eyes had remained in California to finish school. A few cats thought about getting at him, or maybe even turning him in to call the dogs off, but Gunn made it very clear that if anything happened to Snake Eyes, the hand of death would fall on the offender. So, with Gunn as his guardian angel, Snake Eyes was able to finish school and pass the bar. Though his main legal practice was based in Miami, he made frequent trips to L.A., where he did consulting out of a small office downtown, off Central Avenue.

"A'ight then," Gutter agreed. "But you keep your ass out of the fire if it gets hot, Snake."

"Man, stop acting like we ain't come up under the same knuckles." Snake Eyes waved him off.

"Now, when we go through there we ain't gonna roll deep, but we gonna bring muscle and insurance. Criminal"—he turned to the youngster—"round up two or three of your best shooters, I got something I need y'all little niggaz to do."

"All day, cuz," Criminal said with vigor.

"Snake." Gutter turned to his longtime friend. "Walk with me, counselor. We've got plans to lay and enemies to blast."

———

"SPEAK ON it," Major Blood said into his cell phone. He listened for a minute as his little cousin Reckless brought him up to speed on what was popping on the west.

"Yeah, they snatched his fat ass out in Torrence," Reckless said. Major could hear the mirth in his voice. "Trik is trying to smooth things over with them sucka-ass niggaz, you want me to go see him?" the young boy asked, eager to lay something down for the cause.

Major Blood thought on it for a minute. "Nah, let that Jheri curl–wearing muthafucka breathe for now. Once I take care of shit out here, we can put the second phase of our plan in motion. Just lay low until it's time to mash niggaz out."

"You got that, big homey. So when we gonna move on the old heads?" Reckless asked. He hated missing out on all the killing he was sure his cousin was putting down on the East Coast.

"In due time, Blood, for right now you just keep your eyes and ears open," Major told him.

"A'ight then, see about me." Reckless ended the call.

Major sat, processing what he had just learned. He wished he could be there to see the look on Gutter's face when the mystery finally unfolded, but it would have to wait. There were things that he still had to put in order before his plan could come full circle. The UBN could fool themselves into believing they were running the show, but when the smoke cleared Major Blood would show them all who was really in power.

chapter 23

D ANNY AND Tears walked into the garage of the Soladine house to find it overrun with soldiers. Men sat on crates or leaned against walls, chatting. The fact that they were all armed told them that something was up. In the center of the mix were Gutter, Snake Eyes, and Criminal. Snake Eyes was leaning in whispering to Gutter, who was loading an AK-47.

"Damn, it looks like Kuwait in this piece," Danny said, handing Gutter the box containing his new cell phone.

Tears gave all the men dap and leaned against the workbench, which held a variety of firearms. "Looks like you niggaz is fixing to ride?"

"We are," Criminal said. Seeing the confused looks on Danny's and Tear's faces Criminal went on to rundown what Pudgy had told him.

"You think these niggaz is on the level?" Tears asked, taking a Mac 11 from the workbench, and checking the clip.

"We'll know in a little while," Snake Eyes said, popping a clip in a 9 and reaching for the next weapon to load. "We're meeting them niggaz in Long Beach."

Danny picked up a shotgun and cocked it. "Now, this is what I'm talking about."

Criminal twisted his brown face in disgust. "Homey, put that strap down before you hurt somebody. This ain't no fucking game, so be cool."

"Come on, man. You act like I ain't gangsta with mine." Danny puffed up.

Criminal studied his East Coast cousin for a minute before responding. "Trip this, cuz; it's easy to sike ya self up to ride on a nigga, but sometimes the coin flips and you can wind up on the other side of the pistol." He raised his shirt so Danny could see the darkened lumps from healed-over gunshot wounds. "My nigga if I don't know nothing else I know you die the way you live and I plan on going all the way with it." Criminal brandished a long pistol.

Danny held Criminal's gaze, but the lifeless eyes staring back at him swept a phantom wind across the back of his neck. "I can respect that, homey. Look, all I'm saying is that if my homey Gutter is riding into a dangerous situation, I'm going too."

"It's cool," Gutter spoke up. He looked at his protégé seriously and asked, "So you really trying to ride the train?"

Danny stared at Gutter and said, "All day. One thing you always told me was that the set came before anything. If you 'bout to sit wit the devil then you might as well get me a chair."

Gutter held out his fist. "Solid, little brother."

"Harlem gangsta to the death, big homey," Danny declared loud enough for everyone to hear, and pounded Gutter's fist.

MAJOR BLOOD sat motionless in the armchair of his hotel room. Though he wasn't ranting, as Miguel thought he'd be, the rage in his eyes was apparent. Resting on his lap was a copy of the *Daily News*. Within its pages two articles caught Major Blood's eye. The first was about two men killed in a gangland shooting. J. B. and Steve had been good soldiers, but at the end of the day they were expendable. What pissed him off about reading of their deaths was the fact that his warning to Pop Top had been ignored. Steps would have to be taken to show Harlem that he meant business.

The most interesting article was about a woman who had been found dead at a Connecticut mental institution. The ironic part about it was that it wasn't Satin. The woman who had been killed was supposed to have been in another room, but somehow ended up in Satin's bed that night. Ms. Angelino had vanished and neither the staff nor the authorities had a clue as to where she'd gone. Major Blood crumbled the newspaper and tossed it into the corner.

"That's some crazy shit, blood," Miguel said. "What do you think happened to the bitch?"

"How the fuck would I know," Major snapped. He had a perfect record as far as contract kills went and Satin had just screwed it up. When he found out who had helped her to escape he vowed that they'll die slower than she will.

"Something has gotta be done, man," Eddie added. "Pop Top waxed Vlad and Pook then he had at least five of ours in Brooklyn murked. If we let those fuckers get away with killing them cats it ain't gonna look good on us."

Major turned his cold stare to Eddie. "You know what, you have a knack for pointing out the obvious, you silly muthafucka. Next time I'll break your jaw instead of your nose, maybe then you won't say such stupid shit."

Eddie touched his swollen nose, and sucked his teeth. He hadn't known Major that long, but he already couldn't stand him.

"Kick back, Eddie," Tito said, trying to defuse the situation. "So, what we gonna do now, Major?" he addressed his namesake.

"We start hacking away at the limbs of Harlem Crip until it's time to take the head," Major told him. "I'm 'bout to call my little nigga B-High and tell him it's time to start leaking muthafuckas. Maybe he can get the point across better than I can," he said with a wicked edge to his voice.

"Man, you keep talking 'bout this lil nigga, but how come don't none of us know him, I assume he Blood?" Eddie asked, which got him a *stupid* look from Major Blood. "Be cool, nigga, the only reason I asked is because I don't know his moniker, what's the skinny on him?"

"Ain't no skinny, that's my nigga from the way. Solid-ass soldier," Major said, not wanting to go into B-High's shaky history. "Man, we can play twenty-one questions later, y'all go do whatever you gotta do for the day because tonight we riding to the strip joint."

"Yeah, I could go for that. Fuck a few of them fine-ass black bitches or something tonight." Miguel rubbed his hands together.

Major Blood looked at him as if Miguel was as dim-witted as Eddie. "Man, we ain't going to catch no bitches, we going to catch some cases."

"What's the plan, Blood?" Tito asked.

Major just grinned and said, "To kill as many muthafuckas as we can without getting caught."

POP TOP paced the storage unit trying to suck the life out of a Newport. The cigarette had already burned almost down to the filter, but it didn't stop him from taking one last drag before tossing it to the ground and fishing around in his pocket for another one. C-style had just delivered the news of China's suicide and of all the homeys he seemed to be taking it the hardest.

Though he gave China more grief than anyone else, he was quite fond of the little soldier. He couldn't help but wonder if he hadn't convinced him to go on the hit then maybe the little boy would still be among them, laughing and rolling the blunts. China was yet another name added to the steadily growing list of casualties.

"Damn, I can't believe the little nigga off'd himself," High Side said from the crate he was sitting on.

"Yo, the boy was straight laid out!" C-style said emotionally.

"Fuck," Pop Top growled, slamming his fist into the wall, rattling the cool metal. "If it ain't bad enough that this Major Blood nigga is picking us off, now you got niggaz cashing in their own chips."

"Man, I say we move on these niggaz, son. I don't like the idea of having to constantly watch my back," High Side said.

"How we gonna move on them when we don't know where the fuck to find them? This Major Blood nigga is like HIV, every time he shows up somebody dies," Hollywood pointed out.

"Dawg, I don't know how y'all feel, but I say we get low until Gutter comes back. He'll know how to handle this," Rob suggested.

"Get low?" Pop Top glared at Rob. "Nigga, this is war, ain't no getting low. Either you a soldier or a pussy? Which one is it?"

"I ain't no pussy," Rob said softly.

"Then stop acting like one." Pop Top went back to his pacing. He hadn't meant to be so short with Young Rob, but he was stressed the fuck out. Gutter had entrusted him with the well-being of the set and he was letting the situation with the Bloods get out of control. The local crews were easy enough to deal with, but Major Blood was another story. Whereas the young cats running around New York were wolves, Major Blood was a snake and proving to be more trouble than Pop Top had expected. His rational mind told him to call Gutter, but Pop Top never moved rationally.

"We gotta get a handle on this, cousins," Pop Top continued. "We've fought too hard to get a lock on Harlem to let some out-of-town nigga come through and fuck it up." He took a minute to light the cigarette dangling between his lips. "I'm gonna put something together to bring an end to this Major Blood nigga, in the meantime y'all just be on point. I want every muthafucka on the set to be armed at all times."

"That's how I roll anyway, cuz, you know that." High Side brandished his pistol. "First nigga come at me sideways is gonna get his muthafucking head popped off."

"Man, y'all can sit around playing cowboys and Indians, but I'm about to hit the bricks and see about my scratch," Hollywood said, heading for the door.

"Where the fuck is you going?" Pop Top asked.

"I gotta go meet the boy, Goldie, and open up shop. Pussy ain't gonna sell itself. Side"—he turned to High Side—"you still coming through later?"

"Hell yeah, nigga. I'm gonna scoop the boy, Kiss, then we'll push through the spot. I wanna see what you lame muthafuckas is working with anyway," High Side teased him.

"Fuck you, nigga, just make sure you bring some of that good crack money to spend wit my bitches!" Hollywood shot back before leaving the unit.

"HOW IS she?" Gutter asked.

"She's still a little out of it from all the drugs they've been pumping into her, but other than that she seems fine," Sharell said into her cell phone, which was cradled between her ear and shoulder. "I still don't know how he managed to get her out of the hospital."

"Cross has a way of getting in and out of places most people can't," Gutter told her.

"Who is he? I mean, I know he was a friend of Lou-Loc's, but he ain't no gangster."

"You're right, he ain't no gangsta," Gutter said, thinking about the eerie Cross. "But who he is ain't important right now, baby. What's important is that Satin is safe."

Sharell could sense that he was uncomfortable talking about Cross so she let it rest. "So, when do you think you'll be back?"

"Shouldn't be more than a day or so. You know we don't sit on bodies more than forty-eight hours before entering them into the Mosoleum."

"Kenyatta, I can't tell you how sorry I am about Gunn. I only wish I could've been there for the funeral. Please tell Rahshida I'm sorry," she said sincerely.

"I will, ma, and don't trip she understands." He paused as he watched Monifa walk past the kitchen and give him a look.

"Kenyatta, is everything okay?" Sharell asked.

"Yeah, everything is cool. I'm just tripping off my uncle being gone," he lied.

"Don't you worry about that, Ken, he's with the Lord now. You just be strong, you hear me?"

"Yeah, I hear you." His eyes followed Monifa's every move. He was so engrossed in her that he only half heard Sharell still talking.

"Kenyatta, did you hear me?"

"Sorry, what'd you say?"

"I said I love you," she repeated.

"Oh, I love you too," his voice was barely above a whisper. "A'ight, let me go on out here and see about Lil Gunn. I'll call you later on, okay?"

"A'ight, you do what you gotta do and come back to me in one piece."

"No doubt, later boo." He ended the call. He smiled at Monifa, who was watching him intently. Instead of returning the gesture she sucked her teeth and walked out the front door. "Can't win for losing," Gutter said as he headed out the back door to the yard.

part III

DOMINO EFFECT

chapter 24

SATIN SAT on the love seat in the plush living room staring out the window at downtown Brooklyn. She thought she had been dreaming that night in the hospital when Cross had come. She was afraid of the dark-skinned man at first, but there was a calming quality to him... almost a familiarity. When she was placed into the back of the darkened van she thought sure that it would be her last ride, but to her surprise he had brought her to Sharell. From what she was able to gather from the conversation he had done it for Lou-Loc. She had no idea what kind of connection the Goth could've had with Lou-Loc, but she would look into that afterward. What mattered now was that she was free to raise her child.

"How're you feeling, Satin?" Sharell descended the stairs. She was dressed in a pair of Bibs and white Air Max. Her stomach looked as if it would burst through the fabric if she moved the wrong way.

Satin smiled up at her. "Considering... yeah, I'm cool."

Sharell sat on the couch and placed a hand over Satin's. "Baby, you've been through a lot so it's gonna take some time to heal. And never forget that me and Kenyatta got your back."

"Gutter," Satin said out loud, listening to the name that she had heard dozens of times. "It's funny, because I've only heard stories about him and I feel like I've known him since forever."

"You don't go listening to what people have to say about my Ken, he ain't that bad," Sharell joked. "Anyhow, I gotta run out real quick, but I'm coming right back. You sure you don't wanna come with me and get some air, sugar?"

"Nah, I'm okay, but thanks. I think I'm just gonna stay in and get my head together," Satin told her.

"Okay, but you know you can't spend the rest of your days hiding in the house. We still gotta get you to the gynecologist to see about my little niece or nephew, but I wanna speak to Kenyatta and Snake Eyes to see what the legal situation is gonna look like."

"God, I'll probably be a fugitive for the rest of my days." Satin put her head in her hands.

"You don't go worrying about that, I'm sure Snake Eyes is gonna get the matter cleared up. At the least he can tie it up in so much red tape that the baby will be starting pre-k by the time you go to trial. We didn't wait this long to get you back, just to have them snatch you away again, Satin. Leave it in the Lord's hands and everything will be fine." She hugged her.

"Thank you, Sharell." Satin squeezed her back. "You hardly know me and you've already done so much. I don't know how I could ever repay you."

"Don't even worry about that, Satin. Lou-Loc was my brother so that makes you my sister. Family will take care of family, baby. Now let me get outta here so I can hurry up and get back." Sharell stood to leave. "There are some leftovers in the fridge in case you get hungry, but I'm gonna bring some manna back with me when I come. You want me to leave Mohammad here with you while I'm gone?"

Satin recalled the dark-haired man who stood between Sharell and Cross, and how empty his eyes were even in the face of certain death. Being around Cross was frightening, but there wasn't much comfort with Mohammad either.

"I'll be cool." Satin rubbed her arms.

"Okay, well I'll see you in a few hours. If you need me just call." Sharell held up her cell phone. Once she was sure that Satin was good she headed out.

When the door locked behind her, Satin curled her legs beneath her on the couch and picked up the remote. It had been so long since she'd watched videos that she hoped she could keep up with the new music scene.

SHARELL STEPPED out of her building, humming a tune with a name she didn't remember, but it brought her plenty of joy as a child. Mohammad nodded at her passing, but didn't get out of his car, nor did she expect him to. Though his eyes seemed as alert as ever, she knew that the incident with Cross had disturbed him. After the encounter he opened his mouth to apologize, but Sharell waved him silent.

She hit the remote, popping the locks on her X5, and tossed her purse in the backseat. When she went to climb behind the wheel a cold chill ran up her back. She glanced around cautiously, but didn't see anything out of the ordinary on the block. Shrugging it off as the nervousness that came with harboring a fugitive, Sharell got behind the wheel and started the car.

———

WHEN B-HIGH raised his face from the armrest, he looked like he'd been given a facial using baking powder. His eyes were wide and glassy, and his limbs were pumped with adrenaline. He tried to clear his nostril, but there was too much cocaine lodged in it. The Spanish cats he scored from were trying to bust his brain wide-open with the sweet white they served up. Reluctantly, he removed a napkin from the floor and blew his nose. He hated to waste good cocaine, but it was better than suffocating himself.

It turned out to be a good thing that the coke got lodged in his nose. Otherwise he might've missed Sharell coming out of her building. The powder he'd snorted supercharged his brain and demanded he take her on the spot, but the killer Major Blood had shaped held him in his seat. There were too many people on the block and he doubted if he could even get to her before her shadow popped off. *Patience over passion,* he told himself.

Sharell wasn't wearing a uniform so he knew that she wasn't going to work. It was probably a short run, because Sharell didn't stray too far from home if it wasn't work-related, and even when it wasn't her shadow was forever present.

B-High had gotten a kick out of the standoff between the two men. He was actually about to turn in for the night when he saw Sharell come out of the building, with her bodyguard standing out in the open. Until then he had been little more than a shade that she whispered to when she thought no one was watching. B-High was always watching, just like Major Blood had taught him. He didn't know what part the disheveled-looking girl played in Major's plan, but people skulking around in the night were always worth looking into.

From a slumped position in his seat he watched Sharell head toward her car. He'd almost thought she spotted him when she looked around suspiciously. Thankfully, she kept moving. Right after Sharell pulled out, the shadow got on her tail. Sliding from his car he moved to Sharell's building. It didn't take much for him to jimmy the lock and slip in. He found a nondescript utility closet and ducked inside. B-High took the small tinfoil package from his pocket. Sharell was sure to be gone for at least a few hours so he decided to party a little while he waited.

chapter 25

IGH SIDE was lounging in front of the corner store on 142nd and Lenox Avenue, drinking a forty ounce. Periodically he would look up from the newspaper on his lap and scan the block for signs of trouble. Though his friend hadn't said it, he knew the situation unfolding around Harlem had him rattled. Next to Gutter, Pop Top was the most dangerous cat in Harlem, so if Major Blood had him spooked then they had a serious problem.

Around the corner, inside of the second building, a young man served the fiends that High Side sent his way. When Lou-Loc had divided up the territories this became High Side's domain. He had occasional trouble with the Blood cats from Seventh, but for the most part they respected him enough not to tread directly on his turf.

"Break ya self, nigga!" Young Rob said, walking up on High Side. He was followed by C-style, and they both looked high as hell.

"Man, you need to quit playing so much. You know we got

drama out here, fool. Playing like that can get yo shit pushed back," High Side told him.

"Nigga stop fronting like you extra G wit it. You're so caught up in that forty and last night's basketball scores that you ain't even on point. What you gonna do if that nigga Major Blood run up on you?"

High Side smiled and lifted the newspaper, exposing the large handgun on his lap. "Put a fucking hole in him."

"Solid." Rob gave him dap. "So, what's the word on the streets?"

High Side shrugged. "Not much. There were a few incidents, but since them Brownsville niggaz put the mash on them two cats, it's been pretty quiet."

"I'm glad to hear that," C-style said. "Since y'all niggaz been banging out the block has been on fire. I can't even pump my little weed in the hood no more."

"You wasn't getting no money anyhow," Rob joked.

Rob and C-style traded insults, while High Side laughed at both of them. From the corner of his eye, he spotted a car pulling up to the light. It wasn't unusual as 142nd was a busy block. The strange part about it was the way the female passenger in the back-seat was looking at him. It wasn't a look of recognition, but one of hatred. At the moment the passenger side door swung open, High Side made his move.

High Side sprang to his feet and threw the crate he was sitting on at the car, shattering the windshield. The young man who had been trying to climb from the car fell back, trying to avoid the spray of glass. The back door opened up and Ruby hopped out, blasting away with her Desert Eagle. The storefront glass shattered, but none of the bullets hit anyone.

Ruby's eyes flashed pure hatred as she tried to lay down her enemies. When she had approached Hawk about sanctioning a hit on Harlem, he brushed her off, saying that Major would handle it. He might've had faith in the assassin handling the problem, but Ruby refused to sit by and wait. The Crips would answer for the murder of her lover.

Rob knocked C-style to the ground just as bullets whistled over their heads. Not bothering to see if she was hit, Rob rolled on his back and began firing his .38. The bullets tore into the car, but he too failed to hit anyone.

Two more men climbed from the now bullet-riddled car as it turned the corner of Lenox Avenue. They opened fire on the block, not really caring who they hit. High Side got low and cut through the crowd of people that were scattering up the block. Firing from one knee, he hit one of the shooters in the throat. The man dropped his gun and clutched at the hole in his neck. Blood spilled over his fingers and down the front of his shirt as he crashed to the ground.

"Die muthafuckas!" Ruby roared, firing her cannon. The Eagle sent shock waves up her arm every time it bucked, but she held it in a death grip. She didn't even bother to take cover as Rob and High Side exchanged fire with her crew. Her own safety was no longer an issue. All that mattered to her was revenge.

Rob tried to get out of the line of fire, but was too slow. Ruby hit him once in the leg and twice in the back. Rob tried to keep his feet, but vertigo overcame him and he hit the ground. Rob was leaking all over the place, but he still tried to crawl to the hysterical C-style.

The remaining shooter had managed to back High Side into the doorway of the bodega. The small man who worked the register quickly slammed the small wooden door, separating himself from the skirmish and grabbed his phone to call the police. The shooter was trying to bring his firing arm around, but High Side held onto his wrist for dear life, while hitting him with a series of left hooks to the skull.

Over the shooter's shoulder he saw his little man, Young Rob, slam face first into the ground. Ruby was easing up on the boy's prone body to finish him off, but High Side was too busy fighting for his own life to do anything about it. He watched in horror as she knelt beside Rob and blew the back of his head off with the Eagle.

High Side's grief lasted for about five seconds before it was replaced with blinding rage. He grabbed the shooter by his arm and slammed his knee into it, at the elbow. The shooter howled in pain as the gun went flying from his hand. High Side cracked him with a savage right to the jaw, sending him spilling out onto the street. High Side went to pen him, but froze when he heard a round being chambered to his right.

Ruby drew a bead on High Side, who was frozen like a deer in headlights, and prepared to finish him off. Though she knew the young man wasn't Gutter, he'd been identified as a shooter for Harlem Crip. High Side had murdered quite a few of her folk, so he definitely had to go. No sooner than Ruby's finger brushed the trigger, pain exploded in her chest. She looked down at her blouse, which now had a red stain in the middle. On shaky legs, Ruby turned to see C-style holding Rob's smoking gun.

"Bitch," Ruby gasped. "You shot me." She was dead before she hit the ground.

With the immediate threat being taken care of, High Side refocused his attention on his attempted murderer. The shooter's arm hung limp at his side as he tried to get up using one arm. High Side drew his pocketknife and grabbed the shooter by the back of his shirt.

"Fuck you think you going?" He yanked the shooter to his feet. "You was gonna kill me huh, muthafucka?" High Side cut his face with the blade. "Yeah, I told you niggaz about fucking around in Harlem." He plunged the knife into the shooter's gut. High Side stabbed him over and over again. Even when the shooter went down, High Side continued to plunge the knife into his chest, arms, legs, or whatever else was exposed. Only when he heard the familiar police sirens in the distance did he stop stabbing the man.

Wiggling the blade deeper into the wound, High Side broke it off in the man's chest then addressed C-style. "Baby girl, we gotta roll!" High Side called, while wiping his bloody hands on the dead shooter's pants.

"Oh, Rob," she sighed over his ruined body.

"C, we gotta go, now!" High Side said more forcefully. When C-style didn't respond, he grabbed her by the arms and yanked her to her feet. "C"—he turned her to face him—"Cory, that nigga gone and you can't honor his memory behind no damn bars. Now bring yo ass on, girl!"

C-style said her final goodbyes to Rob and allowed High Side to lead her away at a jog. In the course of a few seconds her life had been irreversibly changed. Rob was dead and she had officially caught her first body. Until then she had been little more than a supporter, but now found herself in it up to her ass.

chapter 26

SHARELL HAD never been happier to see her little Brooklyn block. What started out as a quick outing ended up with her shopping on 125th for her and Satin, and hitting the bootlegger for some movies. She knew that the girl was going through a lot and she wanted to plan a girls' night out to help her on the road to recovery. After being near catatonic for so long she needed to refamiliarize herself with the world.

She locked her door and pulled her jacket closed to protect her from the whipping winds. It seemed like out of nowhere the weather had dropped since earlier. Just as she reached the front of the building a fashion magazine that she'd been holding blew away. She thought about chasing it, but it was chilly and she wanted to get inside with the bags.

Outside her apartment door she could hear the sounds of rap videos coming from the television. Good, Satin was still awake so she could see her new outfits. The moment Sharell turned the key in the lock she heard a door behind her swing open. When she turned around she found herself nose to barrel with a wild-eyed man holding a gun.

"Bitch, if you even think about screaming I'm gonna peel yo shit," B-High warned. The coke had him charged so his hand trembled a bit.

"Please, just take it. Don't hurt me!" Sharell pleaded, trying to hand him her shopping bags and purse.

"I don't want ya fucking goodie bag." He slapped the bags away viciously. "Back into the crib, bitch, now!" he ordered.

"Sharell, is that you?" Satin called from the couch, where she had been perched most of the day. She knew she heard Sharell unlock the door, but wondered who she could be talking to? When she got off the couch to investigate, Sharell spilled into the living room, almost knocking her over. Hot on her heels was a man with a gun. Satin thought about going to the kitchen for a knife, but the man must've been reading her mind because he took the gun off Sharell and trained it on Satin.

"Don't get cute, bitch," he warned. "Both of y'all get on the couch." He waved the pistol. Sharell complied, but Satin stood where she was. It wasn't that she was trying to be defiant, but her legs wouldn't cooperate with her.

"You hear me talking to you." B-High stepped forward and placed the gun against Satin's forehead. Tears ran freely from the girl's terror-filled eyes, thinking that she was going to die that night and her escape from the institution would've been in vain.

"Don't! She's fresh out of a mental hospital and probably isn't processing what you're telling her!" Sharell screamed. She was trying to buy them some time so she could figure a way out of the mess. Her gun was inside her purse, lying on the hallway floor outside the apartment. She also had a pager that would alert Mohammad to trouble, but it was useless, hanging from her keychain, which was still dangling from the lock in the front door. Unless she figured something out they'd both be dead.

"Let's see if she processes this." B-High slapped Satin viciously in the face.

She spun and had it not been for the couch she'd have hit the floor. Satin touched her hand to her lip and it came away bloody. Satin had fought her brothers all throughout her childhood for trying to put their hands on her, but a stranger doing it was even more of an insult. Though she knew she was holding the short end of the stick, she couldn't help but wish that she'd still had the gun she'd used to murder her brother.

"That's better." B-High smiled. He reached into his jacket pocket and pulled out a roll of duct tape. "Here you go." He tossed the roll next to Satin. "Tape your friend up, and make sure you do it good, because if she causes any shit before I'm done I'm gonna have to shoot her sooner than I intended."

"What do you want?" Sharell asked with tears running from her eyes.

"I want your faggot-ass man's head on a stick for what his family did to my peoples, but I'll settle for a piece of that fine Spanish tail." He nodded at Satin.

"Don't you touch her." Sharell moved to cover Satin. Satin was sitting on the couch with her knees curled to her chest, rocking. Sharell didn't know what was going through Satin's mind at the time, but if looks could kill the man would've dropped dead on the spot.

"Bitch, get yo ass out the way." B-High grabbed a handful of Sharell's hair and yanked her viciously from the couch. When she was on her feet, he slapped her twice across the face and tossed her across the living room. Satin moved to help Sharell but B-High grabbed a handful of the oversized T-shirt she was wearing and threw her back onto the couch. "Where the fuck do you think you're going?" He stepped closer to her.

"Don't touch her!" Sharell screamed. Her side hurt like hell, but luckily for her, and B-High, she didn't fall on her stomach.

"Shut you fat ass up." B-High pointed the gun at Sharell. "When I'm done with her, I'll get to you. I hear pregnant pussy is pretty good." He snickered and turned back to Satin. "If you don't fight, I'll make sure I shoot you in the head so at least you'll die quick."

Satin tried to crawl under the sofa cushion as B-High undid his belt. The hungry look in his eyes reminded her of the way the orderlies looked at her at the institution. On more than one occasion the men working the graveyard shift had come into her room and fondled her. A time or two they had even penetrated her, but thankfully they used protection. Though she was nonresponsive most of the time, Satin was aware of just about everything around her. Just the thought of her body being violated again made Satin snap.

When B-High placed his gun on the floor to balance himself, Satin was on him like a wild cat. B-High tried to grab her wrists, but her arms were flailing too wildly. She raked her nails across his face and sank her teeth into his collarbone, drawing a scream from him that sounded like a wounded animal as she tore a chunk of flesh from him.

"Crazy bitch." He punched her in the face. Satin bounced off the couch and landed on the floor. "Now I'm gonna shove it in your ass instead of your pussy. Then I'm gonna blow your stinking hole out," he promised, retrieving his pistol from the floor.

B-High lowered himself to the ground over Satin, keeping the gun pointed at her head as he worked her T-shirt up. She was wearing a pair of cheap cotton panties that he ripped away with little effort. B-High admired her unkept bush and thought how warm her hole must be. Not caring if she was wet or not he began forcing himself inside her. Satin whimpered like a wounded puppy as she felt B-High's thick penis splitting her open. She had been through a great many things in her young life, but this was by far the worst. As the head of B-High's penis slipped past her dry lips she wondered if death would've been so bad after all. Closing her eyes, she prepared for the worst.

THERE WAS a popping sound, followed by something warm splashing on Satin's face. She opened her eyes in time to see B-High clutch at his shoulder just before rolling off her. Behind him, Sharell stood, holding her smoking .22.

"Damn it, are both of you bitches crazy!" B-High barked, staggering to his feet.

"As God is my witness, if you don't get out of my house I will kill you!" Sharell warned in a shaky voice.

"Okay, take it easy, shorty." B-High raised his hands over his head and began easing along the wall toward the door. "I'm leaving, just don't shoot again."

Seeing that he was complying, Sharell relaxed a bit, which was a mistake. B-High lunged at her almost faster than she could pull the trigger. She tried to shoot him in the face, but the shot went wild and struck the wall. Before she could get off another round, B-High's fist slammed into her jaw with a sickening crunch, sending her crashing to the floor and the gun across the living room. She tried to get back to her feet, but B-High was on her with his hands wrapped around her throat.

"You stinking bitch, I'm gonna break your fucking neck!" he snarled, raining spit into her face. Sharell started seeing spots as it became harder and harder for her to breathe. Just before the darkness took her B-High suddenly stopped choking her. When her vision cleared she saw Mohammad towering over both of them, strangling B-High from behind. The man's eyes were slits of pure hate as his powerful hands worked B-High's neck. Satin noticed B-High trying to bring his gun up to take a shot at Mohammad and kicked his arm. The shot missed Mohammad's face, but grazed his cheek.

"Fucking worm!" Mohammad snarled, tossing the smaller man across the living room. B-High crashed into the entertainment system, breaking the screen on the plasma television. He looked like he was going to try and get up again, but ended up collapsing back to the ground.

"Are you okay?" Mohammad helped Sharell to her feet.

"Sore as hell, but I'll live. Thank you." She gave him a weak smile.

"No thanks needed, I gave my oath that no harm would come to you. Now, I've got to get you ladies out of here. Can you walk?" he asked Satin, who nodded. "Good, we've gotta go." He ushered them toward the door.

MOHAMMAD STEPPED from the building, sweeping the street with his pistol. His face stung and his shirt was covered in blood from his wound, but he would have to attend it later. What was important was getting his charges to safety.

Sharell followed him, dragging Satin by the hand. She tried to keep up, but the harsh concrete was tearing her bare feet up. The best she could do was hobble behind Sharell. After months of living in a dream, reality was coming at her at a faster pace than she was ready for.

"Start the car," Mohammad ordered, looking up and down the

block in case the would-be assassin had an accomplice. From the way people were running and screaming at the sight of the bloodied and armed man, it would only be a matter of time before the police showed up, and they didn't have time to explain what happened. The city was no longer safe for them.

Sharell's hand shook so violently that it took her four attempts to disarm the alarm and unlock the door. She hopped behind the wheel while Satin climbed in on the passenger side. The girl had a wild-eyed look to her and her body trembled uncontrollably.

"You okay?" Sharell asked as she started the car.

"What was that all about?" Satin asked, wrapping her arms around herself. She felt like her heart was going to leap from her chest due to all the excitement. If God was playing a joke by continuously throwing obstacles in her way, she sure as hell didn't find it funny.

"I don't know, but we sure ain't gonna stick around to find out." Sharell threw the car in gear. She hit the car behind her and the one in front of her trying to get out of the parking spot. With a dented fender and a busted headlight she was finally able to get out into the street. "Mohammad!" she called her shadow.

"I'm coming." He trotted around to the passenger's side. Before Mohammad could get all the way into the car, pain exploded in his back. He tried to right himself, but a second bullet hit him in the thigh, dropping him to one knee. He turned around and saw B-High standing in the doorway of the building, aiming his gun at the car. *Never leave a kill unfinished*, Sharif's words rang in his head as B-High shot out a window on the car.

"You fucking bitches!" he rasped. Mohammad had cracked his ribs, and he was sure to be suffering from a concussion, but the cocaine had him feeling like Superman.

"Mohammad!" Sharell screamed frantically.

"I'm good," he lied. "If you have to, go without me." He slammed the door. Mohammad rolled onto the hood of the car, upper body stretched across. Ignoring the pain that now racked his body, Mohammad drew a bead on B-High.

"Thought you could kill me?" B-High ranted, firing off a shot. "It over for you niggaz, Major Blood is gonna shut this shit down!" He fired another shot. "You muthafuckas..." that was as far as B-High got before a bullet went into his right eye and exited just behind his ear.

Mohammad collapsed across the hood of the car, finally overcome by his injuries. It took the combined efforts of Satin and Sharell to get him into the backseat. Satin sat with him, trying to stop the bleeding, while Sharell hopped behind the wheel and peeled off.

"We've gotta get you to a hospital," Sharell said, struggling to see the road in front of her through the tears.

"No...no hospitals," Mohammad said weakly. "Here." He handed her a bloody piece of paper that been in his pocket. "Put that address in the navigation system, that's our destination."

"Where are we going?" she asked, jumping on the B.Q.E. at Camden Plaza, heading for the Long Island Expressway.

"The only place where Gutter and Anwar felt you'd be truly safe," he said, before laying his head back and closing his eyes. His body had long ago gone numb from blood loss, but the first chills were starting to set into his muscles. He knew they were the first icy pulls of death, but he wouldn't accept it. He would live to see Sharell to the safe house, but when his task was done Anwar and Sharif would honor their promises.

chapter 27

THE **HUNTS** Point area of the Bronx was popular for two things: its factories and its sex trade. During the day it was lousy with trucks dropping and picking up deliveries, but when the sun set it got interesting. Whorehouses, strip clubs, and of course your street corner prostitutes, all opened for business when night fell. With all the nightly traffic Hunts Point generated it seemed like a no-brainer what to do with the property they'd purchased up there, they turned it into a strip club. The Blue Light was shaping up to be one of the premier spots in the area and Hollywood wore the fact that he owned a piece of it with more pride than a proud parent.

"Umm-hmm, this is my kind of place!" Dirty Bill exclaimed, eyeballing a chocolate doll strutting past in a black thong and high heels. He had gotten his name because no matter how many baths he took he still looked dirty.

"You know Wood got an eye for these bitches," Goldie replied. Much like Hollywood he was a young, fly nigga. You could always find Goldie dipped in jewels while the latest in designer wear draped his lanky frame. He was a handsome cat with smooth chocolate skin and could've easily been a model, but the streets took hold of him early in life.

It had initially been Goldie's idea to open a gentlemen's club, but he didn't have the capital. Hollywood, already being a part of the circuit, saw the potential in the idea and was quick to offer up what he had in the stash. It took some doing, but the two entrepreneurs managed to get the Blue Light off the ground and the buzz was getting crazy.

"Wood, we sho nuff gonna make some cake off this joint." Goldie rubbed his hands together.

"That's the general idea, cuz. Shit, there was times I had to keep these bitches humping around the clock to get that change up, but I can't even front, this shit was worth it," Hollywood said, watching the crowd. "I can't wait till High Side's and Bruticus's thirsty asses get here so they can peep this shit!"

"Say, speaking of High Side, y'all heard about that shoot-out on 142nd?" Dirty Bill asked.

"I heard a lil something-something. You know the hood talks." Goldie shrugged it off.

"Yeah, I heard that nigga, High Side, was out there tearing off slob asses!" Bill said excitedly. "Wood, you know how that nigga be on it, right?"

"Yeah, High Side is a true soldier, but I ain't heard nothing about him shooting nobody," Hollywood lied. He knew what had happened as soon as it went down because High Side and C-style had come through his brownstone after the shooting, but it wasn't his place to tell Bill that.

"Man, do you ever think about anything other than hood politics?" Goldie asked, clearly getting irritated with Dirty Bill.

"Hell nah." Bill looked at him as if he was crazy. "G, I eat, sleep, and breathe the hood. You gotta keep your ear to the streets if you plan on winning this game, and I've always been a sore loser."

"What's good, cat daddy?" a Puerto Rican girl with blond hair approached them. She was wearing a white bikini top and a see-through wrap skirt. Even if the material hadn't been transparent there was no way she could've hidden the horse-sized ass beneath it.

"Lexi, right?" Goldie smiled, exposing two rows of gold teeth.

"Ah, so you remember?" She smiled back.

"But of course. You look way different out of your clothes." Goldie openly eyed her.

"Everything is different when the clothes come off, poppy." It was only Lexi's second night at the club so Goldie hadn't really had a chance to pick her brain yet. Normally either he or Holly-wood would handpick the girls who worked at the club, but Lexi had interviewed with Joe and only met Goldie in passing. Joe raved about the girl's body and seeing her damn near naked Goldie understood why.

"I might just have to see about that," he replied.

"Mind if I sit down?" She motioned to the vacant stool between him and Hollywood. Goldie nodded. To his and especially Holly-wood's surprise she didn't sit on the stool, but on Hollywood's lap. Hollywood acted as if he didn't even notice her.

"Damn, Wood, you need some help with that?" Dirty Bill rubbed an ashy hand across Lexi's thigh. She smiled before slap-ping his hand away.

"You gotta pay to play." She pushed her breasts together, teas-ing him.

"If that's the case then you might as well rise the fuck up off me, because I sure as hell ain't no trick," Hollywood told her in an icy tone.

Lexi slid her ass further into Hollywood's groin. Even though he was wearing his game face she could feel his dick getting hard under her ass. "Baby, just because I'm young doesn't mean I'm stupid. I would never disrespect a true player like that," she said, looking over her shoulder at him.

"And what makes you think I'm a *true* player?" he asked.

Lexi flicked her tongue out then gave him a sly smile. "Everyone knows *big* Wood from Harlem. My home girl Janice says you're the man to see if a bitch wanna clock some real paper."

Hollywood quickly flipped through his mental rolodex and placed a face with the name. Janice was a young bitch he had met a while back at a dive called the News Room off Grand Concourse. She was a young mud-kicker dying to live the fast life, but was lazy as hell so she didn't make the grade.

"Well, in case you ain't heard, ya girl fell a lil short." He chuckled softly.

Lexi turned around and straddled his lap. There was a fierceness in her eyes that stirred something low in Hollywood's groin. "I said that was peoples, not my style." She took Hollywood's hand and placed it on her ass. "Wit all this junk I can't do nothing but get money."

Hollywood had to smile at her snappy comeback. "I'll tell you what." He eased her off his lap and slid off the stool. "Let's go on in the office and rap for a taste. Maybe we can come to some type of understanding."

"I thought you'd never ask." She swayed her big ass toward the office. Hollywood admired her ass for a second before following.

THE MINUTE their SUV touched the Bronx, Eddie was struck by a sinking feeling. Tito was behind the wheel with a cigarette dangling from his mouth, silently watching the streets, while Miguel sat next to him, using a handkerchief to load the clips to the various weapons they were carrying. Trailing them in a Camry was a cat named Boo and some wild-ass niggaz from Newark, who claimed Sex, Money, and Murder Bloods. There were six of them in total, making up what Major Blood had referred to as a war party.

Eddie watched Major as he bobbed his head to Mack 10's "Bang or Ball," mouthing along with the song. His heart seemed to swell with pride as he stacked his set in fluid motions that came from years of throwing it up. From the moment Eddie had laid eyes on the man at the airport he knew that he was going to be trouble, and the trail of bodies he was leaving was proof of that. Gutter's house was slowly slipping into chaos.

"Say, Blood, you hear me talking to you?" Major asked, snapping Eddie out of his daydream.

"Huh?"

"I said be the fuck on point," Major repeated. "We 'bout to roll into a fucking nest of vipers and I don't want no fuck-shit throwing my plan to the left."

"Fuck the left, it's right all night, we straight," Eddie said in a nasally tone. Since his nose had been broken it always felt like it was stopped up, making him sound like he had a cold.

"Fool, stop trying to act you niggaz out here is properly educated. Just be on point, ya raccoon-looking muthafucka," Major taunted Eddie who was also sporting two black eyes, caused by the broken nose. Eddie knew better than to try and get fly out of his mouth with Major Blood, but Miguel snickering gave him a new target to direct his anger at.

"Fuck you laughing at, Blood?" Eddie glared at Miguel.

"*You*, nigga. I can't front, you do kinda look like a raccoon with them shiners, kid," Miguel pointed out.

"Fuck you, ho-ass nigga. I'd like to see ya ass try and go toe-to-toe with me!" Eddie snapped.

"Toe-to-toe my ass, Eddie, you know damn well you can't fight!" Miguel shot back. Miguel was an easygoing cat, but next to Tito and Major he was the most thorough cat in the car.

"Man, why don't the both of y'all shut the fuck up." Tito glanced back at them. "Major is right. We 'bout to go at these niggaz on they own turf and I don't plan on none of my home boys getting left behind. We ride or die together."

"Ain't y'all the cutest, kicking that real comrade shit. Look, fellas," Major addressed everyone in the car, "this murder shit ain't rocket science, but there's an art to it. All we gotta do is go in that bitch and wet everything moving then bounce, simple," Major said as if it was just another day at the office, which to him it was.

"Shit, I'm down wit that one-eighty-seven all day, but this ain't gonna be easy. All them niggaz gonna be in there strapped and, of course, they gonna have security at the door. How we gonna bust on the bouncers and still be able to creep on them crabs? As soon as they hear the gunshots it's gonna be like the Fourth of fucking July," Miguel pointed out.

Major turned his attention to Miguel. "Lil brother, would I lead you on a suicide mission? Blood, one thing I've learned in my life is that money truly is the root of all evil. We ain't gonna have to lick one shot until we get right up on them marks."

Tito chuckled, blowing smoke from the edge of his mouth. "Kick back, Blood. The big homey got it all worked out." Both Tito and Major Blood had reassuring smirks on their faces, but it did nothing to put Eddie's mind at ease.

About a block from the Blue Light, Tito stopped the car. In the rearview he could see two shadows slithering out of the Camry and vanishing into an alley next to the gentlemen's club.

"Time to rock and roll, poppy," Major Blood said over his shoulder, handing Eddie the Mac that had been on his lap. Eddie looked at the gun as if he didn't understand so Major explained. "You're gonna go post up by that store." Major nodded to a darkened doorway across the street. "Anybody come out but us, hit 'em hard and fast."

Eddie looked at the gun that was now resting on his lap, and swallowed. He'd hoped that his job would be to watch the car, or possibly subdue security, but Major had other plans. He looked at his elder G, who was watching him intently, and knew that he had to follow the order. Major was testing him and if he didn't answer the call to arms there was no doubt that he would end up going out like B. T. or worse. With a silent nod he stepped out of the car and went to take his post.

Major watched as Eddie crossed the street with his shoulders sagging, before turning back to Tito and Miguel. "You niggaz ready to push a muthafucka?"

In response, Tito laughed and stepped out of the car. Everybody from Harlem to Kansas City knew the reputation of Cisco's executioner, even with the rumors of L.C. going soft no one ever doubted his willingness to kill. Whether Miguel felt the same or not was the question.

"Sup, home boy?" Major asked. Miguel didn't respond, he just got out of the car and followed Tito.

Major and his team strolled to the entrance of the club chatting among themselves. When the bouncer spotted them, he started moving in their direction. Miguel thought he was about to pop off, so he reached for his gun, but Major Blood stayed his hand. To his surprise the bouncer walked right past them as if they weren't even there. Miguel looked to Major who just winked.

The lights in the club were dim, but it wasn't dark yet. They would go almost completely out later in the night when the crowd picked up and the freaky shit started jumping off. There was a main stage in the back, and several smaller stages positioned around the main floor. Though most the smaller stages were vacant at the moment there were three big booty chicks entertaining the crowd from the main stage. Though the Blue Light was a Crip establishment, the trio of Bloods had to admit that the spot was popping.

Major Blood scanned the club for Hollywood, but he was nowhere to be found. *At least somebody was on their job,* he thought, looking over at Miguel who was trying to grope one of the strippers. If he decided to stick around New York and reap the benefits of his work there would have to be some serious personnel changes. The pretty boy wasn't a killer like Gutter and Pop Top, but he was said to be a major cog in the Crip machine, which is why he had to be taken out. He wanted to strip Gutter of all his friends and family before he killed him. If things worked out as he planned, Hollywood's murder would go as smooth as silk.

Miguel's head whipped back and forth as he watched the parade of flesh at the Blue Light. A dark-skinned girl with an ass that belonged on a horse tried to engage him in conversation, but a subtle elbow from Tito put him back on point. The place was crawling with Crips so they had to take extra caution.

"Let's hit the bar!" Major shouted to Tito over the music. Major Blood picked his way through the light crowd, never taking his eyes off the four men who were huddled at the bar. Though no one saw him draw, two .9s appeared in Major's hands. The men at the bar were chopping it up with two strippers, having a good time.

Little did they know Major Blood was about to change all that. None of them were Hollywood, but they were all from the wrong side of the track, which was reason enough to trip.

"Let's announce ourselves, boys," Major said to his crew, before breaking his rival's circle.

chapter 28

THE RIDE was shorter than he had remembered it, Gutter thought to himself as the Regal exited off the East Pacific Coast Highway, near the community hospital. Though the area had changed quite a bit since Gutter had last been there it still brought back memories. From gunfights to chasing trim, he and Lou-Loc had seen more of their fair share of action on the Long Beach streets.

Snake Eyes drove, while Gutter occupied the passenger seat. Rahkim was glaring out the window, smoking cigarette after cigarette, while Danny shifted around nervously under the weight of the carbine rifle on his lap. Gutter wondered for the umpteenth time if he made the right decision in letting Danny come to California with him. The war was still in full swing, but the rules had changed. There was no more etiquette between the crews, just who had the highest body count. It had been years since Gutter had found himself in the thick of it, but the animal that had rocketed him to ghetto star status still lurked beneath the surface and would react accordingly when and if it came to it, but would Danny be able to stand the test of fire? At the end it had been Danny's choice. Gutter made no secrets about the lifestyle he led and what it meant to be a true banger. Twenty-four/seven you rode for the cause in any and all things. From mayhem to murder, you either put in work or you didn't join up, simple as that.

Trailing them in the blue Escalade were Tears, Criminal, Jynx, and the big homey Ren from Four Duce Gangster. Jynx had a presence in Long Beach, so that automatically put the odds in their favor with that as the meet spot. Big Ren was the blue-collar cat, always willing to ride for the cause. He had been putting in work for almost twenty years and showed no signs of slowing down. Though he was a brutal cat, Gutter had brought him along for more strategic reasons. He would be their insurance policy to make sure Trik played fair.

"You think these niggaz gonna keep it funky, or try to pull something?" Danny asked from the backseat, snapping Gutter out of his daze.

He turned to his protégé. "I don't really know, but I know we gonna be prepared for whatever."

"Shit, I hope these niggaz do trip so I can put something hot in a bitch-ass oh-la." Rahkim brandished his Desert Eagle.

"Why don't you put that shit away, Rah, before you accidentally shoot one of us or get us pulled over," Snake Eyes suggested. He had been tight with the Soladines for years, but because Rah was always in and out of prison he had never gotten a chance to know him. Rahkim was a wild card and Snake Eyes didn't quite know what to expect from him. What he did know was that if Gunn's little brother decided to trip it would lead to unnecessary bloodshed, something nobody wanted.

"Little cousin, I've been on one since you and Gutter's asses was both just wanna-Cs, don't tell me how to go about mine," Rah responded, placing the gun on his lap.

"Rah, ain't nobody trying to tell you how to do nothing, but Snake Eyes is right. The streets is already on fire over this shit that happened with Gunn and the last thing we need is to get pulled over for some dumb shit," Gutter told him.

"Whatever, nephew." Rahkim sucked his teeth and went back to staring out the window.

Gutter just shook his head. He knew that Rahkim was going to be a headache, but there was no way he could've left him behind. Next to himself, Rah was the most experienced combat solider, so if things got ugly he would be invaluable. Not only that, Gunn had been his older brother and the man responsible for putting him on the set. He had just as much right, if not more, to be included as anybody.

When they reached the hood, they didn't bother reading the street signs to see where they were because the walls told it all. Insane, Rolling 20's, Dawgz, S.S. (Sons of Samoa), the ruling factions of Long Beach, California, made sure you knew exactly where you were and who was on top.

When they turned down Nineteenth Street you could immediately feel the tension. Various groups of Mexicans were partying in their yards, slinging or just enjoying the weather. Though neither set represented in the two cars had a current beef with the Chicanos, the relations between blacks and browns in Long Beach had always been fragile. Danny must've picked up on it too because he got a firmer grip on his rifle. When they stopped at the red light, a vato who had been resting on a deck stood up and eyeballed them. Gutter turned his sinister eyes on the Mexican, but didn't try to provoke a situation. The Mexican shouted something to one of his home boys that nobody really heard over the music, but whatever it was caused the man to stand next to his comrade and join in the staring contest. When Gutter refused to turn away under the glare of the two hard-asses, the second Mexican threw up Eighteenth Street, which was one of the most notorious Latino sets on the West Coast.

Rahkim gripped his pistol and reached for the window switch on the Regal, but Gutter locked it, giving him a stern look. Reluctantly, Rahkim let the young man slide as they passed through the green light and continued on their way. He understood that Rahkim was fuming over what had happened to his brother and was ready to bust on just about anyone, but the brash young soldiers from Eighteenth Street weren't their targets that night, the Swans were.

"Don't trip on it, Unc, them young boys is just stunting," Gutter said, trying to soothe Rah. "If they mug us again when we bail through, then we can kill 'em *together*, right now we got more pressing business."

Rahkim nodded, but didn't necessarily like it. He had been in prison during the time the treaty was signed and things had died down among the sets. Much like his older brother he came up in the era when banging was in full effect. Whether it was an enemy, or a rival set trying to front, you laid your murder or knuckle game down; diplomacy was a foreign thing to him.

When the Regal turned into the church parking lot there were three cars already there, idling. In the darkened lot there was no way to tell how many people were in the cars, but Gutter was sure that the vehicles were lousy with Brims. The Crips were the ruling force in Long Beach so there was no way a Blood as notorious as Trik would come through the city without a heavy security detail, as Gutter had already anticipated, which is why Lil Blue and a few of the other locs had come down ahead of them and were strategically placed around the block. If Trik and his people had come to do anything other than talk they were going to be in for quite a surprise as Lil Blue and his team had orders to shoot to kill.

"Shit, how many of them do you think it is?" Danny asked.

"I don't know, cuz, so you just make sure you're on point for the bullshit," Gutter said.

"These muthafuckas frog-up you better let that muthafucka bark," Rahkim told Danny, motioning toward the carbine on his lap. "On Crip, cuz, lay everything down that ain't the right color!"

Gutter stepped out of the Regal, followed by Snake Eyes and Rahkim. Tears, Jynx, and Ren got out of the Escalade and came to stand at Gutter's side. No one spoke, but everyone knew what time it was. Gutter, Jynx, Rahkim, Ren, and Snake Eyes moved carefully toward the line of cars, while Tears and the others watched for signs of trouble.

In the quiet darkness the sounds of car doors opening and closing could be heard. There were five men approaching, to match the numbers Gutter had with him. The first three he only knew to be foot soldiers from Swan, but the last two Gutter was familiar with. Mongo was Pudgy's little brother, but there was nothing small about the man. He stood a towering six feet six and was built like the Incredible Hulk, with bulging arms and legs like tree trunks. Whereas Pudgy was more the diplomat, Mongo was a straight beast. He had killed more than his fair share of Crips and Bloods during his twenty-one years on earth and the look on his face said that he was thinking about adding to his list of bodies that night.

Bringing up the rear was a man who, though he was of a very average size, radiated menace. He was dressed in freshly pressed tan khakis and a red-and-black flannel shirt that was buttoned at the neck. His long, Jheri-curled hair hung from beneath his wool Raiders skully like only the world outside him had changed since

1989. His black eyes were tired and haggard as if some weird death scene played over and over behind them. Stopping a few feet short of where Gutter and his people were, he gestured that the next move was theirs.

Being a war vet himself Gutter understood that the man was still unsure about how far he could trust them. Since the war first kicked off the older cat had been on the front line racking up a long dossier of enemies. People like him were forever doomed to live on the edge of life and death, not knowing when or where their numbers would be called. As Gutter examined him he wondered if he wasn't looking at a sneak preview of what he was to become, if he even lived to see that age.

The tension between the two clicks was so tight that you could almost feel the very air constricting around your throat. Gutter nodded to his comrades and matched the man's steps, until they were within a few feet of each other. In the still of the night in a darkened Long Beach parking lot Gutter stood toe-to-toe with not only a sworn enemy, but the man who held the secret to Gunn's murder: O.G. Trik.

chapter 29

DIRTY BILL was finally starting to have fun. The girls saw him with Goldie and Hollywood so they thought he was someone important. For the past twenty minutes he had been in the ear of a sensual chocolate gem, trying to get her head rates to drop from sixty to thirty-five. He was finally starting to make headway when he felt someone bump past him to get to the bar.

"Pardon me, *Blood*," Major Blood said, squeezing up to the bar.

"Loc, I ain't ya Blood, that shit don't rock up here. This Harlem, cuz," Dirty Bill said, not even recognizing the threat.

"Word? I thought we were in the Bronx?" Major said sarcastically with his hand casually at his side.

In every group there was one. A cat so quick to make a show that he doesn't bother to assess the situation or measure the odds. Nine times out of ten it's gonna end nasty, but the poor bastard has gotta make a show of it. This was the case when a cat that had been kicking it with Bill decided to add his two cents to the mix. "Harlem Crip, nigga. Fuck is you smoking?" the kid snarled.

"Crabs!" Major said, placing one of his guns under the kid's chin. The kid opened his mouth to say something, but Major Blood put a bullet through his chin and out the top of his head.

Goldie moved with the grace of a jungle cat as he grabbed the stripper closest to him and held her in front of him like a shield. In true gangsta style he hoisted his pistol and started busting back at Major Blood, who was scrambling to get out of the way.

"Not in my muthafucking house!" Desire, who was the bartender, shouted as she came up from behind the bar with a pump. The twenty-two-year-old bartender might've weighed about a hundred and ten pounds on a good day, but she had the heart of a giant. The burst went wild, shredding through a beam and an unlucky patron, but never touching anything from the red side. Tito bounded on top of the bar and placed his gun to her forehead. Desire pursed her lips to spit in his face, but ended up kissing the barrel as her brains squirted onto the Coronas in the cooler.

HOLLYWOOD LAY back in the leather recliner with one foot slung across the arm, while Lexi gave him some gangsta-ass head. Hollywood suspected that she was about her business from the way she came at him, but the love boat ride she was currently giving him would net a mint on the streets. He needed to have this little freak bitch with him.

Hollywood was about to crack for the pussy when a faint noise caught his attention. The office was soundproofed from the music on the main floor, but there was no mistaking the sound of a gunshot. He lifted his head to say something to Lexi and barely got out of the way as a switchblade came whizzing past his chin. Lexi looked up with murder in her eye and bellowed, *"Die crab!"*

Hollywood was stunned by what was unfolding, but he shouldn't have been. From the time Lexi opened her mouth at the bar she smelled like a snake, but Hollywood let his dick send mixed signals to his brain and now he was caught literally with his pants down.

"That's on Blood I'm gonna open yo pretty ass up," Lexi vowed, jabbing at him with the blade. When she came with a wild swipe, Hollywood made his move. Throwing himself backward in the recliner he brought his knees up into Lexi's chin, snapping her head back and throwing her off balance. Instead of trying to get farther away from Lexi and her blade, Hollywood threw himself in her direction. He tried to knock Lexi to the floor so he could pen her, but miscalculated his lunge and was only able to subdue one arm. By the time he realized his mistake the razor was grazing his jaw.

Hollywood never felt the cut, but he knew something was terribly wrong when his face got moist. Lexi had opened him up from his earlobe to his lower lip with more precision than a surgeon. Hollywood didn't have to see it to know that his beautiful face was ruined, and thus his pockets would take a hit. To this day nobody really knows if it was the vanity in Hollywood or the fact that Lexi had cut him, but he slammed his fist into her skull so hard that it cracked, breaking his hand in the process.

"Con'n bitch." Hollywood kicked her in the ribs as he took stock of his hand. There was no doubt that his right hand would be no good to him that night, but he could shoot just as well with his left he thought as he grabbed his hammer off the desk where he'd left it before the near fatal blow job, and headed for the office door.

As soon as Hollywood opened the office door, a bullet slammed into it. The club he had vested so much in was being shot up and torn apart like a saloon. Three Spanish-looking cats were by the entrance wilding the fuck out. He recognized Tito and Miguel, but the light-skinned kid with the braids was a new face. From the way he was clapping shit up that had to be the infamous Major Blood. The way they were cutting loose it would only be a matter of time before the Crips were overrun.

Hollywood boogied back to the office desk and wrapped on it a series of times, popping a false panel out of the side. Nestled in the panel was the grand opening gift Wiz had given him. Tucking his pistol into his waistband and checking the barrel of the gift, Hollywood stepped out onto the main floor.

THERE WERE five of them in all; five lambs who had successfully escaped the slaughter. They had all began the night with different reasons for hitting the spot, but they were exiting with a common thought; *survival*. When the shooting had started everyone broke for it. Drinks were abandoned and some of the girls jetted wearing nothing but thong and clear heels. Outside meant life, so in a massive wave they pushed for the door.

Eddie knew they'd be coming, but he was still startled when the club doors flew open and people began spilling out onto the street. None of them were Crip soldiers, but they had all been sentenced to death. How many innocents would die that night to claim the life of one enemy?

"Live by it, die by it," Eddie told himself, stepping off the curb.

A big butt stripper, whose weave was sitting at a funny angle from her frantic exit, was making swift strides in Eddie's direction. Eddie laughed at how funny she looked trucking on the six-inch heels to keep his mind off her face, which had twisted into a horrid mask as the bullets from the Mac ripped up her chest. As her blood drained into the gutter at Eddie's feet he thought how Major had

surely condemned him to hell. But he would rather pay in the af-
terlife than go against Major Blood in this one. With that thought
in mind Eddie began sweeping the crowd with the machine gun.

THERE WERE so many people trying to get out of the crosshairs that
Miguel could barely raise his gun, let alone get a shot at the wild
man, Goldie. It seemed like every time he even thought about
pulling the trigger someone darted out in front of him. The whole
spot was thrown into utter chaos, and from the look on Major Blood's
face he was enjoying every minute of it.

Through the tangle of arms and heads Miguel could see Goldie
now had his back to him. With a smirk at the stripes he would get
for smoking Goldie, he took aim and pulled the trigger.... A split
second later he felt the intense heat.

"IS THIS a private party, or can anybody join in?" Hollywood capped
before pulling the trigger on the oddly shaped sawed-off.

The recoil from the Dragon-Mouth round was so powerful
that the gun almost flew out of Hollywood's hand. Even with the
stalk braced against his hip the weapon was difficult to control with
only one hand. The aftermath of the blast was thick smoke hanging in the air and the smell of sulfur damn near choking Hollywood, but seeing the carnage the blast had caused made it almost
worth the vomit that was trying to escape the back of his throat.
Wiz had warned against firing the thing in close quarters and now
he understood why.

The young Chicano had come up with some very interesting
gadgets over the years, but the Dragon-Mouths were the best yet.
A Dragon-Mouth was a shotgun shell that had magnesium shav-

ings and mercury packed in with the gunpowder. When the pellets burst from the casing they ignited, making the spray look like a horde of tiny fireballs.

Miguel was barely able to throw himself out of the way as the embers ignited his clothing and singed his cheek. The more he swatted at the flames the more they seemed to spread. Man's natural fear of fire caused him to momentarily forget his enemies and try to strip out of his jacket. This gave Goldie a clear window.

The first bullet hit Miguel high in the shoulder and sent him stumbling forward. When he turned around, Goldie hit him twice more in the chest. Miguel crashed into the bar, sending abandoned glasses and bottles spilling to the floor. The last thing he would see in his young life was the grin on Goldie's face as he sent a fatal round through his cheek.

HOLLYWOOD NARROWLY missed the barrage of bullets Tito sent his way, as the edge of the bar provided him with a minute to breathe. It felt like slugs were coming from every direction at once, and even with the Dragon-Mouth he and Goldie were in a tight spot.

"Cuz, we gotta make for the back!" Goldie shouted from over his shoulder.

"You'll get no argument from me," Hollywood said, sliding another shell into the gun. "When I let this bitch rock, be ready to bust a move!"

"Solid," Goldie said, still clutching the girl.

Hollywood popped from behind the bar and fired, holding the sawed-off in a one-handed grip. The kick knocked his aim off a bit, but it didn't affect the damage inflicted as the fiery pellets ignited everything in their path. While Major Blood and Tito dove for cover, Hollywood broke for the back door.

Dirty Bill, who had all but been forgotten, saw his chance and made the mad dash. He fired his gun over his shoulder, not really hitting anything, and moved as fast as he could toward the back door. Seeing his comrade dart out into his line of fire gave Goldie pause, and this was all the time Major Blood needed to react. He gave Goldie one to the chest and flipped him backward. Dirty Bill never even cast a glance at the man who he called friend as he disappeared toward the back.

BILL ALMOST broke his neck getting to the fire door. When the bullet struck the wall just above his head he almost shitted his pants. Hollywood was hot on his heels. He knew the homeys were sure to brand him a sucker for the stunt he pulled so he reasoned he might as well kill Hollywood to keep the story from getting out.

Without breaking his stride Bill lowered his shoulder and crashed through the fire door. The emergency siren went off, but Billy couldn't hear it over the sound of his own heart thudding in his ears. He knew he was free at the moment the cool air hit him, but the thought quickly left his brain as a bullet exploded in it.

"HOW'S HE holding up?" Sharell called over her shoulder.

"I can't stop the bleeding," Satin said nervously as she pressed her hands over the hole in Mohammad's back. He was lying across the floor of the backseat with a dreamy look in his eyes.

"Mohammad, we should really get you to a hospital," Sharell said, weaving the X5 in and out of traffic.

"No," Mohammad said weakly. "We can't risk the police getting involved. Here." He handed her his cell, which was slick with blood. "Call Anwar, and tell him where we're going. He'll send someone."

"But what if you bleed to death before help comes?" Satin asked.

"Then it will be what it will be. Just keep driving until we get to the address. Anwar will take care of everything," he told her before closing his eyes.

"Mohammad, Mohammad!" Satin shook him. At first she thought he was dead, but his eyes fluttered open.

"Not to worry, Sharif won't let the reaper have me. He's promised as much," Mohammad assured her.

"Sharell, delirium is setting in. I don't think he's going to make it."

"Mohammad, don't you go dying on us, you hear me?" Sharell called to him, but there was no answer. She spared a glance over her shoulder to see that he was still breathing, but barely. "Lord, please don't take him," she whispered, flipping Mohammad's phone open to call Anwar.

▪▫▪▫▪▫▪▫▪▫▪▫▪▫▪▫▪▫▪▫▪▫▪▫▪▫▪▫▪▫

chapter 30

HOLLYWOOD DIDN'T have to look over his shoulder to know that Tito and Major Blood were hot on his heels. If their heavy footfalls hadn't given them away the plaster spraying on him from all sides did.

Just ahead of him he saw Dirty Bill hit the fire door and go spilling into the darkened alley, two seconds later he was flopping back inside. A small hole appeared in the middle of his forehead, though the blood had yet to show itself.

Trapped, was the first word that popped into Hollywood's mind. With the two Blood assassins at his back and God only knew how many enemies in the alley he had just become the filling of a shit sandwich. Faced with the choice of having to deal with two seasoned killers or the unknown odds outside, Hollywood chose the latter.

"Die young and leave a good-looking corpse," he mumbled before rushing the fire door, with the Dragon-Mouth at the ready.

The two young men who had been staked out in the alley were

so focused on Bill that they didn't even notice Hollywood swing the Dragon around until its roar bounced off the walls of the alley. Boo managed to dive out of the way at the last second, but his partner wasn't so lucky. He flapped around on the ground like a wounded fish as the flames ate away at his chest and face. His agony was intense, but short-lived as Hollywood tossed the spent sawed-off and finished him with his pistol. Seeing the streetlights at the end of the alley, Hollywood rushed for freedom, only to be fired on before he made it out of the alley.

HAD HOLLYWOOD not slipped on a beer bottle, Boo would've parted his skull like the Red Sea with the shot he let off. Hollywood fell hard on his ass, just before a bullet struck the wall above his head. The impact from the fall jarred his gun loose and sent a jolt of pain through his broken hand as he landed on it. He now found himself a bit dazed and at the mercy of the coal-black young man advancing on him. Just when it seemed like it was over, the whole alley was flooded with light and angry shouts.

HOLLYWOOD BARELY had time to roll out of the way as the Honda jumped the curb and slammed into Boo. The car pinned his small frame to the wall with a bone-cracking sound, sending blood spraying from his mouth and onto the windshield. In a rare act of mercy Bruticus got out on the passenger's side and blasted Boo once in the head.

"Yo, Wood..." Bruticus turned to say something to his comrade and a slug slammed into his lower back, sending him crashing into the hood of the car. Another spray of bullets came from across the street where Eddie had been hiding, riddling the side of the car.

After retrieving his pistol Hollywood staggered toward the car, sending an occasional shot at the fire door to keep Tito and Major at bay. He was barely able to duck into the backseat before Eddie shredded the top of the car.

Leaning from the driver's seat, High Side spit off with his 9, laying cover fire for Bruticus to make it back inside the car. Before all the doors could be closed, High Side threw the car in reverse, clipping a fire hydrant when they hit the street, blanketing the block in water. He felt like a coward for running, but a good run was always better than a bad stand.

"Cuz, what was that shit all about?" High Side asked, swerving in traffic.

"It was about some faggot-ass slobs stepping way out of bounds," Hollywood panted. "Man, this shit is getting out of hand real quick." He felt his ruined face. Even if he dropped a few stacks on getting plastic surgery there would probably still be a scar.

"Son, I'm calling Pop Top and telling him what went down." High Side flipped his cell phone open.

"Fuck Pop Top, nigga. Get Gutter on the line!" Bruticus demanded, trying not to pass out from the loss of blood.

chapter 31

SEE YOU still slumming, *cuz*," Ren said, with his face twisted into a mad-dog stare. He stood with his heels touching and feet pointing out like the top half of a number four.

"I could say the same, *Blood*," Trik replied. There was no emotion in his voice and his eyes remained cold as he stared at Ren. The men were equal in height as well as build, but whereas Ren was known as a brawler, Trik was a stone killer.

There was an uneasy moment where neither man said a word. There was the faint sound of thunder in the distance, but there didn't seem to be a cloud in sight. Mongo tensed like he was about to make a move, but Jynx had him covered. When the air had finally come to a boil, both Ren and Trik burst into broad grins.

"What's popping, family?" Trik embraced Ren.

"Same shit, different day." Ren hugged him equally tight. "Nigga, I ain't seen you since Christmas!"

"You know the streets keep a nigga busy." Trik shrugged. "Tell my auntie I'm gonna come check her for her birthday though."

Jynx looked totally confused, but Gutter and Snake Eyes shared a quiet chuckle. The main reason that Gutter had brought Ren along was because he and Trik were first cousins. Sure, they racked up one hell of a body count on opposing sides, but it never came between the cousins. Gutter reasoned that if Trik did have something dirty up his sleeve he'd have been hesitant to spring trap if his family was involved.

"So, what's this all about, cousin?" Ren asked Trik.

"It's about us offering some crab muthafuckas a hand up and they pull a bitch move. Fuck you on snatching my brother, Blood?" Mongo spat viciously.

"Man, you need to slow ya muthafucking lip and remember where you at." Jynx stepped forward with a scowl. "Only blood pump through the beach is *blue* blood." Years before Mongo had shot one of Jynx's home boys when he was coming out of the movie theater with his girl. Jynx had always wanted to even the score, but hadn't had the good fortune to bump into him.

"Man, we gonna roll around in the dirt like some schoolkids or we gonna swap some stories?" Gutter's voice boomed. He didn't speak above his normal tone, but the power in his words is what gave it volume.

Trik turned to the speaker and narrowed his eyes. His features had hardened since the last time he'd seen him; he knew the youngest male Soladine. "Sup, Gutter?"

Gutter shrugged. "I was hoping you could tell me? Word is you got some intel on who put the heat to my uncle."

"Man, skip all that. We ain't telling you crabs nothing until I see my brother!" Mongo cut in. The veins in his thick neck were bulging like they would burst at any moment. He was trying to lay the guerrilla down, but Gutter wasn't moved.

The fire in Gutter's eyes was the only sign that he was becoming irritated with Mongo. "Dawg, why don't you kick back with that loud shit, fo it get tense 'round here? Unlike some muthafuckas, I respect the rules of conduct, so I wouldn't do you or your envoy like that. But if you niggaz is running some bullshit you can rest assured the Soladines ain't gonna be the only ones burying one of their own."

"Why don't everybody just kick back for a minute," Trik spoke up. "Gutter, let's cut to the chase 'cause ain't neither one of us got time for it. The bottom line is I came here to see if we can put a cease to the bloodshed."

"Trik, you must be out ya mind to come over here talking some peace shit when my brother is about to be laid into the ground, cuz. Nah, this shit is about to go full-scale," Rahkim said emotionally.

"Young Rah, I done lost two brothers and a nephew to this shit, so make no mistake about my understanding your loss," Trik said. "Gunn was born on the wrong side of the fence, but me and all the home boys respected him as a stand-up nigga and we also respected the fact that he wasn't active no more."

Snake Eyes spoke up for the first time. "Trik, I've known you for a long time and you've always been a man of your word, but if the homeys respected Gunn's inactive status then how the fuck did he get hit? And why is the finger being pointed at y'all?"

"I don't know all the details, but what I can tell you is that nobody from this side sanctioned that hit," Trik assured them.

"Man fuck dancing around the subject. If y'all didn't do it, I wanna know who killed my uncle," Gutter said seriously.

"Come on, G, you know I ain't in the business of snitching," Trik told him.

"Well, that's too fucking bad, because I'm in the business of killing and if you had us come out here for nothing I'm gonna put in some overtime," Gutter shot back. Trik looked like he wanted to say something, but kept looking to his homeys for a reaction. "Trik, what is your face telling me that ya mouth ain't?"

Trik ground his teeth together. He looked from his troops to theirs and weighed his options. Sure, they could all bang out and make a bad situation worse, but Trik wanted a solution, not a bigger problem. Taking a short breath, he addressed Gutter, "Walk with me for a minute, Gutter." Trik motioned toward a darkened corner away from everyone else.

"Nigga, fuck that shit. Trik, you better start talking before these fullies do!" Rahkim snarled.

"It's all good, Unc." Gutter placed a reassuring hand on his enraged uncle's shoulder. "Come on, Trik." Gutter broke away from his group. When they were out of earshot, Trik began speaking in a hushed tone.

"First of all, let's get one thing straight, *lil* homey, I earned my stripes just like you and everybody else out the Soladine house, so I don't take kindly to being spoken to like a common street punk," Trik told him.

"I hear you, Trik, our family is dead, and the finger is being pointed at you, not nobody else. Now, if you've got some info you wanna share, I'm listening. If not, the next time we meet we'll be speaking over pistols," Gutter told him. It wasn't a threat, but an actual fact and Trik knew that.

Had this been ten years ago it would've surely been on and popping for the threat Gutter had launched at Trik. In his day he had commanded respect and been quick to violence, but it was no longer his day. The young wolves had changed the code of conduct and every gangster, young and old, could be a potential victim of their wrath. Trik was a battle-worn vet, one of the few who had lived to see his forties, and was just trying to live peacefully for the rest of his days, and a confrontation with the youngest remaining Soladine wasn't something he wanted. No, it was better to just give him what he wanted and be done with it. With any luck Gutter and the wild assassin from the red side would kill each other and be out of Trik's hair for good.

"A'ight, trip this." Trik leaned in to whisper to Gutter. "I ain't gonna deny the fact that a Blood blasted your uncle, but it wasn't about no turf. This shit was about a murder that's over twenty years old. The muthafucka who wasted Gunn had a personal grudge, one that even the nation couldn't make him let go."

"How the fuck am I supposed to know who could've been holding a grudge against Gunn for twenty years?" Gutter didn't bother to hide his irritation at Trik's riddles.

"Shit, you're a smart kid. Ask your uncle Rahkim about it. You think on the only nigga crazy enough to clip a dude like Gunn after he was declared inactive, and you couple it with what you learn from your uncle. It'll come to you."

"Trik, that ain't good enough. You said you wanted to end the violence, so I need a name to make that happen," Gutter told him.

Trik sighed. "I want this shit to stop, but I ain't about to just give up one of my own, Gutter, you should know this. Wrong or right, he's still damu and I just can't send him off to the slaughter like that, so you're on your own with the name. Now, if you wanna get down over it"—Trik spread his arms—"cool, but I'd rather keep this shit individual instead of riling the sets. It's hard enough to get these little niggaz to quit tripping as it is."

Gutter weighed Trik's words. He could've tried to force the issue, but to what end? Trik obviously wasn't giving up the name, and besides he had already risked more than he had to trying to put a stop to the fighting. Some people might've taken the fact that Trik was meeting with Crips in Long Beach as a sign of not being down, which could've netted him a bigger problem than the So-ladines. For him to risk his life like that Gutter knew that Trik truly did want to put an end to the violence.

"A'ight, O.G. Trik." Gutter nodded. "Me and mines is gonna bail back to the 'rib and try to put the pieces of this puzzle to-gether."

"G, you know if anybody finds out I put you on the trail..."

"Don't worry about that, Trik. I ain't gonna throw you under the bus for what you did here today."

Trik laughed. "Young general, this ain't got nothing to do with worrying, it's about finally saying enough is enough. I've been kill-ing and watching homeys die longer than most of these niggaz been alive. Set love used to be about something bigger than the turf, but somewhere along the line the game got twisted. If I don't never go to another funeral, it'll still be one too many. I'm tired of this shit, homey, you feel me?"

Gutter thought about his own life and what it was amounting to. "Yeah." He nodded. "I'm starting to," he said, going back to join his soldiers.

"What's good, cuz?" Snake Eyes asked, noticing the worried expression on Gutter's face after speaking with Trik.

"Mount up, niggaz, we outta here," Gutter addressed his crew.

"Fuck you mean y'all out of here? What about my brother?" Mongo demanded.

"As soon as we're clear, Pudgy will be released," Gutter told him, as he climbed behind the wheel of the Regal.

"So what's up, Hoover and Swan cool or what?" Trik called af-ter him.

Gutter smirked. "For the moment. But trip this, big homey, if what you told me was some bullshit, I'm gonna come through yo hood and kill you personally, but that's after I stink your wife and anybody else in the house that's old enough to vote." With that being said, Gutter backed the car out of the lot and mashed to the highway.

"SO WHAT'S the business, nephew? We blasting on Swans tonight or some other fag-ass set?" Rahkim asked from the backseat.

"I'm still trying to figure it out," Gutter told him. "Say, Unc, what you know about a slob Gunn blasted on back in the eighties?"

Rahkim laughed. "Shit, you know how many niggaz my brother done killed in the last twenty years? You'd be better off asking me who the mayor of Mexico City is."

"Nah, this would've been different. From what I gathered from Trik this has to do with a grudge of some sort. Think on it, Unc, is there anything that Gunn could've done back then that somebody would've been willing to wait twenty years to retaliate?"

Rahkim was silent for a minute, going over the list of kills he knew about. Suddenly he recalled something that might be relevant. "Actually I do remember some shit, a real fucked-up situation that went down at the fair. The Hoovers got into it with some niggaz and they bitches from the 900s, which turned into a firefight. A bitch got shot while her kid was in the backseat of the car. Gunn didn't know shorty was there at the time, but when he found out it had him fucked-up for a long time."

"The Nines?" Gutter tugged at his beard. Gutter flipped through his mental rolodex of killers in California and found that the list was longer than he was comfortable with. Death was a rite of passage for the children of the Pacific Coast, same as pee-wee football for suburban kids. Though the 900 block Bloods weren't the largest set, they had a reputation for brutality, but he still couldn't think of one who would've been stupid enough to touch Gunn... then it hit him. One 900 block rider was just that fool.

"Major Blood," Gutter hissed. For as long as he could remember Major Blood had been a thorn in his and Lou-Loc's sides. Neither of them could ever figure why he was so hell-bent on giving them grief, but after hearing Trik's and Rahkim's tales it finally made sense. "The woman Gunn killed had to be Major Blood's mother, or at least an aunt or some shit. He's the shooter."

"Major Blood?" Snake Eyes asked, his voice going up an octave. At the mention of the man's name Snake Eye's mental gang file popped open. Major Blood was a cross between Lou-Loc and Gutter, with a splash of Charles Manson. He had never met the man, but he knew of Major Blood and his exploits all too well.

"Oh, hell nah!" Rahkim slammed his fist into the door, rattling the windows. "That lil half-spic son of a bitch couldn't have touched mine? Floor this bitch to Compton, Ken. On Hoover, I'm gonna smoke his ho ass and everybody close to him."

"Oh, we gonna ride on them niggaz real proper, Unc, don't worry about that. Before I leave California I'm gonna send Major Blood and his whole gang a great big fuck you. But the question still remains, where the fuck is he?" He was about to add to the question when his new cell phone vibrated. When he looked at the screen and saw the 646 area code he got a sinking feeling in the pit of his stomach.

"ARRIVED AT destination," the computerized voice of the navigation system informed them.

The residential block looked like something out of *Home & Garden,* with its manicured lawns and SUVs in the driveways. She looked back at Mohammad who was still moaning softly. He was in a great deal of pain, but at least he was still alive. When she turned into the driveway there were three cars already there, and she could see men moving about in the darkness. She was about to throw the X5 in reverse when she felt something touch her arm.

"Family," Mohammad breathed softly, leaving a bloody smear on the sleeve of her jacket. He slumped back down to the floor and seemed to go unnaturally still. Satin touched his neck and gave Sharell a sad look.

The one leading the pack had to be Anwar. She had never met him personally, but she knew he was a youthful-looking man and the dark-haired youngster approaching the X5 didn't look to be a day over seventeen or eighteen. Behind him was a stocky brute, wearing black fatigues and the beginnings of a smile on his face. The last man in the group was tall, wearing a black kufi. His dark eyes looked concerned as he scanned the interior of the car. When they were right on top of the car she pulled Mohammad's gun and aimed it out the window.

"You won't be needing that, I am Anwar, prince of the Al Mukalla, I believe you know of me?" Anwar stopped, but didn't back down from the gun. Sharell hesitated for a minute, but eventually lowered the gun and opened the door. The smiling boy-prince extended his hand and helped her from behind the wheel.

The bearded man, who was called Sharif, rushed to the backseat to attend Mohammad. He pulled him gently from the back of the car and placed him on the lawn. Ignoring his bloodstained clothes, Sharif placed his ear to Mohammad's chest. He looked up from Mohammad to Sharell and asked, "How long?"

"A few minutes, if that," Sharell said with tears now spilling from her eyes. Yet another life had been taken by Gutter's personal war. Mohammad had sacrificed himself to protect her and she would make sure that he was honored properly. "I'm so sorry for your loss," she said, barely above a whisper.

Sharif glanced at her, but didn't reply. Instead he looked to Anwar with questioning eyes. Anwar turned to the stocky man, Roc, who shook his head in protest. There was some kind of conflict going on between the men, but Sharell didn't know what it was.

"It was his wish and his right," Sharif said defensively.

Anwar sighed. "Do what you must, Sharif, but do not let your promises interfere with your duties."

Sharif nodded. He scooped Mohammad from the ground, and though the dead man clearly outweighed him, he did it as if he weighed little more than a child. As gently as a parent could, he lowered Mohammad into the backseat of a black sedan and got behind the wheel. "I'll have someone here by sundown," he called to Anwar, who didn't bother to respond. The sedan backed out of the driveway, and disappeared into the night.

"Let's get you two in the house," Anwar said to the frightened young women. Noticing that Sharell was still holding Mohammad's bloody gun, he offered to take it.

"No, thanks," Sharell said, making sure a round was chambered. "I think I'll hold on to this for a while."

chapter 32

GUTTER PACED the front yard of Gunn's house, sucking a blunt and swigging a beer. He had always been a notorious pothead, but it seemed like he'd taken to drinking more since he'd been in California. It was probably because of the increased stress he'd found himself under being back on the West.

Shortly after meeting with Trik he got a call from a frantic Sharell. Apparently somebody had tracked her to their hideaway in Brooklyn and tried to kill her and Satin. His boo had put a slug in the intruder, just as he'd taught her, but it had been Mohammad who had saved them. Gutter's heart went out to the young soldier who had laid his life on the line for Sharell. She said that his wounds were pretty serious and doubted that he would make it, but Gutter felt otherwise, even though he didn't say it. He knew things about Mohammad that no one outside of Anwar and Sharif did. In time, Mohammad's body would be whole again, but it was more than he could say for the man's soul.

Gutter wanted to hop on the next thing smoking back to New

York, but Anwar assured him that all was well. Roc and two of his men were with her at a predetermined location. They would stay with Sharell until Gutter could get some of the homeys out that way to post up. She was as safe as could be, but Gutter was still uneasy about being away from her when she needed him most. He had to get home ASAP. He would attend his uncle's funeral, but when everyone left for the burial he and Danny would be on their way to the airport. When he got to New York, heads would roll.

The next piece of business he had to deal with was the poor job Pop Top had been doing with the set. Not long after he spoke to Anwar, Hollywood was on his line. He was about to brush the late-night call off until Hollywood explained that not only was he in the emergency room, but Rob, China, and B. T. were dead. He wasn't moved by B. T.'s death. In fact, he had often wondered at how trustworthy the man was. What hurt him was the fact that they had lost two more men ... no, boys, on the front line. It seemed just like yesterday they were getting high together while Gutter lectured them about what it meant to be a *true* banger. He had no idea how he would face their mothers when it came time to bury their sons.

During the course of his conversation he'd also discovered why Major Blood was nowhere to be found. He had all the homeys out looking for him, but nobody was able to turn up anything. The reason for that was the fact that he was in New York killing Gutter's men. Gunn's death settled the old score, but more important it got Gutter to come to Cali. It was all a ruse to get the rooster out of the henhouse while the weasel slaughtered the chickens.

All morning he had been on the Internet, searching news articles online. The numbers of gang-related deaths and arrests were staggering. *Newsday* even added their two cents about the sudden growth spurt of gang violence that had broken out all over New

York. Major Blood had been putting in serious work going at the Crips in New York, but Pop Top had made sure quite a few of theirs would be sidelined indefinitely. The war raged on with both sides taking heavy losses.

Gutter cursed himself for not being there to lead his army. He had successfully turned Harlem Crip into a solid organization, but they weren't prepared to deal with a cat like Major Blood. He killed without thought or remorse and was always willing to go a little harder than the next man. People like Major Blood had no problem killing mothers or other family members just to get his point across. The question still remained: if he was there to kill Gutter then why lure him to Cali while he was in New York?

Immediately after speaking to Hollywood, Gutter called Pop Top and demanded to know what was going down.

"It's blue, cuz, I got it under control," Pop Top assured him.

"Nigga, how the fuck is it blue when three of my homeys got dropped since I been gone?" Gutter demanded.

"Man, B. T. was a straight bitch from the jump and as far as the other two...they were just casualties of war. Shit happens, man, ain't no need to worry," Pop Top said as if it were nothing.

"See that's your problem, cuz, you don't worry. You got a nigga like Major Blood picking off soldiers left and right and you don't see a need to worry?"

"Man, that nigga ain't special. He bleed like everybody else, Gutter."

"Dawg, that's what I'm trying to tell you, Major Blood *ain't* like everybody else. This nigga is bad news. That little tit-for-tat shit you're playing with him is not only getting us hot, but it's getting niggaz killed."

"G, it's under control. Don't trip, I'm gonna put a lid on it, no problem," Pop Top said, getting tired of talking to Gutter.

"Muthafucka, is you crazy? This shit is all over the news! Son, you got the police on us, the sets on us, and if you fuck around the Feds might not be far behind!" Gutter barked.

Pop Top sucked his teeth. "Man, what you tripping for, cuz? You left me to run the set while you handle ya little family problems, so let me do my thing."

"Top"—Gutter sighed—"I left you in charge because I thought you'd keep it running while I had to dip to the West. As soon as Major Blood popped up you should've called me and I could've gave you the four-one-one on that buster."

"I'll take care of him."

"You know what, don't even sweat it, Top. I got something more important that I need you to take care of. Niggaz tried to get at Sharell last night."

"What? Is she okay? Who needs to die, cuz?" Pop Top asked.

"Kick back, man. I'm gonna be home tomorrow to take care of all that shit. Right now she's good, Roc got her stashed away at my house in Long Island. I need you and some of the homeys to go out there and help out," Gutter told him.

"Come on, cuz. I ain't no babysitter, I'm a field general, I belong in the trenches, you know that," Pop Top protested.

"Top, right now what's going on in the trenches ain't important. I'll see to that when I get back. I need you to tell the homeys to fall back until I get there. Major Blood don't play like everybody else, and I don't wanna lose no more soldiers, Top."

"This is some bullshit, man. In one breath you tell me to keep up the war effort and in the next you tell me to run from Major Blood like I'm some fucking pussy? I ain't wit this shit, cuz."

"Loc, fuck what you wit!" Gutter shouted. "I'm asking you to do me this solid, and you're giving me grief? Check this shit, Top, you're leading the set in name only. I'm the iron fist behind Harlem

Crip. Now, if you can't do me this solid, cool, I'll get somebody else. But make no mistake, my nigga, I won't have you questioning my actions. Dig me?"

"Whatever, man. I got you," Pop Top said, and hung up the phone.

"Silly muthafucka," Gutter spat, slipping his phone back into his pocket.

"You a'ight, G?" Snake Eyes asked, climbing out of his car. Gutter had been so lost in thought that he hadn't even noticed him pull up.

"Yeah, I'm straight." Gutter pounded his fist. "Just tripping off this nigga Pop Top. That muthafucka act like he run Harlem, homey."

"Well, for a good while he did. You know what they say about when a dog tastes blood, cuz. You might wanna keep your eye on that dude."

"Man, Top crazy as hell, but he ain't stupid." Gutter waved him off. "You send that bread off for me, my nigga?"

"Yeah, man." Snake Eyes handed him a Western Union receipt. "Rob's sister is handling all the arrangements. She say that Ms. Lucy too broke up to do much other than cry, so she on it. I think they're gonna have the services tomorrow."

"Damn, that was quick."

"I know, but they wanna get it out of the way, homey. I can only imagine what those women must be going through," Snake Eyes said sadly.

"Muthafucking Major Blood," Gutter spat. "It wasn't enough that that crazy bitch Ruby took my lil homey off the set, but then this nigga Major Blood had the nerve to go at my bitch? Man, that's gonna be the first nigga I see when I get back to the Coast."

"Yeah, ya boy's been getting his murder on, but he ain't try to kill Sharell, this nigga did." Snake Eyes handed him a folder he had

been holding. "You might recognize the little bastard in the picture as B-High, who used to kick it back in the days." Snake Eyes
narrated while Gutter scanned the folder's contents.

"Didn't they cross that nigga out for hitting two of his own?"
Gutter asked, glaring at the picture.

"They tried, but he vanished." Snake Eyes pulled a small legal
pad from his pocket and began flipping the pages. "Spent some
time in Miami and at some point slipped into New York. With his
track record I'm surprised you haven't had any trouble out of him
before this. Between him, Reckless, and Major Blood, they kept
some shit jumping in Compton."

"Yeah, we gonna see how much Reckless got jumping after a
real muthafucking gangsta touch the turf. After I lay this bitch
nigga, I'm gonna grease his faggot-ass cousin, Major." Gutter tossed
the file back to Snake Eyes. "He might not have tried Sharell his
self, but that don't change the fact that he put somebody on the
case. That's my word if them niggaz touch my wife...."

"Easy, homey." Snake Eyes placed a reassuring hand on Gutter's shoulder. "You and I both know that she's good where she's at.
Nobody but us and Anwar knows where she's tucked."

"Nobody but us and Anwar knew where she was tucked before," Gutter reminded him. "Cuz, I'll just feel better when this
nigga is outta my city, real talk."

"Soon enough, cousin. I've made arrangements for the funeral
and wake for Big Gunn to go down tomorrow, all in one shot. The
family understands about you having to bail early because of the
emergency in New York. Speaking of cutting out, what you think
about taking Tariq with you?"

"Who, Lil Gunn? Man, fuck am I gonna do, give him package
and teach him to blast muthafuckas? Nah, I don't think that's a
good idea." Gutter laughed it off.

"Well, I do. Come on, G, look what that nigga is dealing with out here. His mama's a winehead and his daddy ain't here no more. Who's gonna raise him, the fucking streets? You see what happened to us."

"Snake, your ass is a lawyer, fuck is you talking about?" Gutter asked him.

"Yeah, but you went on to become a gang banger, and so did Poppa, Ray, Baby Crunk, and Lou-Loc. Now three of the people on that list I just ran down to you are dead, one is in jail, and the other one is trying to get himself killed. So what's that telling you, that one out of every six of us will make a little something of their life?"

"Yo, dawg—"

"Nah, hear me out for a minute, Gutter. That boy is without a doubt his father's child; if you leave him here it's only a matter of time before he falls into the bullshit. I mean, it ain't like he's gonna have a whole lot of choices if he stays, G."

"Man, we banging in New York too!" Gutter pointed out.

"Yeah, but not like these niggaz." Snake Eyes motioned toward the garage, where most of the crew was assembled inside. "Besides, you know when Sharell drops her load this shit is gonna have to slow up anyhow. Get the little nigga outta here before the police or the meat wagon does."

Gutter measured his words, wondering if his friend's suggestion would make things worse or better. He was right when he said that things would change when Sharell gave birth. She had already started tightening the reins, and they'd get even tighter with a new baby. It wasn't such a bad thing though because Gutter needed to slow down. Maybe bringing Lil Gunn to the East Coast would help him do that. He knew how easy it was to be fourteen on the set, with nobody but the hood to guide you.

"You might have a point, Snake, but who's to say that Gunn even wants to go?" Gutter asked.

"He says," Snake Eyes informed him. "You know me and Lil Gunn are way cool because just about once a month I gotta fly up to get him outta some shit, so he talks to me. His mama ain't doing nothing but pushing him from the nest and into harm's way, but you know Stacia ain't trying to hear she has flaws. I asked the little nigga if he could move, would he? And he say in a heartbeat."

Gutter shook his head at his old friend's cunning. "A'ight, loc. Let me holla at Sharell about it and we'll see what pops. Right now, I gotta go holla at these niggaz, before Rahkim gets them all hyped up." Gutter headed for the garage.

WHEN HAWK was finally allowed to leave the precinct he was less than a happy camper. They had picked him up the previous night and brought him in for questioning on the recent rash of murders. Hawk had been on the police radar as a known gang affiliate and general piece of shit, but until then they'd never been able to come up with a solid reason to pick him up. Apparently they thought that he would be able to shed some light on the rash of gang-related shootings that had taken place over the last few days. Of course, Hawk refused to talk until his lawyer arrived.

The cops were so pissed that they took him from the precinct and drove around Harlem for hours to make it harder for the lawyer to locate him. The bullshit part of the whole thing was the fact that they had picked up several of the Crip leaders also, and thought it would be funny to release everybody at the same time. There was almost a full-scale riot between the two factions right in front of the precinct. Hawk was lucky to slide out before anything serious jumped off, but it still didn't change the fact that Major Blood's cowboy-ass antics had brought unnecessary heat down on him.

"Man, this nigga done stirred up more shit in two days then Cisco did the whole summer." Red tossed a newspaper across the room to Hawk. All throughout it were details about the murders. Crips killed Bloods and Bloods killed Crips. Murder was an everyday thing in New York City, but when it involved the two rival gangs it narrowed the list of suspects considerably. There had been seven murders reported over the last three days and more coming in.

The most tragic piece was the one about a woman getting shot in Harlem. Hawk had warned Ruby over and over, but she wouldn't listen. He should've known that her hatred of the Crips and love of Supreme wouldn't let her sit by and watch, but he never expected this. Major Blood was proving to be more of a detriment to them than an asset.

"This muthafucka is over the top." Hawk flipped the paper closed and tossed it onto the floor. "What the fuck were they thinking about calling him in?" Hawk wondered out loud.

"Dawg, you know the phone is gonna be jumping in a minute. When the big boys feel all this heat they're gonna need somebody to point the finger at," Shotta told Hawk.

Hawk knew he was 100 percent right. He was responsible for Major Blood while he was in the city and though he had not ordered the murders personally, he would surely take the blame for not keeping the killer on a shorter leash.

"Man, I knew that muthafucka was gonna be trouble the minute he showed up in New York," Red said. "Son, them Cali niggaz don't know how to chill the fuck out, now when his ass is long gone we still gonna be catching the flack."

"Don't even trip," Hawk said, grabbing his car keys off the coffee table. Next he went to the closet closest to the front door and retrieved his Glock from the iron box where he kept it. "We gonna go see Major Blood and have a little chat. We out." Hawk led his crew from the apartment.

"WHAT THE fuck is wrong with your face?" High Side asked, noticing his partner's sudden mood change when he got off the phone.

"Man, this bitch-ass nigga Gutter is tripping," Pop Top told him. "Old fag-ass nigga Hollywood went and dry-snitched, now Gutter on some next shit."

"Dawg, you know how me and you do, but I think Gutter should've been told about this shit a long time ago," High Side admitted.

"So now you sucking Gutter's dick too?"

High Side narrowed his eyes. "Man, watch yo fucking mouth. Cuz, all I'm doing is pointing out the obvious to you. We was having a hard enough time with all the different red sets popping up and this Major Blood nigga ain't do nothing but make it worse. Maybe we need to kick back until Gutter gets back?"

"Fuck all that shit, Side. When Gutter's ass was laid up, Lou-Loc put me in charge of Harlem, now I ain't good enough to run it?"

"Dawg, that was before Major Blood came on the scene putting batteries in niggaz backs," High Side pointed out.

"Man, fuck Major Blood and fuck Gutter. Them niggaz don't run Pop Top." He spat on the ground.

"So what you gonna do now?"

"This nigga screaming some he need me to go watch his bitch out in Long Island," Pop Top said, clearly not feeling it.

"Damn, nigga, you ain't never strike me as the babysitting type," High Side teased him.

"Nigga, fuck you!"

"Man, fall back you know I'm only fucking wit you." High Side laughed, but Pop Top didn't.

"Well, don't fuck wit me, I done had enough of that shit to last me a lifetime. That fool got me tight, son. This nigga from Cali and act like he know what it is in New York 'cause he been here a few years. Shit we was born and raised in New York!"

"Man, go ahead wit that shit, Pop Top. Gutter is running the show and that's just the way it is." Unlike Pop Top, High Side didn't have delusions of grandeur. He was good with the few corners he'd been given and didn't really care who was at the helm.

"But it ain't gotta be, son," Pop Top said, with a wicked plan forming in his head.

"Man, what kinda shit you talking?" High Side asked in a suspicious voice.

"Check this, all I'm saying is that maybe it's time we had a little more say in the way things are run? I mean, we are from Harlem, ain't we?"

High Side thought on it for a minute. "Yeah, but what's that got to do with it?"

"Man, it has everything to do with it, Side. We homegrown, baby, but Gutter is the one who gets all the props. Check, when him and Lou-Loc first started that unified set shit, who helped them rally the troops?"

"Us," High Side said.

"And when muthafuckas jump up, who put 'em down?"

"Us."

"Exactly." Pop Top slapped his palms together. "We opened the door for a nigga and we can't get a set of keys? Don't get me wrong, High Side, I got love for the homey too, but he ain't the only nigga putting in work."

"I see your point, but what we supposed to do about it, Top?" High Side asked.

"Fuck you think, nigga? If I can't get a piece up under Gutter, I might as well take the whole pie." Pop Top flipped open his cell phone.

"Who you calling?" High Side asked.

"Bronx Presbyterian Hospital."

chapter 33

THERE WERE so many young men gathered in the garage that the door had to be kept open to accommodate them. Weed smoke filled the air while bottles clanged together and weapons were visible on just about everyone. Most of the men, Gutter knew, but the rest had just come to get their pound of flesh.

"Cousins," Gutter began, forgoing the formalities. "Yesterday we lost a down-ass soldier. A soldier who put many of us on the turf, and handed damn near all of us beat-downs when we were out of bounds. Gunn was not only my uncle, but he played the father figure to a great many of us. We all knew Gunn wasn't in no more, hell everybody on the Coast knew he wasn't active, but that didn't stop that ho-ass nigga Major Blood from laying my folk." The people who had gone with him to see Trik knew who was behind the killing, but this was the first time Gutter had said it publicly.

"Major Blood?" someone whispered.

"I thought he was in the can?" another voice added.

"Nah, they smoked him for killing Bad Ass!" someone else added to the mix.

"Nah, that fag is alive and kicking, causing me even more grief on the East Coast," Gutter said.

"Man, I say we mount up for a road trip, loc!" Criminal said eagerly. It had been awhile since he killed something for the hood and didn't know how much longer he could contain himself. Gutter and Rahkim were icons to young Criminal and he was dying to get his stripes up.

"Nah, little cousin, that's a problem that I'm gonna deal with personally. Oh, but before I do, I want that slob to feel what we feel right now," Gutter said emotionally. "I want him to know what it's like to bury a homey or a muthafucking relative!" he shouted. "Tonight, we rolling through Compton and I'm gonna show these niggaz from the other side how to catch a fucking body. When we bail through, I want any and everything in that hood to lay down!"

The crowd roared at Gutter's proclamation. The sounds of sets being shouted and guns clicking were all that could be heard. They didn't even see Rahshida when she pulled up in the driveway with Monifa. Seeing twenty young men gathered on her property, with Gutter and Rahkim in their midst, meant another mother would be burying her child soon.

"What are y'all doing out here congregating?" she addressed them, putting her shopping bag down on the hood of the car. Monifa came to stand beside her.

"Ain't nobody congregating, Auntie. The homeys just came by to pay their respects to Big Gunn." Gutter leaned in and kissed her on the cheek. She frowned at the smell of liquor coming off his breath.

"Kenyatta, don't play me, all right?" she warned him. "I know y'all ain't fixing to go in them streets and act crazy?" When nobody responded her suspicions were confirmed. "When are y'all gonna ever learn?"

"Rah, you tripping—" Rahkim began.

"I'm not tripping, Rahkim, you're the one that's tripping. As old as you are and as much as you've been through I'd think you'd be trying to defuse these kinds of situations instead of agitating them. Rahkim, that is not what Islam teaches," she tried to reason with him.

"Man, fuck that. A nigga blasted on my brother and I ain't supposed to do nothing? We can all be devout Muslims at Gunn's ceremony tomorrow morning, but tonight I'm a muthafucking gangster." Rahkim stormed past his twin.

Rahshida let out a deep sigh. "Hasn't there been enough death already?" She was looking at the men assembled. "Criminal, wasn't it your brother who got shot last month at the bus stop? Tears, how did you feel when those boys from Six Duce almost blew your face off in front of your son?" No one responded. "Don't you see it? Us killing them and them killing us is getting us nowhere. The only people that thinking is beneficial to is white folks who don't want you to rise above this foolishness. When it is gonna end?"

"When there's only one side left," Gunn called from the flowerpot he'd been sitting on. Rahshida hadn't even noticed him until he spoke. There was a coldness to his eyes that she had seen in her little brother's eyes just before someone died.

"And you, Tariq. What are you doing? It's bad enough that I had to lose my brother to this madness. Will I lose you too?" Her voice was heavy with emotion.

"Nah, you ain't gotta worry about Tariq, Auntie." Gutter put an arm around her. "Tariq is coming back to the Coast with me, I'm gonna make sure he's good."

A glimmer of hope shone in Rahshida's eyes. "Kenyatta, please don't let him get turned out to this craziness. Teach him a better way."

"I'll do my best, Auntie," he said, looking over at Gunn whose eyes were cold and focused. "I'll do my best."

IT TOOK nearly a half hour, but the young men finally went on their way. Snake Eyes was gone again, this time tracking down a current address for Major Blood. He'd heard through the grapevine that he'd purchased a property on the east side of Compton. Rahshida had taken Lil Gunn inside the house to have a heart-to-heart talk. He'd been elated when Gutter made the announcement that he'd be moving east with him. Gunn saw it as an opportunity to learn the art of gang-banging from a true street legend so naturally he was all for it. What he didn't know was that his cousin had a whole different plan in mind.

Gutter had thought of himself as untouchable, especially after his resurrection, but the man formerly known as B-High had shown him different. The first thing Gutter intended to do when he got back to New York was move everyone out. He had recently closed on the house in Long Island and wanted it to be a surprise for Sharell, but the botched hit sped things up. Now her dream house was a safe house. He realized that he needed to do a better job at keeping his family and his hood separate and Brooklyn just wasn't far enough.

"Can I holla at you for a minute?" Monifa walked up on him.

"Sup, ma?" he asked a little dryly. From the look in her eyes he could tell she had something heavy on her mind and he really wasn't for it at that moment.

"Y'all really riding tonight?"

He looked at her as if it were a stupid question. "Come on, Mo, you know the answer to that."

"Kenyatta, I understand you're hurting over Gunn, as we all are, but ain't much can be done about it right off. You said it yourself that he ain't even in California so what good will it do for you to roll tonight?" The shameful look Gutter gave her put a nasty thought in her mind. "Gutter, you can't. They're civilians!"

"So was Gunn, he was inactive."

Monifa gave him a disbelieving look. "Homey, the last time I checked you couldn't retire from this life like a nine-to-five. I'm not saying it was right for Gunn to die, but he knew the risks. If you wanna ride on Major Blood, I feel you … but leave everybody else out of it."

For a minute Gutter's face softened, but when he saw Criminal standing off to the side waiting to see him his war face came back. "Mo, I hear what you talking, but I ain't got no understanding of that shit right now. They done took the two people closest to me in under a year and if I don't put my murder game down now, these niggaz ain't never gonna learn."

"Gutter"—she moved closer and spoke in a hushed tone—"you don't have to do it like this. Revenge is one thing, but this … Kenyatta, I can remember a time where there were lines that even you wouldn't cross."

Gutter took a step back and stared at her. "This is a whole new day, baby, and I'm a whole new man, smell me? It's kill or be killed, ma, ain't no more passes."

Monifa searched his eyes for some semblance of the youth or innocence that they once held, but all she saw were two pale green pools. No life, no warmth, only color. "You are truly lost, aren't you?"

"Nah, I ain't lost, baby." He kissed her on the forehead. "I'm just really finding myself." He stepped around Monifa and went to join Criminal.

Monifa watched him leave and wondered who the man was that she'd just spoken to. Gutter had always been a killer, or at least that's what she'd heard, but even he was within reason. She didn't know the man standing not ten feet away from her and she didn't know the man that she'd given her body to. If Kenyatta Soladine still lurked anywhere inside that shell, he was buried too deep for her to discover. There was a time when she was the most important thing in Kenyatta's life, but to Gutter she would always come second to the set.

"YOU GOT that done already?" Gutter asked in surprise.

"Shit, you should've known that wouldn't take long. The biggest problem was having too many volunteers. The hood loved yo uncle, cuz," Criminal said.

"Yeah, that's all well and good, but I don't need no bunch of ragtag niggaz at my back when I bust this move, C."

"Kick back, cuz, you know I wouldn't even do you like that. These niggaz is handpicked by me, cuz. Niggaz I ride wit on the regular, I know what they made of," he assured Gutter.

"That's why I fuck wit you, cuz, you always been a straight rider." Gutter draped his arm around Criminal lovingly. "Man, you ready to put in some *real* work?"

"Cuz, you know I stay down for that one-eight." He flashed the butt of the gun jammed down the front of his oversized jeans. "I been waiting for a reason to trip on a nigga anyway, but them touching Gunn means it's no-holds-barred. Man, I'm gonna smoke any muthafucka out there, that's on the turf!"

Gutter smiled at Criminal. Of all the young homeys, he really dug Criminal. He was a loyal soldier and spent more time listening than he did talking. Not only was he about his business, but he loved the set more than anything. He showed the same kind of vigor about gang-banging as Lou-Loc and Gutter had. If he survived the night he was surely going to become a big man in the hood, Gutter would see to that.

"Sup, locs?" Lil Gunn addressed the two men.

"What it is, lil nigga." Criminal pounded his fist. "How you holding up?"

Lil Gunn shrugged. "I'll be a'ight, man. Niggaz die every day."

Gutter placed a hand on Lil Gunn's shoulder. "Cuz, you daddy wasn't just no nigga, he was a legend. You might not have been as tight with him as you should've, but don't never doubt that your father was a great man. Outside of this banging shit, Gunn was a good nigga and did a lot of good for the neighborhood."

"I hear you, cuz," Lil Gunn said.

"Man, don't even trip that shit 'cause you know we fixing to ride for the big homey," Criminal told him, trying to pick his spirits up.

"That's what I'm talking about; I'm ready to blast on something!" Lil Gunn said eagerly.

"Man, you ain't gonna do shit but stay your ass in the house where women and children are supposed to be. This ain't something for kids, man," Gutter told him.

"Man, Criminal ain't but a year or two older than me," Lil Gunn pointed out.

"But he ain't my little cousin." Gutter mushed him playfully. "Dig, I know you can handle yourself, Gunn, but I promised Auntie that I'd try to deprogram some of that street shit outta you."

"Come on, G, that's my pops!"

"Yeah, and you done already went and made your mark for

him, which I'm still thinking about fucking you up about. Gunn, you're still a shorty, man, no matter how many niggaz you done shot. Enjoy being a kid for a while, because when you blink it'll be all gone, feel me?"

"Yeah, man," Lil Gunn mumbled.

"Don't feel bad, cuz. Just think, tomorrow night we'll be on in New York City. If you thought L.A. was live, wait till you get a taste of the city. Them bitches love Cali niggaz."

"Straight up?" Lil Gunn asked excitedly.

"Square biz, loc. Besides, you a Soladine nigga, pulling hoes is in your genes. Now go on in the house and start getting your shit ready. We still got a lot to do before we bail and I still gotta convince ya mama to let you roll."

"She ain't gonna give a damn. Not having to look after me will just give her more time to get faded." Lil Gunn stomped off to the house.

"Watch your mouth!" Gutter called after Gunn, who slammed the screen door behind him.

"Man, you really ain't gonna let that nigga get it in for his pops?" Criminal asked.

"Hell, nah, I ain't letting him ride. That there is a child, Criminal, this shit ain't for him."

Criminal shrugged. "It ain't really for none of us, but it's what we got. Maybe if you let him ride out he'll get it out of his system."

"Let me tell you something." Gutter grabbed Criminal by the collar of his T-shirt. "That's my uncle's boy and he ain't gonna fall in line with this dumb shit. If I ever hear talk of a nigga letting Gunn ride again, I'm gonna be a real firm supporter of Crip-on-Crip violence, you understand me?"

"A'ight, homey, damn!" Criminal cringed. He'd heard stories

about Gutter's wrath and didn't want to be on the receiving end of it.

"Good." He let him go and then smoothed Criminal's T-shirt. "Look, man, sorry about all that. Check, y'all go out and start rounding up them cars. When the sun goes down we ride on oh-las."

chapter 34

MAJOR BLOOD paced back and forth under the L on 128th and Twelfth. There was planning to be done and enemies to lay and Hawk wanted a sit-down. He had no idea what the man wanted to talk about and frankly didn't care. All he wanted to do was get it over with so he could go back to busting Crip skulls. The news of B-High's death didn't sit well with him.

B-High was a two-bit junkie and a killer, but one of the few friends Major Blood had left. It should've been a simple task for him to follow Sharell and then kill her, but something had gone wrong. Now Major Blood would most likely have to kill the bitch his self, if he could even find out where she'd disappeared to. She and Satin had vanished and nobody seemed to know where they were, but they couldn't hide forever and he always filled his contracts, no matter how long they took.

"Man, what you think he wants?" Eddie asked nervously.

"Like I fucking care. They smoked Miguel, man. I don't wanna hear nothing other than a full-out strike come outta that dude's mouth," Tito said.

"Oh, don't worry about that, my nigga. We've played enough, now we crush Harlem and bring the glory back to the five. This is the part of the movie where the thugs cry," he vowed.

"There he go right there." Eddie nodded to a black Mercedes truck that was coming down the block. Before the car had even come to a complete stop, Hawk was on the curb and making hurried steps toward the trio.

"Hawk, what's popping, baby?" Eddie grinned.

"You, shut the fuck up." He pointed at Eddie, wiping the smile from his face. "Blood," he addressed Major, "I need to holla at you."

Major Blood shrugged his shoulders. "So talk."

"What the fuck are you out here doing?" Hawk questioned. Red and Shotta had parked the car and were a few paces away watching the scene.

"My job, nigga. Fuck you think I'm doing?" Major Blood shot back.

"I don't recall you making all of us hot being a part of your job description. Do you know I just got outta lockup?"

"They just springing you from the Island?" Major asked in an uninterested tone.

"No, the precinct."

"Then what the fuck is you crying about, Hawk. So you had to spend a few hours in the can, personally I think it's good for your character." Major snickered.

Hawk took a deep breath. "Look, homey, don't break fly with me. I'm talking about this sick-ass game you're playing with Gutter's people. You've got the police crawling all over the hood behind this shit. Why don't you just whack who you gotta whack and be done with it?"

"Oh, I'm gonna kill Gutter all right, but I'm gonna do it in my own time, on my own terms," Major said.

Seeing that reasoning with Major wasn't working, Hawk decided to throw his weight around. "Check this, Blood, you a respected member of this thing of ours, but I'm calling the shots in Harlem. Now, you done turned a fruitful-ass spot into a shooting gallery all because of some sick-ass game you're trying to play with Gutter. My advice to you is to do what you came for and get on the next thing smoking back west."

Major stared at him in disbelief. "Your advice? Muthafucka, who is you to advise me of anything? Blood, them niggaz smoked my little man, so this grudge is personal now. First I'm gonna finish smashing on Harlem, then I'm gonna kill Gutter's bitch, and just when that nigga think it can't get no worse I'm gonna pop his fucking head off. So my advice to you, is to try and stay out of the cross fire. I'd hate to see you end up like Bad Ass."

Hawk felt a chill at that statement. It was rumored that Major had had the O.G. killed, but the evidence was never solid enough to bring him before the nation on charges of treason. Hawk knew that Major was trying to intimidate him and if he let him the killer would surely have free rein in New York.

"Man, I ain't Bad Ass!" Hawk shot back. "I've been putting in work for a long time, Blood, don't test me."

"Fuck outta here." Major laughed him off. "When is the last time you shot some fucking body? See, that's the problem with you old niggaz." Major inched closer to him.

"Watch ya self, son," Red spoke up. He moved closer to Hawk, but Major Blood ignored him.

"When y'all come up on a few dollars," Major Blood continued, "you lose that edge, and that is a sign of weakness." Without warning he shot Red in the chest, dropping him. Shotta moved to draw, but Tito had him covered.

"You know what they say about the weak and the strong." Major rubbed the hot barrel across Hawk's face.

"You loony muthafucka, if you kill me then your ass will never make it out of New York. You'll spend the rest of your days as a hunted man." It was a weak threat, but it was all Hawk could think of to say to save his life.

Major just laughed at him. "Baby boy, your name don't hold that kinda weight anymore. It's a new day in Harlem, Blood," Major squeezed the trigger and hit Hawk once in the chest, surprising all in attendance.

Hawk clutched at the gaping hole and stared up at Major Blood in disbelief. He knew that the killer's services came at a high price, but he never expected it to be his life. Shotta tried to break and run, but Major gunned him down.

"Man, they're gonna send a fucking hit squad after us," Tito said nervously.

"Let them," Major said as if it were nothing. "In two or three days my cousin Reckless will be here with a few of the homeys from the set. Niggaz from the East Coast can either side with us, or die with Hawk. At this point I don't give too much of a fuck."

"This is bad, man. Real bad," Eddie said, pacing nervously.

"The old ways are done," Major Blood said to the corpse at his feet. "It's time to bring in some fresh blood." With a smoking barrel in his hand he turned to Tito and Eddie. "What's it gonna be, homey, the new regime or the old?" he asked, pointing the gun at Tito's head.

"Shit, I'm wit you all day Blood," Tito said hurriedly.

"What about you?" Major Blood turned the gun on Eddie.

Eddie swallowed his heart, which was trying to crawl up from his throat. "All I wanna know is what we're gonna call the new set?"

"That's what I like to hear from my generals," Major Blood said proudly, tucking the gun back into his waistband. "This night marks a new beginning for our little family. Death to all those who oppose us, Crip, Blood, or civilian. Come on, y'all"—he draped his arms around them—"let's go get twisted, because tonight. . . . We've got a funeral to attend."

GUTTER STARED at himself in the mirror for a long while before he finally managed to get off the bed. All of his jewelry and identification were wrapped in a sock and tucked in the top drawer. He was dressed in dark blue jeans and a black sweatshirt. Over his freshly done braids he wore a stocking cap so as not to worry about leaving hair follicles behind. He watched enough *CSI* to know that the police technology allowed them a million different ways to catch a nigga if they wanted them bad enough, and for what they were about to pull, they'd sure as hell be hot on their heels.

Making sure his twin Glocks were secured in the holsters around his belt he headed out the bedroom and descended the stairs. Monifa was sitting in the living room with Rahshida and Lil Gunn watching some old movie on television. He tried to smile at her, but she turned away. *Fuck her too,* he thought to himself. If she thought because she'd gotten a little dick from him in a moment of weakness meant she could dictate what he did, she was dead wrong. Gutter loved Monifa, but it was a love that had been slowly fading over the years. His love for the set was everlasting.

"I'm heading out, Auntie," he called to Rahshida. She glanced up at him then went back to watching her movie. "You need anything?" She didn't even acknowledge him. "A'ight, I see how it's going down. Fuck it, I'm out." Gutter had made it to the front door when Lil Gunn came running up behind him.

"Cuz, I need to holla at you about something." Gunn whispered. "Walk with me to the kitchen." Gutter looked over his shoulder and both Monifa and Rahshida were watching him.

"Gunn, I told you that I ain't letting you ride with us tonight," Gutter scolded him as they walked into the kitchen.

"Nah, man. I know I can't ride, but I need you to do something for me." The youngster dipped under the sink and came up holding something wrapped in a pillowcase. He unwrapped it to expose the six-shot .44 hidden inside.

Gutter gave him a quizzical look.

"It belonged to my daddy," he explained. "When you bust on them niggaz, do it with my daddy's fo-fo," Gunn pleaded. Tears had welled up in his young eyes.

"You got that, cousin," Gutter assured him, placing the .44 down the front of his pants, weighing them down further.

"That ain't good enough, Gutter, you gotta put it on something. Put it on the hood that you gonna kill them niggaz that killed my daddy."

"Gunn—" Gutter began but was cut off.

"Fuck that, cuz. You either put in on the turf or the moment y'all leave the block, I'm gonna sneak outta here and handle it myself!" Gunn said seriously.

Little Gunn had backed him into a corner. Putting something on your hood was the most serious oath you could take. If you put something on your hood and didn't follow through then your word didn't count for shit.

Gutter took Gunn by his shoulders and looked him in the eye.

"On Harlem Crip, I'm gonna make sure your father's murder doesn't go unpunished. I'm gonna bring it to them niggaz, cousin."

To Gutter's surprise, Lil Gunn grabbed him in a bear hug. The young man squeezed as hard as he could, while sobbing into Gutter's chest. "I know you will. My daddy used to always tell me that you and me was more like brothers than cousins and I know you'd never let your little brother down." Gunn pulled away and wiped his nose and eyes with the back of his T-shirt.

"Go on back in the living room before your aunt thinks I'm trying to teach you how to cook crack or some shit." Gutter mushed him. The two men walked back into the living room, and all eyes were still on Gutter. He just shook his head and stepped out the front door, where he was greeted by ten armed and dangerous men.

part IV

WHEN THUGS CRY

FUNERALS, JUST as a rule, are sad as hell. But to attend a funeral for a child was a whole new kind of pain. Gutter had paid for the entire funeral, including the seemingly infinite flowers that were spread over the caskets and along the walls, but it couldn't bring back the lives of the two men who were sent to their final wake.

China and Rob were laid out side by side in two beautifully crafted caskets of a heavenly blue hue. Their faces no longer wore the scowls the streets made them hide behind, but the calmness of two boys who may have just laid down for a nap.

Rob's mother wore a grim face, occasionally dabbing at the tears that seemed to flow lightly but consistently down her face. Her heart was crushed beyond measure at losing her little boy, but she tried to hold it together as best she could. Ms. Lucy was another case. She bawled like a hungry infant, thrashing her head and occasionally falling. Twice her sister had to keep her from hitting the ground.

C-style sat alone in the corner, taking in the scene. All the homeys had showed up to the funeral. The one decent thing Pop Top had done under his rule was insist that no one showed up to the funeral in street clothes. Though Ms. Lucy knew what was up, Rob's mother was a square, and they didn't want to disrespect her. Everybody wore grim faces as they thought of the two lives lost to the set.

The set, C-style thought to herself. Look what the set had taken from her. Rob might not have been the be-all and end-all as far as men went, but he was hers. They had a bond that was supposed to stand the test of time, it wasn't enough though. He was gone...he died trying to protect her from the enemy...the same enemy C-style had blasted out of existence. It was either kill or be killed was the way she saw it.

There were so many things going through her head that she didn't really know what to feel; sad for the loss of her lover, guilty because she was now a murderer, or stupid for buying into Gutter's war? C-style looked down at the cold face of her lover and now imagined herself in the casket. Harlem suddenly started to feel way too small for her.

Pop Top stood off to the back, flanked by High Side and Bruticus. Hollywood sat on the other side of the pew with a fresh-faced young thing snuggled against him. He wore a bandage over the side of his face where Lexi had cut him and dark glasses. Ever since he'd alerted Gutter to Pop Top's bullshit there had been tension between them. Hollywood didn't give too much of a shit about his attitude though, his face and his business were ruined.

Every so often High Side could be seen casting a suspicious glance at Pop Top. His friend had something cooking and High Side was sure it'd go poorly. He and Pop Top went back like two flats, and had held each other down against seemingly impossible odds, but he was talking some other shit. If they tried a mutiny and it didn't go right they'd be dead men.

"Sup, cuz?" Pop Top asked High Side, noticing the conflicted look on his face.

High Side shrugged. "Ain't shit, man, just thinking. Seems like we're losing more of ours than taking out theirs. It's fucked-up what happened to the lil homeys." He nodded at the caskets.

"Yeah, man. A real fucking shame," Pop Top agreed. "Don't trip though, they gonna get theirs, all we need is a new strategy. After the funeral I'm gonna dip out to L.I. for a minute with Sharell."

"What happened to 'fuck Gutter, I ain't no babysitter'?" High Side questioned.

"You know there's always a method to my madness, cuz. Just be ready to roll when I come scoop you."

High Side looked at him. "Man, Gutter asked you to go, not me."

"High Side, it's gonna rain out this bitch and I don't want none of mine to get wet. We just gonna sit up for a while and plot our next move." Pop Top tried to sway him.

"Man, a nigga got business on the streets; I ain't got time to be laid up in the suburbs. Do what you gotta do, man, I'm out here."

"What y'all rapping 'bout?" Bruticus asked, moving closer. He was still a bit stiff from the bullet he'd taken in his lower back, but thanks to the medication he'd been prescribed he wasn't feeling much pain.

"Ain't shit, just thinking back on the homeys," Pop Top lied.

"Damn, cuz, I can't believe them lil niggaz is gone," Bruticus said.

"I know, son," Pop Top agreed. "Man, I don't know what made China off his self, but the boy Rob went out like a gangsta!" Pop Top said proudly.

"Ain't no honor in death, kid," Hollywood said. No one had

even seen him get up and walk over. "Them young boys is outta here, cuz…gone from it," he said emotionally. "They didn't deserve to go out like that, fam."

"Yeah, but we gonna ride for them kids. Word to mine, it's on!" Bruticus declared.

"All day, cuz." Pop Top was speaking to Bruticus, but staring at Hollywood. "So what's up, you gonna call Gutter on speaker phone so he can get the play-by-play on this too?" he asked sarcastically.

Hollywood looked at him stone-faced from behind his shades. "Man, go ahead with that shit, Top. This ain't the time or place."

"Then pick a time and a place," Pop Top challenged.

Hollywood glared at Pop Top. He was surely armed, but Hollywood didn't come empty-handed. He had a two-shot tucked in his cast that he could get to easily if need be, but to cause a scene at a funeral? "Let me get with you outside for a minute." Hollywood stepped outside with Pop Top and the others on his heels. Before the chapel doors were even closed behind them, Pop Top started right in.

"Fuck that shit. A bitch cut ya face and you get all scared and shit and call Gutter. What's up, Wood, I thought you was 'bout the movement?" Pop Top accused.

"Man, don't ever question my dedication to Harlem, I'm just as down as any of these niggaz, if not more so." He motioned to the scar on his face and the cast on his hand. "This shit was about dealing with a problem that was getting out of hand."

"I had the problem under control!" Pop Top snarled.

"How you had it under control, Top, when we taking more losses than them? Look"—Hollywood tried to compose himself—"we all crew so it ain't no sense in beefing about it, but we had to let the homey G know what was going down, Top."

Pop Top sucked his teeth. "Whatever, man."

"Why don't you two niggaz kiss and make up?" Bruticus teased.

"Fuck you." Pop Top spat on the ground. "So, what Gutter say to you about this Major Blood cat?" he asked Hollywood.

"He's bad news times ten. The best way to deal with a cat like Major Blood is to kill him on sight, no questions asked." Hollywood recounted what Gutter had told him.

"Shit, we've been trying like a muthafucka," High Side added.

"Man, it's time to lay this bitch-ass nigga out once and for all. Me and—" That was as far as Bruticus got before the back of his head was knocked clean off.

THE REVEREND had stopped speaking and everyone crouched in their seats when the sounds of gunshots erupted outside. C-style took a quick glance around the room and saw that her crew that had gathered in the back was nowhere to be found, so that meant they were the source of the gunshots, but the question remained of what side of the bullets they were on. Some of the homeys started drawing weapons and charging the door, sending the mourners further into panic. Fingering the small pistol in her purse, C-style fell in step behind her gang.

EDDIE STEERED the car while Tito sat in the passenger seat rolling a blunt. Major was silent in the backseat, which unnerved Eddie. The whole time Major Blood had been in New York, he'd been boastful and arrogant, but now he was as silent as the grave. Now he just sat, staring out the window and petting a C-15 .223 caliber like it was a cat. Eddie wasn't sure where he'd gotten the machine gun and wasn't about to ask, considering the mood Major Blood had been in since killing Hawk.

Eddie turned right on 125th and Eighth, heading north. Along the block he could see the cars lined up and people milling about in front of the funeral home. Among those people were Pop Top and his gang. Seeing his enemies Major Blood sat up in the seat.

"Slow down, my nigga," Major said, moving to a kneeling position in the backseat.

"You ain't gonna kill these niggaz in front of the funeral home, are you?" Eddie asked nervously.

Major chuckled. "Watch me." As Eddie neared the funeral home, Major leaned out the window and started dumping.

ALL HOLLYWOOD could do was stand there in shock as bits of Bruticus's skull sprayed on his face. One minute they had been talking and the next his comrade had gone down. Major Blood was leaning out of the back of Hawk's truck firing on them with reckless abandon.

A crackhead coming out of the store, holding a forty ounce of Country Club, was the only thing that saved Hollywood from getting caught too. The bullet tore through the fiend's chest, slamming him into the bodega window. Willing himself to move, Hollywood dove behind the funeral home's hearse, which Tito proceeded to spray with slugs from a black Mac.

"It's on!" Pop Top roared, drawing his own weapon. He fired on the truck, while trying to back up to the safety of the funeral home. At the sound of gunfire the homeys had started filing out of the funeral home, and most of them got caught in the cross fire and were gunned down. A few were able to let off return fire, while others ran for cover.

Answering the call to arms, High Side returned fire on his enemies. He and Pop Top looked like two gunslingers; taking turns ducking and returning fire. The windows of the truck shattered, but there was no way to tell if they'd hit anyone. The tires on the truck squealed as Major Blood and company sped off up Eighth.

C-STYLE STEPPED out onto the curb and was horrified at the scene. Bodies were strewn all in front of the funeral home, which was now riddled with bullets. Hollywood was picking himself up off the ground with a terrified look in his eyes. Pop Top and High Side looked rattled, but otherwise okay. Too bad the same couldn't be said for Bruticus. The former Decepticon was stretched out on the concrete with a gaping hole in the back of his head. When C-style saw the goop oozing out the back of his head she ran around the corner and vomited.

"Oh, shit they laid the homey!" a nameless face said, motioning toward Bruticus's body.

Pop Top walked over and looked down at his slain friend. "Damn," he whispered, hearing Gutter's warning about Major Blood ringing off in his head. "What kinda nigga shoots up a fucking funeral home?"

"The kind Gutter warned us about," Hollywood said, making the sign of the cross over the fallen homeys.

"What the fuck we gonna do now, Top?" High Side asked.

"Make sure we don't end up like that." He nodded at Bruticus. "Wood," he addressed the pretty boy with a plan forming in his head. "The homey got something he need done and I'm gonna need you with me on this."

"All day, homey. What you need?" Hollywood asked, forgetting that they'd been about to come to blows a few minutes before.

"I'm gonna call you with an address and have you come meet me. Once we rally the troops, we take action. It's time I did something to bring an end to this shit and restore some type of order to Harlem Crip. I'm getting Major Blood off our asses and ending this fucking war once and for all."

"We 'bout to go after Major Blood?" Hollywood asked.

"Something like that. I'll put it to you like this, in a few days this little war will be over and Major Blood will be officially out of our hair," Pop Top assured them before walking around the corner.

Hollywood looked to High Side for an explanation, but he just shrugged. There was something going on with Pop Top that Hollywood couldn't place his finger on, but he had a bad feeling about it. "I'm up, fam. I ain't trying to be around when the police come asking what happened."

"Shit, me either. I'm getting the fuck from around here," High Side said, watching as people finally got the courage to come out of the bullet-riddled funeral home.

"C, it might be a good idea for you to get out of here too. If you want I can give you a ride?" Hollywood offered.

C-style managed to tear her watery eyes away from the carnage. "Nah, I'm gonna stay for a while."

Hollywood knew that she was still going through the motions over Rob so it would be useless to argue the point of why she shouldn't stick around after a shoot-out. "A'ight, ma, but let me take that from you." He reached over and took the gun she had forgotten was in her hand. "C, you sure you're good?" The girl nodded weakly. "Cool, baby. Do what you gotta do and stay off the block for a while. I got a bad feeling about this shit," Hollywood warned before dipping off to his car with High Side on his heels.

C-style just stood there for a while, staring at the ruined funeral home and the horrified looks on the mourners' faces. Two of the homeys were escorting Rob's mother and Ms. Lucy from the funeral home to the limo. She could tell they were terrified and rightfully so. It was bad enough that they had lost their babies, but the war wouldn't even allow them to mourn in peace.

C-style took her blue bandanna from her purse and went to wipe her face, but stopped in midmotion. It was the same bandanna she'd been given when Big Keke and the home girls had put her on the set. Her heart had swelled with pride when she received it and Gutter embraced her as one of his lil home girls, but now it represented the ugliness that being in a gang had brought into her life. Until that moment it had been one of her most prized possessions.

"It wasn't supposed to be like this," she whispered to herself. C-style let the bandanna slip from her hand and float to the ground. This drew some disapproving looks from some of the home boys that were still gathered around, but at that point she didn't care. She was done with the set.

LEXI WAS propped against the lumpy white pillows, trying her best to get comfortable. Her head felt like a herd of elephants was on parade inside it. Hollywood had treated her to a hairline fracture and a severe concussion. To add insult to injury Major Blood had botched the hit on him. She was pissed, but her visitor had eased the pain a bit.

When she'd gotten the initial phone call she thought it to be a prank or even a setup, but as she brushed her hand against the manila envelope containing the five g's she knew it to be real. If her source was on the up-and-up then Gutter had finally gone too far and Major Blood would get a second chance at Hollywood. Soon she would call him to set the final wheels in motion, but the morphine drip in her IV told her it could wait until after her nap.

▮▯▮▯▮▯▮▯▮▯▮▯▮▯▮▯▮▯▮▯▮▯▮

chapter 36

THE EAST SIDE OF COMPTON: SOUTH ATLANTIC
AND EAST COMPTON BOULEVARD

MAN, WHAT the fuck is this nigga doing way over on this side?" Criminal asked from the backseat.

"Fuck if I know," Blue Bird said, taking a hit off the dipped cigarette and trying to pass it to Tears, but he declined so Criminal readily snatched it. "What I do know is that these niggaz is out of bounds, aiding and abetting a fucking fugitive!"

"Man, y'all need to put that shit out and get focused on the muthafucking task at hand," Tears said, rolling down the windows. "We deep in enemy territory, cuz. I'm sure if Major has brought a crib out this way there's probably some 900s 'round here too." Tears pulled up to a red light at the corner of East Compton Boulevard and South Atlantic Avenue.

"Fuck 900s and for damn sure fuck Lime Street, I'm dumping on sight," Criminal said, way louder than he needed to. The PCP was obviously kicking in.

A group of young men standing in front of the store caught Blue Bird's attention. He recognized them all as members of East Side Lime Street except the one in the wheelchair. He was a 900. Being the troublemaker he was, he looked back at Criminal and said, "Say, cuz, there go some Nines right there. You gonna let them marks clown you by posting up when they know we riding?"

"Nigga what? Watch this muthafucka bark." Criminal brandished a long-nosed Colt. Tears knew what was about to go down and had it not been for the red light he would've pulled off. Before he could even protest Criminal was out of the car and heading in the direction of the store.

IT WAS a beautiful night on the Pacific Coast. The sack chasers were out sacking, and the dope boys were out getting their sling on. Just another day in the hood... At least it was for the moment.

"What's up, East Side?" A man in a wheelchair asked, rolling up to the store. He was dressed in black Dickies pants and a red T-shirt.

"Oh, shit, Big Bo from the Nine!" He snatched his green Seattle Supersonics hat off for emphasis. "Man, fuck you doing way over here?"

"Same thing you doing, nigga, trying to cop a bottle and get blown," Bo told him, wheeling up to the window to place his order.

"They ain't got no liquor stores where you stay at?" A man in a Raider's cap asked sarcastically.

"Hell yeah, you know the hood ain't got nothing but hard times and liquor stores. Me and the homeys is kicking it off San Luis at the rest."

"Y'all posted up over here? You must be ready to flip that Lime?" another young man asked. He was dressed in jeans and a T-shirt, but there was a green sports band around his arm, the kind you would get at a club.

Bo looked up at him. "You know I ain't no set flipper, Blood. It's Nine or nothing, y'all know my style." He threw up his set.

"Man, your old ass still out here tripping, wheelchair and all," Lil Bay teased him.

"Please believe it, my nigga. They might've put me down"—he dipped under the seat of his wheelchair, and came up holding a small pistol—"but not out, you feel me, dawg? I ain't tripping though. My nigga Major copped a pad for his people down that way, so we just come through and coast. Me, Mo-Mo, and the nigga Reckless."

"Reckless? I thought I seen him come through here a time or two. I just thought he was on one."

"Man, stop that bullshit. My folk is cool," Bo said, knowing he was telling a bold-faced lie. Though Reckless was barely a day over twenty, he had Major Blood's temper and bloodlust.

"Shit the way Reckless be on it I doubt if it'll be a secret for very long. It's only a matter of time before that fool smokes somebody, much of that sherm as he smoke," Bay said, taking a swig of his forty ounce.

"Man, the nut don't fall too far from the tree," Supersonics cap said. "I don't know who the fuck is worse, between him and Major."

"Say, Blood, who that?" sports band asked, nodding toward a dark-skinned young man who was coming across the street. His question was answered when he heard the battle cry.

"*Crrrrriiiiiiiipppp!*" Criminal bellowed right before he lit the block up.

A SERVICE STATION OFF NORTH HOLLY AVENUE

"RUN MUTHAFUCKA grab you shit and duck, I'm from the crew of O.G.s where niggaz don't give a fuck!" Mad Man sang along with the Dogg Pound song blasting from the stereo. "Man, this niggaz can't C faded!" He slapped Lil Blue on the arm.

"Man, turn that shit down before you get us pulled over, nigga!" Lil Blue snapped. "These niggaz send us off on this fucking dummy mission and yo ass is having a sing along."

"Kick back, cuz. You act like it's something to bust on these ho-ass niggaz."

"Man, this is some real fuck shit!" Lil Blue said from the passenger seat of the stolen Pontiac. "Them niggaz is gonna get all the glory, while we do the grunt work."

"Quit bitching, cuz, this shit should be fun," Mad Man told him, as he surveyed the gas station. A middle-aged man was jiggling the pump inside his '91 Ford, and a gray Le Sabre was double-parked in front of the station. "Come on, man. Let's go in here and rip this bitch off so the homeys can get it popping."

The plan had been for Mad Man and Lil Blue to go around committing petty crimes and leading the police on a chase while Gutter and his team would roll through and put the smash on Reckless and his family. Lil Blue Bird was still upset that they wouldn't be a part of the murders, but Mad Man didn't care. As far as he was concerned, stripes were stripes.

"I still don't like being no damn diversion," Lil Blue complained, taking the gun from under his seat and jamming it into the pocket of his pullover. Still mumbling under his breath, he followed Mad Man across the gas station.

There wasn't much going on inside the filling station. A group of young men congregated around the beer cooler, arguing about what kind of malt liquor they were gonna chip in for. Behind the bulletproofed glass a young girl clicked her gum, and chatted away on her cell phone, not really caring about the loitering young men. All she wanted to do was make it through her shift unmolested. From the way the young men were dressed Mad Man knew they were bangers and a wonderful plan formed in his mind.

"Looks like we might get some real action after all, cuz." Mad Man nudged Lil Blue and nodded at the young men around the cooler. Lil Blue Bird just smiled and continued on to the potato chip rack, while Mad Man moved to get a Pepsi.

"What's cracking, baby?" Mad Man capped to the attendant, opening the Pepsi before paying for it. He took a deep swig and watched for her reaction.

The girl rolled her eyes and clicked her gum one last time before asking the caller to hold on. "Can I help you?" She glared at Mad Man.

"Yeah, I came in to get some blunts and something to drink, but I'll settle for your phone number." Mad Man smiled, at which she just frowned.

"Nigga, please"—she rolled her eyes—"what you need to do is get yo ass from around here with all that blue on." She motioned toward his blue-on-blue Chucks. The girl tossed two Phillies in the little sliding drawer and punched in a series of keys on the register.

"Bitch, please, my pass is international!" Mad Man snarled. "Yo cuz," he called to Lil Blue Bird, loud enough for the young men by the cooler to hear. "This bitch sound like shorty that was wit that tampon we rolled on at the drive-through. You remember the bitch who fries you ate!"

"Straight up, cuz." He picked up on his friend's train of thought.

"Bitch ass rolled through the wrong hood and got caught, you know the rules." The last insult thrown spurred the young men to approach them.

"Sup, Blood. You know where you at?" said a young man wearing jeans two sizes too big for his slim hips. His fitted cap was cocked deep to the right, and the set of his jaw said trouble.

Lil Blue took up the challenge with his chest poked out. "Nigga, we know where we at. The question should be, do we give a fuck?"

"Y'all don't start tripping in here. You know I got a half hour left on my shift, so save that shit for then!" the cashier shouted from behind the glass.

"Bitch, shut up," Mad Man said, tossing his Pepsi against the glass. When he turned around to add his two cents to the mix, he was holding his hammer. "Now tell me where the fuck we at?" Mad Man demanded, pointing it at the man who'd approached Lil Blue Bird.

The young man's scowl faded and he was once again the little boy his mother would kiss on the forehead before school every morning. "Lime Street," he mumbled.

"What, nigga? Tell me again?" Mad Man pressed the barrel against his forehead.

The young man who had been sipping the forty looked like he was having a moment, but Blue Bird pushed the notion from his mind by pressing the barrel of the Beretta in his back. "Don't do it to yourself, homey," he warned.

"Now," Mad Man continued, "tell me where we at?"

The kid looked like he would fall out if he didn't think a sudden movement would've gotten him shot. "Lime . . . Street," he forced out. "East Lime Street."

Mad Man grinned at him before slamming the butt of the gun

into his head. The kid collapsed into a heap, trying to stop the gush of blood that was spewing from his head. "Fuck you hood, nigga!" Mad Man spat. He hadn't had to be so brutal, but he wanted to make sure that he left the young man with a clear picture of what he had signed on for choosing a side. One thing Mad Man hated more than an enemy was some that represented the life without fully understanding it.

"I done told you fool about set tripping in here, I'm 'bout to call the police!" the cashier threatened.

Lil Blue Bird spun and let off a shot. The barrier webbed, but didn't shatter, which was enough to get the cashier to jump beneath the counter. "Bitch, weren't you told to shut up? Now"—he turned to the young men—"you muthafuckas turn you pockets out," he said, waving the gun. "The big homey Gunn has passed on and he demands tribute."

Ten minutes later Mad Man and Lil Blue Bird were hopping back to the Pontiac, laughing like two schoolkids. They had robbed all the young men and the cashier before snatching an armful of cigarettes and fleeing. The police were surely on their way to the crime scene, which was expected. But when they got to the gas station and demanded to see the tape they'd only find out what Mad Man and Lil Blue already knew. The camera hadn't worked in three months. When they got back to the hood they would break Tia off for her stellar performance, but right then they had more mischief to cause. The chase was on.

THE MOTEL room at the Holland Motor Inn was several steps down from the room at the W Hotel in Manhattan, but it would have to do. Being anywhere within the five boroughs was too risky. Not only did he have to worry about the Crips, but the police were riding on every gang in an attempt to restore order and the Bloods wanted answers as to what had happened to Hawk. New York was on fire and Major Blood had struck the match.

"That shit is all over the news," Tito said proudly as he watched an Asian woman on the screen recount the shooting that evening in Harlem.

"Anybody reach out about Hawk yet?" Eddie asked.

Tito looked at his cell phone. "Yeah, niggaz been blowing my jack up all night, but I'm looping the calls."

"Man, they gonna know we was behind that shit," Eddie told him.

"So?" Major Blood spoke up. "Blood, Hawk was connected, but he ain't have no real street power in years. Niggaz is gonna be tight for a while, but when we bring down Harlem and start the new unification they'll get over it. Hell, we'll be heroes!"

"Or dead men," Eddie mumbled.

"I'm getting tired of your negative attitude, Eduardo." Major pointed a finger at him. He was about to start ranking on Eddie again, but his cell phone made him hold the thought. He listened for a while, trying to decipher the caller's slurred speech, then asked, "Lexi?"

chapter 37

SOUTH LIME AND EAST SAN LUIS

JUST BEING so deep in enemy territory, armed and out for blood, made Gutter think of Lou-Loc. There had been times when he and Lou-Loc would arm up to ride, looking to gain stripes or push a dangerous enemy off the planet. Although the enemies they sought that night were dangerous, it wasn't stripes that fueled him, it was revenge.

"You good, nephew?" Rahkim asked from the backseat.

"Yeah, man, I'm cool," Gutter replied, continuing to stare out the window.

"Damn, it's a bunch of niggaz out here," Danny said, watching the homeys on the block watch him. The residents of South Lime eyed the strangers suspiciously.

"Shit, all that means is that it'll be a higher body count," Jynx told him. "These Lime Street niggaz ain't 'bout shit, but the boy Reckless is as dangerous as a rattlesnake. If you see him, smoke his ass because he's damn sure gonna try and smoke you."

"I can dig it. Let's just do this and get up out. I ain't never been to the can in New York and I sure as hell don't wanna go while I'm out here."

"Don't trip, lil cuz. Mad Man and them are gonna have the police tied up for a while so we got a window of time," Rahkim informed him.

"Ain't that the house right there?" Jynx pointed at a two-story stucco number. There were two young men standing in front, one of which they recognized as Major Blood's nephew, Reckless.

"Yeah, there it go. And peep ya boy slipping," Rahkim said excitedly. "We got the drop on 'em, nephew; all we gotta do is lay 'em down." No sooner than Rahkim had made the statement there were gunshots in the distance. The element of surprise was gone and Reckless and his partner were now armed and alert to danger.

"Sounds like Tears and them done kicked it off already," Jynx said.

"Then we might as well claim our fifteen minutes of fame," Rahkim said, leaning out the window and leveling his gun. "What's up now, niggaz!"

SONIC'S HAT took one high in the chest, spinning him. Criminal popped him once more in the back of his head, tipping him forward and through the store window. Bay bolted for the street only to have Tears clip him with the car. He was hobbled but still found the strength to keep moving. This is when Blue Bird stepped from the vehicle.

"Come here, muthafucka." Blue Bird grabbed Bay by the front of his shirt. "Where the fuck you going, huh?" He slapped Bay twice in the face with his gun. When Bay crumpled to the ground Blue Bird shot him twice in the chest and looked around for his next victim.

Sports Band tried to run, but the PCP-charged Criminal was

on him. Sweeping Sports Band's legs, Criminal sent him crashing down on his face. Before Sports Band could fully roll over and plead for his life, Criminal aired him out.

The man in the Raider cap tried to run in the store, but the Korean owner had locked the door at the first signs of trouble. He turned around and found himself face-to-face with a grinning Blue Bird.

"Yeah, what that Hoover like?" Blue Bird demanded, pressing the hot barrel into Supersonics cap's cheek. His eyes were wild and his movements jerky from the PCP.

"Man, we ain't got no beef with Hoover." Raider cap winced against the burning.

"Tough shit, dick head. Next time be more careful of the muthafuckas you let lay in yo hood." Blue Bird shoved Raider's cap against the storefront and pulled the trigger. Raider cap's chest exploded in a nasty spray. Even after he was down, Blue Bird gave him two more for good measure.

Bo tried to use the element of surprise and draw his gun, but Tears was on him. He kicked the wheelchair over viciously, spilling Bo to the ground. "Hold that down, baby. The party is just about to get crunk."

"Well, well, what do we have here?" Blue Bird walked up. He grabbed Bo by the collar and hoisted him back into the chair. "What up, cuz?"

"Man, you niggaz is tripping, you know who you fucking wit?" Bo jerked away from Blue Bird. He tried to sound tough, but couldn't keep his voice steady. This wasn't the first time he'd looked into Blue Bird's eyes, but he feared it'd be the last.

"Gangsta Bo, you and yo peoples done finally stepped outta line." Blue Bird patted him on the cheek.

"Blue, what you talking man, y'all the ones who outta bounds right now. You popped off for nothing."

"Oh, I don't call laying the homey Gunn nothing." Tears stepped up. "Yo partner Major violated and now we gotta settle up."

"What you think we should do wit this nigga?" Blue Bird asked no one in particular, as he rocked Bo's wheelchair back and forth.

"Say, loc, let's see how fast he can move this muthafucka." Criminal kicked the chair.

"So what's up, Bo, you think you faster than a streetlight?" Blue Bird positioned himself behind the wheelchair and rolled Bo to the curb.

"Come on, Blue, stall me out!" Bo pleaded, trying to stop the chair's wheels with his hands, nicking his fingers up. Bo tried to climb out of the chair, but Blue Bird kept yanking him back down.

Blue Bird leaned down to whisper into Bo's ear. "Don't worry about it, homey. You won't be alone in hell for too long." Just as the light was about to turn green Blue Bird shoved Bo into the street.

Bo almost made it clean to the other side before his chair hit a pothole and deposited him onto the street. He looked on in horror as dozens of headlights bore down on him.

"Holy shit." Tears winced as a Cressida flipped Bo high into the air. He didn't even have the heart to look as the skidding Lincoln Navigator finished him off.

"Buck up, nigga, it ain't that bad." Blue Bird chuckled. "Let's make it back to the car and hit the block. Don't make no sense in Gutter and them having all the glory."

"Man, he said Reckless belonged to him," Tears reminded Blue Bird of Gutter's order.

Criminal shrugged. "Then we kill everybody who ain't Reckless."

THOUGH RECKLESS and Major Blood were first cousins, they looked nothing alike. Whereas Major was stocky and high yellow, Reckless was rail thin with skin like polished onyx. After Maria's death, Essie helped her parents to raise the orphaned Major along with her own child. Reckless grew up idolizing Major Blood and his exploits, and when he was old enough Major Blood turned him out to the life. Kill for kill Reckless hadn't quite reached Major Blood's status, but he was off to a damn good start, terrorizing the residents of L.A. and pushing his enemies off the map.

"So what's the word from Major?" Mo-Mo asked, sipping his forty ounce.

Reckless shrugged. "You know my big cousin is on his job. We lost B-High, but he dropped that funky nigga Hawk, so it's officially on with the homeys."

"B-High? I thought that nigga was dead?"

"The boy has been laying low on the East, but it looks like the East done laid him low."

"Church." Mo-Mo shook his head. "So when we supposed to be hitting New York?"

"Shouldn't be more than a few days. He's got some things to tie up before we push out," Reckless told him.

"Dude, I can't wait to get out there to the East. They say the money out there is sweeter than anything we've ever seen out here. And let's not even talk about the bitches. I hear damn near every bitch in Harlem got an ass like a horse. They ain't built like that out here, Blood, huh?"

"A bitch is a bitch to me," Reckless said, staring at his hands as if he had just discovered them. He loved to get high and analyze things. He had once spent an hour observing a roach he had trapped under a shot glass.

"Blood, that water got you straight tripping." Mo-Mo laughed. The humorous moment was short-lived when they heard gunshots and screams off in the distance. Before Mo-Mo could say anything, Reckless was as sober as a judge and on his feet, gun at the ready.

"Fuck was that?" Reckless asked, eyes sweeping the block.

"Man, Bay and them niggaz probably tripping," Mo-Mo said, not bothering to reach for his gun, which was lying next to his chair. Though he was also a killer he didn't function as well under the influence as Reckless.

"Them dumb-ass niggaz is always making the block hot." Reckless relaxed, but didn't put his pistol away. "I'm gonna check that dumb-ass little nigga when I see him later on."

"Kick back, Blood, you know how it goes in the hood." Mo-Mo relit the cigarette. He had just lifted the forty back to his lips when the bottle exploded, spraying him with beer and glass.

"What's up now, niggaz?" Rahkim roared, firing on the two young men. Rahkim was so anxious that he missed both targets, but he blew away damn near the entire wooden porch. Mo-Mo managed to fall off the chair while Reckless dipped behind a large flowerpot and returned fire.

The car came to a catercorner stop, blocking half the street. The homeys filed out of the car and moved to strategic positions from where they could lay Reckless or anyone else who thought to aid them. They were on foreign soil so it was free fire on all aggressors. Ducking and firing, Gutter found cover behind a sturdy oak, and assessed the situation.

Bullets flew with abandon, bringing chaos to the quiet block. It was almost as if Gutter had a front row seat to the premiere of his own movie. Danny was huddled against the car, clutching a shotgun to his chest. Gutter expected to see fear etched across his face, but instead he saw determination. His young protégé spun off the bumper and let a shell rip. Rahkim and Jynx took turns spraying the front of the house in an attempt to kill everyone inside. They had no intentions of taking prisoners. Seeing his homeys in combat stirred the monster in him. The promise of blood would finally be honored.

chapter 38

WHERE THE fuck these nigga come from?" Mo-Mo shouted to Reckless over the gunfire.

"I don't know where they came from, but I know where I'm about to send them!" Reckless snarled, firing from behind the flowerpot. He wished his cousin had been there beside him, but Mo-Mo would have to do...or at least he hoped. While Mo-Mo was only fighting for one life, Reckless was fighting for three because his girlfriend and infant son were inside the house.

Frustrated with the seemingly useless defensive stance, Reckless decided to press his enemies. When he saw an opening he darted out and tried to finish Rahkim, which would've equated to a dead enemy, had Gutter not shot him first. Reckless stumbled backward and crashed hard onto the porch.

"Nigga caught me," Reckless gasped as pain rocked the whole left side of his body. He tried to press his free hand over the wound to slow the bleeding, but it didn't help.

"Make for the pad!" Mo-Mo ducked and squeezed. The first

shot shattered a car windshield, but the second struck Jynx in the thigh, spilling him to the concrete. Reckless slipped into the house, stumbling across the threshold.

"They trying to turn tail, nephew, let's finish these cowards!" Rahkim shouted, advancing on the house.

Gutter's movements were so swift that his uncle had to do a double take. He had heard stories while he was in prison about how efficient a killer his nephew had become, but seeing it with his own two eyes was like watching *The Matrix*. Gutter moved with the grace of a dancer, but the skill of a war vet. Dirt flew in the air from where Mo-Mo's bullets struck, but he always seemed to be a fraction of a second too late to hit his target. Gutter faked left and went right, tossing himself to the dirt-filled front lawn, mashing the Glock's triggers as he went.

Mo-Mo's right shoulder exploded, slamming him into the door frame of the house. He was able to keep the grip on his pistol, but couldn't find the strength to raise his arm. Half falling into the house, Mo-Mo tried to slam the door behind him, but Rahkim was on his heels.

"No, the fuck you don't. I've waited too long for this here." Rahkim kicked the door in.

People were starting to stir from their houses to see what was going on, but a short blast from Danny's shotgun sent them scattering. In the distance he could see a group of young men gathering, surely the soldiers of Lime Street rallying to combat the invading Crips.

"Danny-Boy, Jynx!" Gutter shouted to them as he ascended the stairs. "Anybody come down here but ours, kill 'em!" he ordered before following Rahkim into the house.

Danny-Boy dragged Jynx up on the porch and helped him into one of the vacated chairs. His leg was soaked, but his gun arm was as strong as ever. Once Jynx was positioned, Danny dropped to one knee, resting the shotgun on the porch rail and awaited his enemies.

The inside of the house was a mass of chaotic sound when Gutter crossed the threshold. The television was tuned to BET and playing slightly louder than it needed to be. The smoke alarm blared as something left on the stove when the shooting started burned. An attractive Latino woman stood in the doorway of the kitchen chanting something Gutter couldn't make out, while a child wailed somewhere in the distance. Mo-Mo tried to run across the living room, but Rahkim kicked him roughly in the ass, sending him bouncing off the wooden steps and onto the carpet.

"Man, why you fucking wit us!" Mo-Mo yelled. He was in so much pain that he couldn't even roll for his pistol, which had slid across the room when he bounced off the steps.

"Cuz y'all fucked wit my family," Gutter shot back, moving to where Mo-Mo was laid out.

"Blood, Gunn drew first blood!" Mo-Mo tried to explain.

"And we're gonna draw the last," Rahkim interrupted. "Now die with some fucking dignity!" There was a thunderous roar, but it hadn't come from Rahkim's gun. He looked at his nephew quizzically, as if he'd just realized the seriousness of what they were about to do. There was a neat hole in the center of his forehead that had just started to leak blood down his cheek. Rahkim opened his mouth to say something, but there was only the sound of him hitting the floor face first.

"No!" Gutter howled, rushing to his uncle's side. Rahkim flapped around on the floor like a wounded fish. The blood had now begun to squirt from his head, soaking into the carpet below, while Gutter looked on in horror. Rahkim's karma had come back around to collect on the debt. No longer able to see his uncle suffer, he

finished him with a heart shot. Rahkim Soladine had taken his last ride.

THE MEN who rushed the house were young...the oldest couldn't have been more than eighteen. They were armed with sticks, bats, and a variety of small-caliber handguns. They had no idea what was going on inside the Drayton residence but they knew that some Crips had invaded their neighborhood, which was reason enough to rush head-on into danger.

Jynx leaned over in the lawn chair and waited for the first victim to step into view. He wore a hard face, but his eyes weren't those of a killer. He was just a young man willing to live or die in service to his set, and Jynx was all too willing to treat him to the latter. The boy didn't even have time to scream as the top of his head came off.

Danny's heart pounded so hard in his chest that he was sure everyone on the block could hear it. When Jynx licked off the mob scattered, but they were still advancing on the house. Sweat ran freely down his face, and his palms were so slick that it's a miracle that the shotgun didn't jump out of his hands. A chubby cat armed with a hunting rifle came creeping from the yard of the next house. His *were* the eyes of a killer. *"Kill or be killed, baby boy,"* he could hear Gutter telling him. Blinking a bead of sweat out of his eye, Danny caught his first body.

HAD IT not been for quick reflexes, Gutter would've gotten hit when Reckless darted out from the back room, firing blind as he hit the stairs. He was a man cornered and would fight until his last breath, but that was fine by Gutter. He wanted him to fight before he made his child a bastard. Drawing Big Gunn's .44 he took off after Reckless.

By the time Gutter made it to the bottom of the stairs, Reckless was just hitting a landing. He fired a shot, hitting his rival high in the back. Reckless staggered forward, but the railing kept him from falling down. Gutter licked a second shot, but Reckless was off down the hall. When Gutter cleared the second-floor landing, he played the wall and peeked around the corner before jetting into the line of fire.

Reckless's jog had slowed to a shamble, bouncing him from wall to wall like a drunk. The sheet he'd been clutching to his chest to stop the bleeding got tangled with his legs and he fell to one knee. Firing the gun blindly over his shoulder, Reckless staggered into a bedroom. A wicked smile crept across Gutter's lips as he knew he had his prey cornered.

"Time to die, pussy," Gutter said, moving toward the bedroom. Playing the wall, he inched along it and peeked inside. Reckless had his back to the door, frantically fumbling with the window, his spent pistol lying on the floor a few feet away.

"This for my family, nigga!" Gutter roared, cutting loose with the .44. The next few moments went in slow motion, but would forever be etched into his mind. The bullet seemed to move like a slow trickle, but its screech was like the wailing of one thousand police sirens. It was then that Reckless turned to meet his end and Gutter felt his soul shift. The thing he'd been clutching to his chest wasn't for the bleeding at all . . . it was his son.

"LOOKS LIKE they came out in full force, huh?" Tears joked, weaving the car left to right down Lime Street. There was a knot of people consisting of angry young men and people trying to be nosey forming a wedge in the middle of the street. On the other side he could see someone bucking a shotgun from the porch.

"Then let's turn this shit into a mass murder," Blue Bird said, sliding the AR from the backseat. After chambering one of the missilelike bullets, he sat on the driver's side window and leaned over the top of the car, bracing the AR against the roof. "Hoover!" he bellowed before scattering the crowd with a barrage of missile-sized bullets. The fortunate bounced off the hood of the car, but the unfortunate would have closed casket funerals.

When Danny spotted the car breaking the crowd he immediately moved to fire on it. Had it not been for him recognizing the silhouette of Blue Bird's enormous head he would've hit the car up.

"Hold your fire, lil nigga!" Blue Bird shouted as he climbed out of the car. "Damn, y'all tore shit up out here." Blue Bird surveyed the damage.

Danny ignored Blue Bird's comment. "Jynx is hit, man, and Rah is dead."

"Hell nah, not my fucking folks!" Blue Bird's face saddened. For a minute it looked like he would fall over, but Tears helped him to right his self.

"Man, we need to wrap this shit up. With all this gunfire and things I doubt if Mad Man and Lil Blue can keep the police outta here but so long," Tears said.

"Get Jynx to the whip. I'm 'bout to check on Gutter," Danny said, disappearing into the house before anyone could protest.

HAD IT not been for the wall behind him, Gutter would've landed flat on his back. It felt like someone was squeezing his windpipe, only allowing air through in spurts. His body trembled uncontrollably as he whispered, "No," over and over. All the rage and hate he had carried in his heart when he entered the house drained away and was replaced by great sorrow as he surveyed the damage he'd wrought.

Reckless was slumped against the wall, just below the window. His eyes were vacant and half of his throat was missing from where the .44 slug hit him. On one side of him lay the pistol that had clicked empty and on the other side, still wrapped in the sheet, was his son.

It was at that moment that Gutter realized that he'd gone too far. Totally forgetting all else he rushed to the child. He was screaming his lungs out and splattered with blood, but from what Gutter could tell he hadn't been hit. Looking at the dead man and his son and thinking of his own impending delivery made him ill. Hugging the child to his chest, he gave thanks that the boy was unharmed.

There was the sound of movement coming from behind him, but by the time Gutter turned around to see what it was he was deafened by the roar of a shotgun. The woman who had been screaming in the kitchen slammed against the bedroom door with Mo-Mo's abandoned pistol in her upraised hand. She tried to right herself, but a second blast splintered the door and sent her flying into the dresser behind it. Gutter looked up in total shock as Danny came into the bedroom holding the smoking shotgun.

Danny moved over to the woman's broken body and nudged her with his foot. He looked over at Gutter who was just staring at him in disbelief and simply said, "She was gonna pop you, man. I had to shoot the bitch. Tears and them is outside, cuz. We gotta dip."

Gutter looked from the monster he'd created to the young life he'd almost snubbed and let out a heavy sigh. When he'd set out, Reckless had been little more than another enemy to be executed, but the child in his arms changed the dynamics of that. By his own hands another black baby would have to grow up without his parents and within the hell of God only knew what kind of foster care system. When Reckless's child came of age would he be the one to cut Gutter down while he held his own child over a twenty-year debt?

Anwar's question rang in his head: *"Are you killing for vengeance, or is it something deeper than that?"* Gutter had killed enough people to avenge just about every homey he'd lost on the set so why was he still killing? Because it was natural to him. Death and rebellion had been the constant in his family... the glue that bound them so to speak. Would this be the legacy he'd pass on to his own seed? No. Gutter's would not be a child of war.

Cali was his home... his place of birth, but he would be glad when he was away from it. He would go home to his wife, his heart, and work on being a better husband and a good father to his unborn. Once Major Blood was either dead or out of his city, Gutter was handing the set over to Pop Top. He had built an army, but found himself no longer willing to pay the price that came with being a general. Pop Top had long coveted his position and as far as Gutter was concerned he was welcome to it.

He took a moment to wipe as much of the blood from the boy as he could with the sheet before placing him on the bed, propping pillows on either side so he wouldn't roll off. Gutter whispered soft blessings over him and hoped that the police wouldn't take too long to get there.

chapter 39

S HARELL SAT on a plastic lawn chair in the backyard, trying to relax, but it wasn't working. Gutter had surprised her with the dream house they'd always wanted, but the circumstances surrounding her being there are what had her on edge. In all the years she'd known Gutter he'd been gang-related, but he never brought it home to her. His street life was kept in the streets, but they should've known it'd only be a matter of time before the two worlds collided.

It had all happened so fast that she hadn't fully had a chance to process it. She had just known that she and Satin were living their last night when that man had them at gunpoint, but through the grace of God she was able to get to her equalizer. She felt bad about shooting that boy, but he was lucky she didn't finish his ass for punching her in the face. Her jaw was swollen and bruised, but in time the wound would heal. What troubled her was that two more young men were dead.

Just thinking about Mohammad made her sad. When Sharif

had taken him she was sure that Mohammad was dead, but there was hope in Sharif's eyes. Even if he was still hanging on, the amount of blood Mohammad had lost would've surely sealed his fate before they could get him medical attention. She would never forget his act of selflessness and would keep Mohammad in her prayers.

"You okay?" Satin asked, coming out into the backyard, carrying a platter with two teacups and a kettle on it.

"I should be asking you that." Sharell smiled. "Satin, you should be resting, not trying to mother me; I get enough of that from Gutter."

"It's okay." Satin took the chair next to hers and sat the platter on the ground between them. "I'm just trying to get back into the swing of life. Besides, you're eating for two." She reached out and touched Sharell's stomach.

"I'm not the only one." Sharell pointed at Satin's stomach. "Looks like we'll be fat and ugly together."

"Yeah," Satin said weakly, and rubbed her stomach.

"What's wrong?"

Satin shook her head. "I don't know. When Lou-Loc was killed I felt like my will to live died with him. I wanted to curl up into my mind and never come out, and then I find out about this." She gestured toward her stomach. "The same man who gave me a reason to die turns around and gives me a reason to live."

Sharell smiled at her. "Lou-Loc was always trying to help people; even in death he's proved that."

Satin lowered her head for a minute. When she looked back up to Sharell there were tears in her eyes. "I miss him so much, Sharell, that it hurts."

"I know, baby." She patted her hand. "Lord knows that men like Lou-Loc are a blessing, but at the same time the lifestyles we lead always hold consequences. He lived by the gun and so it was by the gun that he died. We will all miss him, but thanks to your love his legacy will live on."

"You ladies, okay?" Pop Top stuck his head out the sliding glass doors. He and Hollywood had arrived that morning.

"We're good, Pop Top, thank you," Sharell told him.

"A'ight, let me know if you need anything." He smiled and disappeared back into the house. Gutter had sent him to relieve Anwar and his men from guard duty. The young Prince offered to leave some of his soldiers at the house, but Pop Top assured him that he and Hollywood would be okay without them.

"That one gives me the creeps," Satin told Sharell, thinking how every time he smiled it reminded her of a crocodile before it yanked some unsuspecting prey under the water.

"Pop Top is kind of crazy, but he's a loyal soldier. If he wasn't Gutter wouldn't have even sent him."

"Speaking of which, when is he due back?"

Sharell looked at her watch. "Sometime tonight. He, Danny, and his nephew are supposed to be flying back after the funeral but they might have to catch a later flight because something else came up." She thought back to the conversation she'd had with Gutter a few hours prior when he notified her that Rahkim had been murdered. He didn't offer any details, but Sharell had an idea of what had happened.

"That man has been through so much, I don't know how he holds up under it all," Satin voiced.

"Gutter is a warrior. For as many times as I thought the Lord was going to call him home he's still with me."

"That's love."

"Not love so much, Satin, as God's will. For as fucked-up a person as Gutter may seem to be, he's here for a purpose, this I'm sure of. It's gonna take some time, but he'll find his way. We're gonna see to that because we're family and family looks out for family, right?"

Satin smiled. "Right."

"Now, let me go in here and see what we're gonna have for dinner. If we leave it up to Pop Top or Hollywood we'll be eating from the cat kitchen." Sharell got up and went into the house, leaving Satin to contemplate the rest of her new life.

"EVERYTHING A'IGHT?" Hollywood asked Pop Top, who had just come in from checking on the ladies.

"Yeah, they having a tea party or some shit." He flopped on the couch. "You got any more of that purp on you?"

"You know that, fam. I stopped through five-six before I shot out." Hollywood produced a White Owl from his pants pocket and a fifty sack. He tossed the cigar to Pop Top and proceeded to break the sticky weed up on a magazine.

"Fuck is up wit you and these White Owls, you don't smoke Dutches no more?" Pop Top teased him.

"Man, you know the proper way to smoke piff is in a White Owl," Hollywood informed him. "Say man, when are the rest of the homeys getting here?"

"I don't know, sometime this afternoon. What, you scared or something?" Pop Top joked.

"Never that, but I thought this was the rally point? Ain't too much of a rally if it's just us two."

"Young Wood, you don't need no army to win a war. All you need is two or three niggaz down to ride and a few of these." He held up a chrome pistol. "Now hurry up wit the bud, I'm ready to get high." Pop Top reclined in the chair, cracking the blunt over a paper bag. There would be a rally in Long Island, but not the kind Hollywood's bitch ass was expecting.

THAT MORNING was a slow one in Harlem. The normally active streets of Harlem were still and quiet. Between the police and the escalating gang feud, people had made themselves scarce. Bruticus was dead, along with Young Rob and China. C-style was nowhere to be found and Pop Top had disappeared to Long Island. He'd tried to persuade High Side to come along, but he wasn't trying to hear it. Being that there was no one on the streets they were wide-open for him. At his usual post, on a crate in front of the bodega on 142nd and Lenox, High Side watched the traffic for a potential sale and the ever-present police.

"Young Side, what it is?" Don B. asked, ambling up to the corner. Don B. was a former hustler who had turned rapper-CEO. Back then, before the events in *Hood Rat, Still Hood,* or *Section 8,* Big Dawg Entertainment was still a fledgling company with Don B. as its only act. But little did either of them know at the time that Big Dawg would not only grow into a multimillion-dollar label, but it would be in the center of a controversy surrounding several murders.

"Don, what da deal my nigga." High Side slapped him five. "I'm surprised to see you on the streets of Harlem. I thought you moved to Switzerland or some shit since you a rapper now," High Side teased him.

Don B. wiped his nose with his thumb. "Switzerland is my summer home, young'n, Harlem is my kingdom. Speaking of niggaz getting ghost, I'm surprised to see you out here."

"I'm on my grind, fam, you know how I do."

"I hear that, but the way I hear it Harlem has been having some

# # #

problems. They say that Gutter is done and it's about to be a new day." Don B. said smugly. He had never had much love for Gutter or his blue-clad soldiers.

"Don't believe everything you hear, Don. Harlem is still as strong as ever. But fuck the socializing, what you need?"

Don B. smiled, knowing that he had plucked High Side's nerves. "I need an ounce of that Barney."

"Is that right? What's the matter, them Spanish niggaz up the hill ain't taking your money no more?" High Side asked.

"Son, my money is universal but my man ain't around right now, so I gotta settle for the shit y'all slinging."

"I hear that hot shit, cuz."

"Watch that cuz shit, High Side. You already know I ride under the five."

"But yo ass is spending money under the six," High Side pointed out.

"Whatever, duke. You got what I need or what?"

"We always got that, but you gotta give me few ticks for an ounce, homey," High Side told him, pulling out his cell to bleep his man.

"Fuck kinda drug dealer is you where the customers gotta wait? Nigga, when I was out here we had it clicking twenty-four seven."

"Well, you ain't on the block no more. Lou-Loc and them niggaz ran all the tampons outta Harlem." High Side said it in a joking manner, but there was a taunting undertone to his voice. Don B. was a Blood, but that wasn't the reason High Side hated him; he hated Don B. because he'd managed to put the hood behind him and make something of himself. In Don B. he saw two things that he would never become: legitimate and successful.

In a rare show of anger Don B. removed his sunglasses and glared down at High Side. "First of all, little nigga, can't nobody run me outta nowhere. And second of all, before Lou-Loc and Gutter came on the scene, you and Pop Top was two bum-ass nig-gaz begging for somebody to give you a pack to pump. Don't try to play me, son."

"Times have changed, baby boy, and a nigga all grown up." High Side flashed his burner.

Don B. wasn't a sucker, but he wasn't stupid. He knew how cats like High Side were on it. A hating muthafucka didn't need much of a reason to try and kill you. "I hear you talking, fam. Tell you what, why don't I come back in about twenty minutes to pick that up."

"Yeah, why don't you do that," High Side said as he watched Don B. walk away. He knew good and well that Don B. wasn't com-ing back and he didn't care. He might've passed up five hundred dollars on the sale, but at least he got to chump Don B. He couldn't wait to tell the homeys.

High Side's attention was drawn from Don B. when a Black Lincoln rolled to the curb. The Senegalese taxi driver kept his eyes straight ahead while the tinted back window rolled down a bit. High Side was about to go for his gun until he saw the pretty Latino girl's face in the back. "How do we get to Harlem Hospi-tal?" she asked in deep, yet sultry voice.

He smiled and got off the crate to get a better look at the girl, neglecting to pick up his gun. "Yeah, baby. Just keep going down Lenox and you'll run right into it." When High Side raised his arm to point, he saw a swift movement behind the girl. By the time he realized what was about to go down the bullet had passed through his armpit and out his shoulder. Soon the pain would come, but right then the fear and adrenaline made him numb. Spinning on his heels, High Side took off down Lenox Avenue.

"Move, bitch!" Major Blood snarled, crawling over the Spanish girl's lap and spilling awkwardly to the sidewalk. High Side had a good head start, but he was a wounded animal with a predator on his trail.

High Side could have won the hundred-yard dash for the way he bolted down Lenox. He had made it to 140th before the cigarettes and the damage to his arm kicked in. He went from a full-out sprint to a jog, seeming to get slower every few yards. Normally there was always a police presence uptown, but when he needed them they were nowhere to be found. As he darted out into the street and a car put him in orbit he wished he'd listened to Pop Top and had went to Long Island. By that time his arm had gone completely numb so when he landed on it he didn't feel much, but when his head bounced off the concrete the world swam.

High Side found himself in a pretty place. The prettiest green buds sprouted from the streetlights, which had become giant Dutch Masters. He was admiring a cognac waterfall, contemplating a drink, when another sharp blow brought him back to the real world. When his vision cleared he found himself staring at what looked like a yellow-skinned devil.

Major Blood yanked High Side to his feet by the front of his shirt. "Y'all should've listened when I told you to shut it down."

High Side swayed like a rag doll in Major Blood's grasp. "Fuck you, chili bean. Pop Top is gonna smoke your ass for this!" he spat.

Major Blood sneered at him. "How the fuck do you think I knew where to find you?" he lied.

Hearing of his friend's betrayal gave High Side renewed strength. He thrashed about, trying to shake Major Blood off, and only when he was slapped viciously across the face did he go still again. "I'll see you in hell!" High Side literally spat at Major Blood. A line of bloody phlegm ran down the side of Major's face, but he didn't seem to mind.

"More than likely," Major admitted, shoving High Side roughly to the ground. On that once quiet morning, on the corner of 140th and Lenox Avenue, Major Blood divorced High Side's brain from his skull.

LATER THAT afternoon the police responded to a report about a car that had been stripped and left on 96th between West End and Broadway, partially blocking a bus stop. When they opened the trunk they discovered the remains of an immigrant cab driver and a pretty Latino girl. Both wore bullet holes over their eyes.

chapter 40

B Y THE time Gutter, Danny, and Tears made it back to Torrance it was mid-morning. The normally blue California sky was gray and threatening to storm. There was a line of cars parked in front of the house, while homeys were posted on the porch, all waiting to roll to the ceremony for Big Gunn. Among them was Snake Eyes, who had a worried expression his face.

"What's good, homey?" Gutter greeted his longtime friend.

"Yo." Snake Eyes tossed him a folded newspaper. "Y'all fools made the morning news."

Gutter flipped the paper open and was shocked to see a picture of the bullet-riddled Drayton home on the front page. The two-page write-up told of how an alleged gang member–drug dealer and his girlfriend were executed in their Compton home, in front of their infant son. Initially, the police believed it was a drug deal gone wrong because they found large quantities of cocaine in the basement, but an unnamed source, who was said to have heavy ties in the gang community, claimed it was a revenge killing. The young couple was dead when the police got there, but the boy was taken to a local hospital where he was treated for cuts and bruises, and was now in the custody of social services. Gutter didn't need to read anymore, because he'd already seen that movie.

"Police are crawling all over the hood," Snake Eyes continued. "They already rushed the house on Hoover and came by my office on Central. Malika told them that I was away on family business and couldn't be reached, but she doesn't think they bought it," he said, thinking of the conversation with Lou-Loc's baby sister, who was home on break from college and working in the law office. "Shit is getting real hot, real fast."

Gutter shook his head, just before tossing the paper into the trash. "Growing up in the hood," he quoted. If Gutter noticed the look Snake Eyes was giving him he gave no indication of it. "Where's everybody at?"

"Gutter!" Lil Gunn yelled, running down the porch steps. He threw his arms around his cousin and squeezed. "I knew you wouldn't let it ride," he whispered into Gutter's chest.

"That can't be that fool-hearted nephew of mine could it?" Rahshida appeared in the doorway. She was wearing a long black dress, which tickled her ankles and a head covering. "The devil is not welcomed into my brother's house!" she snarled, taking measured steps down the porch. Gutter had seen his aunt angry before, but the fire that burned in her eyes that morning made him take a step back.

"Auntie—" he began, but a vicious slap cut his words off.

"There is nothing you can say to me right now, Kenyatta, that will calm my rage," she almost hissed. "Eighteen and twenty, Kenyatta, that's how old they were. Babies with a baby."

"Auntie, they were enemies," Gutter whispered.

"Why, because those fools' ass-rags, or because the street signs say so? Kenyatta, you didn't just kill enemies last night, you killed children…black children."

"I didn't think—" he began but she cut him off again, this time with words.

"Y'all never do, Kenyatta. I'm from the turf too, so I know full well what this war is about, but it's still bullshit. Since we've been in this country you and my fool-ass brothers have forgotten that this is not how we were raised. Life is the most precious of gifts, but you don't honor it, you abuse and take it. Let a little black girl get killed across the ocean and y'all quiet, but if somebody get killed in the hood and y'all out for blood. Don't any of you fool-ass boys get it? The war y'all are fighting ain't *ours*." She gestured at everyone assembled.

"Kenyatta"—she touched his face lovingly—"when Gunn is laid to rest, I want you out of California." Gutter tried to speak, but she raised her hand for silence. "It's not that you're not welcomed here, Ken. This is your home and you know that, but the longer you stay the worse it's gonna get. Y'all killed people while there was a baby in the house. If the Brims don't kill you, the police sure as hell will!"

"I'm a soldier, Rahshida, you know that. For every one of mine they take, I'll take three of theirs." Gutter wasn't boasting, just stating a fact.

"See, that's the foolishness I'm talking about. Y'all kill them and they kill y'all, it's a never-ending cycle. In less than a week I've lost both of my brothers and almost my faith, because of this thing going on in the streets and I don't want that for you, or Tariq." She draped her arm around Lil Gunn.

"It ain't, Auntie," he said.

She tried to smile, but didn't have the strength. "Go home and be the man my brother raised you to be. Be a good father to your child and a mentor to Tariq. We're all we have left, Ken, the last surviving members of a once proud clan."

"Rahshida, the limo is ready to go," Monifa interrupted. Rahshida hugged her nephews and made her way to the black stretch Escalade. Monifa lingered momentarily, casting cold eyes on Gutter.

"What?" he asked, matching her glare.

"Nothing, I'm just trying to figure out where it all went wrong, Gutter?" she told him. "As I stand here looking into your eyes, the eyes that were always so beautiful to me, I find myself wondering where the life has gone? What happened to the boy I used to love?"

"He grew up to become the man that America hates," he said. His tone was sharp, but not quite hostile. "I've been to the grave and back Monifa and even on the other side we're still niggers. This world ain't got a lot of love for me, and I ain't big on it. Whatever happens happens."

She shook her head. "That sounds real intelligent for somebody that's about to be a father. What you trying to say, that it don't matter if you're here for your child or not?"

"Girl, you tripping, me blasting on muthafuckas ain't gonna affect my seed. I'm always gonna be around for mine and can't nobody change that," he said proudly.

"I'm sure Reckless said the same thing before y'all killed him," she pointed out. "You know, when you used to talk about being a Crip, you did so with such a sense of passion that people couldn't help but to follow you. But as I got older I began to see it for what it was. Gutter, you ain't no great liberator of the Crip movement, you're a killer like the rest of them."

"You got some fucking nerve, coming out here trying to drop jewels on me, Mo, real talk. Yeah, I'm a killer and I accept that. But how many bodies you got under your belt?"

"I've never killed anybody, Gutter," she defended herself.

"Is that right?" He raised an eyebrow. "You sitting here tripping off me blasting muthafuckas, but how many of them pistols have you loaded for me?" She was silent so he continued, "So you see, I ain't the only one with blood on their hands." It was a low blow, but she cast the first stone.

"Fuck you, Gutter, I don't know what I ever saw in you!" she hissed, breaking her promise to herself as the first tears hit her cheeks.

"You saw greatness," he continued. "You saw a nigga from the ghetto that was determined to make it out of the ghetto, by any means necessary."

"You're a fraud, Kenyatta Soladine. You let the set corrupt everything we . . . you used to stand for." She tried to walk away, but he grabbed her arm. He leaned in so close that she could see spittle flying as he spoke.

"Everybody wanna blame the set for what I've become but what I didn't realize until last night was that the monster has *always* lived here." He pounded his chest. "Long before I smoked my first enemy, I was a fucking abomination . . . death is a part of me. Mo, it ain't no secret that I was born into this life, but never forget that this life does *not* define me!"

She broke away from him and took a step back. As she stared at him that loving fire that used to burn between them dwindled to a smolder. If she hadn't been convinced before, she knew then that their era had truly come and gone.

"I gotta go, Rah is waiting for me." Monifa turned to head for the limo, but his voice gave her pause.

"Will you come say goodbye to me at the airport?" For a minute he thought she was going to stop, but it was only a break in her stride. They had already said their goodbyes and Gutter knew it, but he just wanted to be sure before he closed his heart off to her.

FIFTEEN MINUTES later Gutter had reemerged from the house, trading in his sweatshirt and jeans for a beautiful three-piece, charcoal-gray suit. He could've rode in the limo with his family, but just then he wasn't feeling much like family, he was feeling like a wolf and needed to be among his pack.

"If it's one thing I can say is that you Soladine niggaz clean up pretty nice," Stacia cracked from the bottom of the porch steps. She was dressed in a tasteful skirt and blazer set, her eyes surprisingly clear.

"I thought you pushed out with the rest of the fam?" Gutter said, hugging her.

"Nah, you know yo peoples is Holy Rollers and I'm trying to smoke a joint before the ceremony. Set it out, I know y'all got that," she joked.

"Fo sho." Gutter smiled. For the next few moments Stacia was quiet. He could tell there was something on her mind, but she struggled to find the words. "Sup, Stace?"

"I don't know, man. I'm just thinking about my baby's daddy and how much I'm gonna miss him," she admitted.

"Shit, you and everybody else in the hood," Gutter said.

"But not like I will, Kenyatta," Stacia told him. In all the years Gutter had known her it was the first time she'd ever called him by his government. "Me and your uncle might've fought like cats and dogs, but Big Gunn was my first love. You see this figure"— she ran her hands down her sides. It wasn't a seductive gesture, more of a visual aid—"I had to love that muthafucka to let him put a baby in me. But that was a long time ago."

"My uncle was crazy about you too. Remember how mad he used to get whenever you stepped out with your girls?" Gutter recalled. Stacia had been one of the baddest bitches on the set in her day and Gunn was a nut over her.

"Yeah, he was a fool about this." Her face brightened. "If a nigga even looked at me too hard, Gunn was ready to go to the pistols."

"I guess it runs in the family," Gutter joked. Stacia smiled but her face darkened a bit. "What's really on your mind, Stacia?" he pressed.

"Listen . . . I'm sorry about what happened to Rahkim. He was a fool, but I still loved him like a brother."

"Rahkim went out like a warrior," Gutter said, trying to push the visions of his mercy killing from his head. "It was an honorable death."

"Honorable? Baby boy, ain't no honor in getting your shit pushed in," Stacia told him. "Rahkim was just a shade over thirty, with no kids. The only thing to mark his passing will be the mural somebody paints for him in the hood. I can't really see the honor in that."

"Here we go again with this shit." Gutter sighed.

"Oh, nah, I ain't wait around to preach to you. Now, I'm sad for that baby having to grow up without his parents, but my baby gotta grow up without one of his. My biggest regret was that it was Reckless y'all killed instead of Major. But I'm sure that problem is gonna work itself out before too long." She stared at him and he just nodded. "I guess what I'm trying to say is, thank you. Not necessarily for killing them children, but for keeping my child from becoming a murderer. Lord knows if y'all hadn't rode on them busters, Tariq was gonna get ahold of a gun and do something stupid."

"Come on, Stacia, you know I ain't trying to let Lil Gunn get caught up in this shit," Gutter assured her.

"I know that, Gutter. You think if I didn't I'd let you take my only child clear across the ocean? Rahshida was down with the game, but her heart wasn't in it like ours. I know how strong the devil's call is, so I understand a little better. Gutter, I know who you are and what you represent, but I also know that you're a good young dude. Tariq needs a strong male figure in his life to save him from what's waiting behind door number two." She motioned toward the men gathered at Gutter's back. "Gutter, my soul died with Gunn and all I got left is my heart." She pointed at Lil Gunn. "Just promise me you'll show him a better way."

"I'll do my best, Stacia," he said.

"When it comes to mine, your best ain't good enough. I need to know that I'm doing the right thing by letting Tariq go back east with you. If I'm sending my son to join your army then I might as well let him stay here and die with me. I need you to give me your word that you won't let him fall into this hell?"

"On my uncle, Stacia. Lil Gunn ain't gonna get swept up in this bullshit," Gutter vowed.

"Then it's settled. When you fly back to New York his little ass will be on the plane with you. Remember now, Gutter, you promised to take care of my boy."

"I got you," he assured her. In less than twenty-four hours he'd been backed into taking two oaths, and still hadn't come up with a solid plan to deal with Major Blood. Just thinking of the killer who waited for him on the other side of the ocean made him wonder if he'd truly be able to honor his promises.

chapter 41

TITO HAD once considered himself one of the most down Bloods in New York, but in under a year he had crossed two set leaders into being murdered. El Diablo's death had been business, but Hawk getting off'd was something he hadn't planned on. A shit storm was sure to come when word got out that Major Blood had assassinated him. Major wasn't pressed. He was a master strategist with a killer's mentality with a general who knew the lay of the land and its power structure. Thus Tito became his reluctant right arm.

"T, how long we gonna circle this muthafucka?" Eddie asked from behind the wheel of the car.

"Until he pokes his fucking head out so I can blow it off," Tito snapped, showing signs of the strain he was under. Major Blood had successfully kicked off a civil war within a war. Not only were they now fighting Harlem Crips, but there was skirmishes breaking out among the Blood sets throughout the five boroughs. With Hawk dead and the governing body seriously crippled, it didn't take long for things to start falling apart. When the dust finally settled Major Blood planned to rebuild the structure. Gentrification, he called it.

Until that morning everything had been going relatively smooth...but then the phone call had come in. It seemed that someone had rocked his cousin Reckless, cancelling his flight to New York. He and his girlfriend were found shot to death, and their son left an orphan. Tito expected Major to go nuts over the news considering how close he knew the cousins were, but Major Blood didn't. His eyes took on a glint that neither he nor Eddie could bear to look at directly when he simply said, "It ends," and started popping cats.

Bruticus was dead, and Pop Top had vanished so the lane was wide-open and Major Blood had taken full advantage. High Side was the first to get it, but he was nowhere near the last. For the better part of the day they had been stealing cars and picking off Crip soldiers. So far they'd shot at or killed at least half a dozen men since and that number promised to triple before it was all said and done.

When Major said he did his homework he wasn't lying. Not only did he know who the key players in Harlem Crip were, but he was also able to uncover where Gutter got his drugs. The heroin he sold came from the Al Mukalla and touching them was a suicide run, but he got his coke and haze from the Heights. There was a big head Dominican kid named Rico who had been hitting Gutter off for the last year and a half. It was time to bring an end to their partnership.

"There that nigga go right there." Eddie pointed toward a group of men who were filing out of a Spanish restaurant, with a chick who was slightly familiar. His mark was a slim kid with dark skin who wore his hair in a throwback, curly fade. He was laughing at something one of the young ladies with their group had said. *He wouldn't be smiling in a minute,* Tito thought to himself, checking the magazine in the compact machine gun resting on his lap.

"Let me out right here, then go lay in the block until I come around the corner," Tito ordered before slipping out of the car.

"SO THIS is what it's come to, mommy?" Rico asked, almost sounding sad.

"Yeah, Rico, I'm done," she said. "I can't take this shit no more, so I'm gonna fall back for a while."

"You and your click have made me a lot of money, ma, especially you. Shit, you flip more weed for me than most of these niggaz do coke."

"Yeah, it was sweet, but all good things come to an end. I mean, I'm sure the arrangement you have with Gutter is still in good standing, but I ain't fucking around."

"Gutter." He shook his head. "It seems like he's more focused on war than money these days."

"You know how it is." She shrugged. "But listen, I'm about to get up outta here. I'll drop whatever I got leftover off to you tomorrow. It ain't but a quarter pound or so."

"I'll tell you what, drop the money off and keep the weed. Whatever you do with it is on you," he told her.

"Thanks." She hugged him.

"You take care of yourself, baby girl."

"I'll try." She broke the embrace. "Let me get going." She went to step off the curb but froze. If it's one thing she had learned during her time on the streets it was how to spot a murderer and the man approaching her was just that. She turned to shout a warning to Rico, but it was too late.

The quiet night burst into colors and screams as Tito cut loose with the machine gun. He showed no mercy as both enemies and civilians fell under the hail of bullets. Rico tried to boat, but found that for as fast as he thought he was there was no outrunning a bullet. His bodyguards tried to draw, but were no match for the skilled killer, and fell along with their boss.

C-style hadn't even realized she was hit until she tried to run and found that her legs didn't work correctly. There was a red spot just above her left breast that seemed to expand every time she took a breath. She tried to steady herself against the window of the bodega, but the blood made it too slick and she fell. Her mind told her that she needed to escape, but her heart and body told her that there was none. She knew that karma would come back on her for the life she'd taken, but she hadn't realized how soon and how viciously. C-style would never get to see the world as she had often dreamt of. She would never finish school, and more important she would never get to be a mother to the life that she had no idea was growing in her belly.

HOLLYWOOD SAT at the kitchen table with Pop Top playing Casino and sipping Rémy. They'd just gotten the word about High Side so there was a grimness in the air. Hollywood had been ready to arm up and go after Major Blood and expected Pop Top to feel the same way, but the stand-in general was surprisingly calm over the death of his best friend. He reasoned that the best way to finally put Major Blood down was to formulate a plan and then execute. Until then they were to keep close to Sharell until Gutter flew back that evening.

"Man, I'm ready to waste this muthafucka," Hollywood said, laying a card down on the table. "It bad enough that he's killing off our soldiers and shooting up funerals, but then to murk High Side like that...my dude, we need to make a move."

"Shit, who you telling? Me and High Side came up on free lunch and now he ain't here no more. Man, when we finally do pop off, I'm gonna stink this nigga personally." Pop Top downed his glass and slammed it on the table. Though he might not have appeared to be, he was grieving over the loss of his comrade. He'd warned High Side to stay off the streets until it blew over, but as usual he didn't listen. Now he was another notch on Major Blood's belt. He hated sitting around on his hands while his people were gunned down in the street, but it was a necessary evil. Once the balance of power was officially shifted over, Major Blood would answer for his crimes.

Just then the doorbell rang, startling them.

"Who the fuck is that?" Hollywood snatched his gun off the table and got to his feet.

"Calm ya scary ass down. It's probably the pizza I ordered." Pop Top laughed at him. "I got tired of Sharell having to cook for us so I decided to give her a break. Since you're up, go get the door, fool."

"Fuck you, nigga," Hollywood said, placing his gun back on the table and heading through the kitchen's swinging door. As he crossed the living room he noticed Sharell standing at the top of the stairs with a worried expression on her face. "Don't worry, Sharell, I got it." He went to the door. When he opened it his mouth dropped open.

"Sup, Wood?" Major Blood greeted him before knocking him out.

chapter 42

THE CEREMONY was held at a small mosque in the South Central section of Los Angeles, not far from the university. Normally the burial ceremony would've been performed at the house of the deceased, but with the heat and gunplay surrounding Gunn's passing it was decided that it would be best to do it at an outside location. Besides that it was doubtful that any of the homes owned by the Soladine family would've been large enough to accommodate the mourners.

It seemed like most of Southern California turned out to pay their respects to Big Gunn. There were at least a dozen or more different Crip sets in attendance and even a few Bloods had managed to sneak in. The tension ran high, but nobody was tripping. The wire had already been sent out that violence would not be tolerated. Whatever beefs that were active on the streets had no place there, and those who weren't willing to respect it would be punished accordingly.

The imam who performed the ceremony was a former Crip

who was once called Big Droopy, but now went by the name Jamal Ali. He had spilled his fair share of blood as a protégé of Big Gunn's in the late seventies and early eighties until Gutter's father helped him find his way. His voice was just as captivating delivering the Salat Ul Janazah as it had been in battle when riding on his enemies.

The room was divided into two sides; comrades and civilians on one side with family and Muslims on the other. The sons and daughters of Allah stood proudly, arms crossed and facing Mecca, praying along with Jamal Ali. Danny was sitting off to the side, chopping it up with Blue Bird and Tears like they were old friends. Looking at him you'd never even know that he'd been party to a mass murder not even twenty-four hours prior.

From the number of women who showed out to mourn Big Gunn, you'd have thought he was a pimp. A few of them tried to cut Stacia dirty looks, but they knew better than to trip. Whether she and Gunn were together or not, she was still Queen Bitch. Rahshida sat down in the front with the rest of the fam. Lil Gunn tried to keep up his tough image, but a blind man could see that he was hurting. Gutter sat quietly in the back, wearing his murder ones, taking it all in.

"You, a'ight, loc?" Snake Eyes asked, sliding closer to Gutter on the wooden bench.

"I'm good," Gutter told him. "How you doing?"

"Shit, you know I'm fucked-up behind this. I owed Gunn more than I'd ever be able to repay." Snake Eyes recalled how many times Gunn had kept his ass out of the fire growing up.

"As much as you've done for the Soladines I think it's safe to call it square." Gutter chuckled softly. "So what now?"

Snake Eyes looked at his watch. "From here, I'm gonna ride with the family to Riverside to place Gunn's body in the tomb.

Tears is gonna take y'all to the airport. How does Lil Gunn feel about cutting out early?"

"I think he's cool with it." Gutter spared a glance at his cousin. "We got a lot to do when we hit New York. There are a lot of things I gotta put in order."

"You going after Major Blood?"

Gutter was silent for a minute. "I guess."

"You guess? That don't sound like the warlord I know. You okay?" Snake Eyes asked.

"Honestly, I don't know. Snake, since we were little nappy head niggaz trying to look hard on Crenshaw, all I ever wanted was to be a street legend. I've got money, power, and an army of dedicated soldiers, everything I've strived for, but with all that's happened and impending fatherhood I ain't so sure anymore. Is the price worth the prize?"

"Heavy is the crown," Snake Eyes remarked.

"You ain't lying about that, brother, but what am I supposed to do? This nigga done killed my uncle; I can't just let it ride. He touched my family, Snake."

"And you touched his," Snake Eyes reminded him. "Loc, don't nobody wanna see Major Blood put to sleep worse than me for what he did, but think about what you'd be losing by continuing the feud. My nigga, I watched you go through the motions after Lou-Loc died and again when Gunn was killed. Major Blood took one of yours and you wiped out everybody he had left. What if instead of you killing Major, he kills you, then what? Lil Gunn picks up a strap and tries to avenge your death, starting the cycle all over again."

"So what you saying, I shouldn't ride for the set?" Gutter asked defensively.

Snake Eyes laughed at Gutter's quick mood change. "Nah, I

ain't saying that. You put in more work for the set than any nigga, red or blue, in the last ten years. L.C. is done, as are most of your enemies, what you got left to prove? Man, let the soldiers deal with that, you've got more important things to attend to."

"What could be more important than riding for mine?"

"*Living* for yours." Snake Eyes jabbed a finger in Gutter's chest. "For the last few years you've had a cause to die for, but now you've got something to live for."

"Snake, you tripping, this don't sound like the homey that smoked that pig with me and Lou-Loc," Gutter accused.

"Because I ain't that nigga no more, I grew up. I got a big house, a fat bank account, and more pussy than I know what to do with; why the fuck would I wanna keep throwing stones at the pen or the grave? Gutter, ain't a muthafucka living or dead that can question your gangsta or your love for the nation. All blood debts owed have been settled ten times over, except the most expensive one and that's to your wife and that baby she's carrying. You ain't gonna be no good to either of them if you're dead or in the can."

"I don't know if I can just let go like that, Snake. I got a responsibility to the homeys in New York," Gutter tried to reason.

Snake Eyes scrunched up his face. "Man, you don't owe nobody a muthafucking thing. You've organized one of the most powerful sets, on either coast, and made all them niggaz hood rich. If they can't maintain without you, then they was some fucking busters to begin with. I love the homeys, Gutter, but I love you more. I've already lost one brother because he waited until the eleventh hour to decide he wanted to get out, and I don't think I could stand to lose another one. Do something with that second chance you've been given."

"I hear you talking, Snake," Gutter said, mulling over his friend's words.

"Do more than hear me, Gutter, *listen*. Take some of that money I've been tucking away for you and do something with it." Snake Eyes stood. "The ceremony will be over soon, so I'm gonna go attend the fam. Listen to your homey, G," Snake Eyes said over his shoulder as he made his way down the aisle.

THE DOORS to the mosque opened up and people began to file out, some orderly and some not, but all respectful. The LAPD and OSS were posted up across the street trying to be inconspicuous as they snapped pictures. Some of the most notorious gang members in all of California had come to see Gunn off, and they were anxious to match the faces they knew against their extensive database and log the ones they didn't into new files. It was for this reason that some of the more unsavory characters chose to just send flowers as opposed to attending.

The crowd parted like the Red Sea as Jamal Ali stepped from the mosque leading the procession. As opposed to a coffin, Gunn was wrapped from head to toe in white linen. Three men on each side wheeled the gurney that held one of the Crip's greatest heroes. Rahshida brought up the rear, flanked by Stacia and Monifa. Lil Gunn came out shortly after. His face was as hard as ever, but Gutter could tell from his ashen cheeks that he'd been crying, as was his right. Spotting Gutter approaching the quartet, Monifa turned and went in the other direction.

"Hey, Auntie"—Gutter ignored Monifa's snub and attended to his aunt—"you cool?" He took her hands in his.

"No, but what can we do? My brother is free now," she said, trying to keep from crying more than she already had.

"That he is," Gutter said. "Listen, I'm sorry I can't go with y'all to the vault."

"Don't worry about it, Kenyatta, I know how it is." She glanced across the street at the police and sheriffs. "They're minding their manners now because they know disrupting the funeral would turn into a riot, but they're gonna swoop down soon enough. It's best you not be here when it happens."

"I know that's right. Tears is gonna take us to the airport and then come back to the house to join y'all. You need anything before I leave?"

"No, I'm fine, Kenyatta. All I need is some peace of mind." She sighed. "Nephew, I'm sorry I was so short with you earlier. I've just got a lot on me right now. Two funerals in two days is a little more than I'm prepared to deal with."

"You sure you don't need me to stay for Rahkim's ceremony?"

"No, Ken. I don't want to chance you getting deeper into this than you already are. If the police don't already know you're in the city, they will before long. The last thing we need is for them to start playing connect the dots and yours might be an extended stay," she told him.

"True." He tugged at his beard. "Well, you know if you need anything I'm just a plane ride away. When all this dies down me and Lil Gunn might fly back out here to check on y'all."

"Don't bother, Ken. After we lay Rahkim to rest I'm gonna have Snake Eyes sell our properties out here and I'm leaving L.A.," she informed him.

"Auntie, if you're worried about retaliation I can make sure y'all are protected round-the-clock," he assured her.

"And live like a prisoner in my own home? No thank you. Besides, I'm not leaving because I'm afraid, I'm leaving because I'm tired. Ever since we came to California death has been a constant companion of the Soladines. I need to put this state and all this ugliness behind me."

"Where will you go?" he asked.

"I don't know. I was thinking about traveling for a while. Maybe visit Algiers for a few months and settle somewhere down south when I come back. I haven't quite made up my mind yet...maybe even take a look around Arizona."

"Well, if you need anything from me just let me know."

Rahshida smiled and touched his face. "Kenyatta, all I need you to do is be here for your family. Change the way you're living so your wife doesn't feel the kind of heartache I'm feeling right now, nephew."

"I've been hearing that a lot lately." He recalled his conversation with Snake Eyes.

"Then maybe you should try listening."

"I just might," he said honestly.

"Well, we've got a little bit of a drive ahead of us so I'm gonna go now, but you be safe, Kenyatta, and know that Allah loves you."

"I know now." He hugged her.

"Take care of my nephew, Kenyatta, and don't let it take another death to bring us back together."

"I got you, Auntie," he said, trying not to break down himself.

Rahshida wiped her eyes and started in the direction of the limo. Gutter looked over and found Monifa staring at him intently. He started to say something to her, but decided against it. They had said their goodbyes already, so there was nothing more to discuss. That chapter of his life was closed and he needed to focus on the new beginning with his wife and family. After saying farewell to the homeys, Gutter, Danny, and Lil Gunn climbed into Tear's truck and headed for the airport.

chapter 43

━ ▬ ━ ▬ ━ ▬ ━ ▬ ━ ▬ ━ ▬ ━ ▬ ━ ▬ ━ ▬ ━ ▬ ━ ▬ ━ ▬ ━

THE SKY was incredibly blue that morning, seemingly more so than Gutter had ever remembered seeing it. At that altitude the clouds appeared solid enough to walk on, but it was an illusion, as was the temporary peace Gutter felt looking at them. He knew that once he touched down it was back to business.

The flight home went far smoother than the one into Long Beach, but that all depends on whom you asked. Danny-Boy sat directly behind Gutter, trying his best to put the moves on a buxom flight attendant. Though she smiled, Gutter could sense her uneasiness. The innocent part of Danny that first drew Gutter to him was gone, replaced by the taint of a killer and whether he knew it or not, he wore it on his sleeve.

During the ride to the airport, up until just before takeoff, Lil Gunn bombarded Gutter with questions about New York City and the game. When the plane took to the skies all questions ceased, and a look of panic came over the young man's face. Gutter was sitting next to Lil Gunn, who was a nervous wreck. Every time the plane lurched he looked as if he was going to be sick. When the Boeing finally bounced roughly on the airstrip he heard his cousin whisper a prayer of thanks that he hadn't perished in the air. Had he gripped the armrest any tighter it was sure to come off.

"Good evening ladies and gentlemen," the captain's voice began over the loudspeaker. "We're now arriving at JFK. The time is four thirty, with the weather being a warm seventy-three degrees. At this time you may power on cell phones and electronics. Once again, thank you for flying JetBlue."

"I never thought I'd be so fucking happy to see the ground," Lil Gunn huffed.

"Buck up, lil cuz. You'll get used to it after a while," Gutter told him.

"Man, fuck that. I ain't never getting on a plane again. The next time we hit the West we're driving and I don't care how long it takes," Lil Gunn declared.

Gutter laughed and powered on his cell. The digital screen alerted him that he had five new voice mails and two text messages. The homeys, no doubt, wondering if he made it back yet. They were going to send a convoy to receive him, but Gutter declined, assuring them that he'd get with them later the following evening to discuss plans to deal with Major Blood. On his first night back, he intended to devote himself to making sure Sharell was good. Before he had a chance to check the messages the phone was vibrating.

"Speak," Gutter answered.

"Kenyatta?" Sharell asked in a shaky voice.

"What's good, baby? I just touched down. Is everything okay?" he asked. She was silent for a minute. "Sharell, you there?"

"Yeah . . . how was your flight?"

"It was a'ight, but I think Lil Gunn might've shitted his pants,"

Gutter joked, but the laugh she gave him was halfhearted. "Sharell, what's wrong?"

"Nothing, I was just worried. How'd things go in California?"

"Not good, but I'll explain it all to you when I get out there. Sharell, I need to talk to you. Some things are about to change, but for the better."

"I need to talk to you too, baby," she told him, her voice still wavering a bit.

"Sharell, what's wrong with you? Is Pop Top still there with you," he asked suspiciously.

"Yes, he's still here, with Hollywood. How soon do you think you can get here?"

"Me, Danny, and Lil Gunn are about to hop in a cab as soon as we grab our bags," he told her.

"Baby, you've been gone for a while and we need to talk about some things," she tried to choose her words carefully, but her nerves were affecting her thinking. "I need a few minutes alone with you before you get back to business."

"Sharell, I know you so I know when something is wrong."

"Gutter, this thing with these people you're warring with has me scared, please just come out here, Gutter."

Gutter? Sharell never called him Gutter. Something was off and though he didn't know what, he intended to find out. "Okay, baby," he said in a neutral tone. "I'll send Danny-Boy and Lil Gunn back to Brooklyn to grab some of our personal items. They can meet us in Long Island afterward."

"Please hurry, Gutter," she pleaded before the line went dead.

"What the business is, cuz?" Lil Gunn asked, noticing the grim expression on Gutter's face.

"I don't know yet. Yo, Danny"—he turned to face his protégé—"I'm gonna get the Charger from the parking lot and I want you and Gunn to hop in a cab to Harlem. Round up the troops and some straps and meet me in Long Island ASAP!"

"What the fuck is going on?" Danny asked, ready to spill more blood.

"I ain't sure just yet, but I know something is funny. I gotta go check Sharell."

"Loc, if you're about to walk into a situation I'm coming with you," Danny said.

"I don't know what it is. Maybe I'm just being paranoid, but if something is popping, we're gonna need more than just the .40 caliber I got stashed in the car. Just get to me as soon as you can," Gutter said, unbuckling his seat belt and bull-rushing his way down the aisle.

"YOU DID good, baby girl," Major Blood sneered. He was standing directly across from Sharell. Satin sat in the chair in front of him with a gun pointed at her head. "In a few hours all this will be over. Play your cards right and you might live through it."

"You think he's gonna go for it?" Pop Top asked from the kitchen doorway. He was chomping on a turkey sandwich.

"Oh, he'll go for it. Even if he does suspect something, he ain't gonna come in here dumping all crazy with his bitch in the house." Major Blood nodded at Sharell. "You made the right choice, Top. Better to live as a traitor than to die as a martyr."

"Pop Top, I always knew you was a scandalous muthafucka, but I never figured you for a rat, cocksucker!" Hollywood barked. He was sitting in a wooden chair near the front door.

Pop Top grinned before slapping Hollywood on his bandaged face. "Shut yo pussy ass up, nigga. Fuck you and fuck Gutter. That nigga got our soldiers dying in the streets over his bullshit. I'm trying to bring the glory back."

"Glory?" Hollywood snickered through bloody lips. "Nigga, not only are you a fucking turncoat, but you're delusional too. I might die in this house today, but best believe your ass won't be too far behind. Gutter is gonna waste you, faggot!"

Pop Top went to swing on Hollywood again, but Major Blood stopped him. "Enough of this bullshit, Pop Top. Gutter will be here soon and we've got plans to make. Tito," Major Blood called to his general who had come to join him after the hit on Rico, "everything set up?"

"Yeah, I got a few nigga spread around the house and a lookout on the corner. As soon as Gutter gets here, we'll know about it," Tito informed him.

"Excellent. Eddie"—he turned to his other general—"take all three of these bitches down to the basement"—he motioned toward Satin, Sharell, and Hollywood—"and sit on 'em. Anybody get fly, you know what to do."

"I got you, Blood," Eddie said, hurrying to do as he was told.

Major beamed at his perfectly laid plan. "Now, all we gotta do is wait for the guest of honor so we can get the party started. I always fill my contracts."

GUTTER BURNED up the Long Island Expressway like a man possessed. For the last twenty minutes he had been trying to contact his crew with no results. High Side, Bruticus, C-style, nobody was picking up. He even tried to call Pop Top, only to get the voice mail. He tried to tell himself that he was just being paranoid, but in

his heart he knew something was wrong. The next call he placed
was to Danny, who confirmed what he'd already suspected, knowing Major Blood and how he operated. Bruticus and C-style were
dead and Harlem was in chaos, which only confirmed Gutter's
suspicions that a bad situation had gotten considerably worse.
Danny, Gunn, and several more homeys from the set were hot on
his heels. They were scheduled to arrive moments after Gutter,
but he couldn't wait for them. He had to get to his wife.

Gutter was so engrossed in his own thoughts that he almost
missed his exit. He almost caused an accident as he cut across
three lanes and took the ramp at twenty miles above the posted
speed limit. The Charger fishtailed; through the grace of Allah he
managed to get it under control before wrecking.

The Charger moved almost soundlessly through the Long Island streets, ignoring stop signs and traffic signals. It was a miracle
that he didn't get pulled over en route, but he had made it to the
house without incident. As he slowed near the house he saw Pop
Top's Ford in the driveway, along with Sharell's ruined X5. He was
so focused on the house that he didn't even notice the young man
sitting in the Lincoln watching him pass by.

Instead of pulling up in the driveway, Gutter parked on the
street. He scanned the house for signs of movement, but didn't see
anything. Checking the clip of his .40 caliber, he slid from the car
and moved cautiously up the driveway. Placing his ear to the door
he couldn't hear anything, which was strange. Pop Top was a loudmouth by nature, so the eerie silence unnerved him. When he
tried the knob he found the door was unlocked, definitely a bad
sign. Sliding a bullet into the chamber he walked into the setup.

chapter 44

EDDIE PACED the basement floor nervously. Through the small window he could see Gutter coming up the driveway with a pistol in his hand. Shit was about to get real ugly, real quick.

"Why the long face?" Hollywood taunted from the chair where he was tied. He craned his neck and saw the bottoms of Gutter's sneakers. "I see death has come calling."

"You shut you fucking mouth, crab!" Eddie shouted.

"You know it ain't too late. All you gotta do is cut us loose and I'll see to it that you don't catch the same hell your homeys are about to."

Eddie looked like he was considering it, then his face went hard again. "I ain't no fucking traitor."

"Aren't you? You know the word is out about Hawk getting killed in Harlem. The UBN might not know off top, but ain't nothing slow about the big homeys. It's only gonna be a matter of time before they put two and two together and what do you think is gonna happen then?" Hollywood smiled. The whole time he taunted Eddie, he was working on the phone cord that bound him to the chair.

"Shut up!" Eddie snarled in his face.

"What, you put off by a little truth? Eddie, you and I both know that you're the low man on the pole, and it's usually the low man who gets it the worst. Major Blood has got you in a whole world of shit that's gonna blow up in your damn face. Right now, I'm your only chance. You let us go and Harlem will make sure you get to higher ground before the flood. If not, you might as well put that pistol in your mouth and take the easy way out, pussy, because either way you're done!"

"Didn't I tell you to shut up?!" Eddie lashed out and kicked Hollywood's chair over, which is what he had hoped. The impact cracked the back of the chair and loosened the phone cord that had been binding his arms.

"Hollywood!" Sharell screamed, drawing Eddie's attention to her.

"Everybody shut the fuck up!" Eddie clutched his temples. When he turned back to Hollywood he was shocked to see that not only had the man managed to free himself, but was charging in his direction.

Eddie tried to raise his gun, but a swipe of Hollywood's cast sent it flying across the room. Though Eddie considered himself a tough guy, he couldn't fight worth a damn. Hollywood delivered a crushing blow to the side of Eddie's head with the cast, knocking him to the ground.

"I told you that ass was done!" Hollywood snarled, slamming the cast into the side of Eddie's head. He struck him again and again until Eddie lay motionless, with blood pooling beneath his head.

"Y'all all right?" Hollywood attended the ladies, who Eddie hadn't bothered to tie up.

"I'm good," Satin told him. "Sharell?" She turned to her friend, who wore a strange expression on her face.

"Something is wrong!" she gasped. There was a gush of fluid and blood spilling from between Sharell's legs.

"She's in labor," Satin said, trying not to panic. "Shit, shit, shit! We gotta get her to a hospital, but how with those guys in the house?"

"No." Sharell grabbed Satin by the shirt. "Take the Camry and go for help. Hollywood"—she turned to him—"warn Gutter. Don't let them kill my baby!" she pleaded.

"I got you, Sharell. Just stay here. I won't let them kill him," Hollywood vowed, snatching up Eddie's gun and heading for the stairs.

GUTTER BURST into the house with his gun drawn, expecting the worst, but it was surprisingly quiet. He made his way from the foyer to the living room, eyes scanning for enemies, but instead he found Pop Top, lounging on the sofa watching videos.

"What it is, homey?" Pop Top asked, not bothering to get up.

"Top, what the fuck is going on? Where is Sharell and why the hell is the door open?" He relaxed a bit seeing a friendly face, but was still alert.

"That nigga Hollywood probably forgot to lock it when he left. Why the fuck you acting so paranoid?" Pop Top asked casually. From the angle Pop Top was sitting at, Gutter couldn't see the gun in his lap.

"Sharell didn't sound good when she called me, so I thought something had popped off."

"Man, you know broads be extra when they're pregnant and

missing their man. Put that damn gun away before you shoot a nigga by accident."

Gutter still felt like something was wrong, but his friend managed to put his mind at ease enough to tuck the gun into his waistband. He was making his way to the living room when the basement door flew open and Hollywood came spilling out, with Satin on his heels.

"Gutter, it's a setup!" Hollywood screamed, but Pop Top was already spinning on them with his gun drawn.

POP TOP opened fire with the .45, trying to lay everything in his path. He tried to murder Gutter, but Hollywood ended up taking the initial bullet, giving Gutter a fraction of a second to react. Without even thinking he clapped back with his .40, splitting Pop Top's wig. With the traitor dead, Gutter turned his attention to Hollywood.

"Wood, talk to me?" Gutter cradled his head in his hands.

"I promised her I wouldn't let them get you," he coughed, dribbling blood down his chin. "I promised" were Hollywood's last words before death claimed him.

"Wood?" Gutter shook him. "Hollywood!" he shouted his comrade's name over and over, but he was gone. "Not another one," Gutter whispered.

"Oh, God no," Satin sobbed, startling Gutter.

"Where's Sharell?" Gutter snapped.

"She's in the basement... her water broke."

"I gotta get to her." Gutter stood.

"No, there's more of them in the house!"

No sooner than the words were out of her mouth the window

behind Gutter shattered. He looked up and saw three men he didn't recognize barreling down the stairs. Rolling across the living room, Gutter blasted the first invader, sending him spilling down the stairs. Another man pushed open the kitchen door, and was rewarded with a bullet to the chest, sending him flying back the way he came.

"Get out of here!" he barked at Satin, as he laid another man down. The war was on and he had no intentions on taking prisoners.

GUTTER BACKED up, still firing the automatic pistol. It seemed like for every man he dropped three more took his place. The door suddenly imploded as the enemies, who were now surrounding the house, sprayed it. Among them he could see Major Blood, smiling triumphantly. It was a smile Gutter fully intended to wipe off his face.

Hollywood lay on his back staring vacantly at the ceiling. If it weren't for the quarter-sized hole in his chest, he could've passed for someone who was just thinking. The whole time he had been down with Harlem he had pledged his life to the set and his reward was to die young, leaving a beautiful corpse. The house seemed to be swarming with enemies and he would be overrun unless reinforcements arrived soon.

"Just a few more minutes," he whispered, tearing into his enemies.

chapter 45

SATIN MADE a mad dash through the kitchen, almost slipping in a puddle of blood left by the man Gutter had killed. The house was covered in it. Some were from the enemy, but most of it was from Hollywood, who had died trying to protect them. The dead man, still clutching his gun, stared at her through vacant eyes, while she fumbled through the kitchen drawer for the car keys.

The air was filled with the sounds of gunfire and screams of the dead, but she tried not to focus on it. She felt bad abandoning Sharell, but there wasn't much she could do for her considering all that was going on. Her best was to go for help and hope that Gutter could hold out until she got back. Even though he was waging a losing war, Gutter refused to give up.

After finding the keys, she broke for the garage door. The entire garage was a hot mess. Faint rays of sunshine dotted the automatic gate from the bullet holes that had almost completely shredded it. Paint and other chemicals were leaking all over the place making it almost impossible to breathe. Clasping her hand over her mouth and nose, she made her way over to Gutter's Camry, which had also been hit up, and prayed it was still operable. God had been good to her that day because it turned over with no problem.

Outside it sounded like the additional guns had joined the fray. Whether they were friend or foe, she had no way to tell. *How many more would have to die?* she thought. Not being able to hold it back anymore, Satin finally broke down into tears. She had lost everything, her brother, her sanity, and the love of her life. She was tired of being the victim. It would end once and for all she vowed as she threw the car in reverse.

"COME ON, muthafuckas!" Gutter snarled. He fired two more shots at the advancing soldiers and made a dive for the couch. No sooner than he was airborne, a hail of bullets whistled through the house. He had managed to avoid most of them, but a stray caught him in the leg. Gutter crashed awkwardly to the ground, but still managed to clear the couch. Taking a minute to examine his leg he noted that the bullet seemed to have passed through it cleanly. The bum leg would tip the scales against him, as if the battle wasn't already lopsided, but it didn't really matter. Kenyatta Soladine was a man who was used to beating the odds.

Gutter refreshed his clip, but that was the last of his ammo. As he crawled to get a better angle on his attacker, he came across the body of Pop Top, the betrayer. He had trusted him with the life of his family and obviously Pop Top's greed overrode his morality. Not only had he endangered the life of Gutter's wife and unborn child, but he'd cost Hollywood his own life. Gutter vowed that Hollywood's death would not be in vain. Summoning every ounce of strength in his body, he grabbed the bottom of the couch and lifted.

TITO CROUCHED behind a recliner, while motioning for the soldiers to keep at it. Bullets tagged the couch where Gutter was hiding, sending cotton and fabric flying all through the air. He knew if he didn't get Gutter this time, he was a dead man. Major Blood had been clear on that.

"Fuck this," Tito said, standing with his shotgun raised. The sound in closed quarters was almost deafening, as he let it go over and over, tearing the living room up. When it finally clicked empty, he motioned for his men to hold their fire.

When the smoke cleared, the room looked like a war zone. Everything that could be destroyed was. The walls, the entertainment system, it was all ruined. The couch was coming apart at the seams. Springs and padding jutted out at every angle. Tito knew there was no way Gutter could've survived. Suddenly, the couch Gutter had been using for cover flew in their direction. Tito was so busy trying to avoid the flying furniture that he never even saw the bullet coming.

THE CAMRY sent the garage door flying outward drawing the attention of everyone on the lawn. Bullets immediately rained on the Camry, causing Satin to swerve and hit a fire hydrant when she tried to jump the curb. She tried to gun the car forward, but it was caught on the hydrant. Through horrified eyes she watched several of the gunmen take aim and thought of how she had failed her baby.

———

"HARLEM!" GUTTER shouted, blazing at his enemies. He spotted Tito trying to get out of the way and paid special attention to him. With a jerk of the trigger, he hit Tito twice in the chest, then burst his head like a rotten tomato. The soldiers were so shocked by seeing their general murdered that they paused, giving Gutter enough time to hurl himself through the window.

The picture windows in the front of the house all exploded in a spray of glass and wood. Gutter hit the ground rolling. His ears were ringing and he was dizzy as hell, but his battle instincts took over. He staggered back, firing at any and everyone that he didn't recognize. The soldiers returned fire, hitting Gutter once in the gut. He fell back, but managed to roll behind the X5 for cover.

He leaned against the SUV, gasping, and trying to plan his next move. Gutter took a moment to assess how badly hurt he really was. His lungs were on fire and his leg had gone totally numb. Surrounded by enemies and on his own he was surely on his way to sit with Allah. He wasn't afraid to die, but he was afraid to leave his wife and unborn child to fend for themselves. Knowing the curtain call when he heard it, Gutter made to take his last stand.

Just as he was about to roll from his hiding place he heard a car speeding in his direction. He peered from behind the tire and saw his truck come jumping the curb. Two more cars followed it, packed with armed and angry homeys. With Danny-Boy leading the charge the tide was suddenly shifted.

Major's men tried to stand against them, but the Harlem riders had come for blood and wouldn't be denied. With automatic weapons of all shapes and sizes, they blasted away at the Bloods. Even Gutter managed to muster up the strength to rejoin the firefight. He and his crew cut down anything moving.

Gutter's attention was drawn by the sound of screeching tires. He looked over and saw his Camry come flying out of the garage.

Satin plowed into a cluster of men while they hit the car up from all angles. She had almost cleared the curb when the car smacked into a fire hydrant. Major Blood abandoned the assault on the Crips and turned his attention to Satin.

Gutter screamed and emptied his clip. Most of the shots went wild, but his last one struck Major Blood in his chest, dropping the would-be killer. Ignoring the pain in his leg, Gutter limped across the street, silently praying that Satin was okay. Thankfully she was badly bruised but alive.

"Baby girl, you hurt?" he asked, examining her.

"I think I'm okay," she said, rubbing her stomach. "You look like hell though."

"Shit, I've been worse. I was in a coma a few months ago, re-member?" he joked. "Stay put, ma, we're gonna get you and Sharell out of here."

Gutter looked around and surveyed the carnage. The streets were littered with bodies and damaged property. The police were gonna have a shit fit, but he'd cross that bridge when he came to it. Satin was safe and so was her child. That was the important thing at the moment. Gutter was so weary he wanted to collapse. His body ached almost as bad as when he had come out of the coma. Though he was hurt physically, his fatigue came from inside. He had seen enough death over the past few weeks than any ten men would see in a lifetime. Reflecting on all that had transpired he fi-nally understood why Lou-Loc wanted to get out.

The game they had played since children yielded more losses than gains. From New York to California there would be mothers buying suits to bury their children in. He had played the roles of god and devil, destroying the same world his child would have to live in. Death was not a legacy he wanted to leave behind. Now that all scores were settled he was going to hang the game up like

Sharell had always urged him to. Until the day he left the world he would be a Crip, but now he would be a father and husband first.

Gutter's moment of reflection was broken up when he heard someone shout a warning. He looked over and saw a bloodied Major Blood weakly aiming his pistol. He started to dive for cover, but Major wasn't aiming at him. He was aiming past him, at Satin.

The whole world moved in slow motion. Satin stared vacantly at Major Blood as he applied pressure to the trigger. The muzzle flashed and the bullets seemed to trickle from it. Without even thinking, Gutter made his move. The first bullet hit him in the arm, tearing through the muscles and snapping the bone. He was falling, but the bullet that entered just above his heart kept him standing. Gutter slid down the side of the Camry, leaving a bloody smear across the window.

"No!" Satin screamed as she watched the bullets tear into Gutter. Forcing her door open Satin crawled from the car to where Gutter was laying. She called his name over and over again, but he just stared at her. Blood oozed from Gutter's nose and mouth, coating Satin's hands and the front of her blouse. "Not again," she whispered.

Gunn looked from his cousin to Major, who was smiling through bloodied teeth. Snatching a piece of broken wood from the wreckage of someone's fence, Gunn marched over to where Major Blood was laid out. He looked down at the man, expecting him to bitch up, but Major Blood laughed.

"I always fill my contracts," Major Blood croaked.

"And the Soladines never leave debts unsettled. This is for my daddy, bitch!" Using all his might, Gunn plunged the wood into Major's chest. Using his foot, he pushed the wood deeper into the murderer of his father, squirting blood on his sneaker. Major twitched and died, still wearing that smug-ass grin.

WITH THE help of one of the homeys, Sharell came staggering from the house. She was bloodied and the contractions were kicking her ass, but she needed to get to her man. The sight before her almost made her break down. Gutter was laying on the ground with blood pouring from several holes in his body.

"No!" Sharell shrieked and made her way over to where Gutter was stretched out, surrounded by homeys. They moved aside and allowed Sharell into the circle.

Satin was kneeling over Gutter, crying uncontrollably. When she noticed Sharell she took her hand and they cried together. Even on the brink of death, Gutter tried to soothe her. He touched Sharell's face, leaving a bloody print on her cheek. He opened his mouth as if he was going to speak, but all that came out was more blood. Gunn barked for one of the men to get an ambulance, while he knelt beside the ladies and Gutter.

"You gonna be all right, cuz," Gunn sobbed.

Gutter looked at his cousin and shook his head. He wanted to believe him, but he knew his time was at an end. Gutter had always heard stories about what death was like, but nothing could've prepared him for what would happen next.

He could feel the numbness starting in his toes and working its way up through his body. He held on to Sharell's and Satin's hands, but he could feel his strength fading. Danny-Boy stood over them with tear-filled eyes, while Gunn was rocking back and forth praying.

"Kenyatta Soladine, you better not die and leave me an unwed mother." Sharell tried to get him to focus, but his eyes were already starting to glaze over. "Kenyatta? Gutter, stay with me!"

Gutter could hear her speaking, but couldn't make out the

words over the roar of the car's engine. For a minute he thought it might be an ambulance, but he had never seen an ambulance sitting on twenty-inch rims. Gutter turned his head to see who else had come to say their goodbyes, but found that he couldn't see through the bright light. When his eyes managed to focus, he found himself staring at the most beautiful electric-blue Cadillac, sitting on gold wires.

"Sup, cuz?" he whispered.

Sharell looked over her shoulder to see who he was talking to, but saw nothing. Satin, on the other hand, had an idea when she smelled the tilled earth.

"Give him my love." Satin kissed Gutter's hand, which was getting cold.

Lou-Loc was slumped low in the driver's seat, wearing a white Los Angeles Dodgers cap. He peered out from behind his sunglasses and smiled at Gutter. No words were needed to convey the message. The madness had finally ended and no one else could hurt him. He was free.

I had broken down several times in the telling of my story, but I was surprised when I looked up and saw that Baby had tears in his eyes too. Cats like Baby didn't cry easy, but I didn't knock him for it. I knew what he felt in his chest, because I had felt the very same thing when I'd first heard the story. I hadn't meant to upset him, but in a way I was glad I had told him the story; the burden didn't feel so heavy anymore.

"You okay?" I touched his shoulder.

"Yeah, I'm cool," he lied. "It's just that, I had no idea how wild them niggaz was. Ya pops dropped mad muthafuckas for his man." He wasn't boasting, just stating a fact. My father had killed many men, and ordered the deaths of even more over the blood debt.

After recalling the story I wasn't sure if I hated my father for being a murderer, or pitied him for being a product of his environment. What I was sure of was that I knew both my parents better after what I'd learned, and had a newfound respect for my mother for what she'd lived through.

"Aren't you going to finish the story?"

I turned around and saw my mother standing in the doorway. I'm not sure how long she had been standing there, but her face was streaked with tears.

"Mom, I—" She placed her finger over my lips.

"No, Kenyatta. It's my story, so please let me tell it." She sat on the edge of my bed between me and Baby. "Later that night, after the shooting, I went into labor. At five forty-nine the next morning I gave birth to my pride and joy." She cupped my cheek gently. "A few months later, Satin pushed your little troublesome self out." She smiled at Baby Loc. "Snake Eyes moved us down here and we tried to bury our pasts and focus on making sure you guys didn't get lost in the shuffle.

"Kenyatta, when I looked at your little wrinkled face, it eased my pain just a little bit. In the moments I pushed you out of my womb, it was all a bad dream and my soul mate was still alive. Kenyatta, I never told you the whole truth about your father, because I didn't want to soil your memory of him. Lord knows I loved that man more than anything, but it doesn't change the fact that he walked with the devil, because it was what he had been programmed to do, same as the rest of some of these young guys. How could I tell my little girl that her father was a murderer?"

She must've noticed my face stiffen because she pulled me in for a hug. "Baby girl, your father had a beautiful soul, and had he had more time here I'm sure he'd have been a great husband and father, but the streets won't give you up that easy, that's why I've busted my ass to keep you away from that side of the coin. Me and Satin know better than anyone how strong the call can be."

Tears had blurred my vision, but I managed to find my mother's hand. "I'm sorry, Mom, I didn't mean to hurt you with my story, I just thought it needed to be told."

"And it does," she agreed, which surprised me since she was ranting about it a few hours prior. "It wasn't that you hurt me by telling the story, it just brought back some old demons. That night at the house, we all almost died. Me, you, Baby, Satin, those men had every intention on killing us and they would've had it not been for Gutter. In a sense, this story is his legacy. If those people want to publish it, I think you should let them."

"You mean it?" I asked, knowing I had heard her wrong.

"Yes." She smiled. "By publishing his story, his memory will live on in the pages of that book long after we're gone."

I wrapped my arms around my mother so tight that I thought I heard her cough.

"Wow, I don't even get that kind of love on Christmas," she joked. "But seriously, I want you to do what your heart tells you to."

"Thank you so much, Mommy. I'm gonna dedicate the book to you!"

"That's nice, baby, but first things first. I'm gonna call your professor so we can set up a meeting with these publishing people, but I'm going to talk to Snake Eyes about it first. Baby"—she turned to my crime partner—"I think you'd better go on home, honey. Kenyatta's father wasn't the only one with a story. Your mom has something she needs to talk to you about."

"A'ight, Auntie." He got off the bed and started for the window. "Dollar, I'll come check you later." He swung one leg out the window.

"And use the door next time!" my mother called after him, as she always did when she caught Baby-Loc climbing in and out of my window. But we both knew that he never would. "Now"—she stood—"I've got some phone calls to make."

As my mom left my room I suddenly felt overcome with joy. I had always dreamt of having something I wrote published somewhere other than the school paper, and it looked like it was finally going to happen. Little Kenyatta Soladine would be a published author. I wondered if they would sign me for just one book, or give me a multibook deal, and if so, what would I write about in my next one? I lay back on my bed and smiled. With all the stories I'd heard about the gangsters in my family over spring break, I was sure I'd think of something.